HIDDEN
LAKES

Also by Melanie P. Smith

Warrior Series

Dusk

After Dark

Serendipity (Anthology)

Dawn

HIDDEN LAKES

A Novel by

Melanie P. Smith

MPSmith Publishing

Dedication:

To my father...

Life has dealt him more than a few obstacles

But he's still a cowboy and farmer at heart.

Not that he will ever read this...

It's a "flippin' girly book" after all.

Chapter One

Melissa pulled into the driveway, shut off the car and just sat looking at the old house. Memories flooded her mind. Happy memories. Life had been so simple as a kid. Summer afternoons taking turns on the slip-n-slide, tag in the dark, truth or dare. All the things a happy, healthy child needed. She glanced in the backseat and smiled. Jeremy was still sleeping. At seven the long drive from Denver to Hidden Lakes must have seemed like a lifetime. Jer had finally settled down and conked out about an hour ago.

Melissa took a deep breath and quietly opened the door to her Ford Escape. It was one of the few luxuries she was able to keep after Mitch's death. Melissa closed her eyes, took a deep breath and tried to push the memories from her mind. Thinking about Mitch was still too difficult. She was so proud of him. Knowing he gave his life to save a young mother and her infant child helped her to accept the loss. But the knowledge didn't take away the loneliness, especially at night when she tried to sleep alone in that big king sized bed of theirs. It had been over a year now, but the pain of losing not only her husband but her best friend was still so acute. She wondered if she would ever have peace again. Mitch wasn't only a good man; he was a wonderful father to Jeremy. Their little family would never be the same. She just hoped this move would give them the change they needed to move forward.

Melissa headed for the front door but stopped to study the wooden stairs leading to the porch. Two of the steps were rotting to the point they had become dangerous. She'd have to fix them right away. Her son was full of spit and vinegar, just like his father. She knew that with all his energy, he'd fall through them in no time. Melissa skipped the damaged steps and walked the length of the porch. Once she reached the far end, she tipped the empty flower pot and retrieved the key. She smiled, her mother had hidden a key under that pot for as long as Melissa could remember. Hidden Lakes was a small, friendly town. Even if the neighbors knew about the key, they would never abuse the knowledge. Melissa placed a hand on the old railing and winced when it swayed. There was so much work that needed to be done to this house. The growing list of neglected repairs demonstrated just how serious her father's condition really was. The doctor's said he would live a long, happy life. But only if he slowed down and made some drastic changes. Thus the move from Hidden Lakes to retirement heaven in sunny Florida. She pulled a hair band from her pocket, gathered her long blond hair into a pony tail and headed for the house. She knew the inside of her new home would be not only clean, but immaculate. Connie Peters was meticulous about her housework. That and the best homemade pies in Colorado were two things Melissa could always count on from her loving mother.

Melissa pushed open the large door and reached for the light switch. She smiled as she studied the humble furnishings. It wasn't the most elaborate house on the block, but it was home. For the first time in over a year, Melissa relaxed a little. Stepping into the familiar home made her feel as if a huge weight had been lifted from her shoulders. She moved to the thermostat and turned up the heat. According to the calendar it was already spring, but Mother Nature had her own schedule in Hidden Lakes, Colorado. Once the sun set, it was downright chilly. Melissa stepped back outside onto the porch to check on Jeremy. Once she was sure her son was still sleeping, she rushed into the house and up the stairs. She automatically headed for her room, but stopped in amazement the moment she switched on the light. Her parents had completely redecorated. The room was painted white with a sports wallpaper boarder running across the top. There was new carpet and the full sized bed was covered with a large comforter that matched the wallpaper. Clearly this was made for Jeremy. Had they set up the master for her? Of course they had. Melissa frantically blinked, trying to prevent the moisture forming in her eyes from falling. She was almost successful.

It was a lost cause the moment she opened the door to the bedroom that had always been her parents. They had completely remodeled. The new bedroom set must have cost them a small fortune. They knew her so well. The walls had been painted in a subtle cream with rich brown boarders. The deep chocolate comforter matched the walls. She wondered when the gas fireplace had been installed. Had her parents added that for their comfort, or hers? She loved them so much and knew she was going to miss them terribly. It felt so strange to live in Hidden Lakes without her parents. It would be just as strange to walk into her father's old hardware store and know he wouldn't be fussing over the books or unloading boxes.

She took several deep breaths, brushed away the tears and headed back to the car. She needed to get unpacked and settled in for the night. Tomorrow she and Jeremy would begin their new life. Hopefully, with time, it would be a good one. An image of Shane Chandler instantly popped into her head. How could it be good when Shane still lived a few miles out of town? Seeing him with

Kristy and their little family was going to kill her. Did they only have one child, or did they have the American dream of two and a half kids and a dog? With any luck, she'd have time to get settled before she had to deal with that unpleasant encounter.

"Hey sport," Melissa said, brushing her son's dark locks away from his face. "We're here." She reached in and smoothly untangled the seatbelt. "Let's get you into bed."

Jeremy rubbed his eyes and moaned. Then he slid from the car and zombie walked into the house.

Melissa smiled. She knew her little man was only half awake. Once the kid went down, he was out for the count. Jer played hard and slept hard, another thing he inherited from his father. Melissa tried to push the thought from her mind, but couldn't. The older Jeremy got, the more he took on the rugged, good looks of his dad. She knew he was going to be a heart breaker. She just hoped that between her and Mitch they'd taught him enough compassion to let the girls down easy. Mitch had been the perfect gentleman, always opening her door and bringing her flowers. Fortunately, he had passed that knowledge on to Jeremy. Melissa knew she'd been lucky to find such an honorable, caring man. And Jeremy had been blessed to have Mitch as a role model. Her son was a quick learner. By the time he was three, he was emulating Mitch's every move. She'd lost track of the number of times Jer had stopped to pick wild flowers on his way home from school this past year. He had tried so hard to fill Mitch's shoes in his absence. Maybe now that they were here, in a new house, in a small town, away from all the memories, she'd be able to move forward and Jeremy could just be a carefree kid again.

Melissa stripped off Jeremy's sweatshirt and jeans then slipped on his PJ's. Normally she'd insist he brush his teeth, but after the long ride, she decided he could skip it just this once. She watched as Jeremy climbed into bed and immediately slipped into a deep sleep. How she wished she could relax as quickly and completely as her son. Her thoughts shifted to another man, one who could also fall asleep in a matter of minutes. She immediately slammed the door on those memories. Thinking about Shane Chandler, remembering their time together, would bring her nothing but heartache. Melissa returned to the car and gathered up the essentials. The rest of their things could wait until morning. She locked up and headed for her new room. She thought it would be another night of restlessness, tossing and turning until the sun came up, but almost the instant her head hit the pillow she was out.

* * * *

Shane finished the last swallow of coffee and headed outside. The morning air was crisp and cool, but fresh. Spring had definitely arrived. Mornings like this made all the hard work and effort worth it. He leaned against the sturdy porch rail and took in the beauty. He loved watching the sun rise over his land. The vibrant yellow rays danced across the creek making the water shimmer with life. There was a slight breeze ruffling the remnants of last year's alfalfa field reminding him it was almost time to plow the field and rotate the crop. This morning everything was covered in a slight, mystic fog. Every season had its beauty but Shane loved spring the most. The ranch seemed to come alive in the springtime.

He pivoted as he heard the screen door creek open and saw his daughter standing bare foot in the opening. He took two large steps and scooped her into his arms. "Morning sunshine," he said, lowering himself onto the old porch swing and settling Meg onto his lap. "What has you up so early?" He pressed his lips to her forehead and frowned.

"I don't feel good," she moaned, holding her stomach.

Shane was immediately on his feet and back in the house. It was too cold for her to be outside with a fever. Once in the kitchen Shane placed his little girl on a chair and began rummaging around for the children's Tylenol. Once he found it, he grabbed a Sprite from the fridge and moved to her side. "Tummy ache?" he asked gently.

"Uh-huh," she nodded. "And I'm cold." Her little body shivered to prove the point.

Shane crouched in front of Megan and held out the Sprite. "I need you to take little sips. It will help settle your stomach. And I need you to take this medicine."

Meg took the Tylenol and washed it down with a sip of Sprite. "I wanted to go riding with you today," she frowned, clearly upset about missing her first ride of the season.

"There's always tomorrow, pumpkin," Shane said lovingly. His daughter was the best part of his life, the one good thing he'd accomplished. He loved her more than anything, even the ranch. It was strange, he never thought he'd love anything more than the ranch and certainly not anyone. His thoughts turned to Melissa Peters. He'd made so many mistakes with Melissa. She was the only woman he had ever truly loved. Back then his feelings had been so intense, he hadn't known how to deal with them. So, being young and stupid, he'd messed things up. On days like today, he wondered how things might have been different. But he couldn't regret his actions. That would mean regretting Megan. And he could never regret such a beautiful, special little girl.

Shane watched Meg take another sip of her soda then lifted her into his arms and carried her to the family room. After grabbing the quilt from the back of the couch, he settled into the large rocking chair and cuddled his daughter against his chest.

Meg burrowed in close, pressing her cheek against Shane's chest. She felt so safe in her father's arms. Her eyes began to droop and she pulled the blanket further under her chin. Then she bolted up and gave her dad a worried look. "You have to go," she said softly. "You don't have time to waste holding me. You have to move the cows today."

Shane pushed his daughter back against his chest. "Don't be ridiculous. I always have time for you. Cora will be here soon and I'll head out once she arrives." He kissed the top of her head. "The cows can wait for an hour or so. How's the tummy?" He began rubbing her back, hoping Megan would relax and go back to sleep.

"Better, I think," she admitted. "I love you dad," she whispered as she drifted back to sleep.

"I love you too, Princess," Shane whispered. "More than you know."

Forty minutes later Cora stepped into the family room. She sighed and smiled. Seeing such a strong, masculine man rocking his little girl warmed her heart. Shane Chandler was special. She'd seen his compassion as a boy, but she was so proud of the man he'd become. Maybe having such a wonderful father would offset the girls' terrible mother. At least the woman was out of their lives for good this time. Shane had seen to that. What kind of mother sold her own child? Kristy, that's who. Before she could get herself worked up, Cora walked to the chair and placed a hand on Shane's shoulder.

Shane jerked, then settled back when he spotted Cora. "She had an upset stomach and a slight fever," he whispered. "I didn't want to leave her until I knew you were here."

Cora brushed a hand over the child's head. "Fever's down," she said with a nod. "Take her to bed now and don't you worry. I'll take good care of her today. It's probably just a little stomach bug.

I'm sure she'll be much better this afternoon. I'll make chicken soup for dinner."

Shane stood, cradling Meg in his arms and smiled. "And fresh baked bread?" he asked.

"Of course," Cora said, trying to sound impatient. "Now go, you have work to do. This ranch won't run itself while you lollygag."

Shane laughed as he carried Meg to her room. Moments later he was back in the kitchen. He stopped to brush a kiss on Cora's cheek. "Thanks, Cora. I'd be lost without you."

Cora heard the sincerity in Shane's words and cut off the sarcastic reply she was about to give. "That little girl will be fine," she said laying a gentle hand on Shane's arm. "I'm sure it's just a bug. Nothing to worry about. She probably got it from one of her school mates. Now shew, I've got work and so do you."

Shane smiled and hurried out the door. He loved Cora like a mother and he was being honest when he told her he couldn't do it without her. Being a single father and running a ranch would be impossible without help. At eight, Meg didn't need as much supervision as she had in the beginning, but on days like today Cora was a life saver. He was still going to worry about his little girl. He knew Megan was in good hands, but he was going to head back and check on her around lunch time, anyway. While the men took a break, he could reassure himself it was just a bug, like Cora said. Shane pulled himself onto his favorite horse and headed across the field.

Chapter Two

Melissa barely stopped herself from moaning as Jeremy bounced on the bed. If he pushed any harder on the edge, she might topple to the ground.

"Mom, wake up!" he insisted.

Smiling, she pulled him into her arms and rubbed his head with her knuckles. Jeremy squirmed and tried to get away. Melissa finally released him and sat up. "I'm up now you little monster," she said lovingly. "What's so important you had to deprive me of sleep?"

"Can I go outside?" he begged. "Pleeeese? I waited for a whole hour before I woke you up."

Melissa laughed. Jeremy had a whole new world to explore and he was anxious to get started. "Breakfast first, then you help me unload the car. After that, you can go check out the backyard." She'd need to inspect the old tree house. If the porch steps were going, the tree house might be a complete loss. She hoped it was salvageable. As a child the tree house had been her sanctuary. She'd spent hours, days sometimes, with her best friend Sarah plotting world domination in their special clubhouse. She wanted Jeremy to have just as many adventures as she had while he was still young.

"There was a real football in my room. Not a kid's toy, but a real football. Can I have it mom? Can I really play with the football?" Jeremy asked, hope shining in his eyes.

"I bet your grandparents left that there just for you." She smiled, thinking of her parents as they headed for the kitchen.

"And there's an X-Box in my room, too. Is that for me?" he asked hopefully.

Melissa hadn't seen the X-box. Her parents had gone overboard. She loved them dearly, but they needed to be spending their money on their new house, not on spoiling their grandson. "It is but it's a privilege, not a right," she warned.

"Yeah, I know. I have to do my work and be good in school and then I can play with the good stuff," he parroted, losing some of his excitement.

Melissa couldn't dampen his spirit already. "Should I make pancakes?" she asked, smiling. Jer loved pancakes.

"Do we have syrup?" he said, regaining his enthusiasm.

"Grandma always has syrup," Melissa said confidently.

"And scrambled eggs?" Jeremy said, hoping he wasn't pushing it.

"Of course," Melissa said, grateful the light had returned to Jeremy's eyes.

* * * *

Hours later, Melissa watched as Jeremy climbed in and out of the tree house. She was surprised that it was in such good shape. She knew she shouldn't be. Her father was thorough and he'd been a good carpenter. That's what made the condition of the house so depressing. It signified just how sick her dad had been the last couple years. But Jake Peters had built that tree house to last. Melissa knew he had grandchildren and maybe even great grandchildren in mind when he'd selected the sturdy redwood boards to build her childhood sanctuary. Well, his wish had finally come true. Jeremy was having a blast filling the place with all his boy stuff. He'd already announced that no girls were allowed. Little did he know, not so long ago, a similar decree had gone out against all the boys in the land.

Melissa pulled out another nail and pried the rotted board from the back porch. She had to make the backyard kid proof. Jeremy was going to spend countless hours back here and she didn't want to worry about his safety. The front yard and the roof were going to have to wait. Maybe longer than she originally thought if the leak she'd discovered this morning was as bad as she feared. Hiring a plumber to fix the ancient pipes in this house was going to be expensive. Probably more than she could afford at the moment.

Melissa stood and brushed off her jeans. It was time to head into town. She hated to do it. Weekends at the lumber yard were always packed. At least Sunday was better than Saturday. "Come on Jer," she called. "We need to head into town and get some new wood for the back porch before the store closes. I have to get this project done today. Tomorrow is Monday. I start work and you start school."

Jeremy jumped from the ladder and ran to the car. "Can we get ice cream?" he asked. "I'm hungry and dinners not for hours. I don't think I can make it."

Melissa laughed. He was probably right. The kid had been going a mile a minute since they'd walked out the door. "Why don't we stop at the grocery store and buy some. That way we can get bananas and caramel and have banana splits."

"Can we have whipped cream, too?" he asked with the hope of a child.

"Absolutely," Melissa said, backing out of the driveway. "And a cherry on top. What's a banana split without whip cream and a big old red cherry?"

"Yay!" Jeremy said, pumping his arms in the air. "I like it here, mom. I'm glad we moved."

For the first time since Melissa had decided to sell their house in Denver, she felt confident she'd made the right decision. Things would be better here, she would make sure of it. For Jeremy's sake, they had to be. Now if she just knew what to do about Shane Chandler.

The closer they got to the lumber store, the more nervous Melissa became. If she was lucky she wouldn't run into anyone she knew. But what were the chances she'd have the same luck at the grocery store? About a million to one, she supposed. "Okay Carpenter Joe," Melissa said as they climbed from the car. "You ready to help me pick out the best lumber in the joint?"

Jeremy smiled. He liked that his mom let him help with stuff. It made him feel like the man of the house. The way his dad had taught him. He remembered the man to man talk he'd had with his dad just after he'd turned six. Mitch told Jeremy that his job was dangerous and if anything ever happened to him, it was Jeremy's job to take care of his mother. And Jeremy had tried to take care of her. Mom had been so sad when dad died. Jeremy had spent almost an hour selecting just the right flowers to try to cheer her up the way dad had done when mom seemed sad. But it hadn't helped, no matter how many times he tried. Nothing he did in Denver ever helped. But things were different now. Hidden Lakes was a new start for them. And mom already seemed happier. The house needed work, but Jer could take care of it. He was the man of the house now, just like dad said. And he was going to pick out the best wood in the store.

Melissa tied a small red cloth to the end of the wood sticking out her back window. She was going to have to leave Jeremy in the car with the supplies since they couldn't lock up. As they pulled onto the road and headed two blocks south to the grocery store she glanced at her son. "We can't leave the stuff in the car unattended. Do you think you can stand guard while I grab the groceries we need at the store?" she asked.

"Okay," Jeremy said, playing with the radio. "Can you leave the keys so I can listen to music while you're gone?"

"I don't think that's a good idea," she said, used to living with the dangers of the big city. She knew this was a small town, but she'd been gone too long. Until she was more comfortable with the people, she wouldn't chance someone stealing her car with her son inside.

"You're probably right," Jeremy said. "Do you remember that kid that got stolen back in Denver because his mom left the car running while she ran in to buy a pack of cigarettes? I probably couldn't stop someone yet if they tried to steal the car."

Melissa frowned, remembering the incident. Sometimes she thought Jeremy was too wise for his age, like he thought he had to be an adult because Mitch was no longer around, like he had to protect her. In Denver, Jeremy had watched the news every night trying to take in all the dangers, so he'd be prepared for the worst. Maybe living in the country would help him to just be a kid again. She pulled into a stall as close to the front doors as she could get. "Okay, I'll be quick. Lock the doors behind me."

"I'm fine mom," Jeremy said distracted. He was playing with the handheld video game Mitch's mother had bought him. Melissa smiled. Jeremy wouldn't even notice she was gone.

* * * *

Melissa rounded the corner and made a bee line to the frozen food section. She just needed ice cream and then she could escape. So far, so good. She'd been able to avoid every person in the store that she recognized. She had just pulled out a carton of ice cream and was closing the door when she nearly collided with Sissy Francis. Melissa barely stopped the groan forming at the back of her throat. "Excuse me," she said ducking her head in hopes that the woman didn't recognize her.

"I thought that was you," Sissy said, blocking Melissa's path with her cart. "I couldn't believe it at first, but the instant I saw you, I knew Melissa Peters was back in town. I just had to come over and say hello."

More like you just had to come over and snoop, Melissa thought. "How are you Sissy?" Melissa said, trying to sound as cordial as possible.

"Oh, I'm just perfect," she said grinning. How had Melissa Peters snuck into town without anyone knowing? She must be staying at her parents' home. "Me and Frank got married a few years back and we're just happy as clams."

"Congratulations!" Melissa said, trying to maneuver her basket around the hot pink obstacle. Sissy always did like pink. The tight hot pink pants and matching pink and purple blouse was way too much for Melissa's liking. Not Sissy's, that girl was always all about splash.

"So I guess you're staying in your parents' old house?" Sissy said, moving slightly to prevent Melissa's escape.

"Uh...yeah," Melissa said, realizing she was stuck. "It's really been great to see you again Sissy, but I'm actually in a hurry."

"I thought your parents moved to Florida," Sissy continued. "Are you here to sell the place?"

"No," Melissa said, caving. She wasn't going to get home until she gave Sissy the scoop and it really didn't matter anyway. Once she started at the Sheriff's Office in the morning, the whole town would know she was back. "I bought my parents' home. I'm staying, permanently. Now if you'll excuse me, I really am in a hurry." Melissa gave her basket a push, which sent Sissy's cart careening into the glass door. "Sorry," Melissa said as she rushed down the aisle.

"Well," Sissy huffed. "That woman always was rude," she grumbled as she headed in the opposite direction. Clearly time away from town hadn't improved Melissa Peter's social graces. Sissy smiled. Shane Chandler was going to be oh, so surprised to learn his old flame was back in town. Sissy couldn't wait to tell him.

As it happens, Sissy got her chance that very evening. She was sitting at the local café when she spotted Shane Chandler entering the pharmacy. "Frank, come on. We need to go."

Frank looked up and gave Sissy a confused look. "What's the rush? I haven't finished my coke."

"Come on," Sissy said, standing. "You have coke at home." She waited impatiently as Frank threw enough money on the table to cover the bill and a generous tip then followed her out the door. They barely made it in time. Sissy was pulling Frank down the sidewalk as Shane exited the building. They almost collided.

"Oh, Shane. I didn't see you there," Sissy lied.

Frank rolled his eyes. He knew what his wife was up to. She'd been going on nonstop about Melissa Peters all day.

Shane tipped his hat in greeting and started to move passed them. He needed to get home. Meg was doing better, but she still had a slight fever and they were out of children's Tylenol. He wanted to get home before she fell asleep so he wouldn't have to wake her just to give her the medication.

"I'm glad we ran into you," Sissy said, following Shane toward his car. "You'll never guess who I ran into today at the grocery store." She paused, waiting for Shane to inquire but when he continued toward his truck she blurted it out. "Melissa Peters." She was so happy to be sharing the news she didn't noticed Shane's slight misstep.

Shane didn't have time for the town busy body. Did she really think he cared who she'd gossiped with in the grocery store? He was almost to the truck when the words hit him like a freight train. Melissa was in town? He wondered why. Her parents had moved to Florida, some retirement community that would give Jake the rest he needed to get well.

"She said she bought her parents' place and will be living here permanently." Sissy continued, oblivious to the turmoil that was churning inside Shane's very soul. "Those were her words...permanently. Did you know she was coming back, Shane? I never heard a word about it. You can imagine my surprise when we practically collided in the frozen food section. She was buying ice cream of all things. You know, that woman better be careful. She might still be small and petite now, but a habit of indulging that way will ruin her figure quicker than spit. None of us are in our prime anymore."

"I'm sorry. Sissy...Frank," Shane said, trying to breathe. "My daughter isn't feeling well. I need to get home to give her this medication before she falls asleep."

"Of course," Frank said, pulling his wife away from Shane. He could tell the man was upset and with good reason. Everyone knew Melissa Peters had broken the guy's heart.

Shane climbed in his truck, started the engine and pulled onto the highway. He had to get away from here. He was on autopilot, habit the only thing leading him in the right direction as he traveled away from the small town toward his ranch. The instant he saw old man Stewart's cornfield, he pulled his truck to the side of the road and parked. He needed to get a grip. He shouldn't have been rattled so innately by the news that Melissa was back in town. But Sissy had been so smug, reveling in the fact that Melissa was here permanently. It was the situation, the messenger, as much as the message that had thrown him. But why the secrecy? Connie hadn't mentioned her daughter's return to anyone. He knew that, it was a small enough town that if Connie had told a living soul the news would have been everywhere.

Shane lowered his forehead to the steering wheel. He'd never gotten over Melissa, he was pretty sure he never would. Unfortunately, he was just as sure that she would never forgive him for his betrayal. How were they going to live in the same town, run into each other at the grocery store or the hardware store and not cause a scene? Him out of frustration because he couldn't have her and her out of anger because she hated him. He knew he deserved her anger and her hatred. He had no one to blame but himself. But knowing it, didn't make the fact any easier to live with. A part of him died the day he left Melissa. A bigger part of him died the day she left town without a word. So much time had passed, just over eight years in fact. He wondered if it was possible to put the past behind them.

Shane slowly pulled the truck back onto the roadway. Megan needed him. He wasn't going to figure anything out tonight, and certainly not while parked on the side of a dark roadway. He'd go back home, take care of his daughter and figure out a plan in the morning.

* * * *

Melissa pulled out of her driveway and headed for the Sheriff's Office. She was lucky to live in a neighborhood that rarely changed. She'd known her next door neighbor, Mrs. Chilcot, all her life but she never would have asked her for help. It all sort of just happened, almost like fate had worked everything out. She'd been surprised

18

when she opened the door and saw Agnes Chilcot standing there with a plate of cookies and a kind word of welcome. Of course, she insisted the elderly lady come in so they could catch up. They'd gotten to visiting and the topic had come up of Melissa's new job. Agnes immediately asked if she needed help with Jeremy since school started almost an hour after Melissa's shift started. Everything had worked out perfectly. The only downside was that Agnes had been ancient when Melissa was growing up. She had to be at least eighty five now. Melissa worried that Jeremy's energy would be too much for Agnes to take, especially that early in the morning. But for today, Melissa was not going to borrow trouble. Things had worked out and she was headed for the first day in her new job.

* * * *

The instant Sarah heard the news she was in her car and headed to the Peter's house. Melissa was back. She was so excited, she could hardly stand it. Sarah pulled into the drive and rushed to the door. There wasn't a car in the driveway and the house looked vacant. Had the rumors been wrong? Was Sissy making things up again to get attention? Sarah was so deep in thought that she jumped when she heard her name. "Oh Mrs. Chilcot, hello."

"Sorry to startle you dear. I assume you're looking for Melissa," the elderly neighbor requested.

"Yes. I am," Sarah said moving from the porch to stand beside the small fence separating the two yards. "Have you seen her?"

"I spoke to her yesterday and again this morning," Agnes said cheerfully. "She's still a beauty, that one. It's a pleasure having her home and her son is a pure delight."

"Son?" Sarah asked. But immediately shifted gears, Mel could tell her about that later. "You don't happen to know where she might be, do you?"

"Oh yes," Agnes said still beaming. "She's at the Sheriff's Office."

"What?" Sarah asked in surprise. "Why? What happened?" She'd have to call Jason and see what he could do to help.

"Sorry dear," Agnes said, realizing Sarah misunderstood. "I didn't mean to alarm you. I assumed you knew because of Jason. Melissa is working for Joe Swenson. Dispatcher, secretary or some such thing. She's taken Dolly's old job."

"Oh, well good," Sarah said. And it was. If Melissa was working for Sheriff Swenson chances were good she'd stay in town awhile. Sarah couldn't be happier. She just wondered why Melissa hadn't called her. She'd missed her friend these past eight years and was anxious to catch up. "You don't happen to know when she gets off do you?"

"I believe she said three," Agnes considered. "Yes, three o'clock because she said she'd be home before Jeremy."

"Jeremy?" Sarah asked, confused.

"Yes, Jeremy. Delightful boy. I admit I was a little worried. Kids that age have so much energy and at my age there's no way I can keep up. But the boy was a real treat. No problem at all. Anyway, I'm sure Melissa said three o'clock and that's why I didn't need to watch for the boy after school."

"I see," but she really didn't. Mel was going to have to fill in the details. So, Melissa Peter's had a son. Sarah wondered how old he was. With any luck he might be old enough to spend time with Scotty. Wouldn't it be wonderful if she and Mel had kids that could grow up together the same as they had? "Thanks Mrs. Chilcot. I'll come back after three."

Sarah climbed into her car and started backing out of the drive when she spotted Shane Chandler's fancy truck. She was a little surprised, but realized she shouldn't be. It was only a matter of time before he found his way over to Mel's house. Sarah paused, considering her options. Before she could decide if she should stop and let Shane know Melissa wasn't home or just drive off, he had blocked her in. Well that answers that, Sarah thought. She pushed open her door and came face to face with one of the most gorgeous men in the county; probably the nearest five for that matter. "Hello, Shane."

"Is she home?" he asked. Shane never was one for small talk.

"Nope," Sarah said, trying to sound casual. "Mrs. Chilcot says she's working at the Sheriff's Office. Apparently Joe gave her Dolly's old job. And believe me, Jason has a lot to answer for. I intend to find out why he didn't tell me they had a new dispatcher." She glanced over the fence and realized Agnes had retreated to the house already.

Shane scowled. How had Mel moved to town, taken up residence and gotten a job all without Shane even knowing she was here? "Did Agnes know when Mel would be home?"

No way was Sarah going into that convoluted explanation before she talked to Mel. "Sometime after three," Sarah said casually. "But I have first dib's. I plan to be right back here in this driveway at 3:05 and if you come knocking we won't be answering. Mel and I have a lot of catching up to do."

Shane smiled. "Understood. I can't make it until later anyway." He started to turn around to head back to his truck then stopped. "I know you're close and all, but would you do me a favor and not mention my visit to Mel?"

Sarah narrowed her eyes. "Why?" she finally asked.

"Oh, I think you already know," Shane said with a sigh. "I just want a chance to talk to her. If you warn her off, it's going to take weeks to track her down. Please, Sarah. Just give me one shot. After that, I'll stay away if that's what Mel wants."

Sarah considered. She could give Shane this one chance. She knew the history and thought they both got a raw deal all around. Shane had more than paid his debt to the Karma God's after putting up with Kristy as long as he had. "Okay. But I won't lie for you," Sarah finally said. "If I can, I'll keep your secret and give you a chance."

"Thanks," Shane said with sincerity. "That's all I'm asking. How's Jason and the kids?"

"Great," Sarah said, then frowned. "Except, you'd think with my connection with the police I would have heard about Mel's return before today...and not from Sissy Francis. It was embarrassing to get the news from that nosy woman."

"Agreed," Shane said relieved that even Sarah hadn't known Melissa was returning to town. "I wonder why all the secrecy? She had to speak to Joe weeks ago to have that job lined up already."

"Well, maybe we'll both find out tonight. Anyway, I've gotta go. Kayla's getting fussy and Brook should be getting home from kindergarten any minute now." Sarah waved as she climbed into the car.

"It was good to see you Sarah," Shane said as he turned and headed for his truck. He always liked Sarah Miller, now Madsen. She was a smart, fun loving, classy lady. Jason Madsen was one lucky man. Shane just hoped the guy realized it and cherished what he had. Everyone wasn't that lucky.

* * * *

Melissa placed the casserole in the oven and headed for the door. It had been too long since she'd checked on Jeremy and it would be dark soon. Catching up with Sarah had been a welcome surprise. As usual, they had both lost track of time and now dinner was late. Mel hadn't realized they were neighbors. And thank goodness they were. Jeremy was well behaved this morning, but Melissa still wasn't comfortable using Mrs. Chilcot as a daily babysitter. Once Sarah realized Jeremy was only a year younger than her oldest son, Scotty, she'd insisted Mel drop Jeremy off at her house before work. Sarah could get them both off to school and the boys could get to know each other better. Somehow things kept working out for the best. Other than the plumbing anyway. Once she'd explained the problem to the only plumber in town, he went off on neglected pipes and terrible homeowners. She just knew the repair was going to cost a fortune. One she didn't have at the moment. Apparently that was what credit was for. Mel hated to put anything on her credit card, but she kept one for emergencies and this was definitely an emergency.

Hidden Lakes

She stepped onto the porch and smiled as Jeremy came barreling down the driveway on his almost new bike. Just another thing she was grateful for. If she and Mitch hadn't bought such an extravagant gift for Jeremy's seventh birthday, she'd be shopping garage sales for something used and probably decrepit. Melissa still felt bad that Mitch hadn't lived to see the pure joy on Jeremy's face when she gave him that gift. Remembering that day, almost a year ago, made her a little sad. But Jeremy was so happy here. Mitch had helped her make that happen. Mel thought about their situation. She had a new car and Jeremy had a new bike. Appearances were everything. This way nobody would know just how broke she really was and Jeremy could start acting like a kid again. He could run and play and ride his bike around the neighborhood. Oh, he could play in the back yard back in Denver, but Mel never let Jeremy wander out alone. Which meant his playtime was limited by her availability. She didn't worry so much here. She knew as long as he stayed in the area, he was safe. She glanced up just in time to see a fancy new truck pull up behind her car. She'd parked on the curb to give Jer more room to ride his bike. Her face fell when she saw Shane Chandler casually exit the cab. He swung the door shut and immediately headed her way. For a moment she panicked. Her eyes shot to Jeremy then back to Shane. She had to stay calm. She could do this. She knew this day would come eventually, she'd just hoped for a little more time.

Shane spotted Melissa on the porch and some of his tension lifted. He knew he could trust Sarah, but he also knew if push came to shove, she was loyal to Mel. He didn't notice the boy until the kid's bike screeched to a halt in front of him, almost stopping on his left boot. Shane glanced down casually, wondering who the kid was and froze when bright blue eyes stared up at him. His eyes. But that wasn't possible. It couldn't be. Half the population had blue eyes, he assured himself. Mel had blue eyes. His head shot to Mel then back to the kid.

"Hi mister," the boy said clearly sizing him up. "Can I help you?"

Shane had to smile. The kid had guts. "I'm just here to see an old friend. Who might you be?"

"Jeremy," the kid said proudly. "Who are you? And who is your friend? We just moved here but I might know him."

"Shane Chandler and my friend is that lovely lady standing on the porch over there."

"Hey! That's my mom," Jeremy said proudly. "You know her?"

Shane studied the boy closer, then turned to look at Melissa. She wasn't moving. He knew that look, something was wrong. "I did a long time ago," he answered, trying to ignore the hurricane churning in his gut.

"I like your name Shane," Jeremy said. "Is it okay if I call you Shane, Mr. Chandler?"

"Absolutely. I like yours too. Is it okay if I call you Jeremy?"

"Of course," Jeremy told the stranger laughing. "That's my name. Sometimes I forget names. But I won't forget yours 'cause it's the same as mine. So that will be easy to remember."

"The same?" Shane said, that sinking feeling in his stomach getting worse by the second.

"Yeah," Jeremy said innocently. "I'm Jeremy Shane Carpenter."

"Jer, I need you to take your bike around back. Dinner's almost ready. Then go in the back door and set the table. I'll be there in a minute," Melissa said, stepping off the porch and approaching Shane.

Shane turned on her the instant she reached the driveway. He glanced toward the back to ensure the boy was long gone, then glared back at Melissa.

Melissa didn't know what to say. Clearly Shane had already figured it out. He was looking at her with such cold fury she was afraid to speak. She'd seen Shane like this before, but not often. He was nowhere near rational when his temper ruled like it was right now.

"Jeremy Shane Carpenter?" he finally hissed. His chest was rising and falling rapidly. He had a son. A son that Melissa didn't bother to give his name. "Don't try to pretend he's not mine. So help me Melissa, I'll force a paternity test if necessary."

"It's not necessary," she said softly. "He's ours."

"Ours?" Shane bellowed. "That's rich. Ours suggests some kind of joint commitment. In this case joint knowledge would have been nice. How could you?"

If all Melissa had seen was anger, she would have had a comeback, but she knew Shane too well. And what she saw in his eyes was pain. "Let's go inside."

"Does he even know? Does he know I'm his father or did you lie to him, too?" Shane asked, not moving.

"No Shane, he doesn't know. I was hoping I would have more time before you found out I was here. Well, that's not true. I knew the instant I showed up for work the whole town would know. I just never thought you'd come over so soon. I planned to talk to him, and you…in time." Melissa stopped, sensing she was only making things worse.

"Eight years wasn't enough time for you?" he said through gritted teeth.

"No! It wasn't," Melissa shot back. "Because during most of that time, Jeremy had a father. A good man that loved him. A man that Jer looked up to and thought was his dad."

"You told my son that some other guy was his father? You let my son grow up thinking that some random guy was..." Shane stopped himself, clenching his fists by his side. He knew he was getting out of control. He couldn't sit down and talk rationally about this. He needed time to think, time to cool off. He closed his eyes and counted to ten. When he opened them, Melissa was still standing there motionless, not saying a word. "I can't do this right now. I'll come back at nine. Go have dinner with 'our' son. I assume he'll be in bed by then?"

"Yes," Melissa confirmed.

"Then I'll be back at nine. Don't mess with me, Melissa. You had better be here when I get back."

"I'm not going anywhere Shane," Melissa said, turning to head back into the house. "This is my home now. I'm staying in Hidden Lakes for the foreseeable future."

"Good, then I'll see you at nine." Shane climbed in his truck and drove away.

Hidden Lakes

Melissa sank to the ground and began to cry.

Jeremy looked out the window, expecting to see the cowboy talking to his mother but instead he saw her crying. His face hardened and he rushed to his mother side, angry at the man for ruining things. They had been so happy here until he came. "Mom?" Jeremy said, putting a hand on her shoulder the way his father used to do when he was upset. Feeling his dad's strength always made Jeremy feel safe. Maybe he could do the same for his mom.

"I'm sorry sweetheart," Melissa said standing and taking her son's hand. "Did you set the table?" She needed to pull it together, for Jeremy's sake if not her own.

"Yes, but why are you crying?" He frowned down the road then looked back at his mom. "Did that man hurt you? Because I sort of liked him, but if he made you cry he's not nice like I thought."

"No sweetie," Melissa said. "Shane didn't make me cry. There's just something very hard that I have to do and it scares me. That's why I was crying."

"Is Shane making you do it?" Jeremy asked following his mother into the kitchen and taking his seat at the table.

"No, not really. It's something I should have done a long time ago, but I was too afraid." Melissa pulled dinner out of the oven and dished up their plates.

"Can I help?" Jeremy finally said. "Maybe if I help you, it won't be so scary."

Mel took Jeremy's little hand and held it tight. "No, it's something I have to do on my own. But don't you worry. Everything is going to be okay."

Jeremy stood and moved to his mother. He reached out and gave her a big hug. "Maybe that will help. Hugs always make me feel better."

Melissa felt the tear slide down her face and quickly brushed it away. Words could never express how much she loved her little boy. He was growing up so fast, too fast. Before she knew it he'd be going off to college. She hated knowing she was going to have to share him with Shane. And she would have to share. There was no way Shane would reject his own son. Wasn't that why he'd married Kristy? Because she was pregnant with his child. That's when it hit her, why was Shane stopping by to visit an old girlfriend? If Kristy knew, she'd skin him alive.

Melissa thought back to the last time she'd seen Kristy. It was the day before she had left town. Melissa knew she couldn't stand to say goodbye to Shane, but she had to do something. So, she bought him a birthday card even though it was early and left it on the windshield of his old truck. She wished him happy birthday and told him she would always be his friend. Unfortunately Kristy found the card, not Shane. She'd stormed into Melissa's father's hardware store looking for a fight. Kristy had gone off the instant she saw Melissa. It was all Melissa could do to get the woman into the back office before they caused a scene. Kristy told her Shane had proposed and that Melissa was to stay away from her fiancé. Melissa had looked pointedly at Kristy's ring finger, which did not have a ring. That had only intensified Kristy's anger. She informed Melissa that she didn't have a ring because she was pregnant. They were waiting until the baby was born. Then they would go shopping for the most beautiful, elegant ring they could find and have a wonderful ceremony, which Melissa was not invited to.

Hidden Lakes

Kristy ranted for quite some time, telling Melissa how wonderful her relationship with Shane was and how stupid Melissa had been. Unlike Melissa, Kristy didn't mind sharing Shane in the short term as long as she won in the end. That's when Kristy let it slip that she had trapped Shane by getting pregnant on purpose. She was tired of wondering which of his girlfriend's Shane would choose so Kristy made sure it was her. She told Melissa if she was smart she would wise up and do the same. If Melissa ever wanted to be happy she would find a man and force him into marriage with an unplanned pregnancy. Melissa had been so stunned and heartbroken she didn't know what to say. So, she just stood there, listening to a mad woman vent. Then Kristy turned and stalked out of the store. Melissa went home and packed. She'd left for Denver the following day. That was over eight years ago and she hadn't seen the woman since. More importantly, she had no desire to see her now. Oh she knew it was inevitable, but that didn't make the prospect any more pleasant. Especially now that Shane knew about their son.

Melissa looked at Jeremy. How was she going to let Shane have time with their child but still keep him away from that dreadful woman? She sighed. It wasn't going to be pleasant, but that was definitely one topic they would be covering in their discussion tonight.

Chapter Three

Shane stomped into the kitchen, slamming the door behind him. He winced when he saw Cora jump. "Sorry," he said, moving to the fridge and grabbing a beer.

"Rough day?" she asked, studying Shane. Something was wrong. Seriously wrong.

"You might say that," Shane grumbled.

"Does this have anything to do with Melissa Peters moving back to town?" Cora asked hesitantly.

"It has everything to do with Melissa." Shane sank into a chair, closing his eyes as he combed a hand through his hair.

Cora picked up a spoon and began stirring the stew. Megan was feeling much better, but not yet a hundred percent. Cora's stew would remedy that. The girl would be back to normal and headed off to school in the morning. "Do you want to talk about it?" Cora finally asked.

"Where is Megan?" Shane said, not wanting to get into anything if his daughter was nearby.

"I sent her up for a nice hot bath. I suspect she's about ready to get out and join us for dinner. She's much better today. It appears she just had a twenty four hour bug. She's ready to go back to school in the morning," Cora assured him.

"Good," Shane said. Then he let out a huge sigh and focused on Cora. She was the closest thing he had to a mother. As far as he was concerned his own mother didn't count. That woman didn't have a maternal bone in her body. "I saw Melissa, just before I came home. I stopped by the old Peter's place."

"And?" Cora asked.

"And it appears we have a son," Shane said, gritting his teeth. Just saying it out loud brought back all the anger and betrayal.

Cora gasped and dropped the spoon onto the tile floor. She was quick to recover, bending to scoop up the mess and toss the spoon into the sink. Then she went to Shane. She didn't say a word, just took him in her arms and rocked him gently. "I know how hard this must be on you, Shane." Her mind was racing, Melissa had been pregnant when she left?

Shane inhaled the sweet smell of a woman he loved more than his own mother. She'd always been there for him since the day he'd arrived in town. She loved him unconditionally and the feeling was mutual. Other than Melissa, she was the only person who knew his secrets. The only one that knew his family history. And that's what made this all so much worse. Melissa knew. She knew how hard it was on him to have a mother that was on her sixth marriage. The constant revolving door of men as he grew up. The isolation he felt. The feeling of never being good enough. And knowing that, knowing how strongly he felt about family, she had packed up and left town carrying his child.

"I knew she was angry. Hell, she had a right to be furious. I screwed up and I knew it. But I didn't realize she hated me that bad. That she despised me enough to deprive me of my own child. Especially when she knew how much that would hurt me," he sighed. "I suppose that was probably the whole point. I hurt her, so she hurt me."

Cora was thinking. She knew Melissa. That girl didn't have a vindictive bone in her body. Cora didn't think it was about hate. She thought it was more likely about love. "I know how hard this is, but I don't think you should jump to any conclusions. What did she tell you? Did she explain why she'd kept something so important from you all this time?"

"I really didn't give her a chance," Shane admitted. "I'm going back tonight after the kids are asleep. I was just so angry I had to leave. You know how I get. If I don't control it, my temper gets me into trouble. I came home to take a ride and try to think before I go any further. If she thinks I'm just going to walk away from this, she's crazy. I will have my son. I might have to have him part time, but he's mine and he is going to know it. He's going to understand that I want him, that he's part of my family."

"Of course he will," Cora said returning to the stew. "Melissa wouldn't try to keep him away from you." She glanced at Shane and saw her mistake and his fury.

"She already did," he growled. "For eight damn years."

Hidden Lakes

"Shane," Cora began then stopped abruptly. "I can hear Megan so I'm going to make this quick. Both of you were young. You both made mistakes. Mistakes you've been paying for in more ways than one, for a very long time. Don't assume Melissa acted out of anger. She was only twenty at the time. She may have simply acted out of desperation. The same as you did when you decided it was your duty to try to make a life with that no good tramp."

"She ran away with my son," Shane said vehemently. "If I'd known, things may have been so different."

"Just give her a chance to explain," Cora begged.

"Hey princess," Shane said, forcing a light tone to his voice. "Cora says you're feeling better."

Megan moved to the table and sat next to her father. "Much better. I'm starving, what's for dinner Cora?" she asked sounding lighthearted and healthy again.

Shane let out a long breath. At least his daughter was better. "So, back to school for you tomorrow then?"

"Uh-huh," Megan said absently as she buttered a slice of freshly baked bread, still hot from the oven. "Are you going riding again this weekend? If you have to go out to the back pasture I'd like to go with. I didn't get my ride yesterday."

"We'll see," Shane said. He couldn't commit to anything until he spoke to Melissa tonight. "You coming straight home from school tomorrow or do you have practice?" Megan had insisted that she needed to learn other things besides ranching. This year, she wanted to play softball. Shane knew it had more to do with her best friend Heidi Roberts than expanding her horizons, but he didn't care. It was good for his daughter to get away from the ranch and do other things. And since Heidi was playing softball, Megan was playing too.

"No practice. I'll be home on the bus. How come?" She finally looked up at her father, realizing this was a strange question. He never asked her about her schedule, they always just checked the calendar.

"No reason. I just thought if you got right home maybe we could go for a ride tomorrow. It would have to be a short one, but I know how much you were looking forward to spending the day on Trigger yesterday," Shane said, buttering a slice of bread for himself. He knew he was going to have to explain things to Megan tomorrow. Since he didn't have a good explanation himself, the task seemed insurmountable at the moment. Maybe if they were doing something Megan loved at the time, it would soften the blow.

"Okay sure," Megan said, trying to sound like it didn't matter. But her face said it all. She was thrilled with the idea.

Cora brought a large bowl of stew to the table and placed it in front of Megan. "Eat up. You need your strength if you're going to spend all day at school and all night wandering the range on that wild beast you call Trigger."

Megan laughed. "Cora, you know you love Trigger almost as much as I do," then she dug in with enthusiasm.

* * * *

It was nine fifteen and Shane still hadn't arrived. Melissa paced the living room, impatiently waiting for the confrontation she'd been dreading for over eight years. She slid back the curtain and glanced at the roadway. This time, she saw his truck. Melissa let out a sigh of relief, but didn't know why. She knew Shane would show. He wasn't the type of man to learn he had a child and turn his back. So why had she doubted him? Because eight years ago she thought he was the type of man that would be faithful. Then she'd learned he'd had an affair. They were talking about their future and he was sleeping with another woman. It was so tempting to fall back into that easy trust, but she knew she couldn't. Shane broke her heart eight years ago. She knew she had to remember that no matter what happened tonight. Her body still reacted to Shane and she hated that, but somehow she'd put it aside. Tonight was about Jeremy, not her and Shane.

Shane hadn't meant to be late. One of his cows had gone into labor and needed his help to turn the calf. It had been a long, hard day and it was about to get even harder. He started up the stairs and noticed the damage. Melissa had a child living here now. She needed to make repairs and ensure his safety. Just one more thing he was going to have to talk to her about. There were so many, he wondered if they'd be finished before morning. He reached out to press the bell, but pulled back his hand when the door flew open.

"I didn't want you to wake Jeremy. Come in." Melissa stood back in invitation.

Shane stepped into the foyer and waited. The place was mostly the same as it had been years ago. He'd gotten so comfortable here, it almost felt like coming home. Almost. But things were different now. Funny, both of them had adamantly declared they loved each other and both of them had betrayed the other.

"I thought we would do this in the living room. Do you want something to drink before we start?" Melissa asked, knowing she sounded stiff and impersonal.

"No thanks," Shane said sounding just as distant. "But do you mind if I wash up?" He'd tried to wipe the blood away with a dry cloth, but remnants of the red liquid had dried and crusted in the crevices of his fingernails.

"Oh, no. Go ahead. You still know where it is, right?" Melissa was babbling. What was wrong with her?

Shane shot her an exasperated look then strolled down the hall, of course he knew where the bathroom was. Once inside, he let out a sigh and flipped on the water. "Whoa!" he said jumping back, but not in time. Water spewed from the faucet hitting him directly in the chest. Before he could get the damn thing shut off, his shirt was drenched. He shook his head and stripped off his shirt. Then he slowly turned the nozzle, trying to determine the problem. It only took seconds to see the whole mechanism was toast. He grabbed the soap and turned to the tub. Once his hands were scrubbed clean, he dried off on the towel and went in search of Melissa.

Melissa gasped when she turned and saw Shane's bare chest. She knew she looked like a moron standing in the middle of the kitchen staring at the dark hair covering that gorgeous torso she used to love so much. She was about to speak but stopped at Shane's words.

"You need a plumber." He held up his wet shirt. "Mind if I use the dryer?"

That shocked her back to reality better than anything else could have. "Not the bathroom too," she moaned, taking his shirt and practically stomping to the laundry room. She opened the dryer and tossed in the garment. Then she twisted the knob with so much force Shane thought she might pull the thing off.

"Easy," he said placing his hand over hers. That was a mistake. All the old electricity was still there. One touch sent his libido into overdrive. He gently pushed Melissa's hand away and started the dryer. "What do you mean, too?"

"Nothing," Melissa said shortly. She knew she was being rude, but that touch had sent her reeling. It was as if she'd traveled back in time and here she was, twenty again and in love. How did Shane do that to her? She hadn't seen him in over eight years and the chemistry was still as strong as it had been the day she packed up and left.

Shane just raised an eyebrow and waited. He knew Melissa. She'd been as rocked by the touch as he had and she didn't seem to like it one bit. Well, neither did he.

"Fine," she finally spit out. "The plumbing seems to be shot." She started out of the kitchen and headed for the living room. "I called 'Don't be dumber, call a plumber' Pete but he can't get me on the schedule for at least two weeks. More likely three."

"You didn't know about the sink, so why did you call him?" Shane asked.

"Water backed up in the basement and the tub won't drain. He said it's all part of the same problem and I'll probably need a complete overhaul," Melissa paused. "Never mind. We're here to talk about Jeremy."

Shane sat down on the couch and waited. He didn't know where to begin and wanted to give Melissa a chance. She obviously didn't want to talk about the state of the house and its numerous repairs. He glanced around and wondered about her finances. She started working at the SO, but did she have the kind of funds it would take for a complete plumbing overhaul? He was pretty sure Melissa would never tell him the answer to that question.

Melissa moved to a large chair across from Shane and sat down. "I'm not really sure where to begin with this. I know that you are going to want to be involved in Jeremy's life. I know you have a right to be. But I'm his mother. I've been solely responsible for him for the past eight years." She took a deep breath. "I guess what I'm saying is I'm very protective of my son. As much as I have to accept this, accept you spending time with him, I'm not comfortable with Kristy. I don't want my son around her at all, but I'm realistic enough to know I probably can't stop it. But Shane, if you leave him alone with her, I will fight you on this. I will mortgage the house and battle you until I have nothing. Do you understand me?"

Shane was shocked. Melissa didn't know about Kristy. How had nobody told her? "Melissa, I will have my son in my life. I'm not just going to visit him once in a while. I want joint custody. I want to know that no matter what you decide to do with your life, I have a legal right to spend time with my son. I'll fight you with everything I have on that issue, too."

"No," Melissa stood and began to pace. "If you have joint custody, Kristy..."

"Kristy's gone," Shane cut in. "Stop worrying about Kristy. This is about you and me and our child. My child. You've kept him from me for almost eight years. I will have rights to my son. That part of this is non-negotiable."

"Gone?" Melissa said, sinking back into her chair. She wasn't sure what she felt, other than weak. She was so relieved that Jeremy never had to spend one minute in that horrid woman's company, but she was also afraid. If Kristy was gone, did that mean Shane was single? Available? And how was she going to resist this nagging, explosive attraction she still had for him? Then an awful thought struck her. She jerked her head up and looked into his eyes. "And your child? Did she take the baby away from you?" No wonder he hated her.

"No," Shane said and smiled. "Megan is mine."

"You have sole custody?" Another thought struck Melissa. Shane was well respected in this town. If they went to court the judge might side with him. She could lose Jeremy completely. Father's didn't typically get sole custody of their children. The courts still believed kids were better off with their mothers. But Shane had won the custody battle against Kristy in their divorce. What would a judge do when he learned she had kept Shane's child from him for almost eight years?

"In a manner of speaking," Shane said cryptically.

"What does that mean exactly?" Melissa asked, terrified of what Shane could do.

"It means Kristy signed away all rights to her daughter. When she left me, she didn't want to be saddled with that kind of responsibility. Megan is mine and mine alone," Shane confessed. He didn't know why he was telling Melissa about Megan, it had nothing to do with their current situation.

"Well, I hope you know I would never do that. Jeremy is a part of me and I won't let him go," Melissa said adamantly.

40

Shane was surprised and confused. What exactly was Melissa thinking here? That he had somehow forced Kristy to give up her kid? That he would try to force her to do the same? "We are talking about two different people here, Melissa. I realize I didn't know you as well as I thought I did back then. The woman I thought I knew never would have snuck away with my son and deprived me of being a father. Be that as it may, you are not Kristy. I didn't believe for one minute that you would give up your kid." Especially not for a single wide trailer and a hand full of change.

"And I never believed you would talk about a future with me while you were screwing another woman. I suspect it's best to leave the past and what we thought we knew out of this conversation," Melissa retorted, her temper rising.

"You're right," Shane agreed. "The situation with Jeremy is too important to get sidelined by the past. So, are you going to fight me on custody?"

"You mean joint custody," She corrected.

"Yes, Melissa. I mean joint custody," Shane said impatiently.

"That depends," Melissa considered. "I don't have any problem with you having joint legal custody. You are his father. You have a right to doctor's information, school records, all of that. Physical custody is another story. I'm working full time. I already feel like I have very little time with Jeremy. It may sound selfish to you, but I'm not willing to give up what little time I have left with him."

"As I see it, you've had eight years." Shane was trying to keep a lid on his rising fury, but it was becoming more and more difficult as the minutes passed by. The longer Melissa spoke, the more she acted like she was doing him a favor and he should just accept the measly crumbs she was willing to drop. "If you think I'm going to be an every other weekend dad, you're nuts."

"Actually, I work weekends. I was thinking he could spend time with you on the ranch while I was at work." Melissa hoped Shane would agree.

"No," Shane said immediately. "I want him all weekend. Friday 'til Monday. He can ride the bus out after school on Friday and catch it back to school on Monday. Every weekend."

Melissa started to panic. She hadn't considered the possibility that Shane might want Jeremy to sleep over. Her breathing was erratic and she thought she might hyperventilate. "I don't think I can do that," she mumbled. "He's my baby. He's never stayed the night away from me."

"Melissa, I'm not budging on this. Either you can give me some of my rights willingly or we'll fight it out in court. He's my son. I have a right to spend time with him. Even the every other weekend minimum by law gives me overnights. You can't win this."

He was right. She knew he was right, but how would Jeremy react to this? Probably just fine. Jeremy already knew that he had another father. Mitch had explained it when he'd had that stupid man to man talk. She could have strangled him for that. Who has a man to man talk with a six year old? Mitch Carpenter, that's who. Jer had never asked to meet his father, but Mitch had assured him if he ever wanted to, Mitch would make sure Melissa didn't stand in the way. "I think we need to move on. That's not something I can agree to until I talk to Jeremy. If he doesn't want to go, I'm not going to force him."

"Melissa...." Shane began.

"No," Melissa interrupted. "I know you have a right to get to know your son. I also know if we went to court, the judge would make me do this. But first I need to talk to Jeremy. I need to see how he feels. I'm not going to traumatize him just to make you happy. He's been through enough in the past year. I won't force this right now."

"What do you mean, he's been through enough this past year?" Shane asked, worried.

"He lost his father," she said softly. "The only man he knew as his father. I know that makes you angry, but it's just the way it is. It's not something I can change."

"You mentioned that earlier," Shane said, gritting his teeth. "Something about him having a father that was a good man that Jeremy looked up to. If he was such a good man, where is he now?"

"Dead," Melissa said, swiping at the tear that escaped despite her best effort.

"I'm sorry," Shane said, softening. He hated knowing that Melissa had found someone else. Someone she clearly loved. And that his son had a father that wasn't him. But seeing the pain in Melissa's eyes, watching her try to fight the sorrow almost killed him. He couldn't stay cold and uncaring any longer. "How did he die?"

Melissa was surprised by Shane's concern. Once again, he reminded her of the old Shane. The one she thought she knew, but had been questioning for the past eight years. "Fire," she finally told him. "Mitch was a firefighter. He died at work, saving a young mother and her infant daughter."

So the guy wasn't just a good man, but a hero that gave his life in the line of duty. How could Shane ever compete with that? What was he saying? Who exactly did he want to compete for, Melissa or Jeremy? Something told him he wanted them both. Heaven help him, he still wanted Melissa as much as he ever had in spite of the betrayal. In spite of her deception and the lies, he still wanted her. He still loved her and somehow knew he always would. "I'm sorry. I can see that you loved him very much. I'm sorry for your loss."

Melissa studied Shane. She wanted to hate him for his deception, for cheating with someone like Kristy of all people. She wanted to tell him she would decide how often he saw her son, she would be in control, but she couldn't. And right now, for some reason she couldn't explain, she wanted to tell Shane she never loved Mitch. But she couldn't because she did love her husband. She had loved Mitch, she had needed Mitch and she had missed Mitch every day for the past fourteen months. "Thank you," she finally settled on. "But now you see why I have to do this right. I have to talk to Jeremy before I make plans for him. He loved Mitch, he looked up to him. I know that eventually he will have those same feelings for you, but I can't force them and neither can you."

"So what are you suggesting?" Shane asked reluctantly.

"I need time to talk to Jeremy. I'd like to sort things out. Get an idea of what you want and then run it by Jer. He deserves to have input in this. We are talking about his life," she practically begged.

"You said he doesn't know about me. So are you saying if he rejects it, which would be a natural response to that kind of shock, I'm just supposed to step back and forget my kid?" Shane knew it had come out harsh, but seriously. Did Melissa not know him at all?

"Of course not," Melissa told him. "In the first place, for you that would be impossible. What I'm saying is if the arrangement you have suggested makes Jeremy uncomfortable I'd like to ease into it. Maybe spend days with you and nights with me. Then once he gets used to you, we can talk about sleep overs."

"It sounds to me like you're already planning an escape route. I wish I could trust you to present this to Jeremy as a positive, but it's obvious to me you don't see it that way. How will I know you didn't influence him? The kid loves you. He'd give you what you want," Shane argued.

Melissa tried not to be offended, there were eight years between them after all. But she wasn't the one that had betrayed Shane. How dare he question her honesty when he'd had an affair? "You trusted me before, I guess you'll just have to do it again."

"No way," Shane said standing to pace. "I did trust you and look where that got me. I very specifically remember asking you that day in the parking lot, the day you had baby things in the car, if you were pregnant. You lied to me. You looked me in the eyes and lied. Now you're asking for trust? I'm sorry. I can't give it to you," Shane paused. "I think you are forgetting one very important thing Melissa. I have another child. A daughter that is going to be impacted by this news just as much as my son. For eight years, Megan has been my only child. Now she has to share me. I'm willing to do whatever it takes to help her through the transition. Whatever it takes to help Jeremy through the transition, but I will not let you stand in my way. I will not let you bulldoze my chances with my son. I have a right to get to know him and he has a right to get to know me. I'm willing to be reasonable, to take Jeremy's feelings into consideration, but I don't trust you, Melissa. I won't take your word for it."

Shane's words hurt. They hurt more than she wanted to admit. She had lied to him, but at the time she thought she was doing the right thing. She thought she was giving him what he needed. She knew lying had been a mistake, but she'd held onto the belief that it was the right thing to do for so long, it was hard to accept she'd been wrong. It was hard to admit that Mitch had been right all along. The only thing they ever fought about was Shane's right to know he had a son. Mitch believed very strongly that they needed to bring Jeremy back to Hidden Lakes, explain everything to Shane and work out a solution. But Melissa had resisted, and she realized she was still resisting. "Okay, don't take my word for it. After I talk to Jeremy, you can talk to him if you want. You can ask him yourself what he wants."

"After you talk to him and tell him what? That his dad didn't want him and now I've changed my mind? How are you going to explain this to him? How are you going to help him understand that the father he loved, the one that died, wasn't really his father after all? And now, his real father wants to spend time with him. Time you don't want me to have?" Shane asked.

"I don't have to," Melissa told him calmly. "Jeremy already knows he has another father."

"I thought you said he didn't know about me. That he believed that this Mitch guy was his dad," Shane said, confused.

"I did. I let him believe that Mitch was his father. Jeremy loved Mitch. As he got older he started to idolize him actually. To the point that I worried about it. But Mitch also loved Jeremy. He believed very strongly in family. I didn't tell Jeremy anything about you. I didn't know how. But Mitch did. You didn't know Mitch so you couldn't understand but he was a very good, honorable man.

Mitch and I fought, pretty regularly, about my keeping Jeremy a secret from you. He said he would be furious if someone did that to him and he wouldn't do it to someone else. He loved kids, loved life and he loved me, but on this one topic I frustrated him. He never could get through to me, so he talked to Jeremy. The week that dad had his heart attack. I came here and Jeremy and Mitch went on a boy's trip. Mitch took him camping. When I found out what he had done, I was furious. First, Mitch told Jeremy that if anything ever happened to him, Jeremy would have to be the man of the house. I worry that Jeremy took that to heart and he's starting to forget how to be a kid. I could have strangled Mitch for that alone, but I was livid about the rest."

"Which was?" Shane asked. The more he heard about Mitch, the more trouble he was having hating the guy. In fact, under different circumstances he and Mitch probably would have been good friends.

"He told Jeremy that sometimes kids have more than one dad. That sometimes there is a biological dad, the one that is related by blood and sometimes there is another dad. One that loves the child just as much, but doesn't have the same blood. He told Jeremy that he had two dads. Mitch and someone else that didn't even know about him. Someone that would love him and be there for him if he knew Jeremy existed. He promised Jeremy that if he ever wanted to meet this other dad, Mitch would make sure I didn't stand in his way. He explained to Jeremy that Mitch was his father, but they didn't have the same blood. His other father was the guy that had the same blood that Jeremy had."

Shane was floored. No wonder Melissa had fallen for the guy. And there was no way Shane, someone that had messed up and broken her heart, could ever compare. "So it's possible that when you tell Jeremy that I'm his other dad, he might be okay with it because it won't be that much of a shock?"

47

"Maybe," Melissa said. "But I have to warn you, he's kind of mad at you."

"Me? Why?" Shane asked, perplexed.

"He thinks you made me cry," she told him, a little embarrassed to admit that.

"You cried?" Shane asked, surprised. "Why?"

"Talking to you about this scares me. I know how passionate you are about family and your responsibilities. Sharing Jeremy with you terrifies me. Right now you have so much more to offer him than I do. He's vulnerable. He needs a male influence. And don't they say that boys are usually closer to their father's than they are their mothers?" she shrugged. "When you left, the fear made me cry."

"I see," Shane said, thinking about the state of the house again. "I know it's none of my business, but since you brought it up I'm going to ask. How are you doing financially?"

"No, Shane. It's not your business," Melissa said, straightening her spine. "But don't worry we'll be fine." She could worry, but Shane didn't need to. She wasn't a charity case.

Shane knew that stubborn streak. She needed help, but she'd never let him help her. He'd just see about that. "Okay, I have a suggestion. Did Joe give you the same days off Dolly had? Are you off Tuesday and Wednesday?"

"Yes," Melissa answered hesitantly.

"Okay, then what if you take tomorrow to talk to Jeremy and I will take tomorrow to talk to Megan. Then we'll meet back up on

Wednesday and come up with a schedule. I have to tell you, I'm pretty firm on the weekend idea though. You have to work and that will give you Tuesday and Wednesday's with him as well as every other night of the week."

"Okay, on the talking and getting together Wednesday part. I'm not sure I can go that long without seeing Jeremy. I'm going to have to think about it and we'll try to work something out," Melissa agreed.

"Then I'll see you on Wednesday," Shane said standing. He had to get out of here. The longer he stayed the more his fingers itched to touch her, the more he wanted to pull her close and kiss her. She may have loved Mitch, but he knew they still had chemistry. Chemistry he couldn't act on. He started for the door and remembered his shirt. He pivoted, and headed for the laundry room.

Melissa watched as Shane walked from the back of the house buttoning his shirt. Thank goodness. She'd always loved Shane's body. He had broad shoulders and not an inch of fat. Working the ranch must keep him in shape. Melissa never knew Shane to go to a gym. She glanced at her tiny arms, maybe she should throw hay every once in a while. She'd lost weight over the past year. Depression and loneliness played havoc with her appetite. She continued to watch as Shane walked to the door and silently closed it behind him. Melissa sighed as she relaxed into the large chair. Finally, she could breathe easy. Sitting for so long across from a half-naked Shane without touching him had been the hardest thing she'd done in a long time.

Chapter Four

Shane saddled the horses and led them out to the coral. Once they were tied, he headed for the kitchen. Cora had packed sandwiches for dinner. He planned to take Megan out to the lake and tell her about Jeremy. She was a good, smart kid. Hopefully she would understand that having a brother wouldn't change anything between them. But kids were unpredictable.

"You worry too much," Cora said casually. "That girl knows you love her. Having a brother will give her someone to play with around here. I always thought you needed more kids. Now you have one."

"How do you know?" Shane teased. "You haven't met the kid. He could be a holy terror. Having him around even part time might finally push you over the edge."

"Nonsense," Cora said, not taking the bait. "No child created between you and Melissa could be a holy terror. Intelligent, yes. Rambunctious, yes. Energetic, of course. But you forget I knew you when you were a child. I had to live next to you when you were the same age as this boy. I can't count how many times I caught you on the roof of my garage and nearly had a heart attack. But you were never a terror. Just curious and full of energy and life. I suspect Jeremy is the same."

"Do you know how shocked I was when I bought the ranch and moved to Hidden Lakes only to discover the sweet neighbor lady that always gave me treats was living right here? I just knew it was fate and I had to hire you," Shane remembered fondly.

"And you did," Cora said. "Now, take that girl riding and tell her how wonderful it's going to be to have a brother."

Shane followed Cora's gaze and spotted Megan coming up the long drive. He kissed Cora's cheek, grabbed the food and headed for the horses. He knew the instant Megan spotted him. Her face shifted into a huge smile and she started to run.

"Hey dad," she said happily as she screeched to a halt.

"Hey yourself," he said lifting her up and throwing her over his shoulder. Megan squealed and kicked her feet. Shane set her back down and kissed the top of her head. "Go change so we can head out. I thought we'd go to the lake, so it's going to be a long ride."

Megan ran to the house, letting the screen door slam behind her. Shane winced, Cora wasn't going to be happy about that. He tucked the food into the saddle bag and waited. Moments later Megan exited, careful to shut the door softly. She walked somberly to the horses, clearly Cora had taken her pound of flesh.

Shane smiled, "Ready?"

"I guess," Megan said grumpily.

"Don't you think you're over reacting just a bit?" he asked casually. "I mean, you knew you were going to get the third degree from Cora the instant that door slammed shut. So get your butt in the saddle and lighten up. Trigger's going to sense it if you're off today."

"I know," Megan said putting her foot into the stirrup. "I didn't mean to slam the door, I was just so excited about riding, I forgot."

Shane gave Megan's behind a little push then handed her the reins. "Then let's get some of that excitement back." He swung into his own saddle then moved from the corral. "Race you to the fence."

Megan giggled and took off. She loved to ride. She loved the ranch. But most of all, she loved her dad. He was the best father in the whole world. She knew that sometimes he got sad. She thought it was because he didn't have a friend like Heidi. If dad had a good friend, he wouldn't be lonely. Maybe she would try to find him one. She stopped worrying when she saw her dad was pulling ahead. After giving Trigger a little nudge they caught up, then passed her dad and Nico. She barely reached the fence before Shane and immediately began to cheer. "I won, I won, I won," she chanted.

Shane laughed. He knew he shouldn't let his daughter win, but he couldn't help himself. Beating him always made her so happy. And he wanted her happy when he talked to her about Jeremy. "Yeah, too bad you're not a good sport about it."

"Too bad you're such a bad loser," Megan countered. Shane moved up beside her and the two of them kept pace until they reached the lake. Megan talked about school and softball and Heidi the whole way.

Shane dismounted and moved to help Megan off Trigger. He was too slow. She was already hopping to the ground and pulling things from the saddle bag. "Hey, are we going to have a picnic?" she asked, clearly delighted.

"Sure are," Shane said absently. He moved back to Nico and pulled out a blanket.

"Is something wrong?" Megan asked Shane.

"Why would you ask that?" Shane said, surprised at Megan's insight.

"Because we haven't had a picnic at the lake since mom told me you bought me from her then left," Megan said casually. "You thought I was going to be upset about that, but I was happy."

"Were you really, Megan?" Shane asked seriously.

"Yes," Megan said softly. "Mom was mean to me."

"Mean how?" Shane asked, holding back his anger.

"She said mean things. Like I wasn't as pretty as she was and she used to pull my hair," Megan admitted.

Shane was furious. "Well, your mom was right. You're not as pretty as she is."

Megan frowned.

"You are about a million times prettier." He grinned and something eased inside when he saw Megan's face light up. "I suppose that's probably why your mom was mean. She was jealous. She knew you were prettier and nicer and smarter than her. She didn't like it."

"I guess," Megan said, pondering. She hadn't thought of that but as she remembered the times her mom had been the meanest, it was always when Megan looked her best. Like the time her dad had bought her a pretty blue dress to go to Heidi's special birthday dinner. Her mom said her blue eyes were ugly and the dress made her ugly eyes stand out more. "Dad, do you like blue eyes?"

Shane frowned. "I like your blue eyes, princess. You're eyes are like sapphires, deep and mysterious."

"Like yours, huh?" Megan asked.

"Exactly like mine," he said pulling her into his lap. "Why did you ask me that?"

Megan reluctantly told him what her mother had said about the dress and Megan's eyes. "Mom said that men didn't like blue eyes, they liked green eyes like hers. That's why she had a man as wonderful as you and I would wind up with small potatoes. What does that mean?"

"It means your mother was a cruel woman and you shouldn't listen to anything she told you. I never loved your mother, Megan. The only good thing that came out of me knowing her was you." He kissed her forehead. "Your mom knew I didn't love her, I think that's why she said mean things to you. Things that aren't true. Because she knew how much I love you and she was jealous," Shane pondered. How could he segue into Jeremy? This was probably as good a way as any.

"I didn't love her either," Megan whispered. "Is that bad?"

"No honey," Shane said, pulling her tighter against him. "It's just the way it is. I didn't love my mother either. Sometimes a parent is just a trial you have to endure. I'm sorry it had to be that way for you. I never wanted that for my kids. I'd give anything for you to have a warm, caring, loving mother."

"I don't need one, daddy. I have you," Megan said honestly.

Shane couldn't speak. He'd always known Megan was a blessing. One he didn't deserve, but he cherished her and would do anything to protect her and make her happy. He hoped finding out about Jeremy wouldn't shatter her rosy outlook. "I do need to talk to you about something kiddo," he said, pushing her back so he could look her in the eye.

"I thought so," she said taking a deep breath.

Shane looked out over the lake for a very long time. He loved it here and was determined to bring Megan more often. He didn't want it to become a place they only went when they had to talk about difficult things. "About eight years ago, there was a woman in my life. Someone I loved very much. But some things happened, no..." Shane shook his head, if he was going to tell Megan the story, he was going to be completely honest. "I did some things that hurt her and she moved away. I just found out yesterday that she had moved back to town," Shane glanced at Megan. She wasn't saying anything, just watching him with that intent look of hers. The one Cora said mimicked him. "I also found out that when she left, she was pregnant. She was going to have a baby and he was mine. I was the baby's father."

"So you have another kid besides me?" Megan asked.

"I do," Shane said, still watching for a reaction.

"You said he, does that mean I have a brother?" she asked, still deep in thought.

"Yes. You have a brother," Shane told her. Waiting. A few minutes passed and Shane couldn't take it any longer. "Megan, I'd like to know how you feel about that."

"There's a new kid at school. I just met him today. Is that my brother?" Megan asked.

"Probably," Shane hadn't thought of that. "His name is Jeremy Carpenter," his brows furrowed. He still hated that his son had somebody else's name.

"Well then, I guess that's okay," Megan finally said. "I mean, he seemed cool."

Shane smiled. "So you met him already?"

"Yeah," Megan said, shifting to lean against her father's chest to get more comfortable. "He was with Scotty Madsen after school. They ride the same bus." Megan was thinking about the boy she just met after school. "Hey, he has blue eyes, too."

"He does," Shane said, leaning back on his elbows. "How would you feel if he spent some time with us here on the ranch? If he spent the night sometimes?"

"Do we have to share a room?" she asked. "I really like having my own room."

Shane laughed. "No, sweetheart. You don't have to share a room. Jeremy will have his own room."

"Then it might be fun," Megan said thoughtfully. "Does he know how to ride a horse? Can we go riding together?"

"I don't know if he's ever ridden. His mother liked to ride, but they used to live in the city. Maybe eventually the two of you can go riding alone, but for a while Hank or I will have to go with you."

"Okay," Megan agreed.

The two of them sat talking, eating and enjoying the evening for hours.

* * * *

Melissa was making chocolate chip cookies when Jeremy got home from school. They were his favorites. She thought they could enjoy cookies and milk and talk about Shane. As much as she was dreading this conversation, she had to admit Mitch had made her task a lot easier. She'd been livid when she'd found out what he'd done. So angry they'd had the worst fight of their marriage over it. She'd thought she had plenty of time to ease into the topic with Jeremy. Now she was glad he had done it. Jeremy wasn't going to be shocked to hear he had another father. And he liked Shane.

Jeremy flew into the house and up the stairs to his room. Melissa could hear him stomping around while he deposited his bag and changed his clothes. She smiled. Jeremy didn't do anything by half measures. He had so much energy. He got that from Shane of course. Cora had told her story after story about living next door to the rambunctious Shane Chandler. Melissa was grateful Jeremy hadn't thought of climbing on the roof or dangling from the tree

Hidden Lakes

house...yet. She knew boys would be boys, but she was terrified of the possibilities.

"Hey mom," Jeremy said cheerfully when he entered the kitchen. "Are you making cookies?"

"Uh-huh," Melissa said, sliding the sheet into the oven.

"Can I have some?" Jeremy asked hopefully.

"Grab the milk," Melissa said, placing several large warm cookies onto a plate and walking to the table. "I thought we could talk while we had a snack."

Jeremy studied his mother wondering if something was wrong. She had that tone, the same one she had when she told him they had to sell the house and move. He squared his shoulders, ready for bad news, grabbed the milk and walked slowly to the table. His mom already had glasses set out, so he poured milk in both of them then put the carton back in the fridge. Jeremy lowered himself to the chair and continued to study his mother. The cookies could wait. He needed to know what was wrong.

Melissa pushed the plate of cookies toward her son. "Dig in while they're still warm." She tried to make her voice sound light and easy. She could tell Jeremy was worried and she hated it. She hated more than anything that her seven year old sometimes acted like he was thirty. She grabbed a cookie for herself then raised an eyebrow at him. "I thought you loved my cookies."

Jeremy forced a smile and took a cookie. "I do," he finally said, taking a big bite to make her happy. "What did you want to talk about?"

Melissa realized procrastinating was only going to make things worse. She needed to get it out there so Jeremy would stop worrying. "Do you remember when grandpa was sick and I came here to spend some time with him?"

"Uh-huh," Jeremy said taking another bite of cookie. "Is he sick again?"

"No honey," Melissa assured him. "Grandpa is doing really well. I talked to grandma today. They love it in Florida and want us to come for a visit."

"Oh," Jeremy said, considering. "But I just started school."

"We'll go visit, but not for a while. Maybe over spring break or something." Jeremy looked so much like Shane right now. He had that thoughtful, calculating look that Shane always got when he was puzzling something out. She shook her head trying to force the memory out of her mind. She hadn't realized just how hard it was going to be living here, remembering all the good times she'd shared with Shane. The love she felt back then, the intense physical attraction, it was all still there. How on earth was she going to push it aside now that she had to share Jeremy? She was going to be seeing Shane on a regular basis. Fighting her attraction was going to drive her insane.

"Okay," Jeremy agreed, taking a big gulp of milk.

"I wanted to talk to you about the things Mitch told you on your camping trip. The one you took when grandpa was sick," Melissa continued.

"About me being the man of the house now?" Jeremy asked. Maybe his mom wanted him to fix the front steps or something.

"No," Melissa said shaking her head. "The other part. The part about you having two dads."

"Oh," Jeremy said, sitting back in this chair. "Okay."

"Mitch was your dad and he loved you very, very much. You know that, right?"

Jeremy nodded once, but didn't respond.

"But you also have another dad. A man that didn't know he had a son," Melissa continued.

"How come he doesn't know?" Jeremy asked. "I mean, I don't really understand that part. How can I have another dad, but he doesn't know he's my dad?"

"Because I didn't tell him," Melissa said, waiting for a response.

"Why didn't you tell him? Did you think he wouldn't like me?" Jeremy asked, frowning.

"Of course not," Melissa said immediately. "At the time things were complicated. Your father was already having a child. He had someone else in his life that was having a baby. I didn't tell him that I was also having a baby because I didn't want him to have to choose between me and the other woman. I thought that it would be better to leave town and take care of you myself. Then I met Mitch and we got married. Since Mitch was your dad, your other dad didn't have to choose."

Jeremy looked out the window, the expression on his face intensified. He was considering what Melissa had said, working it out in his mind. She'd know when he came to terms with what she had told him and then they could move on.

Jeremy took a deep breath and turned back to face his mother. "Dad told me that my other father would have been sad if he knew I was his son. He said that my blood father would have wanted to get to know me and spend time with me. And that you didn't want to share me because you and dad loved me so much. Is that true? If my blood father knew about me, would he want me to spend time with him?"

"Yes," Melissa said, unsure how she felt about what Mitch had told Jeremy. "In fact, your blood father found out about you and that's what I need to talk to you about."

"He wants me to visit him?" Jeremy asked, taking another bite of cookie. "So he can get to know me?"

"Yes," Melissa told him. "He wants you to spend time with him every week. He would like it if you would sleep at his house sometimes."

"Does he live close by?" Jeremy asked. "Because now that dad's gone, I can't go very far without you."

Melissa sighed. "Jeremy," she said exasperated. "Your father does live close by, but even if he didn't that's not important. I need you to ignore Mitch's ridiculous request that you become the man of the house. I'm the adult, you just need to be a kid. Stop worrying about taking care of me. It's my job to take care of you."

Jeremy frowned. His mom didn't want him to take care of her? Did she think he couldn't do it? He knew he could. He'd just have to prove it to her. He considered. How could he prove to her that he could be the man of the house? He couldn't fix the stairs because the wood had to be cut and his mom would be really mad if he used the saw. Maybe he could fix the roof. How hard could that be? He just had to nail down those shingles his mom had bought. He'd take care of that this weekend. Then she'd see that he was big enough to take care of her.

"Jeremy?" Melissa pressed.

"Huh?" Jeremy asked, realizing he'd been thinking about the roof and didn't know what his mother had been saying.

"Shane Chandler is your blood father. The man that came to visit yesterday. I need to know how you would feel about spending some time getting to know him," Melissa waited.

"Shane?" Jeremy considered. "Is that why we have the same name?"

"Yes," Melissa agreed. "That is why your middle name is Shane. I wanted to give you something of your father's."

"But he made you cry," Jeremy said, scowling.

"No. He didn't," Melissa said firmly. "I told you, he just reminded me that I had to do something that was hard. I had to talk to him about you, and now I have to talk to you about him. That was hard for me. I didn't want you to be upset and not knowing how you would react made me cry."

Jeremy considered that. "Is he nice?" he finally asked. "He looks like a cowboy and he seemed nice when I met him. Is he?"

How was she supposed to answer that? Other than being a lying, cheating pig she supposed Shane was nice. He would definitely be nice to Jeremy. She knew that. Shane would love and cherish and protect Jeremy. "Yes. He's very nice," she finally told him.

"Okay," Jeremy agreed.

"Okay what?" Melissa asked. "Okay, you want to get to know him?"

"Uh-huh. And I guess I could sleep over there," Jeremy decided. "If he's a cowboy does he have horses?"

Melissa's heart sank. She was afraid this would happen. Jeremy loved horses, always had. What if he saw the ranch and wanted to stay forever? What if he wanted to live with Shane and just visit her on the weekends? "Shane, your father, lives on a ranch. I haven't been there for a long time, but I'm sure he still has horses...and cattle. Probably a dog, too."

"Really?" Jeremy asked, excited for the first time. "Can I ride the horses?"

"I'll talk to Shane about it," she promised. "But I don't want you trying to ride them alone. Until I say it's okay, you can only ride if there's an adult riding with you."

"When do I get to go?" Jeremy asked.

"Shane would like you to come spend the weekend with him," Melissa admitted. "I don't know how I feel about that. He wants you to ride out after school on Friday and stay until you go to school on Monday. But if you do that, I'm going to miss you."

Jeremy considered. How was he going to fix the roof if he was visiting his blood father? But he wanted to ride horses and play with a dog. Maybe he could spend the weekend with Shane and then fix the roof after school one day. It was getting hot, he would have time. "I know you will miss me but you have to work," Jeremy finally said. "I'll miss you, too. But I think I'd like to try it. I'd like to spend some time with my dad if you'll let me."

Melissa fought the tears that wanted to escape. She knew her life was going to change forever and there was nothing she could do about it. But she wouldn't prevent Jeremy from getting to know Shane. He might be a lousy boyfriend, but she knew he'd be a wonderful father. And maybe, just maybe, if Jeremy had a father he'd stop trying to be the stupid man of the house. "Jeremy, there's something else you need to know. Shane, your dad, has a daughter. Her name is Megan and she lives with her dad. If you go to visit, she'll be there too."

"I met a girl named Megan today. She was nice," Jeremy told his mother. "She's not in my class, she has Mrs. Brown. Scotty said she's cool," his eyes widened. "And she has the coolest dad around. Except Scotty's because Scotty's dad is a deputy. If Megan's dad is my dad, then I have the coolest dad around."

Melissa smiled. "I guess you do. So, you think you can get along with Megan for the weekend?"

"Sure," Jeremy said. "I mean she's a girl and all, but she was nice. I don't think we'll fight or anything."

"Then I'll let you spend the weekend with Shane. But you have to promise me you won't try to go riding with Megan alone. Not even if she asks you to or says it's okay," Melissa insisted.

"I know," Jeremy sighed. "Only with an adult."

"Come here," Melissa said, turning her chair and holding out her arms. Jeremy moved forward, accepting her hug. She loved him so much and sharing him was going to kill her. But she knew that Shane had a right to his son. She also knew if she gave a little, Shane would be reasonable. The more she thought about the situation, the more certain she was that not going to court was far better than putting her life in a judge's hands. Shane was loved in this town. Everyone had liked him eight years ago, but now they practically worshiped him. His cattle company had grown quickly and Shane took care of his neighbors. In a fight, his neighbors would take care of him.

Chapter Five

Once again, Shane stood on Melissa's front steps. He took a moment to study the damage. No way could the wood be repaired. She needed a whole new set of stairs. Shane stepped over the weak spots and walked to the door. The steps would have to wait. Melissa was already going to throw a fit over the plumbing. He knew her. He knew how proud and stubborn the woman was. Getting her to accept his decision was going to be a fight. He wouldn't mention the stairs tonight. Seconds later, he rang the bell and waited.

Melissa took a deep breath and moved to answer the door. She hoped this conversation went better than the last one had. She could admit to herself she had been less than accommodating and Shane had left angry. Jeremy was willing to spend the weekend at the ranch, but Melissa still wasn't sure she would allow it. How could she spend three and a half days away from her little boy? She pulled open the door and tried to force a smile. "Come on in," she stepped back in invitation.

"Is Jeremy here?" Shane asked, stepping into the living room and realizing it was empty.

"He's in his room," Melissa said, taking a seat in the large chair. "I asked him to stay up there until I called for him. I wanted some time with you first."

Shane settled onto the couch and waited. He wasn't going to start the conversation. He didn't want to anger her right off the bat.

"I talked to Jeremy," she began. "He's looking forward to getting to know you. Scotty told him about your horses and Jeremy wants to learn to ride. I'll allow that, but only if there's an adult with him. You can't let Jeremy and Megan go off on their own," she insisted.

"Melissa," Shane said, taking a deep breath. She was already pissing him off. "It may have escaped your notice, but I know how to be a father. I've been one for eight years. I know what's appropriate and what's not."

Melissa narrowed her eyes at Shane. He was already being difficult.

"If you're under the impression you can dictate my every move, you are mistaken. I'll listen to your concerns. I'll even discuss them with you if I disagree, but I am Jeremy's father. When he's under my care, I make the decisions. I will decide when he's ready to ride alone or with my daughter. Acting like you're doing me a favor and thinking I'll cave to your every whim is only going to put us at odds at every turn. I don't need your permission. Telling me what you will and will not allow is only going to piss me off." Shane waited for the blow up. He didn't have to wait long.

"I don't really care if I piss you off Shane," Melissa said, trying to control her anger. "I am Jeremy's mother. If I'm going to let you spend time with him, I'm going to dictate the terms."

Shane sat back, unconcerned. "You can try," he finally said.

"Shane," Melissa said, standing and moving to the window. "This isn't easy for me. I won't let him go if you won't assure his safety. If you won't agree to my terms."

Shane watched her as she began to pace. After a couple turns around the room, he stood and blocked her path. "I can and will assure his safety. You know I would never let Jeremy do anything reckless. You also know I'm not going to plop him on a horse and say have a nice ride. You're being insulting. I'm his father, Melissa. Do you honestly believe I'd be negligent? You know me better than that. Oh you might want to pretend like you don't, but that is beside the point. And knowing me like you do, you also understand that I will not take orders from anyone. Keep making demands and we'll have to move this to the courtroom."

Melissa clenched her hands and closed her eyes. She would lose in the courtroom. She had no doubt about that. She also knew the judge would deem her unreasonable. This was just so hard. It was hard to relinquish some of the control. They were talking about her baby boy. But she did know Shane. He wasn't making idle threats. And he wouldn't be dictated to. "Fine," she said, plopping back down into the chair. "I'll be sure to ask nicely next time. Satisfied?"

Shane smiled. "For now," he said returning to the sofa. "What did you decide about the weekend visits?"

"I haven't decided," Melissa said honestly. "Jeremy is all for it. On principle anyway. But he's never been away from me for that long. I don't know how he'll handle it."

"You mean you don't know how you will handle it," Shane corrected. "And you were here for an entire week when your dad was in the hospital. So he has been away for longer."

"That's different. Mitch was there," Melissa said, brushing off his argument as insignificant. She glanced up and saw that had been a mistake. Shane was still furious about Mitch. She considered what she had said and realized she was being unfair. Was she really telling Shane that she could trust Mitch with her son, but not his real father? "I'm sorry," she said immediately before Shane went off on her. "That was wrong and insensitive."

"And then some," Shane said, tamping down his temper as he studied her. "I came up with a compromise. It's not ideal, but I'm willing to try it if you want."

"Oh?" Melissa asked, curious.

"I have a cabin," Shane told her. "I originally built it for..." Kristy he thought but stopped before he ruined it. Melissa would never stay in a cabin that was built for the other woman. "I offered it to Hank, but he didn't want it. He said he wasn't willing to give twenty four hours a day to the ranch and if he lived in the cabin, that's what would end up happening. It's been empty since I built it. Nobody has ever lived there. It's furnished with the basics, but nothing else. I'm willing to let you stay there for one night on the weekends. But only one. If you're there for my entire visit, I won't get the time I want with Jeremy. It satisfies your concern of going so long without seeing your son."

Melissa didn't like the idea much either but it might be doable. "Can he spend some time with me while I'm there?"

"That was the idea," Shane said annoyed. Melissa was trying his patience. "I'd like him to sleep in the house, but I'd be willing to let him spend some time with you on Saturday after you get off work and maybe he could stay for dinner. Then he'd return to the house and spend the evening with me before bed. I think it's a good compromise."

Melissa considered. "This weekend is going to be busy. I have some things I need to take care of at the house on my time off. Let's do a test run and see how it goes. Next weekend we can discuss the cabin if it's too hard for me or Jeremy to be away from each other that long."

"I can live with that." He could more than live with that. He didn't want to share his visits. He'd missed so much of Jeremy's life. He wanted a little time with the kid all to himself. And he thought it was important to give Megan and Jeremy some time to get to know each other as well. "Now, we need to talk about child support."

"No," Melissa said immediately. "I don't want any money from you."

"Too bad," Shane said casually. "I'm paying it anyway."

"Fine," Melissa relented. "Go open a savings account and dump the money in there. Once Jer is eighteen he can use it for college or something."

"Not a bad idea," Shane agreed. "But you'll have to go with me. I want your name on the account too. No, don't argue with me. I can see you're on a fixed budget. What are you going to do when Jeremy gets into high school and wants to play football or baseball. Outfitting him is going to be expensive. You need access to the funds to pay for his activities. You know I'm right. You won't let Jeremy suffer and go without for spite or your stupid pride."

Melissa sighed. Shane was right. If Jeremy wanted to play sports, she'd dip into the funds to make him happy. "Fine, let me know when you want to open the account and I'll meet you at the bank."

"Good," Shane said leaning to the side and pulling out a check. He dropped it on the coffee table. "That's for back child support."

Melissa immediately began shaking her head. "Take it back, or I'll just tear it up."

"I'm not taking it back and you would be stupid to tear it up," he said softly. "If you don't want to use it to buy the things you obviously need right now, like a new set of stairs, then deposit the check into the account once we open it."

"Fine, it's going into the account." Melissa was itching to see how much he'd written the check for, but she refrained. She didn't want Shane to see just how much she needed the money.

"It's only part of the payment," Shane said, watching her closely. "I also called Pete. He's going to be here next week. I told him to send the bill to me. I'm paying for the plumbing."

"No way," Melissa said jumping to her feet. "I will not owe you Shane Chandler."

"Child support Melissa," Shane said, also standing. "I won't have my son living in a house that doesn't have basic plumbing. This isn't for you, it's for Jeremy. And, you don't have a say. Pete is clear. He'll be here to take care of the problem and he'll be sending me the bill directly."

Hidden Lakes

"Maybe I won't let him in," Melissa said defiantly.

Shane didn't respond to that. Melissa wouldn't go that far and they both knew it.

Melissa gritted her teeth. She didn't want to accept charity from anyone, but she especially hated it coming from Shane.

Shane pulled out another check. He placed it on the table next to the first one. "Child support for this month. If you want to put it in the bank, go ahead. But I'm paying to support my child. I'd prefer you use it to fix the front steps. That's a safety concern. I don't want Jeremy injured because you couldn't afford to hire a carpenter to fix the steps."

Melissa just sat there, forcing air into her lungs then pushing it back out. The simple act of breathing was taking so much effort. She knew Shane was legally required to pay child support. That was logic. Unfortunately, her emotional side couldn't get passed the fact that he was giving her money. Money she desperately needed, but didn't want to accept. Somehow it made her feel tied to him, indebted to him. She didn't like it.

"Stop thinking about the money," Shane finally said. "Was there anything else you wanted to talk about? If not, I'd like to see Jeremy before I leave."

Melissa stood and left the room. Moments later she returned with Jeremy.

Shane stood. His stomach gave a little flip and he realized his palms were sweaty. He wasn't this nervous as a teenager on his first date. "Hi Jeremy," Shane finally said, trying to hide his nerves.

"Hey," Jeremy said, sitting on the couch next to where Shane had been sitting.

Shane sat back down and smiled at his son. He still couldn't believe it. He had a son. "So, your mom explained everything to you?"

"Yeah," Jeremy said, a million questions on his mind.

"And she said you're willing to spend the weekend at my place?" Shane asked.

"Uh-huh," Jeremy said. What was he supposed to call his new father? Dad? Shane? He just didn't know. And he didn't know how to ask.

"Hey," Shane said placing a hand on Jeremy's knee. "You okay?" Jeremy was acting strange. A lot different than the first time they'd met.

"I'm okay," Jeremy said, finally looking Shane in the eye.

"So what's up?" Shane asked. "Do I make you nervous?"

Jeremy smiled. "No, not really."

"Then what?" Shane asked.

"I don't know what to call you," Jeremy blurted.

"Oh," Shane said, relieved. "I can see how that might be a problem. Eventually I hope you will feel comfortable calling me dad. For now, if that seems strange, you can call me Shane. It's entirely up to you, bud. What would you like to call me?"

Jeremy got that far away look. He was silent for a full minute. Then he turned to Melissa. "Would it bother you if I called Shane dad? I mean, I used to call Mitch dad. Would it make you sad? I know how much you miss dad. I don't want you to be upset."

"No honey," Melissa said, touched Jeremy would make that sacrifice for her. "Shane is your dad. I think it would be appropriate to call him that. It might feel strange to start out calling him Shane and then switch to dad later. I know you loved Mitch and he knew it, too. In fact, I think Mitch would want it this way. Mitch really wanted you to meet Shane."

Jeremy turned back to Shane. "Then I think I'd like to call you dad."

Shane's heart soared. He hadn't realized just how much it meant to him that his son acknowledged the relationship. "Is there anything you want to ask me about all this?"

Jeremy considered. "I don't think so. Not right now. But if I have questions can I ask you later? Maybe this weekend when I stay at your house?"

"Of course," Shane assured him. He glanced at Melissa. "I hear you might be interested in learning how to ride a horse. Is that true?"

Jeremy grinned. "I love horses. Can I really learn how to ride?"

"Absolutely," Shane said, patting his son's knee. "Now, it's getting late. I need to get home. I'm looking forward to this weekend, Jeremy. I hope you are, too." He turned to Melissa, "I'll be in touch."

Melissa walked silently to the door. Once Shane was gone, she turned to Jeremy. "You sure you're okay with all this?"

"I'm fine mom," Jeremy said as he bolted up the stairs. "See you in the morning."

* * * *

Shane couldn't help himself. He'd been watching the clock all day. He didn't think time had ever moved this slowly in his life. He threw another bale of hay out of the truck. He should be exhausted, but he wasn't. He was anxious and excited. He glanced at his watch again. Any minute the bus would arrive. Shane jumped from the truck and moved into the barn. After splashing his face with water, he stepped back outside and saw Megan and Jeremy. The sliding doors closed and the yellow school bus jerked forward. Shane swallowed the lump that had formed in his throat. The sight of his children walking down the drive was indescribable. He felt like a fist was squeezing around his heart. He shook his head. He was definitely losing it. When had he become such a girl? Just then, Megan spotted him and broke into a run. "Dad!" she called as she headed right for him. Shane walked toward his children, a silly grin spread across his face.

He caught Megan easily. They'd been doing this for years. Shane hugged her tight then lowered her to the ground. "Hey sport," he said turning to Jeremy. He ruffled the kid's hair and waited for a reaction. "How was school?"

"Good," Jeremy answered looking at Megan, then at Shane. Father and son watched each other, both unsure what to do next.

Megan resolved the problem for them. "Come on Jeremy," she said pulling on his arm. "I'll show you where your room is.

Cora changed the sheets already. You can change and then we'll grab a snack. I want to show you the barn and all the horses. Trigger's mine," Megan continued talking as the two walked into the house.

Shane followed them as far as the kitchen. "Cora?" he called.

"I'm in here," Cora's voice came from the pantry.

"Hiding?" Shane asked, grinning.

"Not on your life," Cora said, narrowing her eyes. "The kids will be hungry. I'm looking for a snack," she turned to Shane and smiled. "Are you as nervous about this weekend as I am? I just keep thinking I need to have the perfect snack, the perfect dinner, the perfect breakfast. If we keep Jeremy happy, he won't get home sick and want to leave."

"I know," Shane agreed. "I think we're all going to be on edge the next few days. But once we get through this first one, the rest will be easier. Megan wants to show Jeremy the barn and all the animals. He's curious and I think a little excited about the adventure. We'll do fine, I know we will." Shane took the items from Cora's arms. "What's for dinner?"

"Fried chicken." She closed the pantry door and moved to the counter. "All kids love fried chicken, right?"

"All of mankind loves fried chicken, especially yours. Good choice," he said, grabbing a cookie from the large jar he'd carried from the pantry. "Don't let them eat too many of these. I want him to have a good meal his first night here."

"Shew," Cora said, giving Shane a little shove. "You act like I've never dealt with a child before."

"No," Shane disagreed. "You're far more experienced than I am with this."

Hours later, Shane walked into Jeremy's new room. "So," he said, sitting on the edge of the bed. "You survived. Everything okay?"

Jeremy smiled. "I had a good time today," he said, sitting up and moving closer to Shane. "I'm glad I came."

"Me too," Shane told him, wondering how to say goodnight.

Jeremy leaned in and gave Shane a quick hug. "Thanks," he said softly. "I think I'm going to like it here."

Shane gave Jeremy a little squeeze then moved back. "I know I'm going to like having you here," then he stood and walked to the door. "You know where I am if you need anything tonight. I know it's a strange place, so don't worry about waking me. I want you to feel comfortable. There's a nightlight in the hallway, so if you need a snack or a drink or anything just head to the kitchen. We're outside the city, so it gets pretty dark out here. The light seems dim now, but in the middle of the night, it's more than enough."

"I'm fine," Jeremy told him. "I don't usually wake up until morning."

"Goodnight," Shane said, as he pulled the door half way closed. He paused in the hall then moved to Megan's room. The instant he sat on her bed, Megan jumped into his arms.

"Goodnight dad," she said enthusiastically. "I'm glad Jeremy's here. It was fun showing him our ranch," she smiled. "I think his favorite was Frisco," Megan paused, thinking about her dog. Hank had found the German Shepherd at the pound when he was just a puppy. Megan loved Frisco and could understand why Jeremy liked him immediately. "Or maybe the horses. Jeremy really wants to ride a horse. Are you going to show him how tomorrow while I'm with Hank?"

"I am," Shane said tucking Megan into the bed. He'd arranged for Hank to take Megan to the auction. They'd be gone most of the day. That would give Shane a chance for some one-on-one time with Jeremy. And Megan was excited to go. She loved to spend time with Hank and his manager loved his daughter. The two of them would have a blast. It was a win, win for everyone. This way Shane would have time with Jeremy and not feel guilty about neglecting Megan. "Now, go to sleep. You have an early day."

Megan pushed herself up and kissed Shane on the cheek. "Goodnight. Love you," she said climbing back into bed and settling in for the night.

"Goodnight sweet pea," Shane said, standing. "I love you, too."

The following morning Shane sat at the table sipping coffee and waiting for Jeremy to wake up while he read the paper. He'd already finished the morning feeding and sent the ranch hands out to repair fences for the day. Cora would be around, but otherwise it was just going to be him and Jeremy. He couldn't wait to get started. Shane glanced up when he heard footsteps coming down the hall. A sleep ruffled Jeremy stepped through the door. "Morning," Shane said then took a sip of coffee.

"Morning," Jeremy yawned as he pulled out a chair and plopped on the seat.

"You hungry?" Shane asked. "Cora's not here yet. She had to drive a neighbor to the doctor, but I can probably handle scrambled eggs if you want."

"Eggs sound good," Jeremy said looking around. "Is Megan still asleep?"

"Nope," Shane said moving to the fridge and pulling out eggs and milk. "You want some OJ?"

"Okay," Jeremy agreed.

"Megan went to an auction with Hank. He's my Ranch Manager. I've been looking for another good bull. Megan and Hank are going to see if they can find one today."

"Oh," Jeremy said, sounding a little disappointed.

"I thought maybe we'd start working on your riding while they're gone," Shane said, hoping to peak Jeremy's interest again.

Jeremy's head shot up, he had a huge smile on his face. "Really? Horseback riding?"

"Yeah," Shane said, glancing Jeremy's way. "I don't think you're ready for bulls yet."

Jeremy giggled. "Don't say that to mom. She'll think you're serious and never let me come back."

Shane dumped the eggs on a plate and dropped two pieces of bread into the toaster. "Does that mean you want to come back?" He set the plate in front of Jeremy.

Jeremy shoveled eggs into his mouth and nodded with enthusiasm. "I like it here," he said with his mouth full.

Shane ruffled Jeremy's hair. Today was going to be a good day.

* * * *

Sunday morning, Jeremy headed for the kitchen in search of Shane. He'd been thinking about his mom. She'd called every night and he knew she missed him, but he was having too much fun. He didn't really want to go home, but last night he decided he needed to. Just before he fell asleep he realized he wasn't taking very good care of his mom. She'd been sad without him and he needed to do something to cheer her up. Remembering what Mitch had told him, Jeremy decided he needed to go home and fix the roof. That would make his mom happy and show her he could be the man of the house like he was supposed to. Shane said he could come back next week, so Jeremy didn't think his new dad would mind letting him go home a little early. Now he just needed to find his dad and let him know.

Shane was sitting in the living room going over inventory. He needed to order more grain soon. The paperwork was Shane's least favorite part of running a ranch. He wished he had someone he could turn the job over to, but he didn't trust anyone enough to handle his money. He'd heard too many stories about accountants skimming the books. Now that his net worth had skyrocketed, he feared that was a definite possibility. It still amazed him how much Thoracol paid him for the rights to his tracking database. He'd developed the thing out of necessity and once it was perfected, he'd marketed the program hoping it would help fellow ranchers. Now, months later he was several million dollars richer. He had insisted on retaining a percentage of the proceeds, Cora's idea. It had seemed silly at the time, but he was now glad he'd listened. Every time he cashed a check, he thought about Megan and the life his money could provide for her. Now, he had another child to support. His cattle business was a huge success, but the added income would provide for his children and grandchildren for the rest of their lives. He glanced up as Jeremy walked into the room. "Hey sport," he said cheerfully. "How'd you sleep?"

"Good," Jeremy said, climbing onto the couch. "I really like it here," he began. "I've had a really nice time and I really want to come back next week if you still want me to."

Shane closed the books and studied Jeremy. Something was up. "Of course I want you to. I'd like it if you spent every weekend with me from now on."

"I'd like that too," Jeremy admitted.

"But?" Shane asked.

"But I think I need to go home." Jeremy watched Shane, hoping he wouldn't make his dad mad so soon. "I have some things I need to take care of. I thought if you took me home this morning I could take care of stuff before mom gets home from work."

Shane leaned back, "What sort of things?"

"Just stuff," Jeremy said evasively. He wasn't sure if he should tell his dad what he had planned. His mom was such a worrier but he didn't know his dad well enough to know how he would react.

"I was hoping you'd want to stay another day," Shane said casually. "I thought we could go for a short ride later this afternoon."

Jeremy wanted that, too. But he needed to fix the roof. "Maybe we could do that next weekend," he offered.

"Sure," Shane agreed. "But if you're going to cut our time short, I think you should tell me why."

Jeremy considered. He needed a ride home and if he refused to tell his dad why he needed to go, Shane might not take him. "Grandpa was sick for a while. He couldn't fix some stuff before they moved. I need to work on the house before mom gets home."

Shane raised one eyebrow. "Have you done much repair work?"

"No," Jeremy admitted. "But my dad..." he paused. "My other dad, told me that I had to be the man of the house. That's what the man of the house does, he fixes stuff. Mom is a lot happier here, but she's still sad sometimes. I want to help her to be happy. If I fix some stuff, it might make her happy."

"I see," Shane said. He was proud of the kid but a little worried. Mitch had put a lot of pressure on a seven year old boy. His son should be chasing the dog and playing baseball. Not worrying about repairing the house. "Well, I might be willing to take you home early if you're willing to let me help."

Jeremy considered. "Don't you have work to do here?" he finally asked.

"Naw," Shane said casually. "I've been up for hours. My work's all done. If you're willing to tell me what to do, I think I could be a lot of help. Do you have the right tools?"

Jeremy thought about that. He scrunched his brow as he considered. "I was planning on patching the roof before it rains. Do you have a ladder? I didn't see one at our house."

Shane swallowed hard. The kid was going to climb onto the roof? Melissa would kill him for sure. "Well in that case, I think we need a few supplies. Did you get something to eat yet?"

"I had a banana and one of Cora's sweet rolls," Jeremy rubbed his stomach. "They were delicious."

"Cora's the best," Shane said, standing. "Let's take some of them with us for later."

"Can we?" Jeremy asked, excited.

"Absolutely," Shane said putting his hand on Jeremy's shoulder and guiding him out the door. "Now, let's head to the barn. We need to load up the truck."

* * * *

Melissa locked up her desk and headed for the door. She wasn't sure how she felt about leaving early. Joe had been great. He knew she had to fix the roof before the next rain fall. According to the weatherman, it was supposed to rain next Thursday. When Joe found out she had a hole in her roof, he insisted she leave at noon. Melissa had tried to argue, but Joe told her to keep her phone handy and he'd call her if he needed her. Otherwise he was ordering her to work from home. She was grateful for his understanding, but felt like she was already taking advantage of her new boss's kindness.

Melissa spotted someone on her roof as she approached her home. Why was there a man on her roof? Her heart began to beat faster the closer she got to the house. If Shane had hired someone to fix her roof, they were going to have a confrontation. It was bad enough he'd arranged for the plumber. She would not accept him paying for the roof repair. And she couldn't afford to pay someone to do something she could handle herself. She jumped from the car and realized the man on her roof was Shane. She'd recognize that gorgeous chest anywhere. That's when she noticed Shane's truck parked on the curb. She stomped to the back of the house in search of the ladder. Enough was enough, that's when she spotted Jeremy. Her anger boiled over. The man had her son on the roof! It reminded her of something Mitch would do. Her ex-husband didn't have the slightest fear of heights and insisted on passing that trait on to their son. But she expected more from Shane.

Melissa began climbing the ladder. She became more and more angry with each step she took. She glared at Shane as her head crested the roof. She opened her mouth to start her lecture then stopped when she spotted Jeremy. Her mouth slammed shut in surprise. Jeremy was wearing a harness. She studied her son and realized Shane had tied him to the chimney. Jeremy was selecting shingles then carrying them to Shane, who secured them to the roof. She paused to take in her surroundings. As she glanced around, she spotted the tools. Melissa instantly knew Shane had done a far better job than she could have done repairing the roof. By the looks of things, he had cut out an entire section and replaced the old rotted wood with new. Now he and Jeremy were tacking down shingles. The job was almost finished. How long had they been here? And why had Shane brought Jeremy home when he had insisted so adamantly that Jeremy would spend the entire weekend at the ranch? She was about to ask when she heard Jeremy speak.

"It's crooked," Jeremy said, standing over Shane, hands on his hips.

Shane smiled. "Oh, yeah?" he asked, acting surprised. "It looks fine to me."

Jeremy sighed. "Dad," he said with exasperation crouching down next to his father. "It's not fine. Look," he pointed to another shingle then reached out and pulled it slightly to the left. "Now it's fine."

"You're right," Shane said, holding back a smile. "It's a good thing I have you here. Otherwise this repair job would be a disaster." Shane spotted Melissa and grinned. "You're mom's home," he whispered.

Jeremy jumped to his feet and whirled around to face Melissa. "Mom!" he exclaimed. "You're early," he scolded. "Why aren't you at work?" he said with a frown. "Are you sick or something?"

Melissa pulled herself onto the roof and shook her head. "No, I'm fine." She moved to stand next to her son, examining the harness and rope. "That's some safety net you've got there sport."

Jeremy smiled. "It was Shane's idea," he rolled his eyes. "I told him I didn't need it. Tell him how many times I got on the roof in Denver with dad."

"More than I want to remember," Melissa admitted. "I like this way better." She turned to Shane, "Thanks for thinking of it."

"No problem," Shane said. It was only partially for Melissa. In fact, he honestly believed they would be finished with the project before Melissa ever got home. He wanted to be able to tell Melissa he'd taken precautions but he'd also done it for his own peace of mind. There was no way he could keep a close eye on Jeremy while he repaired the roof. This way, he didn't have to worry about the kid falling off. "I thought you worked until three."

"Joe sent me home early. He said it's supposed to rain next week and he wanted to give me plenty of time to fix the roof," Melissa smiled. "I guess I should go back to work, but I'm not going to." She pulled Jeremy into a tight bear hug. "I'm going to spend time with my son. You have no idea how much I've missed you."

Jeremy ducked his head and glanced at Shane. He was embarrassed and wished Shane hadn't seen his mom making such a fuss.

"Jeremy's a tough boss," Shane said, standing. He'd just nailed down the last shingle. "I'm ready for a break. Got anything to drink?" He could see Jeremy was self-conscious about his mom's affection. A change of subject would get the kids mind on something else.

"Oh yeah," Melissa said. She should have thought of that. It was a warm day. Her eyes settled on Shane's bare chest. It was covered in sweat. It took all of her self-control not to reach out and run her hand across his masculine torso. She started to leave then remembered Jeremy was tied in. She turned back to her son and began studying the elaborate system.

Shane moved in next to Melissa. He reached down and unhooked the carabineer. Melissa realized the rope was actually a lead. If a horse couldn't escape, the thick rope would certainly hold her son. She smiled and moved to head down the ladder. Jeremy went next.

"Stay out of the way," Shane called. "I'm going to drop down the tools." Moments later, Shane descended the ladder then immediately removed the harness still secured to Jeremy's hips. He rubbed Jeremy's head and smiled. "Good work son," Shane said proudly. "We make a good team."

Jeremy looked at his mom. "I told you I was the man of the house now. We fixed the roof so you don't have to. I was going to do it by myself, but Shane...I mean dad insisted on helping me."

Melissa was horrified. Jeremy planned on fixing the roof himself? She closed her eyes and cursed Mitch all over again. Not only for his ridiculous man of the house speech, but for allowing Jeremy on their roof in Denver. She glanced at Shane, remembering Cora's story of the first time she'd caught Shane on the roof of her garage. "Well, I guess we owe Shane dinner then." She gave Jeremy a little shove. "Why don't you go wash up? Being a carpenter is hot, dirty work."

Jeremy ran to his room and gathered up clean clothes. He paused at the top of the stairs. "Dad, you will stay for dinner won't you?"

Shane glanced at Melissa then back to Jeremy. "I need to get home to Megan. Do you think you have enough for two? I can bring her back with me and the four of us could have a nice meal together."

"Can he mom? Please?" Jeremy begged.

"Sure," Melissa said, watching Shane. "Any special requests?" She was a little apprehensive about spending the evening with Kristy's daughter.

"I'm easy," he grinned, trying to tease her. He could sense her discomfort and assumed it was pride. She didn't like him working on her house. "When it comes to you anyway. But you already knew that."

"Does Megan like spaghetti?" Melissa asked, ignoring the blatant reminder. "I can run to the store and get some fresh bread to go with it."

"We both love spaghetti," Shane smiled. "What time should we come back?"

"Let's say six," Melissa decided. "That will give Jeremy time to clean up and me time to get to the store and back."

"Six it is," Shane agreed. "See you then."

"Go get in the shower," Melissa called to Jeremy. She waited until she heard the bathroom door shut then followed Shane out the door.

"Shane," she called. "I appreciate the work you did today."

"Are you sure?" Shane asked. "I saw your face when you got out of the car. You were pissed."

Melissa sighed. "At first," she admitted. "I thought you were trying to make me indebted. First the plumbing arrangements, now the roof. But I realized you were protecting Jeremy when he told me his plans." She covered her face with her hands. "I can't believe he was going to try to fix the roof on his own. Just thinking about what could have happened terrifies me."

"The kid is fearless," he hesitated then decided to ask. "Did Mitch teach him that?"

"Partly," Melissa admitted. "Mitch was fearless. I guess firefighters have to be. I told Mitch that Jeremy was too young to be on the roof, but he wouldn't hear it. His father allowed him to help when he was only three. According to Mitch, that's what boys do. They watch and emulate their father. Jeremy certainly did that. Anyway, thanks for fixing the leak and that harness thing was brilliant."

"Does that mean you trust me now?" Shane grinned. "Have you finally figured out I'd protect that kid with my life?"

"I'm sorry I doubted you," Melissa said, chagrined. "I never really doubted you. I know you'll protect Jeremy. I just panicked at the thought of being away from him for so long. Which reminds me, why did you cut your weekend short?"

"Jeremy insisted the roof had to be fixed today. He also insisted it was his job," Shane frowned. "From what you've told me your ex was a pretty great guy, but I don't like the pressure he put on that kid. Jeremy honestly believes he has to be the man of the house and that means taking care of all your problems. You're going to need to watch him for a while. I made him promise me he won't try to use the saw. He said you already covered that. I don't think he'll go back on that one. But there are so many other ways he can get into trouble. I don't like it."

"I know," Melissa agreed. "I was so angry with Mitch when I found out what he did. But I told myself it was okay. I thought Mitch and I would grow old together. I never really believed he would die. When he did, everything changed. I was shocked and depressed. I didn't realize what Jeremy was doing until it was too late. Now I don't know how to reverse it. I just want him to be a kid again. A seven year old boy whose biggest worry is whether he wins at kick ball. How do I get that back, Shane? I want it back."

"I don't know," Shane admitted. "But we will. Somehow, in time, we will." Shane started to reach out, then dropped his hand. Things were going too well to mess this up. "We'll be back at six," then he climbed in his truck and drove away.

Hidden Lakes

Melissa stood in the driveway for a very long time. She was torn. When Shane reached out she'd been terrified. Terrified he would touch her and terrified he wouldn't. She felt so empty inside as she watched him drive away. But she couldn't go there again. She'd trusted Shane once and he'd broken her heart. He was so easy to love. She wasn't sure she had ever stopped loving him. But she couldn't trust him and what was love without trust? It was a waste, that's what. She had to get a grip. She had to figure out a way to live in the same town as Shane and not be pulled in to the chemistry between them.

Chapter Six

Shane waited for Megan to fasten her seatbelt then shifted into drive and headed to dinner. Megan was unusually quiet. He wondered what was going on in that brilliant mind of hers. He knew what was going on in his. He was happier than he had been in a very long time. The prospect of having dinner with Melissa and his two kids was like a dream come true. He couldn't remember the last time he'd been this excited for a date. Did that make him old? Probably. Or pathetic. He knew he shouldn't get his hopes up. Melissa still hadn't forgiven him, but he wanted another chance with her. He wanted that more than anything. Having a nice dinner together seemed like a good beginning. Maybe the start of a new family. Shane shot another glance at his daughter. She was worried about something and he didn't like it.

Megan sat staring out the side window, her hands fidgeting in her lap. What if Jeremy's mom hated her? She could tell this was important to her father and she didn't want to ruin everything. It was fun having a brother. She liked teaching Jeremy about the ranch and the animals but mostly she liked seeing her father happy. She'd never seen her dad this happy before. But Megan was afraid she might ruin everything. Hadn't her own mother hated her? Mom had said she was an awful, ugly child and that nobody would ever like her. According to her mom, Megan wasn't worthy of love. The day her mom left had been the worst. Her mom specifically came to Megan's room to brag about the arrangement she'd made with Megan's father. She wanted Megan to know her dad had bought her. Not because he loved her, but because he was angry with her mother. Megan didn't believe her. She knew her dad loved her. The same way she knew her mother despised her.

The one thing Megan couldn't get out of her head was her mom's smug, confident declaration that no woman in Shane's life would ever love Megan. That Megan would always stand in the way of her father's happiness. Her mom had paused in the doorway, grinning. "I know what a worthless, spoiled brat you are Megan. It makes me happier than you could ever imagine knowing that you are the one thing that stands in the way of Shane and true happiness. You're going to be in the way. There's not a woman alive that will put up with you, not even for Shane. I only tolerated you because I had to, but not anymore." Her mother had laughed then. "When Shane refused to marry me, I was devastated. Not only had I lost my meal ticket, but I was stuck with a kid. Not anymore, Shane's stuck with you now. The laughs on him and coincidentally, you ended up being my meal ticket after all. I get everything I ever wanted and Shane gets stuck with you. He'll regret the day he ran me off. He'll rue the day he agreed to keep you. Years from now when he's a lonely old man, wallowing in self-pity, he'll have to admit the worst thing he ever did was agree to keep you. When that happens little girl, your father is going to hate you as much as I do. He's going to resent all he had to give up for a spoiled brat.

Knowing that is going to make every day of my life a happy one," then she'd walked out the door.

What if her mother had been right? What if Jeremy's mother hated her? Her dad was happy about Jeremy, but Megan also knew her father liked Jeremy's mom. She snuck a glance his way, he was so happy he was almost glowing. What if she ruined that for him? What if, like her own mother, Jeremy's mom thought she was an ugly spoiled brat? What if Jeremy's mom wouldn't date her dad because of her? Megan couldn't let that happen. She'd go to dinner and be the best girl in the world. She wouldn't ask for anything or cause any trouble at all. Then maybe her dad would have a chance to be happy.

Shane reached over and placed his large hand over Megan's. She'd been fidgeting since they got in the car. "What's wrong, princess?" he asked softly.

Megan's head shot up. She looked at her father then turned away. "What if she doesn't like me?" she finally asked quietly.

"She's going to love you," Shane assured her, wondering what had brought this on. "What's not to love?" he said lightly.

"But what if she doesn't? She might not want to spend time with you if she doesn't like me. That will make you sad," Megan mumbled. "I don't want to make you sad."

"Megan...sweetheart," Shane said gently. "Melissa is going to like you." Shane sighed, not sure how to continue. "If Melissa and I spend time together it's because we both want to. If we don't, it's because we decided it's not what's best for us. What happens between the two of us will have nothing to do with you. Does this have something to do with your mother?" Shane knew there were things that Megan hadn't told him. Things that Kristy had said or done to undermine his daughter's self-esteem. He hated Kristy for that.

"Maybe a little," Megan admitted. "She didn't like me. She left because she hated me. She made you pay her money to keep me. If my own mom hated me, Jeremy's mom probably won't like me either."

Shane clutched the steering wheel so tight his knuckles turned white. Sometimes he wanted to kill Kristy. To track her down and choke the life out of her with his bare hands. "Melissa's not like your mother Megan," Shane sighed. Melissa was apprehensive about this meeting. Maybe he was making a mistake. Was he being selfish? He knew it would be hard for Melissa to meet his daughter. It was going to remind her of Kristy and all they had lost because of that woman. But he had to believe she'd be kind. That she wouldn't take her anger out on an innocent child. "She's a nice lady. But Melissa is going through a tough time. Her husband died and it's lonely for her without Jeremy. He spent the last few days with us. Now it's our turn to spend some time with his mom so she doesn't feel so alone. Can you do that for me?" he asked, hoping Megan would understand if Melissa was less than enthusiastic this first time together.

Megan considered what her dad was saying. "Is Jeremy's mom sad?" she finally asked.

"I think she is sometimes," Shane said, patting Megan's knee. "So what do you say we try to cheer her up tonight?"

"Okay," Megan reluctantly agreed.

Shane pulled into Melissa's driveway then rounded the truck to take his daughter's hand. No matter what happened here tonight, he was going to protect his little girl. He knew having Jeremy around would make things easier. The kids were great together. But he was afraid of Melissa's reaction and how his daughter would interpret the slightest discomfort. They walked slowly up the stairs, careful to avoid the rotting boards. Then Shane rang the bell and waited. He didn't realize he was holding his breath until Jeremy flung open the door and joyously pulled Megan into the house. Shane took a deep breath and followed them inside.

Melissa was in the kitchen putting the finishing touches on the table. She looked up when the three of them walked into the room. "Dinner's almost ready. By the time you wash up, I'll have the bread out of the oven." She wiped her hands on a dish towel then walked to Megan. Melissa held out her hand and forced a smile. "Hi, I'm Melissa and you must be Megan. I've heard a lot about you. Jeremy had a blast at the ranch this weekend. Thank you for showing him around." Shane's daughter looked as much like him as she did her mother, maybe more. That would make this easier. If she'd been a younger replica of Kristy, Melissa wasn't sure she'd be able to get through the night.

Megan slowly took Melissa's hand and shook it. Then a smile spread across her face. "It was fun," she answered. "I think I like having a brother."

Shane watched them closely. He was so proud of his brave little girl. He saw a slight hesitation in Melissa's eyes when Megan talked about Jeremy being her brother, but it passed as quickly as it had come. They were both trying and that was all he could ask. "Come on you two," Shane said, putting a hand on each child's back as he led them out the door. "I for one am starving. Let's get washed up, I want spaghetti."

Jeremy giggled and ran down the hallway. "Come on Megan, follow me." Megan did as she was told. Shane followed behind.

Hidden Lakes

A few hours later, Megan and Jeremy sat in Jeremy's room. Dinner was over. Melissa's spaghetti was even better than Cora's, but Megan would never admit that to anyone. She wouldn't want to hurt Cora's feelings. After dinner Jeremy got his mom to let them play video games while the grownups did the dishes. Megan had relaxed, but she was still a little nervous. She'd wondered if Melissa would like her better if she did the dishes instead of leaving them for the adults. She asked Jeremy but he had insisted they head to his room, he was excited to show her his video games. Megan played one game, but didn't like the fighting. Now she was sitting at a small table drawing a picture of Jeremy on Trigger with a broken pencil. Frisco was standing beside the horse. Megan loved to draw. Her dad said she was a natural, but Megan didn't believe him. He was her dad, he had to say that. She was concentrating on the picture so intently she didn't notice when Jeremy stopped playing his game and moved to stand behind her.

"That's good," Jeremy said in awe.

Megan looked up, her cheeks flushed, embarrassed. "It's nothing," she said, trying to hide the picture.

"Don't," Jeremy said, trying to get a better look. "It's really good. Is that me?" he asked enthusiastically.

"Uh-huh," Megan said, squirming. She sat back, the picture wasn't perfect, but it was pretty close to what she wanted.

Jeremy reached out to grab the picture and accidentally knocked over Megan's soda. Orange liquid flew across the table, soaking Megan's sweatshirt and jeans. Luckily Jeremy had saved the drawing in time.

Megan jumped to her feet, knocking over her chair. She began to frantically look around for something to clean up the mess. Melissa would blame her for this. If she ruined the carpet, Melissa would blame her. She had to do something. Her sweatshirt was already wet. She had a tank top on underneath, she could use her shirt to clean up the mess. Megan didn't think, she just whipped off her shirt and began to wipe up the liquid.

Jeremy stared at Megan, amazed and confused. He had knocked over the drink, but she was frantically using her own shirt to wipe up the mess. There was no way she'd be able to put that sweatshirt back on. He placed the picture on the dresser then ran to the closet and pulled out a dirty towel. "Move! Let me do that," he said shoving the towel onto the table.

Megan dropped her shirt and grabbed for the towel. Jeremy didn't let go. They were fighting for the towel when the table tipped over. Megan fell to the ground, Jeremy landed on top of her and began to laugh. Megan stared at him in horror, then she burst into giggles.

Shane was sitting at the kitchen table sipping coffee. Melissa was positioned across from him. They could hear the kids moving around in Jeremy's room upstairs. He was grateful they were getting along so well. "It hit me on the way over that Jeremy's birthday has to be coming up soon."

Melissa glanced at Shane then looked away. "It is," she admitted. "July 12th. I'm going to try to have a party for him. I'm hoping to get the steps and the porch repaired by then. I can't have a bunch of kids over unless the yard is safe."

"We could have it at the ranch," Shane suggested, holding his breath. He wasn't sure how Melissa would react to that idea.

"Can I think about it?" Melissa asked. Their lives were becoming so entwined. She wasn't sure if she could handle it. How could she keep an emotional distance from Shane if they were constantly spending time together? Dinners? Birthday parties? Everything was just becoming so confusing.

"Okay," Shane agreed, reaching out and placing his hand over hers. "But if it's not at the ranch, I'd like to participate, and I know that Cora would like that, too. And maybe Hank."

"We have plenty of time to put something together. Let me get back to you in a few days," Melissa couldn't think. Shane's touch had sent her emotions into overdrive. Sitting here with him like this felt so intimate. And she still hadn't gotten the image of him standing on her roof in faded jeans and no shirt out of her mind. He had been sexy eight years ago, but he was over the top gorgeous now. His shoulders seemed wider somehow and all those tight muscles had her fingers itching to explore. The two of them had always had such potent chemistry. If she didn't get a grip, they would end up in bed and that couldn't happen. Not with two impressionable children in the house.

Just then there was a loud thud. It was obvious it had come from Jeremy's room. Melissa jumped to her feet and darted up the stairs.

Shane laughed. She was so much like Cora, a good mother, but such a worrier. He gathered up the mugs and walked them to the sink. He'd clean up the kitchen while she dealt with the kids. Then it would be time to head home. He couldn't take another minute alone with Melissa. Touching her had been a mistake. The instant their hands made contact, electric currents shot through his body. If it wasn't for the kids he would have pushed her onto the table and had his way with her. He needed to take a step back. He needed to figure out how to control his emotions while in her presence. Jumping in like a freight train was only going to send her running.

Melissa took the steps two at a time and rushed to Jeremy's room expecting to find blood or a cracked skull. She pushed the door open and froze in shock. The small table and a chair were tipped over and Megan was on the floor half undressed, shirt lying by her side. Jeremy was on the floor next to her, both of them were laughing. A horrifying thought popped into her head. While Shane was downstairs seducing her, had his daughter been up here seducing her son? Jeremy was only seven years old! Megan truly was her mother's daughter. "Get out," Melissa yelled.

Megan and Jeremy froze. Then Jeremy stood up. "Mom. It was my fault," he began. "I'm sorry."

"Be quiet Jeremy," Melissa said, breathing hard as she glared at Megan. "We'll talk about this later. Megan, you and your father need to leave. Now!" she said, raising her voice. "I can't believe I let someone like you spend time alone in my son's bedroom."

Megan began to cry. Jeremy's mom did hate her. The same hatred and disgust Megan had lived with from her mother was shining in Melissa's eyes. She had ruined everything. When Melissa said 'someone like you' she really meant an ugly spoiled child, just like her mother had. Megan turned and ran down the stairs then out the front door. She had to get away. She was a bad person, just like her mother said. She was going to ruin her father's life. Her dad was going to hate her. Megan didn't know where to go so she just climbed in the truck and wept. It was so cold and her clothes were all wet. She'd forgotten her sweatshirt in Jeremy's room, but she couldn't wear it now anyway. Not after she'd wiped up the spill with it.

Shane stepped into the hallway just in time to see Megan rush from the house. She was clearly upset about something. Melissa stood at the top of the stairs glaring down at him. "I want you out of my house and don't come back. I won't have that....that...hussy around my son."

"Now wait a damn minute," Shane said, his anger flaring. She was talking about his daughter. "You need to calm down and tell me what happened."

"Mom!" Jeremy said, pulling on Melissa's shirt.

"I told you to stay in your room," she barked, taking Jeremy's hand and practically throwing him towards the door. "Don't come out," she growled as she slammed the door. Then she turned back to Shane. "I knew better. How could I have been so stupid? I let you into my home!"

Shane stood, glaring at Melissa. She was crazy. Whatever had happened, she was clearly over reacting.

"But worse, I let that woman's daughter into my home. What was I thinking?" Melissa began to pace the small hallway at the top of the stairs. "I exposed my son to..." she stopped and glared at Shane. "I won't allow this. Jeremy is never sleeping at your house again. You can still see him, but there is no way I'm letting him near that girl again. I knew the apple didn't fall far from the tree. I knew letting that sleazy, manipulative hussy's daughter into my home was a bad idea, but I did it anyway. I should be shot."

"That's the first thing you've said that I agree with," Shane said, so angry he couldn't stand it. He clenched his fist before he picked up her frilly lamp and tossed it across the room. Nobody talked about his daughter that way. "Which tree are you talking about, Melissa? Kristy's or mine? Am I a product of my mother, the bad apple that makes my eight year old daughter a hussy in your eyes?" he hissed.

Melissa continued to glare. "You're right," she finally said. "That girl didn't have a chance. With a father like you and a mother like Kristy, what did I expect? I have to hand it to her, she's definitely a fast learner. You've always been smooth and great in bed, but with all that practice who wouldn't be? Megan's just a child. I shudder to think what she's going to be like as a teenager. Get out of my house Shane and don't come back."

All the blood rushed from Shane's face. How had he ever believed Melissa loved him? While he was falling in love, she was using him for sex. While he was sharing his deepest, darkest secrets, she was judging him. Now she was judging his daughter. It wasn't Megan's fault her mother was pond scum. And it wasn't his fault his mother was either. "I guess that doesn't say much for our son now does it? His mother's bat shit crazy and it seems I'm the devil incarnate." He turned and stalked out, slamming the door behind him.

Shane was relieved to find Megan huddled in the truck. He'd failed her tonight. He'd lied to her. She'd been so worried about meeting Jeremy's mother and Shane had been selfish. He'd wanted Melissa to accept them, wanted her to love them so badly that he'd risked his daughter to get what he wanted. Seeing Megan this way broke his heart and infuriated him all at once. He yanked open the door and realized Megan was shaking. At first he thought it was from her crying, but as he lifted her into his arms he noticed the missing sweatshirt. She had a flimsy little tank top on and it was soaked, so were her jeans. She had to be freezing.

Shane immediately pulled off the tank then wrapped Megan in his flannel shirt. "Come on. Let's get the pants off too," he said, glancing over his shoulder to make sure Melissa hadn't followed him outside. He needed to get his daughter away from here. Then he could decide what to do about his son. If Melissa thought she could keep Jeremy from him, she was in for a shock. Once Shane had buttoned his shirt, he secured the seatbelt and shut the door. Tonight had been a disaster. He'd get Megan home, do his best to assure her everything was going to be okay, then work on a plan for their future. A future that was going to include Jeremy.

Shane spun out, leaving skid marks on Melissa's driveway. He didn't care. The woman was nuts. Once they were on the road he glanced at his daughter. She was so quiet. Too quiet. He didn't like it. He reached over and undid her seatbelt. "Come here princess," he said pulling her little body against his. Megan snuggled against him, wrapping her arms around his waist. Shane reached down and clicked the seatbelt around Megan's waist then wrapped his arm around her. "I'm sorry," he choked.

Megan raised her head, wiped away a tear and sobbed. She was the one that was sorry. She had to stop crying so she could tell her dad. She was sorry she'd been bad. She was sorry she was an ugly brat. She was sorry Jeremy's mother hated her. "I'm so sorry daddy," she sobbed.

Shane put his hand under his daughter's chin and lifted her head, forcing her to look at him. As he looked into her swollen red eyes, he wanted to punch something. For the second time in Megan's short life, Shane had allowed a woman to hurt her. Never again. He would never let any woman shatter his daughter again. "I love you princess. You didn't do anything wrong. I don't want you to say you're sorry. This was all my fault, not yours."

Tears ran down Megan's face. She couldn't talk. Not now. She felt guilty for making her dad sad, she hated that she'd done something that made Jeremy's mom so angry with her. But how could she fix it now? She had tried to clean up the mess, but Jeremy got in the way. Had Melissa been that mad over the spilt soda? Or was it the mess in Jeremy's room. Megan just didn't know. She curled into her father's side and cried.

Shane pulled up to the ranch house and climbed from the truck, pulling Megan into his arms. He strolled into the house and up to Megan's room. Once inside, he set her on the floor and pulled a set of pajamas out of her drawer. "I think you should take a quick shower. Your sticky and won't sleep well unless you do," he said, turning her around so he could tie her hair into a pony tail. "Try not to get your hair wet."

Megan picked up her clothes and slowly walked to the bathroom. Shane waited until he heard the water running then sank onto her bed. What had happened tonight? What had gone on in that room that made Melissa go so nuts? It really didn't matter. There was nothing on earth that could justify what Melissa had done to Megan. Nothing Melissa could say or do that would make him forgive her for putting that broken look in his daughter's eyes. For the past eight years he'd believed he'd made a mistake. For eight years, he had loved the woman that he'd lost. Now he knew he'd loved a lie. Melissa hadn't loved him. As bad as tonight had been, at least he'd found that out before it was too late. Seeing the real Melissa couldn't save his heart, but at least he could save his daughter.

Megan walked from the bathroom and climbed into bed. "I didn't know what to do with the clothes," she whispered. "I left them on the floor."

"Cora will take care of them tomorrow." He stretched out next to Megan and pulled her against his chest. "Go to sleep." He kissed the top of her head. "I'm not going to let anyone hurt you ever again. You're my little princess and I love you." Shane closed his eyes, trying to block out the pain. He'd failed his daughter, again.

"I'm sorry I made Melissa mad, daddy." Megan brushed away another tear. "I don't know what I did, but I'm really sorry."

Shane pulled Megan closer. "Don't be. Whatever happened is no excuse for Melissa to yell at you. Melissa should be saying she's sorry, not you baby." Right now more than ever, Shane wished he could go back in time and make different decisions. He should have gotten rid of Kristy when Megan was a baby. He should have offered money to get her out of their lives before she could damage his daughter with her hatred and her venom. But he couldn't change the past. All he could do was protect her future. He could make sure nobody ever made Megan feel unwanted again. And he was going to start with Melissa. That woman would never be alone with his daughter again. And if she thought she could keep his son away from him, she was in for the fight of her life. The first thing he needed to do was call his attorney. No more overnights my butt. Shane was going to file for joint custody and this time he might not settle for weekends.

* * * *

Melissa entered Jeremy's room and frowned. Her son was on the floor, scrubbing the carpet furiously. She walked in and sat on the bed. "Jeremy, come sit next to me for a minute. We need to talk."

Jeremy looked up, then quickly turned away. He blinked several times, not wanting to cry. He still didn't know what had made his mom so angry. Why had she yelled at Megan like that? He'd spilled drinks before, but his mom hadn't gone crazy over it.

Melissa saw the tears forming in her sons eyes. She hated this. How was she going to explain? "Jeremy," she said more sternly. "You can finish that later."

"But it made you so angry," he said, glancing at her. "I'm sorry I spilled the soda. It was my fault, not Megan's. I did this. You shouldn't have yelled at her like that," he stood, raising his chin in defiance. His mom had been unfair.

"I wasn't angry about the soda," Melissa said, furrowing her brows. She hadn't even noticed the spill. She patted the bed. "Come on, we need to talk."

Jeremy moved to the bed and slowly sat down. "Then why were you angry?" Jeremy asked, confused.

Melissa glanced around the room and spotted Megan's sweatshirt. For the first time, she noticed the white cloth was covered in orange splotches. Had she completely misread the situation? No, that was impossible. She had seen what she'd seen. The children were acting inappropriately and it was all Megan's fault. "I heard a loud thud and came up to see what happened. Maybe you could explain to me what you and Megan were doing."

Jeremy lowered his head and studied his hands. "I was playing the X Box. Megan got bored and didn't want to play. She said fighting games were boring. But I was doing good, so I kept playing. When my guy got killed, I played again. Maybe twice, I can't remember. Megan moved to the table and started drawing. Then I got killed again, so I went over to see what she was doing." He looked up at his mother. "She's really good." He jumped up

105

and moved to the dresser, bringing back a piece of paper. He handed the drawing to his mother.

Melissa hesitantly took the paper. Jeremy was getting off the subject, she'd need to reign him back in. She glanced down, intending to brush it aside then stared wide eyed at the drawing. It was good. Megan had drawn Jeremy sitting on top of a horse with a German Shepherd sitting obediently at the horses side. The dog was looking sideways, towards the artist's vantage point. The girl was an artist, a talented artist. At eight, she could draw better than many of the paintings Melissa had seen in galleries back in Denver. "Megan drew this tonight?" Melissa asked, amazed.

"Uh-huh," Jeremy said, grinning. "I told you she was good. I wanted to ask her if I could have it, but then you came in..." Jeremy trailed off.

Melissa stood and set the drawing back on the dresser. She'd make sure it got back to Megan. Melissa returned to the bed and waited. When Jeremy didn't continue she prompted him. "So, you finished playing the game and went to check on Megan."

"Yeah," Jeremy said, then sighed. "When I saw the picture I was really surprised. I mean that's me and it's good. Megan seemed embarrassed about it, like maybe she doesn't usually show people the things she draws. She was kind of hiding it so..." he paused, looking at his mother guiltily. "Well, I grabbed the picture to get a better look."

"I see," Melissa said, she had a sinking feeling and started to worry. Somehow she knew she wasn't going to like what Jeremy had to say.

"When I grabbed the paper, I accidentally knocked over Megan's soda." Jeremy glanced up, but couldn't read his mom's expression so he continued. "It made a big mess and splattered all over Megan. She panicked. She jumped up and started darting around the room. Then, before I really knew what she was doing, she pulled off her sweatshirt and started mopping up the orange drink. I didn't want her to ruin her clothes because of me so I pulled a towel out of the hamper. I moved over to wipe up the mess, but Megan started grabbing for the towel. She was really upset, I don't know why," Jeremy furrowed his brow. "Do you think she gets in a lot of trouble for spilling at her house? Not by dad, he would never yell at her." Jeremy paused to glare at his mother, "Not like you did. You shouldn't have yelled at Megan, mom. It wasn't her fault, it was mine. I tried to tell you that but you wouldn't listen."

Melissa was becoming more horrified at what she'd done by the second. With every word Jeremy said, she felt smaller and more guilty. Why had she jumped to conclusions? Why had she yelled at Megan like that? It wasn't like her.

When Melissa didn't react to Jeremy's scolding he continued. "I didn't want her to have to clean up my mess. So, we were fighting over the towel. Well, not really fighting, just she had one end and I had the other. We were both pulling at it and somehow we knocked over the table. She tripped and fell to the floor and since I was holding the towel I fell on top of her. Then I started laughing. I don't know why really, it just seemed funny, the room was a mess and we were fighting over a stupid towel. Megan was covered in orange soda, she'd knocked over the chair when she jumped up and then we knocked over the table. I was just glad I had the picture in my hand so it didn't get ruined, too. And Megan was so serious about the whole thing, then when I started laughing, she started laughing and that's when you came in. I really don't understand what we did that was so wrong. Especially Megan, mom. Why did you get so mad at her? You've never been that mad before when I made a mess. Is it because grandma and grandpa spent so much money on new carpet? I just don't understand."

Melissa felt awful. She'd terrorized a little girl. How could she explain something to Jeremy that she didn't even understand herself? "I'm sorry," she said, pulling Jeremy against her. "I'm sorry I yelled. You're right. I shouldn't have yelled at Megan, I shouldn't have yelled at you and I shouldn't have yelled at Shane." She'd been so awful to Shane.

Jeremy frowned. "You said I can't stay with dad anymore but I want to. You wouldn't really keep me from dad would you? I was just getting to know him. I like him. It was fun at the ranch. You promised I could spend time with him on the weekends. You can't take that back," Jeremy said defiantly.

"Go put the towel and Megan's shirt in the laundry. We'll talk about this more tomorrow. It's late and you have school in the morning." She leaned over and kissed Jeremy on the forehead. "I'm sorry I yelled at you."

"You should tell Megan sorry. You made her cry," Jeremy said, dumping the laundry in the basket and pulling out his pajamas. He walked back to the bed and stood in front of his mom. "You always make me say sorry when I'm wrong. You should say you're sorry. And I'm still spending time with dad. If you try to stop me, I'll just ride the bus to the ranch after school."

"We'll figure something out. I won't keep you away from Shane," Melissa said, pulling Jeremy into her arms. He wasn't even eight yet and he was already a better person than she was. "Goodnight," she stood, kissing the top of his head. "I love you."

"Love you too," Jeremy said closing the door behind her before he dressed for bed.

Melissa walked slowly to her room then dropped onto the bed. She was a horrible person, a bully. Tears began to roll down her cheek as she remembered the sad, terrified look on Megan's face as she yelled at her and ordered her out of the house. Then the pale, shocked expression on Shane's as she'd compared him to his mother. She curled into a ball and let herself cry. At around two o'clock Melissa had an epiphany. She was still in love with Shane, and she'd lost him forever. She used to believe it was impossible to love two people at the same time. Now she knew she'd been wrong. She'd never stopped loving Shane, even while she had loved Mitch. Had Shane felt the same about her and Kristy all those years ago? That could explain how he'd gotten both of them pregnant at almost the same time. Kristy claimed he cared for both of them, but she hadn't wanted to listen. And if he had loved both of them, did that excuse his actions? She didn't have an answer for that. And really, would it matter now? She'd terrorized his little girl. Not because Megan deserved it, but because Kristy was her mother. Shane would never forgive her.

* * * *

Shane climbed out of bed at four and meandered down to the kitchen. He hadn't slept at all last night. He was tired and frustrated and needed to get an early start. Once he fed the livestock, he'd head for Bramble. Hopefully, Steve Olson would have time for him today. He hadn't needed the man for years, not since he'd made Kristy sign over all parental rights for money, but the guy was good at his job. If anyone could get him joint custody of Jeremy, Steve could. That and Judge Stone might be enough. It had to be enough.

He would not lose Jeremy. Now that he knew he had a son, he would do everything in his power to keep him in his life.

Cora parked in front of the ranch house and spotted Shane as she climbed from the car. He didn't look happy. She slowly approached him, wondering if he would tell her what was going on. Shane was a proud stubborn man. He wouldn't talk until he was ready.

"Hey," Shane greeted as Cora approached. "I'm glad you got here early. I have a busy day and need to head out."

"You gonna tell me what's wrong?" she asked pointedly.

"Probably not," Shane shrugged. "You tend to defend Melissa no matter what she does. Things didn't go as planned last night, let's just leave it at that." He grabbed a bale of hay and headed for the barn.

Cora followed, frowning. This had something to do with Melissa? What could the girl have done now? She moved in close to Shane and leaned against the stall. "Try me," she pressed.

"Look Cora," Shane sighed. "I know you were always close to Melissa. You want to see the best in people. I'm just not up for excuses this morning." He latched the stall door and turned to face the woman he adored. Just once he wished she would be on his side. He loved her dearly and always would. She was the closest thing to a mother he had ever had. "Megan's still upset so I let her stay home from school. She's going to head out with Hank today. They're branding in the north field. Don't worry, she won't be in your way."

Cora frowned. Shane let Megan stay home from school? The situation was worse than she originally believed. Megan had to be seriously ill for Shane to even consider keeping her home. "What about you?" she asked.

"Like I said, I have a busy day." He studied her. "I'm going to see Steve Olson. I wanted to ask if you'd mind staying a little late tonight. I'll be back as soon as I can, but the drive alone is going to take five hours. I have a lot to go over with Steve so if you could stay a little late, maybe get Megan dinner before you go, it would really help me out."

"Shane, you know I'm here for you, right?" she studied him. "I'm on your side. Sure, I care about Melissa, but I love you and Megan. If I've done something to make you doubt that I'd like to know what."

Shane leaned against the stall door, lowered his head to his hands and sighed. "No, I guess you haven't." He drew in a deep breath then let it out slowly. "I'm just tired and frustrated and I have a long, difficult day ahead. I know I can count on you. Thanks for that."

Cora wasn't satisfied, but for now she'd let it be. "I'll be here when you get back. Take as long as you need. If it's too late, I'll just bunk in one of the guest rooms. You're stressed, I can see that. Don't rush back, drive safe and do what you need to do."

"Thanks, Cora. Hank's out fixing a downed fence with Woody, but I expect him back any minute. Megan's supposed to be getting dressed. Now that you're here, I'm going to head out."

Cora reached out and touched Shane's arm. Before she could speak Shane leaned in and kissed the top of her head. "I owe you one. I know I didn't give you a lot of notice. It's nice to know I can always count on you. It means a lot to me. See you tonight," then he was gone.

Hidden Lakes

Cora frowned as she walked toward the house. She knew she always played devil's advocate when it came to Melissa. She hadn't realized Shane walked away from those discussions thinking she was taking sides, Melissa's side. Had she made excuses for the girl's actions? Maybe. She had always liked Mel and couldn't bring herself to believe the girl would hurt Shane on purpose. So what had happened last night? Cora stepped into the kitchen and froze. Megan was sitting at the table in front of a bowl of cereal. She wasn't eating, she was just staring out the window. It was obvious Megan had been crying. Her eyes were swollen and her face was splotchy. Cora stepped into the room and placed her bag on the counter. "I hear someone gets to skip school today." She walked to the fridge and pulled out a gallon of orange juice.

"Hi Cora," Megan said quietly. "I'm going out to help Hank today," she sniffled.

Cora slid into the chair next to Megan. "You want to talk about it?" Megan was silent for so long, Cora didn't think she was going to answer.

"Why am I unlikable?" Megan finally asked, tears filling her eyes. "What's wrong with me and can I change it?"

"Now you're just talking nonsense," Cora said, furious. "What makes you think there's anything wrong with you?"

"My mom told me I would ruin my dad's life, but I thought she was just being cruel. After last night, I know she was right. Dad was happy. Now he's angry at Melissa and it's all my fault. I just don't know what I did. Mom told me that dad would always be lonely because of me. I don't want dad to be lonely. I want him to be happy," tears were streaming down her face now.

"Hey," Cora said, taking Megan's hand and pulling her in for a hug. "First of all, never start a sentence with 'my mom told me'. That woman was selfish and petty. Your father loves you more than anything in the world. Kristy resented that. She said cruel things to make you doubt yourself. She lied, sweetheart. You need to understand that. You need to stop thinking about those mean, cruel things she said because none of them are true."

"But Melissa hates me," she sniffled. "Now dad's mad at her and Melissa won't let Jeremy visit anymore because she doesn't want him around me." She was sobbing now.

"Can you tell me what happened last night?" Cora asked, worried. No wonder Shane was meeting with an attorney this morning. "Start at the beginning. You and your dad arrive at Melissa's house. What happens then?"

Through the tears and the sobs, Megan walked Cora through the evening. Megan might not know what happened, but Cora understood. And she was furious with Melissa. Of all the ridiculous notions. To believe a child could do something inappropriate. Then her eyes widened and she froze, shocked. What had Melissa said to Shane after Megan left the house? If she'd compared him to his mother, Shane would never forgive her. She glanced up and spotted Hank standing in the doorway. "Hanks here," she whispered. She didn't know how long he'd been standing there, but from the look on his face, it had been awhile. "Go grab a jacket. It's warm down here, but it might be chilly in the north field."

"Okay," Megan said, standing and wiping her face with her sleeve.

Once Megan was out of the room, Cora turned to Hank. "Take care of her Hank. That girl is upset and preoccupied. Trigger's gentle with her, but he can still spook like any other horse. I'm not sure she's up for that today."

Hank stepped into the room and poured himself a cup of coffee. "I love that kid as much as you do, Cora. I understand the situation and don't intent to let her out of my sight today."

"Good," Cora said, standing. "You hungry? I can fry you up a couple eggs."

"Thanks, but no. We've got to get started. We have a long day ahead of us. I had a muffin about an hour ago."

Cora ignored him and scrambled some eggs. She browned a tortilla, rolled in the eggs and some salsa, then wrapped it all in a paper towel. Hank grinned as he accepted the breakfast burrito. "Not bad," he admitted. "It would be better with sausage or bacon, but this will do in a pinch." He stood as Megan stepped back into the room. "Ready squirt?" he asked, guiding her to the doorway. He glanced back at Cora and gave her a quick wink before disappearing out the door.

Cora sank back onto the chair. She was worried about Shane and Megan. The girl was taking too much on herself. Her memories turned to Kristy. That woman was nothing but trouble. She had no business being a mother. Cora hadn't agreed with the way Shane handled the situation, but at least paying her off had gotten her out of Megan's life for good.

Chapter Seven

Melissa pulled into the small lot of the police department and shut off her car. She felt awful and knew she looked just as bad. But Joe had let her leave early yesterday, there was no way she was going to call in sick today. She climbed from the car and slowly made her way into her office. She'd only been there a few minutes when Joe appeared. He placed both hands on her desk and leaned forward, glaring at her. Melissa swallowed hard and forced a smile.

"Go home. You look like hell," Joe barked and stood, not expecting an argument.

"I left early yesterday," Melissa began. "I can't afford to go home again today. I need a full paycheck."

"Who said anything about losing pay?" Joe said, narrowing his eyes at her. "In fact, I came out to see if you'd mind working a few hours extra tonight. Now, I don't know..."

"I'll work extra hours," Melissa offered. "Where's Tina?"

"Her mom fell and broke her hip. It was lucky her neighbor found her when he did. Otherwise she might have laid there for hours. Anyway, I told Tina not to worry about work. She's in Bramble at the hospital, waiting for her mother to have surgery. Susan has to have a hip replacement. Tina might be out for a week. She said she'd play it by ear, but she wants to be there for her mother until Susan is transferred to rehab. Hopefully the doctor's will let Susan transfer out here," Joe shrugged. "Anyway, we're shorthanded tonight. Normally I'd just have one of the guys man the radio, but Scott's wife, Beth is on bed rest and ready to have the baby any minute. I gave him a couple days off to take care of her. That only leaves two guys on tonight. If I pull one of them in to dispatch that leaves the other deputy without a back. That's unacceptable. I won't risk my men's safety that way."

Melissa considered. "If you can give me a couple hours to make arrangements for Jeremy, I can handle Tina's shift tonight. In fact, if you want I can work late all week."

"Go," Joe said with a nod. "But don't come back until this afternoon. You're exhausted. Make arrangements for Jeremy then get some sleep. I want you alert and ready for work when you come back. I got the phones and the radio today."

Melissa paused and was about to argue when Joe interrupted. "Don't argue with me girlie. Get. If you come back before two, you're fired." Then he turned and headed for his office. Clearly the conversation was over.

Melissa ran her hands through her hair, then stood and slowly made her way back to her car. She had until two to get a short nap and talk to Shane about Jeremy. She knew Shane would be surprised. Only a few hours ago, Melissa had threatened to restrict

Jeremy's visits. Maybe this would help to smooth things over between them. One could always hope. She climbed into her car and headed home.

A few hours later Melissa pulled down the long drive that led to Shane's ranch house. She was pretty sure he wouldn't be at the house but she hoped Cora would tell her where he was working, and that it would be accessible by vehicle. She shut down the car and slowly made her way to the back door. She assumed Cora would be in the kitchen. If she remembered correctly, it would be lunchtime for the hands. The door was opened and she could see Cora at the counter. She raised her hand to knock but stopped when she heard Cora's words.

"You're not welcome here, Melissa. Get in that fancy car of yours and go on back home." Cora didn't even turn to look in Melissa's direction. She was still too angry with the girl.

"So you're mad at me too," Melissa said through the screen on the door. "I should have known Shane would talk to you about last night. I admit I didn't behave well, actually I was awful," Melissa paused. "I don't know if it matters, but I'm truly sorry for the horrible things I said. I was wrong and I wanted to apologize for my actions."

Now Cora turned. "Shane's not here. And if he were, I doubt he'd listen. You hurt his baby. How could you think...?" Cora shook her head. "Never mind. It's none of my business. Just go home. That family has been victimized enough by the women in their lives. Do everyone a favor and just leave them be."

"What about me, Cora? Have I been victimized enough?" Melissa demanded, hurt by Cora's words. She knew Cora was devoted to Shane, but he'd hurt her too. He'd betrayed her. He'd cheated on her.

Hidden Lakes

Cora studied Melissa. "I'm not making excuses for you this time. Shane pointed out this morning how often I do that. I made excuses when you left eight years ago and then I made excuses when you returned and announced that Shane had a son. I wanted to believe in you, I wanted to be right about you. I can see now I was wrong all along. Shane missed out on almost eight years of that boys' life. I honestly believed you loved him, but I guess I was wrong about that too. If you had loved him, you would have stood by him. You would have been there when he needed you most."

"I never realized your loyalty to Shane was blind loyalty. How can you stand there and criticize me? Shane cheated on me! He didn't just get another woman pregnant, he got Kristy pregnant. Do you have any idea how much that hurt me? Can you stop making excuses for Shane for one minute and consider how I felt? Okay, I agree I shouldn't have kept Jeremy a secret from Shane, but he was marrying Kristy! He betrayed me, not the other way around. He cheated on me. He was dating two women at the same time. He was pretending to plan a life with me while he was sleeping with Kristy McGrath of all people. How can you stand there and expect me to feel sorry for him?"

"Go home Melissa," Cora said, turning back to the counter. She gathered up the sandwiches and placed them into a large cooler. "You're not welcome here. Shane doesn't need this. Believe whatever you want about that man. You couldn't be more wrong about him and clearly you don't deserve him." Then she picked up the cooler, pushed past Melissa and headed for an old truck. "I expect you to be gone when I get back. Otherwise, I'll have to call the Sheriff."

Melissa stood there in shock. She understood Cora being angry with her. She deserved that after the way she'd acted the night before, but she never would have expected this. How could she blame Melissa for the mess Shane had caused all those years ago? And what did she mean when she said Shane had been victimized by the women in his life. She'd never victimized Shane. He cheated on her. She moved to the front steps and sat. Cora could just call the sheriff. She wasn't leaving until she got some answers. As she sat there thinking about her past she realized she didn't really know what had happened back then. She had Kristy's version of events, but that didn't mean anything. Shane had started to give her an explanation, but she hadn't let him finish. The instant he told her Kristy was pregnant, she'd lost it. She rushed off, not wanting Shane to see her cry over him. The one thing she did remember was Shane's claim that it had only been one night. A big mistake that he had made at a party of some kind. He'd started to make excuses about being drunk but she hadn't wanted to hear it.

Was it possible that Shane had gone to a party, gotten drunk and ended up in bed with Kristy? And if that's what happened did it really matter? He'd still cheated. And that's what didn't make sense about Cora's outburst. Cora didn't make excuses. Sure, she'd be the first one to defend someone she loved, and she definitely loved Shane, but she also believed in facing the consequences of your actions. Cora never would have said Melissa didn't deserve Shane unless there was more to the story. Which was even more reason to risk arrest to get answers.

Melissa was still considering the past, trying to remember every little detail, when an old beat up car pulled down the drive. It sputtered and creaked as it made its way over the gravel path. The instant it came to a stop, the engine died. Melissa watched in amazement as a woman dressed in a sky blue silk shirt and white leather pants climbed out of the car. She was wearing spiky heals and her blood red nail polish matched her lips. The woman turned and shoved the rusty door, which was hanging from one hinge. The door swung shut, then slammed against the side of the car. The woman began to curse under her breath, lifted the door slightly and slammed it shut. She flung a large bag over her shoulder and headed for the front door.

Melissa knew the instant the woman spotted her. She'd been mumbling under her breath, clearly annoyed at the entire situation. She froze for half a second, then made a beeline for Melissa. Somehow Melissa knew this encounter was not going to be pleasant.

"Excuse me," the woman said with a fake smile. "I have two bags in the trunk. Please take them to the guest room."

Melissa raised an eyebrow, but didn't move.

"You do work for my son, don't you?" the woman asked, no longer smiling. "I can see you must be on a break, but I've been traveling for hours and I could really use a drink and a comfortable place to rest for a while. Shane would want you to take care of me. I'd hate to have to tell him you were less than helpful."

"I don't work for your son," Melissa said, realizing who this woman was. "And I doubt he'd expect me to be helpful."

"Oh," the woman said, taken by surprise. She quickly regrouped and held out a hand. "I'm sorry, like I said it's been a long day. Then who are you? Are you dating Shane? You must be. Well as you might have guessed, I'm his mother, Gloria. And you are?" she asked when Melissa didn't jump at the chance to take her hand.

"Melissa," she said, glancing at Gloria's outstretched hand then back to her face.

"Well," Gloria said, pushing the strap of her large bag higher on her shoulder. "As I said, I'm beat. Could I get you to let me inside so I can relax until Shane gets home?"

"I don't have the authority to let you into Shane's house," Melissa said, scowling. Shane had told her about his mother back when they were dating. She'd always believed he'd over exaggerated things to make his mother sound worse than she really was. Now she realized, he'd down played how fake and manipulative she was. This woman reminded her of Kristy. She was conceited, self-centered and extremely fake. Melissa instantly disliked her.

"I understand," Gloria said, studying Melissa. "Shane told you we don't get along."

"That's putting it mildly," Melissa said, still watching Gloria.

Gloria moved to the steps and sat next to Melissa. "That's why I'm here," she began. "I miss my boy. I know, he's a man now, but I'll always think of him as my precious little boy. He was such a delightful child. I wasn't always the best mother, and I know that. But I love my son. I want to make things right. Not only for me but for Shane and his little girl. I've been looking forward to spending time with my granddaughter."

"Have you met Marnie?" Melissa asked. She wanted to find out if Gloria really knew Megan or if she was bluffing. She was pretty sure this was another game.

"Oh yes," Gloria smiled. "We haven't met in person, yet. Shane hasn't allowed that. If you know about me, the two of you must be close. You have to know how stubborn my boy can be. But Marnie and I have become very close over the past few months. We talk on the phone all the time. She's the biggest reason I made the trip out here. I have a right to know that precious little girl," Gloria

121

smiled inwardly. She hadn't known the girls name until now. This little conversation was going to pay off in the long run. Women were such easy targets.

"Really?" Melissa said, angry now. The woman had no scruples. She planned to use Megan to get at Shane. Not if Melissa could help it. "I heard you grumbling about the state of your car as you walked toward me. Is that why you're here? You want Shane to buy you a new car?"

Gloria narrowed her eyes at Melissa. She didn't like this woman and realized trying to gain her as an ally was a waste of time. "As you can see, my car is old and falling apart. I do think Shane should buy me a new one. I cared for that boy. I loved him and sacrificed for him. I always thought of him first and how does he thank me? He shuts me out of his life and refuses to provide for me in my time of need. He has so much, but because he's angry with me, he lets me suffer. So yeah, I think the least he could do is buy me a new car. But if you're implying that's why I'm here, you are mistaken. I told you, I'm here to spend time with my granddaughter. Talking on the phone is great if that's all I can have, but I want more. I want Marnie to know me, personally. I want to show her I'm not a bad person. If Shane has influenced your opinion of me, a complete stranger, just think of what he might have said to his daughter. He's being unfair. I intend to rectify that."

"What about Shane's wishes?" Melissa asked flatly. "If you love him so much, don't you want to take his feelings into consideration?"

Gloria took a long, deep breath then let it out slowly. "Are you trying to provoke me or are you just naturally rude and insensitive?"

Melissa smiled then shrugged. "I'm just trying to figure you out. I know what Shane has told me about you. Meeting you in the flesh has certainly been enlightening. I just think that if you were really here to make amends with your son, you would have called first. You might have warned him you were coming. Instead, you decided to surprise him. I assume you were counting on his daughter to support your cause."

Gloria smiled. "Yes," she admitted. "I'm counting on my relationship with Marnie to sway Shane. They're the only family I have. I'm willing to do anything to be a part of their lives."

"And you want my help?" Melissa asked.

"I was hoping for it but I don't think I need it," Gloria said, trying to figure out this woman's angle.

Melissa stood. "The best way to sway Shane is to demonstrate you're not just here for his money. If you are serious about wanting a fresh start, head to Bramble and get a job, rent an apartment, start with that. Show Shane you want him in your life, but give him a little space."

Gloria stared into the distance for a long time. She wasn't sure how to play this. Go to Bramble and get a job, yeah right. That was so not going to happen. She tried for her most pathetic, contrite look and turned back to Melissa. "Bramble is a long ways away. I understand what you're saying and you're probably right, but it's impossible. I used up my last dime getting here. My car is on empty and the last time I ate was yesterday afternoon," she forced tears into her eyes. "I'm desperate."

Melissa walked to her car and pulled out her purse. She returned to the porch and handed Gloria two crisp one hundred dollar bills. "That should get you to Bramble, pay for dinner and get you into a room for a few days. I happen to know there are a couple waitressing jobs available. Try the Penny Pig first. Helen's room above the garage might still be vacant. If she hires you, I'm sure she'll let you stay there as part of your employment."

Cora frowned when she spotted Melissa's car. She'd hoped the girl would have left by now. Then she noticed the other vehicle in the driveway. She studied the area and spotted Gloria. Just what they needed, one more thing to deal with. She brought the truck to a stop and jumped from the cab. She knew Gloria spotted her when she grabbed something from Melissa's hand and rushed to her car. By the time Cora reached Melissa, Gloria was halfway up the driveway.

"Please tell me you didn't give that woman money," Cora demanded.

Melissa turned to Cora. "Is Joe on the way?"

"Melissa," Cora demanded. "Did you give her money?"

Melissa sighed. "Yes, Cora. I gave her money."

"Girl, you have no idea what you just did," Cora said with regret.

"Yeah. I think I do," Melissa said, slumping onto the porch stairs. "I had to get rid of her. She planned to use Megan to get at Shane," Melissa scowled. "She tried her best to get me to let her into the house. I think she was counting on Megan getting home from school before Shane came home for the night. She wanted time to manipulate Megan. I couldn't let that happen. She agreed to go to Bramble and try to work at Shane from a distance."

"How much?" Cora asked. "We both know you can't afford to give away money. How much did she get from you?"

"Two hundred," Melissa admitted. "I was only going to offer one but I figured that wasn't enough to make her go away."

"Oh Melissa," Cora said, sitting down next to her. "You needed that money to fix your stairs. That woman is nothing but trouble. You do realize she's not going anywhere. She won't go to Bramble. She's going to head to town and try to shack up with William," Cora jumped up. "Don't go anywhere. I'll be right back."

"You headed in to call Joe now?" Melissa said, only half teasing.

"I'm not calling Joe on you. But that's not a bad idea. I should probably warn him that Gloria's back in town." Cora stepped into the house and in seconds came back outside, phone in hand. "Hey Joe, I just thought I'd let you know Gloria just left. She conned Melissa out of a couple hundred bucks and claimed she's heading to Bramble but we both know that's a load of bull."

Melissa rolled her eyes. "Cora, she didn't con me out of anything. I gave her the money so she'd go away. As far as I'm concerned it was money well spent."

"I guess great minds think alike," Cora said into the phone. "I was going to call, but it would be better to warn him in person. Okay, keep me posted."

"Joe's heading to William's place I presume?" Melissa asked.

"Yep," Cora said with a smile. "Problem solved."

Hidden Lakes

"I thought William was with Emily," Melissa asked. "From what I heard they're pretty serious."

"He is," Cora agreed. "And I trust William, I just don't trust Gloria."

"So they have a history?" Melissa asked, surprised.

"Gloria came to town a while back," she paused. "I guess it would almost be four years now. She was between husbands and wanted Shane to front her some money until she could find husband number six I believe. Anyway, she hooked up with William and used him for a few months while she tried to get at Shane. William's a great guy, but an easy target for someone like Gloria. Don't get me wrong, he's completely devoted to Emily and I'm not worried about fidelity or anything like that. I just worry that she'll con him out of more money. She got a couple hundred from you, but William would give her thousands if he thought it would get her out of town. I don't want to see that happen. Joe will take care of it and he'll warn Emily. Don't worry, Williams safe."

"Cora, I had no idea Gloria was so horrible," she sighed. "Shane told me a little bit about her, but I always thought he was exaggerating. You know my parents. I just couldn't imagine a mother treating her son that way. Now that I've met her, I can see he down played his stories. He must have had the worst childhood. I'm glad at least you were there for him."

"I am too," Cora said, studying Melissa. "I want to forgive you, but I think you should know I'm still pretty angry about last night."

"How much did Shane tell you?" Melissa asked quietly.

"Nothing," Cora said soberly. "Shane was upset. He wouldn't talk to me because he thought I'd make excuses for you and he wasn't ready to hear them."

"Did you tell him I'm here?" Melissa asked.

"He's not here," Cora told her. "He's in Bramble talking to his lawyer. Megan told me you said Jeremy can't stay here again. You had to know that would set him off."

"At the time I wasn't thinking that clearly," Melissa admitted. "Now that I know, I'm not surprised. I'm not going to keep Jeremy from him. In fact, that was one reason I came out here. Joe needs me to work for Tina. I don't know if you heard, but Susan fell and had to go in for hip surgery. Tina's going to be off for at least a week. I was hoping Jeremy could ride the bus home with Megan until Tina gets back. I know that's going to put more work on you. If it's too much, I'll talk to Sarah."

"Jeremy is always welcome here," Cora stated. "Will you be picking him up after work?"

"I'm going to be pretty late tonight. If you don't mind, I thought he could just sleep here. Then, we can play it by ear the rest of the week. If it's early enough, I want him to come home but I don't want to keep him up late on a school night. I know that sounds fickle, but I should know more tomorrow." Melissa wasn't used to asking for help, but she knew this was the right thing to do.

"Whatever you decide is fine," Cora assured her.

"Do you have to ask Shane first?" Melissa asked, worried.

"No. He'll agree," Cora paused. "Are you willing to tell me what went on between the two of you? Megan told me what she

127

knows, but she also said her dad was inside with you for a while after she went to the truck."

Melissa inhaled but decided to confess everything. "Cora, I have no idea what got into me. I don't even believe those things. Shane is nothing like his mother. I knew that before. But now that I've met her, it's so much worse. He must hate me."

"Shane doesn't forgive easily," Cora agreed. "But he doesn't hate you, he loves you and always has. That makes this worse. He's a man. He'll never admit it, but you hurt him. Which is another reason I'm angry with you. He really has had a difficult life. When you left all those years ago, I was so sure you'd come back. I believed in you but you never returned."

"Cora," Melissa began hesitantly. "I know you. You love Shane, you'd do almost anything for him, but you also believe in accepting the consequences for your actions. I don't understand what you said this morning. You made it sound like all of this was my fault. Like I didn't love him enough to stand by him. But he cheated on me. He got another woman pregnant. How could that be my fault? You say Shane has always loved me, you think he still loves me, but how could he? If he truly loved me, he wouldn't have slept with Kristy of all people."

"Do you really not know what happened?" Cora asked skeptically. "Shane said he told you it was only one night at a party, but you left him anyway."

"Shane did say that. He started to make excuses but I didn't want to hear them. He broke my heart and I just couldn't take it," Melissa admitted. "But even if he only cheated one night, he still cheated."

"No. He didn't," Cora disagreed. "I'm not sure I should tell you what I know. It feels like I'm betraying Shane's trust. But on the other hand, I think you need to know. He didn't cheat on you. How could you not know that? How could you believe the worst of him?"

"Uh, maybe because Kristy was six months pregnant and Shane was confident it was his," Melissa said sarcastically.

"Shane was so in love with you from the moment he laid eyes on you. I've known him a long time and he has never been as happy as he was with you. You meant everything to that man," Cora said, clearly lost in thoughts of the past.

"When he told me it was only once, I wanted to believe him, but I just didn't know. And even if it was only once, it hurt so much to know he'd made love to someone else. Then Kristy came to see me. She told me that Shane had been seeing her all along. That they'd dated for years. That's why I left. She convinced me it was her that Shane wanted and I was just getting in the way," Melissa said softly.

"And you believed that? Why could I see how much that man loved you but you couldn't see it?" Cora asked, perplexed.

"Because I never thought I was enough," Melissa whispered. "I was just a small town girl, Shane was larger than life. I never understood why he chose me."

Cora gave Melissa a nod. She realized if she didn't tell Melissa the story, it would remain a secret forever. Shane certainly wouldn't bring it up again and if he did, he'd just take the blame for everything. "Shane was in love with you, but his feelings were so intense it scared him."

"I believe that. It scared me too," Melissa told her.

Hidden Lakes

"He had decided to ask you to marry him, but with a mother like Gloria, he was nervous and apprehensive. He'd been stressing about it for weeks. It's funny, I mean ironic, that you were afraid you wouldn't be enough for him because he had the same fears about you. He didn't think he had anything to offer. He'd purchased the farm, but he was heavily in debt. He had dreams and goals, but what if he failed? The two of you would have a rundown farm house and debt up to your eyeballs," Cora sighed.

"I had no idea he was worried about that," Melissa closed her eyes. "We were so young. Well, I was. Those kinds of things never even crossed my mind. Now I can see it. Shane is so noble and dependable. Of course he would have worried about that."

"One night Brad called. They had just learned about Trent's deployment to Iraq. Those boys were close and Brad wanted to give him a wonderful going away party. Shane wasn't going to go at first. He never liked that sort of thing, not even as a teen. But he wanted to support Trent. Nobody knew how things would turn out. We all hoped for the best, but deep down knew it was dangerous and we might never see him again. Because of that, Shane decided to go." Cora wondered how Trent was doing now. He'd returned from Iraq, met a girl and last she'd heard they were expecting their first child.

"Shane never told me he went to a party for Trent. I wasn't even invited. I guess Kristy was though," Melissa said, more annoyed than she should be.

"Kristy wasn't invited," Cora told her. "From what I understand it was supposed to be guys only. She just showed up on her own. Anyway, like I said Shane was stressed over things with you. He loved you, but he was putting so much pressure on himself to be successful. He wanted to be stable, he wanted to make sure you felt secure. He wanted to give you the world. He started drinking with the guys and before long he was drunk. He let lose for once, lost control and Brad wouldn't let him drive home. He insisted Shane crash in his guest room. Shane was so drunk, Brad and Trent had to help him up the stairs. That's when Kristy arrived. She told Brad it was an emergency. At first he said no, but she insisted she had to see Shane that night."

"And she had sex with him? In his condition, how is that even possible?" Melissa asked, could Cora's story be accurate? If it was, Shane hadn't cheated on her. He had no idea what he was doing. "If what you say is true, why did he act so guilty when he told me?"

"Because he felt guilty. Shane blamed himself for what happened. He didn't remember having sex with Kristy. He just woke up naked, in bed with her and knew what had happened. He was so ashamed and of course he couldn't forgive himself. I told him to talk to you about it. I couldn't stand watching him try to deal with the guilt of betraying you any longer. He struggled with the problem for six months. He was so sure he'd lose you if you ever found out."

Melissa sank back against the railing. Of course Shane would blame himself. He would believe that he was responsible for whatever happened because he'd allowed himself to get out of control for one night. In his eyes, he drank too much and betrayed her. It wouldn't even cross his mind that he was the one that had been taken advantage of. "Cora, if that's what really happened, Kristy basically raped Shane. How could he marry her after she took advantage of him like that?"

"What?" Cora asked in surprise.

Hidden Lakes

"Why did Shane marry Kristy?" she asked again. "She trapped him. Forced herself on him while he was drunk. How did he ever think they could have a lasting marriage after that?"

"Shane never married Kristy," Cora was shocked that Melissa didn't know that. "Didn't your parents tell you? Shane wanted to do the right thing. That's why he told you about the pregnancy, but even then he knew he couldn't marry Kristy. He couldn't marry someone he despised so intensely. Not when he was hopelessly in love with you."

"I wouldn't let my parents talk about Shane. Mom started to tell me something a few days after I moved. I told her not to bring him up to me and if she did, she'd never hear from me again. She believed me and never mentioned Shane again." Melissa was beginning to think she'd made more mistakes than she originally believed. "Did he tell her? Did Kristy know Shane wasn't going to marry her?"

"Yes," Cora said nodding her head.

"Do you think that's why she came to dad's store? She wanted to make sure I was out of the way? And I played right into her hands. I did exactly what she wanted me to do," Melissa rested her head on her knees. She'd been so stupid. She should have had more faith in Shane, in herself. She should have done so many things differently. But if she had, she never would have met Mitch. She couldn't imagine her life without him. He had taught her so much about herself. He'd helped her to grow up, helped her to become a better person, taught Jeremy so many important things.

"I think that's a very strong possibility," Cora scowled. "Kristy was selfish, manipulative and very vindictive. You were the enemy because you stood in her way. She would have done anything, said anything to get rid of you. I'm just surprised you trusted anything she said."

"I didn't at first," Melissa said, ashamed. "But she knew things. Things that made me believe what she said. Then there was Shane's guilt. It all added up. I was young and knowing they had been together hurt me so much. I couldn't think straight. It took months before I began to question the things Kristy said, before I realized she probably lied. Like I said, she told me they had been dating and sleeping together all along. She said she was confident Shane would eventually choose her, but she didn't want to wait. She claimed Shane thought she was on birth control, but she'd stopped taking it. She got pregnant on purpose to trap him. She didn't feel bad about it because she knew he loved her and they could be happy together."

"And you bought that nonsense?" Cora shook her head. "I'm surprised at you, but I guess I understand. Hearing those things would have been a shock," Cora sighed. "I just thought you'd come back. I truly believed once you thought about the whole mess, you'd trust in Shane's love and be there for him. He needed you, but you never came back. I guess I only have one more question for you now."

"What?" Melissa asked.

"Now what?" Cora said soberly. "What are your intentions where Shane is concerned? He's never stopped loving you and I can't stand by and watch you hurt that boy again."

"Cora, I don't expect you to believe me or even understand, but I have always loved Shane too. Don't get me wrong, I loved Mitch. I was happily married for a long time. I never could have married Mitch if I hadn't loved him, but a part of me always belonged to Shane. It always will. But Shane doesn't forgive easily.

133

I've done so many things wrong. I took his son away and then I yelled at his daughter and insulted him. Every time I turn around I'm making another huge mistake. I don't blame him for hating me. If the tables were turned, I'd feel the same. Because of that, I don't know. I don't have an answer to your question. The chemistry is still there. I can't come within ten feet of the man and not want to jump him. But it really doesn't matter what I want, does it? I have a son, Shane has a daughter. What we do now will impact both of them. It's not as simple as it was nine or ten years ago. There are two innocent lives to consider." Melissa glanced at her watch then stood. "I need to go. I have to get to work. Thanks for not calling the cops on me. I need my job and I'm pretty sure getting arrested for trespassing might jeopardize that. Joe is only so understanding."

"I was bluffing," Cora admitted. "It would take a lot more than just showing up for me to call the cops on you. I am devoted to Shane, but I always liked you Melissa. I hope the two of you can figure this thing out. Not only for your sake but for the kids' sake as well," Cora stood and headed for the house.

* * * *

Shane questioned himself for about the hundredth time. What was he doing? He should just turn the truck around and head back to the ranch, to his kids. But he couldn't. He had to find out what Melissa was up to. He needed answers. Things had gone well in Bramble. It had taken longer than he'd anticipated, but he left Steve Olsen's office feeling confident in his position for the first time since he laid eyes on Melissa again. Since he'd discovered he had a son. Then he'd stepped into the house and spotted Megan and Jeremy camped out in front of the big screen watching Spiderman.

Cora was in the kitchen making popcorn. She'd filled him in on the day's events and before he knew what he was doing, he was back on the road headed for town.

He wanted to believe Melissa. He wanted to trust her, but after everything that had happened, how could he? So, here he was speeding toward the old Peter's home, gut roiling in anticipation, wondering what he was going to say or do when he got there. More to the point, he was wondering what Melissa's reaction to him showing up on her doorstep would be. Shane turned into the sub-division and slowly made his way to Melissa's driveway. The instant her house came into view he snapped. She was playing games with his life again, but this time she wasn't going to win.

Shane jumped from the truck and stomped over to Melissa who was standing at the back of her vehicle loading up boxes. "I wondered what game you were playing when I spotted Jeremy at my house, but I never guessed you were planning to run."

"Shane," Melissa began.

"Don't Shane me," he growled. "I guess old habits die hard with you. Things get a little complicated and you pack up and disappear. Well, not this time sweetheart. This time I have a son involved and I'm not letting you take him away again. If I have to, I'll get Judge Stone to issue an injunction. You run with my kid and I'll make sure you're arrested for kidnapping."

Melissa inhaled sharply, then turned to face Shane. Her eyes were red and swollen, tears running down her face. "That's not necessary." She closed her eyes, trying to regain control of her emotions. "I was hoping Jeremy could stay with you for a while. At least a week, maybe longer." When he didn't respond, she pushed past him and headed for the house.

"Melissa?" Shane called.

She paused, then slowly turned back to face him. "I know I've made mistakes, I know you hate me, everyone seems to hate me. I know you don't trust me and I don't blame you for that." She paused again, the tears falling faster now. "Please Shane, just go. Go home and take care of our son," then she spun around and practically ran for the back door.

Shane was stunned. Melissa would never leave Jeremy, so what was going on here? She looked so sad and defeated, he couldn't just leave. He followed Melissa's path, stepping through the back gate, up the stairs and froze in the doorway. "What the hell?" The house was a mess. At least a foot of water was covering the floor. Debris was floating around in the dirty water. Melissa stood just inside the kitchen, brushing away tears. Shane stepped inside. "Did you call Pete?"

Melissa closed her eyes again and leaned against the closest wall. "Yes," she choked out. "I've called Pete. I've called and called and called, then I had Mrs. Chilcot call. I can only deduce from his lack of response that he couldn't care less if I drown in this mess." Then, she slumped to the floor and began to sob. "Shane, I can't take this. Not now. Please just go away. I've gotten the message, loud and clear. I'm not wanted here. Not by you and not by this town. It's ironic really. I'm the one that was born here, this should be my town. These people loved my parents, stood by them for years, but they all love you now. And I hurt you. I took your son away, so I'm the bad guy. I get it, the town hates me. I'm all alone, but I can't take this tonight. Please Shane, if there's even an ounce of compassion left after our history, please just go away." She was practically begging now. She glanced at him with tear filled eyes for the slightest second then she pressed her forehead to her knees and sobbed, her little body shaking uncontrollably.

Shane couldn't stand it. She looked so fragile and broken, like life had finally dealt out more than she could take. She just sat there, crumpled on the floor with at least a foot of filthy water settling around her. He sloshed over and lifted her into his arms. "You're not alone." He grinned at the surprised look on her face as he stepped outside and sat with her on the porch swing. She was cold and wet and now so was he, but at the moment he didn't care. "The first thing we need to do is get the water shut off. Do you know where the valve is located?"

"I thought I shut it off, but there must be two because the flow hasn't stopped. It hasn't even slowed." She wiped away more tears and looked at him, perplexed. This man hated her. Why was he helping her?

"Then let's not waste any more time looking. I'll just find the main shut off up front and stop all water from flowing into the house. It's better that way anyhow. Then we'll get Pete out here to take a look and go from there." Before he realized what he was doing, Shane reached up and brushed a tear from Melissa's cheek. He had to stop this and somehow get a grip on his emotions. They'd always had chemistry. Shane had remembered that, but somehow he'd forgotten how potent it was. How all-consuming and intense that connection could be. The instant he'd lifted Melissa into his arms all he'd wanted to do was kiss her. Kiss away the tears and the pain and protect her. How could he still love this woman after everything she'd done to him? He didn't want to, but there was no denying it. He still loved her. He still wanted her. But he didn't have to give in to the insanity. He didn't have to hand her his heart so she could crush it into a million pieces again. He would do the neighborly thing and help her while she was in crisis, then do his best to keep his distance.

Melissa slipped off Shane's lap. She didn't have that much self-control. She wanted to snuggle against him. Let him hold her, protect her, love her. But he didn't. He hated her and she couldn't blame him. He was just being kind because she was so pathetic. Shane could never walk away from someone in need, especially if that someone was a woman. His gentle assurances didn't mean a thing. She was on her own. As much as she wanted to hold on tight and believe this time they could have their happily ever after, they couldn't. And fantasizing about kissing Shane was only going to get her into trouble. "Okay," she took another steadying breath then stood. "I think the main valve is out by the lilac bushes. I've shut off all the breakers, so now that it's dark we won't be able to see a thing."

Shane stood and headed for the shed. He might need a shovel to cut away the lawn. Chances were pretty good that nobody had accessed the main valve for years. And it would give him a couple minutes alone to regain his sanity.

Melissa plucked a box off the kitchen table and headed for her car. She needed air and space. She was a mess and she knew it but she had to be strong. They'd take care of the crisis, get the water shut off then she'd figure out where to spend the next few weeks. Shane would keep Jeremy, she had no doubt about that. If nothing else, she'd sleep in her car and shower at the station. But how would Joe react to that lovely scene? What would she do if one of the deputies caught her sleeping in a parking lot like a homeless woman? But wait, she didn't have to leave the house. She could park in the driveway and sleep in her car. Or maybe just stay in the house. Her bedroom was upstairs. It would be cold and musty and she couldn't use the power until the water was gone, but she could survive. She'd survived worse those first few days in Denver. Melissa closed the back door, pivoted around and came face to face with Gloria.

"Melissa dear," Gloria said in that fake, sweet tone of hers. "I hope you don't mind, but I really needed to talk to you. I was at that quaint little café and Betty Clawson mentioned you had moved into your parents old home." Gloria paused, pretending hesitancy. "I hate to ask, but you see that money you gave me..." she paused again. "Well, you see I'm afraid it didn't go as far as I hoped it would."

"I thought you were headed for Bramble," Melissa said coldly.

"Well, I was. But after filling the car with gas, that took a third of the cash right there, then the café and well, you know how expensive things are these days. Anyway, I can't go to Bramble now. I don't have enough for a room when I get there. You wouldn't want me to have to sleep on the street would you?" Gloria lowered her lashes and glanced up then away again. "I know how generous you were earlier, and I thought maybe...well I hoped..."

"That you could con her out of a few hundred more?" Shane growled, furious at his mother's nerve.

Melissa stepped back in surprise. Then she took a few more steps in retreat. She'd let Shane handle his mother. It was ironic really, here she was worried about herself, thinking she'd be homeless and desperate for the next week, but if she hadn't given away that two hundred dollars things would be different. That was the cash she kept on hand for emergencies. If she hadn't been careless and given it to Shane's mother, she would have had the funds to check into a motel. Apparently no good deed did go unpunished. Melissa stepped forward, took the shovel from Shane and escaped to the lilacs. She'd make herself useful while Shane dealt with Gloria.

"Shane!" Gloria said, clearly surprised. "Well, good. I'm glad you're here. As I was telling Melissa, I'm in a bind. Stanton left me. He was able to pull off a quick divorce because we had that stupid prenup. I knew that was a bad idea, but there's nothing I can do about it now. Anyway I was forced to leave without a thing. Just that junky old car I owned when we got together. It took everything I had just to get here, to you. I know you've been angry with me, but I'm desperate and you have so much. You're not honestly going to send me out in the cold, alone without a penny to my name. I'm your mother."

"Funny, I remember the terms of that prenup pretty well. What happened to the twenty five grand he was willing to give you just to go away?" Shane asked unmoved by her little speech. "And the two hundred Melissa fronted you this morning?"

Gloria sputtered, she was unaware Shane knew the details of the marriage contract. "Shane," Gloria said in her most forceful condescending tone. "I've told you at least a hundred times that catching a wealthy man takes money. I met what I thought was a wonderful man. I simply adored him and honestly believed he was good husband material. Unfortunately, I'd gone through most of the twenty five before I realized he was a con. I had just enough left to travel across the country to get to you. I know you're a hard, cold man but you won't really abandon me now. Not when I'm starving and homeless."

"I'll make you a deal Gloria," Shane said through gritted teeth. "I'll give as much thought to your nutritional wellbeing as you gave me when I was eight. I'll put forth just as much effort to care for you, have just as much compassion and..."

"Stop it," Gloria hissed. "Cora fed you, watched over you, pampered you. Don't try to pretend you were some poor neglected child."

"Yes, Cora provided for me. Cora loved me. Cora fed me, not you. If it was up to you, I'd have starved to death years ago. I told you last time you came to town that I was done with you. We both know you violated the restraining order today when you showed up at the ranch. Do it again and I promise you will find yourself in jail." Shane started to turn, but stopped when Gloria put a hand on his arm.

"What do you think Marnie will say about all this? How will your daughter feel when she finds out her grandmother was in town. That I traveled thousands of miles to get to know her and you threw me out like a pesky rodent?" Gloria was sure Shane would cave.

"My daughter's name is Megan, not Marnie. A caring grandmother would know that though, wouldn't she?" Shane didn't miss the daggers Gloria shot Melissa's way. Melissa just shrugged and kept on digging. Shane smiled. "You thought you conned Melissa. You thought you maneuvered her, and weaseled my daughter's name out of her to use against me when it benefitted you most, well I guess the joke's on you. Melissa isn't stupid mother. She didn't give you that money because she's an easy mark. She gave it to you because she was protecting me and my daughter. But it didn't work. You are still here. Listen carefully, that well's run dry. You won't be getting another dime from Melissa. I'm paying Judge Stone a visit tomorrow. Melissa and her home will be added to the current order. Go anywhere near Melissa, show up at her house again, the school, my place, come anywhere near Melissa or my family and I will make sure you regret it for the rest of your life."

Gloria forced herself to breathe, slow steady breaths. Melissa was going to pay, she was going to pay dearly. Nobody misled Gloria and got away with it. And Shane, her son had clearly forgotten who he was dealing with. "I don't have to violate the order to get at Megan, Shane. And just my being in town is an aggravation to you. Why don't you do us both a favor and give me what I want.

Hidden Lakes

Buy me a new car and give me ten thousand dollars and I'll go away. I'll take the money and use it to find myself another husband. I'm happy, you're happy, it's a killer deal and we both know you can afford it."

"Melissa?" Shane called.

"Yeah," Melissa said hesitantly.

"Do you want this woman to leave?" he asked.

"More than you could possibly imagine," she said smirking at Gloria, who was now glaring at Melissa with undisguised hatred.

"Did you hear her?" Shane pressed. "You have about three seconds to leave before I call the cops and have you arrested for trespassing."

Gloria knew she'd lost this round. But that didn't mean she was leaving town. She'd get what she wanted, she always did. Shane would regret crossing her in the end. She was his mother for heaven's sake. The man had millions, he owed it to her to share and she wasn't leaving until he did. Shane might call the police on sight, but Cora wouldn't and she was pretty sure Melissa wouldn't either. "I'll be staying at Clyde's motel for a while. Feel free to stop by and visit any time," then she whirled around and made her way up the sidewalk.

Shane stepped in beside Melissa and took the shovel. "I'm sorry about that," he reached into his wallet and pulled out two one hundred dollar bills. "Here."

"Shane, I don't want that. I gave your mom money to go away. It didn't work but as far as I'm concerned it was worth it. Keep your money," she insisted.

"No way," Shane said, slipping the bills into the front pocket of Melissa's jeans. He smiled, "You might want to move that to your purse or at least the car. I've tried to pry wet bills from wet jeans before. Believe me, it's not an easy task if you want the bills to stay in one piece." He gave her a little shove then promptly pried the metal cover up and within seconds had the water shut off.

Melissa didn't move. She was glaring at Shane, unwilling to do as she was told like a good little girl. She'd wasted her money on Gloria, it wasn't Shane's responsibility to pay for her miscalculation.

"Melissa," Shane sighed. "You know I'm rich, right? And I know you're not. Take the money. Gloria is my problem. I'll handle her, but I won't allow you to spend your emergency funds on her new shoes when you need it for an emergency." He took her shoulders and turned her toward the house. "In case you've forgotten, you have a real emergency on your hands tonight."

"I haven't forgotten," Melissa said, considering. Now that she had her two hundred back, she could spend at least two nights at the motel, maybe three if she was careful about what she ate.

"What are you thinking?" Shane asked, taking her arm and leading her back toward the house.

"Nothing," she said too quickly. "Now what? Is there a way to force the water out of the house? If we don't get it to drain, there's going to be mold. This disaster is going to cost me a fortune already, I can't afford to pay a hazmat team to de-mold my basement."

Hidden Lakes

"You go get the push broom out of the shed. Push as much water as you can out the back door. I'm going to pay a personal visit to Pete. We'll be back in twenty minutes tops," he studied her. She wasn't as pale as she'd been before, but she still looked defeated. "It's going to be okay, Mel. I promise, we'll get this worked out. I have an idea to run by you, but I want to get Pete first. Go work on pushing out the water. I'll be back as soon as I can," then he was gone.

Melissa listened as Shane started the engine on his fancy truck then backed out of her driveway. What idea did he have? And he had said we? We'll get through this. She wanted to believe him. She wanted to grasp onto the hope and hold on tight, but she couldn't. She was still all alone. Sure, Shane would do what he needed to do to take care of Jeremy and she was grateful for that. She might have to sleep in a musty old house with no water and no electricity, but at least her son would have a real home to live in. But what if he never wanted to come back? Shane's house was new, a big fancy ranch house complete with horses and cows and a spunky dog, not to mention a new sister. And nobody could resist Cora. Jeremy might decide he's happier with his father and then Melissa really would be alone. All alone with a few weekly visits, but nothing else. Is this how Shane had felt when she offered him a few nights a week but no sleep overs? Of course it was and that was just another example of how badly she'd messed up with him. She didn't know what she would do if Jeremy wanted to live with his father, but that was a problem for another day. For now, she needed to get as much water out of this house as possible.

Shane pounded on Pete's door and waited. He'd started out angry but now he was furious. The man had ignored the frantic calls for help from a single mother, alone. Well, Melissa wasn't alone and never would be as long as he was around, but that wasn't the point. She thought she was alone and apparently so did the rest of this town.

Pete stomped to the door and yanked it open with a scowl, which quickly turned to a frown. "What's crawled up your butt, boy? I have a doorbell. It's not necessary to rattle the walls to get my attention."

"I'd say that's debatable," Shane snapped. "You do realize you're the only plumber in town. The only plumber for miles, don't you?"

"Of course I do," Pete snapped back. "What's got you so riled?"

"So, being the responsible business owner you pretend to be, I would have to assume you've checked your messages. You do monitor your phone calls just in case someone has an emergency?" Shane continued.

"The only call I got tonight was from that woman that wronged you. I know you can't be here on her behalf so spit it out all ready, kid. What's got you so pissed all of a sudden?" He hadn't gotten any other requests, so what was going on?

"Melissa Peters, now Carpenter. She's called how many times, Pete? Five? Six? How about Mrs. Chilcot, I know she called at least twice. Maybe after all those calls you just might figure out this isn't about something frivolous. Maybe say seven or eight calls about the same problem might be what I call a clue that someone, one of your neighbors in fact, has a real emergency," Shane practically yelled.

"Shane, she took your kid," Pete was starting to worry. He'd ignored Melissa out of loyalty to Shane. "Unless you say otherwise, that woman's on her own."

"I say otherwise Pete," Shane said, exasperated. He hadn't believed Melissa when she'd said everyone hated her because they loved him. Had there been others? Had Melissa been having problems since she'd gotten back to town and just kept it to herself? She would, he knew it. Hell would freeze over before Melissa would complain to him about the way she was being treated. "You have two minutes to get in the truck. You're going to need your tools so come prepared. You're not leaving until I'm satisfied with your results."

"If it's an emergency, I'll need my truck," Pete said, feeling around in his front pocket for his keys. "Maybe you could give me a clue here, Shane. What kind of emergency are we dealing with?"

"A broken pipe I think," Shane said soberly. "There's at least a foot of water on the floor. The house is flooded. I was able to shut off the main valve but I need you to take a look and see what needs to be done," Shane paused to glare at Pete. "I want this done right, no cutting corners, no hassling Melissa. My kid lives in that house. If you have to rip out every inch of pipe in that home and replace it, that's what you're going to do. And, no matter what Melissa tells you, you are going to send the bill to me. Are we clear on that?"

"We're clear," Pete said, confused. "But...well, I mean...Shane, I ignored her for you. I had no idea the problem was that big, but even if I did I would have hesitated to help. That woman wronged you. She ran off with your kid. She..."

"That woman has a name, it's Melissa Carpenter. You know that Pete, she grew up in this town. Her parents lived here most of their lives. How many times exactly did Jake Peters rush over to the hardware store after hours because you had an emergency? How many times did he drop whatever he was doing because you asked him to? And you repay him by ignoring his only daughter? By leaving her stranded at home, alone to deal with a broken pipe and a flood? I wonder how Jake would feel about that. I wonder how Jake and Connie would feel if they knew the whole town had turned their backs on their only daughter. Somehow Pete, I don't think they'd understand."

"But she..." Pete began as he climbed into his truck.

"But nothing. Melissa is a Peters. She was born and raised here. She deserves respect. Disrespect her again, and I'm going to take it personally. If you disrespect her, you disrespect me. Are we clear?"

"We're clear," Pete said before he slammed his truck door and backed onto the road.

Melissa was wet and frozen when Shane returned with Pete. She'd been sweeping out the water for the past twenty minutes, but she needed a break. She'd just sat down on the back of her vehicle when Pete pulled in. She immediately stood and walked to the truck. "Thanks for coming, Pete. I know it's late and you probably had plans but as you can see, I'm in a real bind. I appreciate any help you can give me tonight."

Pete just nodded and headed for the back of the house. Melissa was still scowling when Shane walked up. "What did you do to him? Shane, I don't need you fighting my battles. If Pete doesn't want to be here, he should go home. I'll figure something out for tonight and call a plumber from Henley or Bramble in the morning."

Shane just took her hand and led her to a chair. "Relax," he said softly. "I explained the situation to Pete and he wanted to come take a look. He'll let us know what we need to do tonight and I'm confident he'll be back in the morning."

"Shane if you..." Melissa argued.

"I didn't do anything," Shane said. "I'll be right back." Moments later Shane returned with a second chair. She wasn't certain where he'd gotten the first one.

"Now...for my idea," Shane said, setting the chair across from Melissa and settling in. "I have this cabin."

"Shane, we've already had this conversation, remember?" Melissa asked. "I assume it's the same cabin you offered me before. The one you said I could use when Jeremy stayed the weekend."

"Yes, but don't just shut me down here Melissa. I want to finish my proposal. I want you to understand this isn't charity. It's a win for both of us. I get to spend time with my kid and you have a place to stay. Plus, the place is an eyesore. I was hoping while you were there, you might clean it up a bit. Maybe plant some flowers in the front garden. You know, make the place look nice. Cora keeps saying she's going to do it, but I keep her pretty busy. She hasn't had time and neither has Hank."

Melissa was thinking, considering. She didn't know how long it would take to fix the plumbing, but if she accepted Shane's offer maybe, just maybe, he could start to forgive her for all her mistakes. Maybe if he had to see her every day, he might soften up a little. They might never be lovers again, but it just might be possible to be friends. "If I said yes, I would want to pay you something for staying there."

"We can start with the cleanup. Then we'll negotiate," Shane said, wondering if he had gone crazy. He wanted to help Melissa. He wanted to make sure Jeremy was provided for, but he had to keep Melissa away from Megan.

"Shane," Melissa insisted.

"We can talk about that later. Once the manual labor is done, we can negotiate terms if necessary," he began. "I want you to stay at the cabin, but there is one stipulation."

"What?" Melissa asked, not liking Shane's tone.

"I will need your promise that you will stay away from Megan. You hurt her last night. You don't understand the situation with her. Maybe I'm just being over protective, but I'm willing to take that chance. I won't risk Megan's emotional wellbeing. I can't risk having her hurt by you again. I can't explain, well I guess more to the point I won't go into it right now, but I'm firm on this. I want you to use the cabin, but only if you can promise me you won't go near my daughter." Shane was watching Melissa. He knew he'd hurt her with his demand, but he couldn't back down, not on this.

"I'll stay away from Megan. And I'm going to accept your offer because I have nowhere else to go. Now that I have the two hundred back from your mother I could probably get a room at Clyde's but I don't want to. Gloria said that's where she's staying and I'd prefer to stay out of that woman's path," Melissa sighed. "Shane, I'm going to pay you something. Maybe it will be work, maybe dinner, something. I don't know, but I have to pay for my stay, those are my terms. And that's not negotiable."

"Fair enough," Shane said standing. "Let's check in with Pete. Then I suggest you find something dry to change into. It's a long drive out to my place and soppy jeans are going to be mighty uncomfortable."

Chapter Eight

Melissa pulled to a stop in front of the log cabin but didn't get out of her car. She just sat there, staring into the darkness. The cabin wasn't huge, but it wasn't exactly small either. Shane had told her there were two bedrooms so it would easily accommodate both her and Jeremy. She sighed and leaned her head against the back of the seat. What in the world was she thinking? She never should have accepted Shane's offer. He was still angry with her. Offering up the cabin hadn't been a gesture of peace, it was charity. Shane would have made the offer to anyone whose house had flooded. Anyone except Gloria that is. It wouldn't matter how long she was here, one day, one week, one month, Shane wasn't going to forgive her.

She had thought maybe they could at least be friends, but who was she kidding. She could never be just friends with Shane. Her feelings ran too deep. It was going to kill her to live here, on his ranch and see him every day knowing she could never have him. Her heart was going to break every time she stepped outside and saw him riding away on his horse, or playing catch with her son. Karma was apparently coming back to bite her and bite her hard. She'd yelled at a small child, so her punishment was to live in hell for the next few weeks until her plumbing was fixed. Well, she was strong enough to deal with whatever fate dished out.

Melissa jumped when her car door flung open. She glanced up and saw Shane smirking at her. Clearly amused that he'd scared her so easily.

Shane reached in, unhooked the seatbelt then took Melissa's hand and pulled her from the car. "Come on," he said casually. "I'll give you a quick tour before I head back up to the house." He stopped at the front entrance, selected a key and smoothly opened the door.

"You keep it locked?" Melissa asked, surprised.

"I do now," Shane told her. "One of the hands decided it would be the perfect place to bring a date for a little one on one time if you know what I mean. I saw the light on and kicked him out, but it's been locked ever since. I didn't want the boys to think the cabin was here for their enjoyment."

"I see," Melissa said, stepping inside. She slowly took in her surroundings. It was rustic, but classy. She smiled inwardly, the place was so much like Shane. There was a large oak table with matching chairs, a dark brown leather sofa and two large matching recliners. The living room had a beautiful stone fireplace with a wonderful oak mantel. The floor was slate and the kitchen counter was a deep chocolate granite. There were stainless steel appliances and Navaho Indian rugs for throws. She walked across the room and looked out the large French doors and saw they led to an elaborate deck. She was sure Shane had Adirondack chairs and a large BBQ out there although she couldn't see them in the dark. She could see the stars. She'd forgotten how beautiful and majestic they were out here on the ranch.

"Wow," Melissa finally said. "I can't believe Hank turned you down when you offered him this place. It's wonderful, Shane."

Shane shrugged, a little embarrassed by her praise. "The bedrooms are back here." He motioned down a hallway then pivoted and headed to the back of the cabin, clearly expecting Melissa to follow.

She did. They passed a door she assumed was the bathroom but didn't stop to investigate. She'd do another walk through once Shane left her alone. He pushed open a door and waited for her to step inside. "This will be Jeremy's room," Shane told her, pausing in the doorway. "It's the smaller of the two rooms. He'll have that bathroom to himself. The master has its own. We have to meet Pete at eight, so I thought I'd take the truck and we could load up the beds from your place and bring them out," he paused. "I have to warn you, the master has a twin bed as well. When I realized the place was going to be unoccupied, I just threw in what I had at the time. I planned to buy a king size bed eventually, but until now I haven't had a need to use the place." He turned and moved to the other closed door.

Melissa followed. She hadn't planned on moving any furniture out here, but she guessed both her and Jeremy would be more comfortable in their own beds. Once she talked to Pete in the morning she'd have a better idea how long they'd be staying. If it was only a couple weeks, maybe she'd just buy Shane a new king sized bed for the place as rent. Jeremy could sleep on the twin bed that was in there now and if she bought Shane a bed, the cabin would be ready for company in the future. It would also help with her guilt. She wouldn't feel like she was taking advantage of Shane's hospitality.

Melissa stepped into the master bedroom and smiled in amazement. There was another set of French doors that led to the same deck and a sky light above the platform obviously made for a large bed. Right now it had a small twin that was clearly too small for this wonderful space. There was a rustic log frame leaning against one wall. It matched the multicolored wooden end tables and a large dresser. There was a large patchwork quilt on the small bed with matching pillow cases. The thing was so large it swamped the tiny bed. Melissa assumed it was made for a king sized frame, but Shane had made do with what he had. "You sure you want to let me move in here?" she asked, glancing at Shane. "I might never leave. Evictions can take years, you know."

"I'm sure," Shane said, smiling. "Does that mean you like it?"

"I love it," Melissa said enthusiastically. "It feels like a fantasy getaway cabin. I'd expect to find something like this in the mountains, near a pretty blue lake and lots and lots of pine trees and wildlife. If I look out the window will I see deer grazing near the forest?"

"Nope," Shane said, smiling. "Just a large wheat field that needs planting, cows and a few blue jays."

"Even better," Melissa said, and meant it. She had always loved the ranch and had dreamt of making a life here since the moment she'd laid eyes on this handsome cowboy years ago. That thought brought her back to reality. She'd never live here. She may never make amends with Shane, so she couldn't start fantasizing about being a rancher's wife when the chance she'd ever be this ranchers friend were slim to none. "Thanks again, Shane for letting me crash here. You have no idea how much this means to me."

"Like I said, we both win," Shane said, pushing thoughts of Melissa out of his mind. It was all he could do to stop himself from pulling her into his arms and kissing her blind. But that could never happen. She'd left him once. He knew she'd leave him again. He wasn't sure he could stand being dumped by this woman twice in his lifetime. It was better to keep his distance. "It's important to me to spend as much time as possible with Jeremy. And the place needs a woman's touch. I have an account at Ace's Garden Center in town. When you have a chance, maybe you could stop by and pick out some flowers. There are the two beds in front and a couple hanging boxes off the deck in back. I was also thinking some hanging pots might look nice, but I'm going to leave that up to you. If I remember correctly, you always loved playing with flowers." He smiled at the memory.

"I do," Melissa said, remembering the hours she'd spent decking out her mother's gardens years ago. "We didn't have a lot of space for flowers in Denver. I had hoped I'd be able to resurrect mom's gardens this year, but it looks like that's going to have to wait until next season. With the plumbing and the front porch, I have enough on my hands to last me all summer." The worried look returned to Melissa's face.

Shane put a hand on her shoulder. "Don't worry," he immediately dropped his hand. Touching Melissa in even the most casual way was a very, very bad idea. "Things are going to work out. Just have a little faith." He glanced at the darkened doorway. He had to look away from Melissa's beautiful blue eyes. He could get lost in those eyes and do something he'd regret. He had to get out of this bedroom. The small bed was pulling him in like a magnet. "It's late. Meet me at seven fifteen by the truck?"

"Okay," Melissa said, relieved that Shane was leaving. Another minute with him alone in this bedroom might prove disastrous.

Shane turned and headed for the front door. "I'll leave the kitchen door unlocked just in case you need anything tonight. I think the place is stocked with the basics, but I may have forgotten something. Like I said, nobody has stayed here so tonight the place is getting the first trial run. There's a coffee pot in the kitchen, but you'll have to come to the main house for coffee. Cora will be here early, so if you want just call her when you get up and she can send one of the men out with a fresh can."

"I'll be fine," Melissa assured him. "I'm beat. I'm just going to grab a couple things from the car and then I'll probably pass out from exhaustion. Thanks again for your help tonight. I had pretty much reached my breaking point when you came along. I don't know how to thank you for your kindness, but I'll try to figure out a way to repay you."

"That's not necessary," Shane said, stepping out onto the porch. "See you in the morning," he called as he descended the small staircase and climbed into his truck.

Melissa stood in the doorway watching as Shane's tail lights grew smaller and smaller, then they disappeared completely when he reached the main house. She took a long deep breath then headed for her car. The first thing she needed to do was try to save her wedding album. She knew some of the pictures were destroyed, but hopefully she could save at least a few. She was heartbroken over the loss. The only two albums she had of her and Mitch's life together had been damaged. A tear rolled down her face. Somehow she was going to preserve those memories if it was the last thing she did. Mitch may not have been Jeremy's biological father, but he had been an important part of her son's life. He needed those pictures as much as she did. Somehow she'd find a way to preserve those memories, she owed at least that much to Mitch. She pulled out a small duffle and the two albums then retreated back into the cabin.

* * * *

Shane stood on the front porch, still debating with himself. No matter how many times he told himself to avoid the woman he somehow continued to find himself knocking on her door. Once he got home last night, he'd fallen into bed and fell into a deep sleep immediately. Unfortunately, it hadn't been a dreamless one. And every erotic dream featured Melissa Carpenter as the lead character. He'd awaken horny and lonely, which made him grumpy and agitated. He'd gotten up with the sun and was already finished with the morning chores. It was only six thirty, but he figured if they were to leave by seven fifteen, Melissa had to be up. He took a deep breath and knocked.

It took a while, but Melissa finally cracked open the door. Shane frowned. He'd been sure she would be awake by now, but it was obvious he woke her up. "Uh...sorry," he began.

Melissa panicked. "What time is it?" she pulled open the door and surveyed the room for a clock. "Did I sleep in? I was so beat when I finally got to sleep, but I was sure the sun would wake me up. I'm sorry Shane, I only need a few minutes and I'll be ready to go."

"Take a deep breath, Mel. It's only six thirty. We have time," he held out the steaming thermos of coffee. "I thought you might need this to get you going. You didn't call Cora or come up to the house so I thought...." he broke off as he glanced around the room. Photos were scattered everywhere. They covered the table, the coffee table, the couch, the large lounge chairs, even the kitchen chairs and countertop. "What's all this?" Shane asked, picking up a photo. His heart sank when he recognized Melissa in a wedding dress. "Oh," he said, promptly placing the photo back on the table.

"They got wet last night," Melissa said, uncomfortably. "Those are my wedding photos, the rest are family photos. I had two albums and both of them are ruined. I'm letting the pictures dry out, but I think most of them will be lost completely." Melissa closed her eyes, she wouldn't let Shane see her cry over Mitch. That would only make their already strained relationship worse.

Shane could see how much losing the photos was hurting Melissa. Oh, she was trying to mask her sorrow, but he knew her too well. Just another indication of how much she had loved her late husband, as if he needed more proof. From all accounts the guy was a saint, and that quick glimpse of him standing there in a tux was enough for Shane to see why Melissa had fallen for him. He was everything Shane wasn't. Shane was rugged and a little wild. Mitch was clean-cut and respectable. He was a fireman of all things, how much more respectable could you get than that? Melissa deserved a man like Mitch, not someone like Shane. Shane would always have to work long hours. He'd always come home dirty and smelly and calloused. Mitch's hands were probably smooth as a baby's butt. The thought of those hands touching Melissa sent a rush of jealousy and pure anger through Shane's system. He didn't want anyone touching Melissa, kissing Melissa, nobody but him. He shook his head to stop that line of thinking. He was never going to touch Melissa again. He had to accept that. He had to find a way to move on, to accept her as a friend or at the very least a neighbor and nothing else.

"I need to get dressed," Melissa said, shaking Shane out of his thoughts.

"Right," Shane said slowly. "Uh, well....here's the coffee. I'll see you at the truck in a half hour," he turned and rushed out the door.

Melissa sat on the back deck of the cabin, stunned. Pete was going to have to do a complete overhaul of her plumbing system. It was going to take thousands of dollars that she didn't have and several months to complete. Shane agreed to let her stay at the cabin while the work was done, but Melissa was apprehensive about the arrangements. She'd felt guilty this morning, once Shane had left her alone. She'd seen his face when he recognized what the pictures were. He'd been hurt by them. For several seconds, Melissa considered gathering up the pictures and hiding them away. She didn't want to hurt Shane, but she also felt Mitch deserved better than that. She wasn't ashamed of her marriage to Mitch. Sure, she'd made mistakes and both her and Shane had been hurt by the events of eight years ago. But that didn't change the fact that she had been married to a wonderful, caring man. A man that loved her and her son more than anything else in life. Would the guilt over the men in her life ever stop? For years she'd felt guilty for loving Shane while she was married to Mitch. Now she felt guilty for loving Mitch. Well, it was going to stop now. Mitch was a part of her past. Maybe Shane was too, but for the next ten years he was going to be a part of her life in some manner or another. Until Jeremy was eighteen, she was just going to have to find a way to push aside her emotions and deal with Shane as an adult. No more fantasies. No more hoping for something they didn't have. No more chemistry.

Yeah, right. As if she could control her reaction to that man if she tried. Well, she didn't have to act on those feelings and she wouldn't. In time, they'd settle into a nice, platonic friendship. She hoped. Because if her libido went into overdrive every time she saw Shane for the next ten years, she'd probably end up in the loony bin.

Melissa stood and took her iced tea inside. She had to clean up the crinkled, disastrous pictures before she went to work. The last things she wanted was for Jeremy to find them. She didn't know what she was going to do with them, but for now they'd go in a box. She could do some research, maybe find someone that restores old photos and see what they could do to save at least a few.

Melissa had just finished boxing up the photos when she heard a loud thud on the front porch. She opened the door to find Shane unloading the beds from his truck. "I thought you said you had work to do this afternoon."

"I did," Shane said, lifting out a mattress and placing it against the wall. "I finished. I thought we'd get the beds put together before you had to head to work."

Melissa stepped forward and began to help. In no time at all they had the truck unloaded and were putting together the large bed. Once they finished Melissa stepped back and studied the room. "Much better," she said with a nod. "That twin bed was way too small for this room. It made things unsymmetrical. When I saw the bedframe leaning against the wall I knew it would be majestic, but now that it's put together I can see it surpassed even my imagination. Where did you get these? They're wonderful."

Shane shrugged. "They were made locally," he hoped he sounded casual. He'd always had a love for woodworking. Making this bedroom set was the only thing that got him through those first couple years without Melissa. It kept his mind focused on something other than the pain of losing the only woman he had ever loved. Of course, Kristy had despised them. Mostly because it kept him away from her. She was so convinced that if she forced herself on him, he'd change his mind and marry her. Once she found out that was never going to happen, the wild parties and public cheating began. If she couldn't have him, she was determined to humiliate him. When the town turned on her instead, that made things even worse.

"Really?" she asked in surprise. She didn't know anyone locally that was into woodworking. "By whom?"

Shane stood. "Do you think we could do Jeremy's bed tomorrow? I have a few things I need to take care of before I call it a night."

"Oh," Melissa said, standing. "Of course. Thanks for the help. You shouldn't have neglected the ranch for this. I could have figured it out myself. It would have taken a lot longer, but I don't want you to feel like you have to take care of me Shane. I'm staying in your cabin, that's enough. Don't put yourself in a bind on account of me."

"Nothing's been neglected. I just have a few things to do before dark. I'll let myself out. Let me know when you want to put Jeremy's bed together and I'll work it in."

"That one I can take care of myself. I think I've put that thing together so many times I could do it in my sleep." Since her parents had already put Jeremy's room together the bed she had brought from Denver was easy to relocate. The same with her mattresses. They were the perfect size for Shane's cabin and she didn't need them at home anymore. "What do you want me to do with the old bed?" she turned up her nose. "I hesitate to mention it because you've been so generous, but that bed, the one in Jeremy's room is pretty much garbage. The springs are broken and the mattress sags worse than an old lady."

"Then just throw the pieces outside. I'll have one of the guys gather it up and throw it in the trash." He brushed off his knees and headed for the door. "Goodnight Melissa," he said as he disappeared down the hallway.

Melissa listened for the sound of the door closing then stood and walked to Jeremy's room. She really didn't need any help with this bed and she was glad Shane agreed to toss the old one. It really was terrible. She glanced at the clock and decided she had just enough time to tear down the old bed and shower before she had to head to work. She'd put Jeremy's bed together once she got home. It would be late again. She worried about the time he was spending at the main house. It scared her to think he might get so used to it he might never want to come home again. Her parents' house, her house now, was nice but it was a shack compared to Shane's big ranch home. And Cora's cooking beat Melissa's hastily thrown together meals any night of the week. The more time she spent here, the more inadequate she felt.

The past hour she'd spent with Shane hadn't helped things any. Being that close to the sexy cowboy, in her bedroom no less, was an exercise in torture. She'd lost count of the number of times his hand had brushed across hers, sending electricity through every nerve in her body. A couple times his thigh had brushed against her leg and her stomach did a full somersault in response. Living here, seeing Shane in his sexy jeans and rugged cowboy boots was keeping her on edge. Trying to ignore him clearly wasn't going to work. Melissa considered her options. If she couldn't resist him, maybe she could try to entice him. She'd caught his eye and his heart once before, she should be able to do it again, right? As she tore down the bed and threw the pieces on the gravel out front she began to formulate a plan.

* * * *

Two weeks later, Shane was still ignoring Melissa. She'd done everything she could think of to catch his attention. Part of the problem was time. Shane had been so busy planting the field, he'd gone to work early every morning and didn't get home until late. Then there was her job. She hadn't had a full day off since Tina's mother had her accident. That was about to change though. Tina was back to work and Melissa was back on her regular schedule. Tomorrow was her first day off. She would get up early and head in to Ace's for flowers. Then, once she got back home, she'd put on those skimpy cut-offs and her favorite red tank and head outside. She knew she'd lost a lot of weight after Mitch's death, but Shane had always liked her curves. She still had a few and that outfit was the best one she had to entice a man in all the right ways. Shane had always said he was a leg man and those tight shorts definitely showed off her legs. Melissa headed for the bedroom to paint her toes with that sparkling pink polish she'd picked out two days ago. For some reason painted toes had always gotten to Shane. Melissa planned to use everything she'd ever learned to get him to notice her. Some might say that was playing dirty, but Melissa believed it was just playing for keeps.

Melissa pulled into the driveway and started for the cabin, then changed her mind. She'd seen so little of Jeremy these past few days. She wanted to say goodnight if he was still awake. She knocked softly on the door and waited. Shane was standing in the doorway within seconds. Melissa studied him for a full minute before she could speak. His hair was damp and he was bare foot. He had pulled on jeans, but the top button was undone and his gorgeous, masculine chest was completely bare.

Shane cleared his throat to get Melissa's attention. Part of him was flattered at her careful perusal, but another part, the part that insisted he had to stay away from this woman, was finding it difficult to keep his distance. "What's up?" he asked, noticing his voice was more husky than usual and not liking it one bit.

"Oh," Melissa said, looking into Shane's eyes. She'd always loved his eyes. They were dark and mysterious and so masculine. "I just got home and wondered if Jeremy was still awake. I've been working so much this past week I've barely seen him. He's at school when I'm home and by the time I get home from work, he's already in bed. Since I'm an hour early, I just thought maybe..." she trailed off wondering if Shane would invite her in or order her off his porch.

"The kids went to bed but I think Jeremy is still awake," Shane said, moving aside. "Go on up," he paused, then motioned to the stairs.

"Thank you," Melissa said sincerely. Then she turned and took the stairs two at a time.

Shane moved into the family room to wait. He wanted to talk to Melissa about his plans for tomorrow. He knew she wouldn't like them. It was her first day off, but Jeremy had been begging him to take him out on a real ride and they were riding the fence line in the morning. They needed to move the cattle to the south pasture before they ruined the section they'd been grazing. He stood when he saw Melissa slowly descending the staircase.

"Jeremy already asked you about tomorrow didn't he?" Shane said when he saw her face.

163

"Uh-huh," Melissa admitted. "Don't worry. I told him he could go," she assured him, glancing away. She was so disappointed, she had to blink several times to stop the tears in her eyes from falling. She had wanted Jeremy to help her in the garden. She thought they could spend the day picking out flowers and working together like old times. But he'd been so excited about his first real ride, she couldn't deny him the opportunity. This wasn't the first time she'd sacrificed what she wanted for her son's happiness and it wouldn't be the last. Her fears about being left behind grew a little larger. She was losing her son to his father. She wanted to believe that was a good thing, that having a hard working example like Shane was teaching Jeremy to be responsible but fear trumped logic and she just wanted to escape. She needed to get out of here before Shane saw how much this was hurting her.

"I'm sorry," he finally told her. "I know you were looking forward to having a whole day with him. But, Matt started talking about riding the fence and moving the cows and Jeremy immediately asked to go. I promised he could before I realized it was your day off. Once it hit me, I tried to back out but Jeremy was so excited about his first ride I decided to wait and talk to you before I dashed his hopes."

"It's fine, really Shane," Melissa said, forcing herself to sound casual. "In fact, it works out perfectly. I planned to go to town and get those flowers you've wanted me to plant and Jeremy would be bored in no time at all. This way he's out of my hair and having a good time to boot." She paused, hoping he fell for the lie. "Anyway, I'm beat. Thanks for letting me tuck him in. Will you have him home for dinner or should I plan on eating alone?" She hadn't looked at him. She couldn't, she knew if she did she'd burst out in tears.

"He'll be back for supper," he assured her. "Melissa if you want me to, I'll cancel. We can do this another day."

"Nonsense," she shook her head. "Like I said, this helps me out. I can finally start paying my way around here. I've been feeling guilty for days. I want to contribute if I'm going to stay at the cabin. I should have the front gardens planted by the end of the day tomorrow," then she turned and headed for the door.

"Melissa," Shane started, but Melissa didn't stop. She rushed out the door, closing it softly, but securely behind her. Moments later Shane heard her car start up and drive toward the cabin.

Shane hadn't slept well. He kept seeing the disappointed look on Melissa's face. Knowing he'd caused that, watching her stand there pretending like everything was okay when it obviously wasn't had made him feel so damn guilty. She'd been close to tears when she'd rushed from his house and he'd been tempted to chase after her and cancel his plans. Then he thought of Jeremy and the disappointment his son would feel if he did. He couldn't do it. He had to choose Jeremy's happiness over Melissa's. He knew she had done the same. She'd chosen her son's happiness over her own. Somehow he was going to make it up to her. He thought of the box of pictures in the closet. He'd seen them there a few days ago when Jeremy had rushed home for a jacket before they took the four wheelers out to check on a birthing cow.

Maybe he could make things up to her with the pictures. Scott Johnson owed him a favor. He'd call him in the morning and see what he could arrange. The man was magic when it came to restoring pictures. Shane had seen some of his work. He was so good, he'd become known internationally, which kept him mighty busy. But if Shane called in a favor, Brad might bump a client or two and work Melissa in early. It was worth a shot, anyway. Shane would pay for the work, he just didn't want to wait several months before presenting the final album to Melissa. He wanted to give her something now to cheer her up. As much as he'd tried to avoid her, he seemed to run into her at every turn. And she always had that melancholy look in her eyes. He knew she missed her husband and maybe restoring their wedding pictures and her other family photos would give her a little happiness.

Shane finished saddling the horses and turned to grab breakfast before heading out. That's when he spotted Megan. She was running for the stables. What was that girl up to? Shane changed course and walked to the barn. Megan was in the tack room, pulling her saddle from the wall hook. "What do you think you're doing?" Shane asked, annoyed at his daughter. He'd told her she couldn't go with them today. He couldn't keep an eye on both kids at the same time. And with this being Jeremy's first real ride, he needed to concentrate on his son. If he was distracted by something Megan did, Jeremy could get injured.

"Saddling Trigger," Megan said, unfazed.

"Megan, we talked about this last night. You can't go with us today," Shane said impatiently.

"It's not fair," Megan pouted. "Why does Jeremy get to go and I can't. I always go with you to ride the fence line when I'm home." She felt like crying and tried to hold back the tears then changed her mind. She wanted her dad to see how upset she was about this. She reached up and brushed the liquid from her cheek making sure her father noticed.

"Crying isn't going to help," Shane told her. "You know why you can't go. I already told you last night. This is Jeremy's first ride. I need to concentrate on his riding to make sure he doesn't get into trouble. You've ridden fence a million times. It's not going to hurt you to stay home this once. I'm not going to tell you again, Megan. Put the saddle back and go in the house. It's too early for you to be up anyway."

Megan was surprised. She'd always been able to get what she wanted before. Her father rarely told her no and when he saw something was important to her, he always gave in. Jeremy had ruined that. At first she thought it was fun to have a brother. Not now. Now she knew that having a brother meant her dad didn't love her anymore. He didn't want to spend time with her. He just wanted to spend time with Jeremy. Was it because he was a boy or because her mother had been right and Megan was ruining her dad's life and making him unhappy? Jeremy's mom still hated her. Maybe her dad was beginning to regret having Megan around. She knew her dad and Jeremy's mom were trying to avoid each other. Was it all because of her? Was she making her dad so unhappy he didn't want her anymore, he just wanted Jeremy? If she were gone, dad could be happy with Melissa. She turned and ran for the house, tears streaming down her face. It was hard to run, her vision was blurry and she was crying so hard she couldn't catch her breath. She ran to her room and watched out the window until Jeremy and her dad mounted their horses and headed up the trail. Then she pulled out her pencils and began to draw.

* * * *

Melissa climbed out of bed and got dressed. Once she'd brushed her hair into a tight pony tail, she headed for the door. She had work to do. Missing Jeremy and regretting the day they wouldn't have wasn't going to get the flower beds planted. She slipped on a ball cap and headed for the car. The ranch seemed eerily quiet this morning. She wondered what Megan was doing. Shane wouldn't take her with him today. He'd have his hands full with Jeremy. That's one thing she knew, she could trust Shane with her son's safety. Jeremy was in good hands and he was having a blast. Melissa would have tonight and tomorrow to spend with her son. That would just have to be enough.

Two hours later, Melissa pulled into the drive. Her mood had improved. She was excited to begin planting all the flowers she'd purchased. There was nothing like picking out colorful flowers and planning a garden layout to brighten the day. As she turned to head passed the house toward the cabin she froze. Cora was standing near a horse, frantically trying to climb onto its back. Melissa slammed on the brakes and jumped from the car. "Cora!" she yelled in a panic. "What are you doing? You know you can't ride with your back."

"It's Megan," Cora said clearly frantic. "She took off on Trigger. I knew she was upset. She wanted to go riding with Shane and didn't understand when he told her no. But Shane had to concentrate on Jeremy, with this being his first time and all. That girl didn't understand. She pouted all morning then she snuck out and I saw her running off on this horse."

Melissa took a closer look and realized Cora was holding onto Trigger, Megan's horse. So where was Megan? "Trigger came back alone?"

"Yes," Cora said, even more frantic now. "Shane's not back. Something had to happen to that girl. She's a good rider, but with Trigger running back to the house alone, I know something bad has happened."

Melissa gave Cora a gentle push. "I'll find her." She climbed into the saddle and tried to adjust to the seat. It was a little small for her, but she could manage. "Do you have any idea where she would have gone? Any special place I should check first? If we're lucky she climbed off to rest and Trigger got away from her and headed home."

"The lake," Cora said immediately. "That's where she goes when she's upset. Maybe you're right. Maybe she's just sitting by the lake and Trigger took off without her." Cora doubted that was the case, but she wanted to hope for the best. "Go find my girl," Cora practically begged. "Please Melissa, find that precious little girl before something happens to her. She's out there all alone."

"I'll find her, I promise," Melissa assured her. "I won't come back until I do," then she gave Trigger a little kick and they were off for the lake.

Melissa knew she was pushing the horse too hard. Trigger was panting and beginning to slow. A second trip to the lake after he'd run here with Megan, then run back to the house was too much. She knew it, but she couldn't slow down. The closer she got to the lake, the more frantic she got. Deep in the pit of her stomach she knew, without a doubt, Megan was in some kind of trouble. She just hoped the little girl wasn't injured. She'd rushed off so fast, she'd forgotten to grab a first aid kit. Suddenly, the lake came into view. Melissa stood in the saddle searching for Megan.

At first Melissa didn't see Megan, then as she crested the hill, she spotted her. The child was standing completely still. Melissa felt her entire body relax. Megan was okay. She was standing upright, not lying on the ground with a broken neck. "Megan!" Melissa yelled. When Megan ignored her the second time, Melissa knew something was terribly wrong. She jumped from Trigger and tied him to a tree. No way would she let the horse escape again. Melissa began to rush toward the frozen girl, but paused to look around for the danger. She knew with every step something was lurking, she just couldn't see what.

"Megan?" Melissa asked, slowly creeping closer. "What is it honey? I can't see anything. Is it a mountain lion? Shane always told me to watch out for them. They usually spook easily unless they're hungry. Megan, I need you to talk to me. Tell me where the danger is."

"S...s...snake," Megan whispered, then shut her mouth when it began to rattle.

Melissa jerked her head to the ground and spotted the large rattler. It was huge and pissed. The thing was coiled tight as a spring, its tail was shaking frantically and it let out a loud hiss. Melissa took a deep breath. "Okay," she said softly. "We can handle this." She was trying to convince herself as much as Megan. "Here's what I'm going to do. I'm going to walk around the back side of the snake. Do you know if it's alone?"

Megan gave the slightest nod, but other than that, she didn't move.

The girl was white as a ghost. Melissa was amazed Megan had been able to stand still so long. She was a brave kid and Melissa was determined to save her. She was realistic enough to know she might get bit in the process, but she would save Shane's daughter if it was the last things she did. The thought of dying from a snake bite brought a tinge of panic back, but she pushed it aside. If she died, Jeremy would have Shane and Megan. He wouldn't be alone now. "Okay Meg. You're doing great. I know you're tired, but you need to hold on just a little longer. I'm going to try to divert his attention to me. If he heads my way, wait until he gets a few feet away then run as fast as you can to Trigger. Jump on his back and wait for me, okay?"

Megan shot a glance at Melissa but didn't answer. Clearly she didn't approve of the plan, but she didn't argue. Melissa slowly made her way around the snake. Once she was directly across from Megan she stopped, hoping the snake would turn and come after her instead. It didn't move. Okay, so that wasn't going to work. She needed another plan. She continued around, making a huge circle to the other side. Once she was standing about a foot to Megan's left she closed her eyes and prayed for a miracle. "Megan?" Melissa whispered. This time the snake did shift. His attention was now focused on Melissa. Good, he perceived her as the bigger threat. "I need you to listen to me. We're only going to have one shot at this."

"Okay," Megan whispered. She didn't like the way the snake was looking at Melissa.

"I'm going to shift and pick you up. On the count of three I need you to jump into my arms. You'll need to wrap your arms around my neck and jump as high as you can then wrap your legs around my waist. Do you understand? It's important you get your legs up as high as you possibly can. Snakes can jump. I'm pretty sure this one will. He's agitated. The moment I lunge for you, I think he's going to jump at me. I need your legs out of the way completely. Do you understand me?" Melissa asked more urgently.

"I understand but I think that's a very bad idea," Megan whispered. "You're going to get bit."

"No, I won't." Melissa was pretty sure she was going to get bit, but she didn't want Megan to know that. Once she got her out of harm's way, she would order Megan to take Trigger and find help. Chances were good nobody would arrive in time, but at least Megan would be safe. How long did it take for a snake bite to affect your nervous system? Melissa had no idea. What if it was instant?

Hidden Lakes

She wouldn't be able to give Megan instructions. "Megan, I need you to make me a promise."

"What?" she asked hesitantly.

"If the snake does bite me, I need you to go find your father. Shane will know how to help me. I need you to jump on Trigger and run as fast as you can to the house. If he's not there, get another horse and go find him in the field. Do you promise?" Melissa pressed.

Megan shook her head no. "I won't leave you." Her eyes grew wide when the snake shifted back to her.

"We don't have time to argue about this. I'm the adult, you need to do what I say. Now I'm going to count to three and you need to jump. Ready?"

Megan nodded.

"One, two...jump!" Melissa yelled as she pivoted and braced herself for impact as she grabbed the small child around the waist. Megan jumped higher than Melissa expected. The little girl wrapped her legs tightly around Melissa's waist at the same time as she encircled Melissa's neck with her tiny arms. Melissa took two steps, confident they were going to make it when she suddenly felt something tugging on her left leg. The leg that had been closest to the snake. She immediately glanced down and spotted the reptile clinging to her pant leg. She gave her leg a tentative shake and realized the snake's fangs were caught in her boot. Her mind focused on her leg. Had she been bitten? She didn't feel any pain. Should she feel pain? Would the venom numb the area of the bite to allow more poison into her system? She wished she knew more about snake bites. But wishing for the impossible wasn't going to help her now. "Meg?" Melissa said pushing slightly to get the girl's attention. "I need to put you down now. I need to put you down as far away from me as you can get. Then I need you to run to Trigger and climb on his back. Can you do that for me?"

Megan's eyes grew wide. "Why?" she asked, clearly afraid.

"I'll tell you once I know you're safe. We don't have a lot of time here. I'm going to push on your hips and swing you out away from me. Once you feel me pushing swing your legs out and let go of my neck. Ready?" Melissa asked.

Megan took a deep breath then choked out, "Ready."

Melissa watched as Megan fell to the ground, then jumped up and ran to Trigger. Once she'd climbed into the saddle, Melissa glanced back at the snake. She closed her eyes and took two deep breaths, trying to regain her composure. "The snake is caught on my pant leg. I'm going to have to pull him off and throw him in the river. You stay there until I get back. Promise me you won't get off that horse until I tell you it's safe."

Megan began to cry. Melissa was going to die all because of her. She was an awful child. Jeremy was going to be so sad. Her dad was going to be mad.

"Megan, I need you to promise me that no matter what happens you will not get off that horse. Answer me…now," Melissa said, trying to remain calm but failing miserably.

"I promise," Megan said, still crying.

Melissa took one step then realized that wasn't going to work. She'd hoped she could make her way to the river then pull the thing off and toss it into the water. But as she took a step, she worried the fangs would come lose and the snake would get another shot at her.

Hidden Lakes

While he was stuck and unable to cause any harm, she would have to grip its head and yank him from her boot. Melissa wondered what she had done in her life that was so bad she had to tangle with a three foot rattler... literally. She took a deep breath then reached down and grabbed the snakes head. It hissed and began to flail its body in all directions. The thing was slithering around so much Melissa was worried she'd lose her grip on its head. She yanked on it again, this time trying to pull up then out. It worked. It was still swinging back and forth, but so far, so good. If she could just get to the river without dropping it, she might survive this nightmare after all. The instant she reached the bank she tossed the snake far away from her and watched as the water carried it down stream.

Melissa didn't hesitate. She broke into a run headed back to Trigger. She realized, almost immediately that Megan had untied the horse. Trigger was stomping his feet, clearly wanting to go. Megan was controlling him, not letting him move more than a foot in any one direction. Cora was right, the kid was a good rider. The instant Melissa reached Trigger she vaulted onto his back behind Megan and gave him a quick kick. The horse darted for home. Megan slumped forward and began to sob.

It took a while for Melissa to realize Megan was crying. She tried to pull her back so she could reassure her, but Megan wouldn't let go of the horn. She was sobbing uncontrollably now, her little body shaking so hard Melissa worried she would fall off the horse. Melissa pulled on the reins and brought the horse to a stop. Then she lowered Megan to the ground.

Megan tried to stand, but her legs were so weak she fell instantly to her knees. She scurried away from Trigger so he wouldn't step on her and wrapped her arms around her waist as she curled into a ball and cried. Melissa was going to die. It would take too long to get back to the house. Even if her dad was there, Melissa would suffer and die all because of her.

Melissa climbed from the horse and looked around. She had to find something to tie the horse to. Megan was starting to scare her. The little girl was so upset she was starting to hyperventilate. She spotted a tree a few yards away, that would have to work. Once she tied the reins tightly around a branch she returned to Megan. Melissa sank to the ground and pulled Megan onto her lap. Megan wrapped her entire body around Melissa and continued to weep.

"I'm so sorry," Megan choked out. "We can't stop. We have to get you back to the house. I don't think we'll make it, but we have to try."

Melissa pushed Megan back so she could look her in the eyes. "What are you talking about?" she asked, furrowing her brows in confusion.

"I saw the snake. It bit you. It bit your leg. The poison is already inside you, but if we hurry, maybe dad..."

"Megan, the snake got my pants and my boot, nothing else. The leather on my boots was thick enough it didn't get through. I'm okay. I'm not bit." Melissa set Megan on the ground and quickly pulled off her boot. She showed Megan her pant leg, the boot, then she pulled up her pants and showed Megan her leg. "See. I'm okay. I promise."

Megan looked into Melissa's eyes then back at her leg. "You swear?"

"Yes," Melissa said, pulling Megan into a huge hug. "I'm so proud of you," she said kissing the top of Megan's head. "You were extremely brave. I'm sorry it took me so long to get to you. I know you had to be scared. But you did everything just right. You stood completely still and didn't look at the snake directly. You didn't panic and run. That gave me enough time to get to you and save you. You are such a brave little girl. I really am proud of you."

Megan began to cry again. Jeremy was so lucky to have Melissa for a mom. Megan just wished they could be friends. But she knew once they got back to the house, Melissa would avoid her again.

"What's wrong, you were hoping to get rid of me or something?" Melissa joked.

Megan shook her head vehemently. "No!" she exclaimed. "It's just..." she wiped away her tears. "It's just that I know you don't like me. Why did you risk your life to save me when you hate me so bad? I'm not worth it. Jeremy needs you."

"Megan, you are worth it," Melissa said in a tone that left no room for doubt. "And I don't hate you. I've never hated you. I know you might not believe that because I yelled at you that night at my house, but I was wrong. I owe you an apology."

"No. You don't," Megan said as she took a long, shuddering breath. "I'm not likable. I know that. My mom told me nobody would ever like me, not really. She warned me that I would chase off anyone dad cared about and he'd be sad and lonely forever because of me."

"Well then, you're mom lied to you," Melissa said, furious with Kristy. "You are likeable. I happen to think you are very special. You are brave and kind and Jeremy showed me that picture you drew of him on the horse. You are a talented artist, you are exceptional at riding a horse and you don't panic under pressure. I know, I just saw you handle that snake like a pro. I really am proud of you and I like you very, very much."

"Then why do you run away from me? Why do you leave the barn when I walk in? Why do you walk back in the cabin if you see me outside?" Megan asked.

"I'm sorry you saw that," Melissa said, even more angry with Shane for the situation he had caused. "It's not because I don't like you. It's because your dad is afraid I will hurt you again. I don't want to upset him, so I've been avoiding you. I'm sorry if that hurt your feelings, it wasn't my intention."

"Dad treats me like I'm a baby because my mom said mean things. He thinks it upsets me that she made dad buy me from her. It doesn't. I was glad she left. I do feel bad that dad had to give her so much money because of me, but I hate my mom. I hope I never have to see her again," Megan said then she covered her mouth with her hand and gasped.

"It's okay," Melissa said, agreeing with the kid. Kristy was worse than she'd originally believed. She told her daughter she was selling her to her father. And that nonsense about Megan not being likeable and ruining Shane's life was criminal. If she ever saw Kristy McGrath again, she just might shoot her. "I probably shouldn't tell you this, but I didn't like your mom very much either."

Megan sat up straight. "You knew my mom?"

"A little," Melissa admitted. "We weren't friends or anything, in fact we didn't like each other at all. I'm sorry she was mean to you, but she lied Megan. You are very likeable and you don't make your dad sad. He's going to be mad when he finds out what you did today, but that's only because he loves you so much."

"Not anymore," Megan whispered. "Now that he has Jeremy, he doesn't need me anymore."

"Megan," Melissa said, shocked at the girl's conviction. "Your dad loves you more than anything in the world. Having Jeremy in his life hasn't changed that. It will never change that."

"But he didn't want me to go with him today. I always go with dad when he rides fences when school's out," Megan argued.

"Do you remember the first time you rode fence with your dad?" Melissa asked.

"Yes," Megan said, thinking back. It was a long time ago, but she still remembered. She had been so excited that her dad finally trusted her to ride with him.

"And what did your dad do while you were riding that day? Did he stay by your side to make sure you didn't get hurt or did he ride off with Hank or one of the other guys like he normally would?" Melissa asked.

"He rode right with me. He told me not to leave his side for a minute. He said sometimes a horse can get spooked if he sees or hears something that scares him. He didn't want to be away from me if that happened. He didn't want me to get hurt. He said he would be right there and if Trigger spooked, he wouldn't let him hurt me," Megan answered. "Why did you want to know that?"

"Because that's the reason Shane wouldn't let you ride with him today. This was Jeremy's first time on a big ride. The horse he's on could get spooked. Jeremy is new to riding, he wouldn't know what to do. He's not as familiar with horses as you are. That means, Shane needs to be right there by Jeremy's side just in case something happened."

"I don't understand. I mean I know he needs to be with Jeremy, but I don't understand why I couldn't go too," Megan said, trying to figure this all out.

"Because Shane is also protective of you sweetheart. I know you've been riding a long time and you are good at it. I saw that right away, the way you controlled Trigger was commendable. But you are Shane's little girl. He loves you more than anything. He would never forgive himself if he was paying so much attention to Jeremy that he let you get hurt somehow," Melissa explained.

Megan's eyes brightened. "Oh," she finally said in understanding. "Then he does still love me?"

"Of course he does silly," Melissa said, rubbing Megan's head.

"But..." Megan furrowed her brows in concentration. Melissa couldn't help but notice it was the same look Shane and Jeremy got when they were trying to reason something out. "I think dad is going to love Jeremy more than me. Jeremy's a boy. He can do things I can't when he gets bigger. Then he'll always choose Jeremy to do stuff with him instead of me. He'll take some of the love he has for me and give it to Jeremy. I don't want him to love Jeremy more than me."

"It doesn't work that way," Melissa disagreed, considering. "Let me explain it this way. Do you love Cora?"

Megan smiled. "Tons. Cora takes care of me. She's kind of like a mom I guess, not mean like my mom, but nice. She takes care of me when I'm sick and she bakes me cookies when I'm sad. I love her a lot."

Hidden Lakes

"So does that mean you don't love your dad as much because you have to give some of that love to Cora?" Melissa asked.

Megan frowned. "No. I can love Cora and my dad. Cora is Cora and dad is my dad."

"Exactly," Melissa said. "Shane can love Jeremy without changing the love he has for you. Jeremy is his son, but you are his daughter. He will always love both of you the same. Having Jeremy come along won't take away from the love Shane has for you. The heart is wonderful that way. The more people you love, the bigger it gets. There's room enough to love everyone."

"I guess that makes sense," Megan finally admitted. "I'm glad you didn't get bit. You're the best mom in the world. Jeremy is lucky. I wish I had a mom like you."

Melissa stood to blink back tears. That was the nicest thing anyone had ever said to her. She brushed off her pants and then held her hand out to Megan. "Come on. Cora was frantic when I left her. She's going to be crazy with worry. Let's get back so she can see for herself you're okay."

"Alright," Megan said, standing to brush off her jeans. Her legs were still a little wobbly. It made her feel good when Melissa took her arm and helped her to Trigger. It felt even better when Melissa picked her up and placed her in the saddle.

"How about you take the reins for a while," Melissa offered. "I'm still a little bit shaken up from my encounter with that snake." She pulled herself onto the back of Trigger and wrapped her arms around Megan's waist. For the first time in eight years, Melissa wished she could spend time with Shane's daughter. It was strange, she always thought she would resent Megan because she was

Kristy's blood but she found herself wishing for a relationship she could never have. Shane would never allow that kind of closeness. The knowledge made her more than a little sad.

* * * *

Shane handed the horses off to Matt and headed for the house. Normally he'd wipe them down himself, but he was anxious to see Megan. She'd been so upset this morning. It was good that Jeremy would be spending the night with Melissa. It would give him some one-on-one time with his daughter. He stepped into the bright afternoon sun and saw the dust from the upper road. Who could be out riding at this time of day? He took several steps toward the approaching horse and froze. Red hot anger boiled inside. Melissa had promised she wouldn't go near Megan. How dare she sneak out the instant his back was turned. She must have decided to punish him for taking her son away. She was disappointed because she couldn't spend the day with Jeremy so she broke the rules and went riding with Megan. He wouldn't tolerate such a betrayal.

Melissa saw Shane before Megan did. She also saw his face. He was furious. Well, she wouldn't let him yell at Megan. The child had been through enough today. He'd just have to put it aside for now. She brought Trigger to a stop and jumped from the horse, reaching up to pull Megan to her feet. "You okay?" she asked Megan, hoping her legs were strong enough to get her inside the house.

"I'm okay," Megan assured her. She turned to go inside but paused when she saw her dad. He was furious. She straightened, willing to accept her punishment. She knew she wasn't supposed to ride alone. She deserved whatever punishment he gave her.

Hidden Lakes

Shane marched right up to Melissa and pressed a finger into her chest. "You had no right!" he bellowed. "I told you to stay away from my daughter. You had no right to go back on your promise. You agreed to stay clear of Megan if I let you stay here. Just because I took Jeremy with me on your day off doesn't give you the right to betray that trust. I guess I'll never learn. Your lack of honor, this complete pettiness to get back at me comes as a surprise. You'd think I'd learn. Nothing you do should surprise me anymore, but here I am shocked to the bone at the utter disregard you have for my wishes. I let you stay on my land. I helped you out when I didn't have to and this is how you repay me?"

"Daddy!" Megan cried. "Stop it."

Shane gave Melissa one more look of disgust, of total loathing, before he spun around lifted Megan into his arms and stomped into the house.

Melissa stood frozen in shock. She'd never seen Shane like that before. She'd never seen anyone look at her with so much hatred. Then the tears began to fall. She turned and ran to the cabin. She didn't even stop when she heard Jeremy calling her name.

Jeremy walked into the cabin and searched for his mom. He was angry with his dad for yelling at her. He was mad and confused. But dad shouldn't have yelled at his mom and made her cry. He finally found her inside her bedroom. She was laying on the bed her head under her pillow. He could hear her crying from the hallway. He stepped into the room and climbed onto the bed, wrapping his arms around his mom. "Please don't cry," he whispered not knowing what to do. Mitch always knew how to make mom happy, but Jeremy never could. He'd tried flowers when they were back in Denver, that seemed to work for Mitch, but it never helped when

Jeremy did it. His mom was so sad. Jeremy worried she'd go back to being sad all the time again, the way she was in Denver. And it was all his dad's fault. "I want to go back to our house," he told her, hoping that would make her happy again. "When can we move back?"

Melissa sat up and wiped away her tears. "We talked about this Jeremy. Our house won't be done for a few more weeks. Stop worrying about me and don't try to deny it. I can see it in that face you're pulling. I'm alright, really. Shane just hurt my feelings a little, but it's okay."

"I don't like him very much right now," Jeremy told her. "He shouldn't yell at you like that and he should never make you cry."

"He was worried about Megan, that's all. I'm glad he yelled at me instead of her. Megan's had a pretty hard day today. In fact, I was hoping you would spend the night up at the house with her. She had a pretty big scare and she needs a good brother to talk to. Do you think you could be strong and go up and spend some time with her? I think it would help her to know you're there." Melissa hoped he'd agree. She needed to be alone. She needed time to think, to decide what she was going to do.

"What scared Megan?" Jeremy asked, worried.

"Why don't you go up and talk to her. I think she might like to tell you about it herself," Melissa waited. She didn't push him while he sorted through his thoughts. She'd learned not to push him, or it would backfire.

"Okay, if you promise me you are really okay," Jeremy finally said.

"I'm really okay," Melissa said, kissing her son on the cheek. "Now hurry up to the house and be there for Megan. It's important.

183

Make her talk to you about today. If she has someone to share it with, she might sleep better tonight."

Jeremy kissed his mom and walked slowly to the house. He wasn't sure he was doing the right thing. His mom had seemed sincere, but he also knew she was upset. He thought he should be there to take care of her, the way Mitch had told him to. But if Megan needed him, maybe he should be there for her. She was just a kid, maybe that was more important. He rushed up the stairs and stopped just inside the door. Cora was slamming around in the kitchen and he didn't want to get in her way.

"Where are you going?" Shane asked, annoyed.

"Home," Cora said, shooting a furious look his way. "You ought to be ashamed of yourself. I love you Shane, I always have. I never thought the day would come that I was ashamed of you. The way you acted out there, I'm embarrassed for you. Clearly you don't have enough sense to be embarrassed for yourself. It's shameful, the way you yelled at that girl." Cora shook her head then stalked out the door. "Don't expect me tomorrow either. You can just fend for yourself for a few days. I'll let you know when I've cooled off enough to come back. I'm spitting mad at you right now Shane Chandler. Spitting mad," with that she slammed the door and walked to her car, slamming that door behind her too.

Now what was that all about? Shane wondered. More of the same he guessed. More of Cora making excuses for Melissa. He started to turn and spotted Jeremy. "I thought you were spending the night with your mother," he asked.

Jeremy glared at his father. He was spitting mad, too. Just like Cora. But he knew he couldn't yell at him like Cora had. He was just a kid and he'd be in trouble if he told his dad what he thought right now. "Mom asked me to spend some time with Megan. She said she needed me. If you'll excuse me, I don't think I want to talk to you right now."

"Jeremy," Shane said sternly. It was enough to get Jeremy to pause and turn to face him. "I know you don't like it that I yelled at your mom, but she was wrong. She promised me she wouldn't spend time with Megan then she broke that promise and went riding with her. She needed to know I was angry and that what she did was wrong."

Jeremy just stood there, not speaking, not moving for the longest time. Then he took a deep breath. "It seems to me that it was wrong of you to tell my mom she had to stay away from Megan. She didn't tell you to stay away from me. I don't understand why mom can live at the ranch but she can't talk to Megan. Are you saying she's not good enough? That she can't be trusted to make sure Megan is safe? Because that's just stupid. And if mom can't be around your kid, you shouldn't be around me."

"I'm not discussing this with you Jeremy. The situation is different. For one thing, you're my kid too. I have just as much right to be around you as your mother does. For another thing..." Shane was cut off by Jeremy.

"I don't have to listen to you," Jeremy said, knowing he was being disrespectful but not caring. "You're just a bully. You got mad and you made my mom cry. I don't like bullies. My dad told me I don't have to like them and I don't have to be nice to them. You were mean to my mom just because you're bigger and stronger than her. I'll stay here tonight because mom asked me to for Megan, but I don't think I want to see you for a while. I want to spend some time with my mom," then he turned and ran up the stairs to Megan's room.

Hidden Lakes

Shane stood there, completely surprised by Jeremy's words. He wasn't a bully. Had he really made Melissa cry? If so, it was just another game she was playing. She was trying to come between him and his son. And it had worked. Jeremy was angry with him and didn't want to spend time with him. Well, he wasn't going to allow it. He wasn't going to let Jeremy get away with disrespecting him either. And Megan had some explaining to do of her own. He stomped up the stairs but stopped just outside Megan's doorway. She was excited about something. That was vastly different from the last words she'd said to him before rushing off to her room. The instant he'd put her down she turned on him. He'd never forget the look on her face. She was so angry with him. She demanded an explanation. She insisted on knowing why he'd ordered Melissa to stay away from her. When he didn't answer, she'd told him she hated him and ran to her room. Megan had never acted that way before. She'd never looked at him with so much anger and she had never told him she hated him. He was perplexed. How had he become the bad guy? The three most important people in his life were angry at him. No, not angry, furious. And it was all Melissa's fault.

He moved closer to Megan's door and listened. How had his life come to this, eavesdropping on his daughter? How pathetic was he anyway? He was about to walk away when Megan's words registered with him. Megan had taken Trigger out alone?

"I was sad when dad left with you and wouldn't let me go. I thought he didn't love me anymore. I thought now that he had you, he didn't need or want me around," Megan said softly.

"That's just stupid," Jeremy told her. "Dad loves you. You're his daughter. My mom always says that sometimes she doesn't like what I do, but she will always love me. No matter how mad she gets, she will never stop loving me. It's the same for dad. He loves you and always will."

"I know that now," Megan admitted. "Melissa explained it to me. Dad wouldn't let me go because he had to make sure you were safe on your first ride. The same as he did with me on my first ride," she paused when she saw the offended look on Jeremy's face. "Don't get mad. He shouldn't have let me go. Sometimes things happen when you ride a horse. They can spook. I learned that first hand today. Anyway, your mom said that if he took both of us and one of us got hurt while he was paying attention to the other, he would never forgive himself. It had to be just you this time. I wish dad had just told me that. I would have understood. Instead he yelled at me and I thought he didn't love me anymore. I came up here to draw and it helped for a few hours, but after a while I just needed to get out. I needed to ride. So I snuck out when Cora was busy and took off on Trigger."

Jeremy frowned. "You shouldn't have left like that. Not all by yourself. Dad says you should never ride alone. Because like you said sometimes things happen and the horse can get spooked."

Shane realized he was holding his breath. If Megan had left alone, why was Melissa with her when they rode back? He was sure he wasn't going to like the rest of this story.

"I know," Megan whispered. "That's what happened. I rode out to the lake. I like to go there. It's the special place dad takes me when we need to talk. I always feel closer to him there, I always feel loved when I'm with him there. I thought maybe it would help me today. Like being there would make me feel loved again."

Shane closed his eyes in shame. He'd really messed up with Megan today. It broke his heart to hear she believed he'd stopped loving her. He should have handled it all differently. He should have talked to her rather than yell and demand.

"When I got there, Trigger got spooked by something. I didn't know what and it took me by surprise. He reared up and knocked me off his back. I fell to the ground then stood up planning to yell at my horse. That's when I heard it. Trigger was gone, he'd already run down the road out of sight," Megan said, her voice shaking a little.

"What did you see?" Jeremy asked in anticipation.

"A rattle snake," she said, a tear running down her cheek. "I was so scared. I didn't know what to do. I was all alone and nobody knew I had even left. The snake was so close I just knew if I moved he'd bite me. I thought I was going to die."

Shane couldn't move. A rattle snake? Megan had been that close to a rattler. How had she avoided getting bit? He wanted to rush in and inspect every inch of his daughter's body, but he stopped himself. If he interrupted, he'd never hear the entire story. Megan was mad at him for one thing. And he knew his little girl, she'd down play the story to him but not to Jeremy. Jeremy was her equal. She'd be completely honest with him.

"What did you do?" Jeremy asked, amazed. If he saw a rattle snake, he'd probably wet his pants. His dad had told him how dangerous they were. He knew someday he'd probably see one, but he hoped it would be from a very long ways away.

"I remembered what dad told me. He said you should stand perfectly still and never ever look them straight in the eye. So that's what I did. I thought he would eventually move away. I hoped that if I was as still as a statue he wouldn't feel threatened and he would slither away. He didn't," Megan said with a shudder. "I was standing as still as I could and never ever looked directly at him. I just kept hoping he would leave, but he just stayed there coiled in a ball watching me, sometimes hissing at me. My legs were starting to get tired and I was afraid I wouldn't be able to stand there much longer but I knew I had to. If I sat down, or fell down the snake would get me."

"Were you scared? I would have been really scared," Jeremy admitted.

"More than scared. I was sure I was going to die," Megan smiled. "That's when your mom got there. She came running up on Trigger. I guess he went home and she figured out something was wrong so she came looking for me," Megan said gratitude evident in her voice.

Shane felt like a clod. Melissa had saved his daughter from a snake. That in itself was a miracle. Melissa was terrified of snakes. And how did he thank her? He called her names and made her cry. He had to go see her, but not until he heard the end of this story.

"Mom's scared of snakes," Jeremy told her. "How did she help?"

"Your mom's not afraid of snakes," Megan disagreed. "First she walked to the other side of the snake and tried to get it to come at her instead of me. She said if it did I was supposed to run and get on Trigger. He didn't move. Then she moved closer to me and told me she was going to pick me up and run. She said to wrap my legs around her waist so it couldn't get me if it jumped. I was sure she was going to get bit. I knew for sure your mom was going to die and it would be all my fault. She counted to three and I jumped into her arms. I was so scared, but she held onto me and wouldn't let me fall."

Hidden Lakes

Jeremy jumped to his feet. "She didn't get bit did she?"

Megan sighed, but didn't answer. She was having too much fun with the story. "She took a couple steps then told me she was going to swing me away from her and made me promise I would run to Trigger. The instant my feet hit the ground I ran. I kept thinking the snake was going to chase after me. Once I was on Trigger I looked for your mom. She was still standing in the same spot. When I looked down, I saw that the snake was attached to her leg."

"What?" Shane asked as he burst into the room. "Melissa got bit by that snake. Why didn't anyone tell me? She needs to get to the hospital."

Megan scowled at her father. "You were listening?" she demanded. "You told me that was wrong. That it was rude to listen outside someone's door."

"Megan, did Melissa get bit?" he demanded.

"No," she said, still scowling. "I thought she did. I started to cry thinking she was going to die and it was all my fault. She pulled the snake off her leg and rushed to the river and tossed it in. Then she ran back to Trigger and we ran away. I was crying, so she stopped and got us off the horse. When I told her I thought she was going to die she showed me how the snake had got stuck on her boot. She was wearing leather cowboy boots. The snake's fangs went through her pants and stuck in her boot. She even took off the boot to show me there were no marks on her leg. I was so relieved. I knew you would never forgive me if your mom died because of me," she glared at her dad. "Then when we got back to the house you yelled at her. She saved my life and you yelled at her. You told her she couldn't talk to me. You made her promise to stay away from me. All this time I thought she hated me like mom said. I thought I was ugly and unlikable but it was you," Megan accused. "You won't let her like me."

"Megan," Shane began.

"No!" she yelled and put her face under her pillow. "I don't want to talk to you. I want you to leave me alone."

Shane considered the situation. Maybe it was better to let her have this night with Jeremy. They could talk in the morning. Right now he needed to talk to Melissa. He had to thank her for saving his little girls life. He still couldn't believe Melissa, the girl that was terrified of a garter snake, faced down a rattler to save his daughter's life. "I'll leave you two for now, but we will talk about this in the morning." He closed the door and rushed outside.

Once he was standing on the front porch he hesitated. What did you say to the woman that saved the life of someone you loved? How did you apologize for yelling at said person? No wonder Cora was ashamed of him. No wonder she was so livid. He took a deep breath then knocked on the door. Melissa didn't answer immediately. When she did, she only cracked the door and peeked out. Her eyes were swollen and bright red. "Can I come in?" he asked humbled by her appearance. He'd done that. Once again, he'd hurt someone he cared about. Someone he loved. It was no use denying it. No use pretending like avoiding her was doing any good. He loved this woman and she'd just saved his daughter's life.

"I'm kind of busy," she said, not moving. "Maybe you could yell at me another time?"

Shane pushed open the door and forced his way inside. He knew this woman. If he didn't force the issue, she'd close the door and ignore him the rest of the night. He was about to speak when he spotted the boxes. Melissa was packing. He looked at her, willing an explanation to form in midair. "You're leaving?" he

191

finally asked. His heart was beating way too fast. She couldn't leave. Not like this.

Melissa sighed. "Yes, Shane. I'm leaving. I know Pete is still working on the house and there isn't any water but as long as you're willing to keep Jeremy out here I can manage at home. It won't be that bad, I can shower at the station."

"Don't go," he heard himself say. There was a hint of desperation in his voice. Well that was something. At least the monumental sized ball of desperation he was feeling in his very soul hadn't shown through.

"Shane, we both know it's better this way," Melissa impatiently brushed away a tear. "You hate me. You dislike me so much you do everything humanly possible to avoid me. When that doesn't work, you can't even stand to look at me. I'm making you uncomfortable and that's not fair to you. This is your ranch, you always loved it here. With me on the premises you can't wait to escape. I need to leave, for all of our sakes."

Shane didn't hate her, he loved her. He avoided her because being close to something you wanted so badly but knew you could never have, was a special kind of hell. He couldn't look at her because her beautiful blue eyes and luscious blonde hair haunted his dreams. He wasn't strong enough to resist them in the day light. "I know it might seem that way but you're wrong. I don't hate you, I could never hate you."

"Shane, I know you're worried that I'm going to keep Jeremy from you. That's why you want me to stay. You don't have to worry about that. I know Jeremy is better off here, for now anyway. It kills me to admit that, being away from him is going to be hard but it's my reality. And regardless of how hard it is on me, I want what's best for my son. For now, staying here with you is what's best for him."

"Now that is going to be a problem," Shane countered. "As he pretty much hates me right now and wants nothing to do with me, if you leave, he's just going to follow."

"Jeremy doesn't hate you," Melissa disagreed. "He might be angry with you. He's pretty protective of me and he thinks you made me cry."

"I did make you cry," Shane challenged. "You saved my daughter's life and I made you cry. I was horrible to you and I don't blame you for wanting to leave, but I'm asking you to please give me another chance. Please let me make this up to you. Please stay," he whispered the last words. He was desperate and pretty sure she was going to tell him where to shove his request.

"Who said I saved Megan's life?" Melissa asked, not wanting Shane to know the whole story. It was too terrifying for words.

"I overheard Megan telling Jeremy about her terrifying adventure. You stepped between her and a rattle snake. You could have been killed yourself. You Melissa, the woman that refused to come off the bleachers because of a garter snake saved my little girl from a rattler." Shane still couldn't believe what she'd done.

"Megan over exaggerated," Melissa began. She stopped, confused when Shane marched down the hall towards her bedroom. "Where are you going?"

"I want to see your boots," he demanded, throwing open her door and rummaging through her closet.

"Uh..." Melissa tried to stall. "Why do you want to see those old things?"

Hidden Lakes

Shane stood and glanced around, considering. Then he pushed past her and headed for the laundry area. She would have taken off the pants the instant she entered the cabin. He froze when he saw where the snake had latched on. "One more inch and he would have gotten to you," he closed his eyes, forcing back the pain and fear. "One tiny inch and you could have been gone forever." He turned back to her, terror and regret showing on his face.

"Maybe, but it didn't happen so stop freaking out about it," she started to shake. "You're not helping my nerves, Shane. The whole thing was scary enough. I don't need you filling my head with could have been's."

Shane was across the room before either of them knew what happened. He pulled her into his arms and just held her close. She was shaking uncontrollably now. Shane wanted to shake himself. He'd been so stupid. He'd been angry and afraid and cruel to the one woman he couldn't stop loving. And she could have easily died out there saving his little girl. "I'm sorry. I'm so sorry I yelled at you." He took her hand and led her to the couch. He had to push aside her clothing, but then he sat down, pulling her down next to him. "You had to be a wreck after that and I jumped right in and made everything so much worse. I don't deserve it but do you think you can ever forgive me for that. I can't believe you pulled that snake off your boot and tossed it in the river," he smiled. "You Melissa. I've never seen anyone as scared as you are of snakes and you pulled a rattlesnake off your boot. From the size of those holes, it must have been a large one."

"It was about three feet," Melissa admitted. Somehow, Shane had made her feel safe again. Something she hadn't felt since she approached the lake and saw Megan frozen like a statue. "You should be proud of Megan. She was so brave. She broke down afterwards, when she thought I was going to die, but the whole time she was so courageous. And that kid is good with a horse. Trigger wanted to run, but Megan held him back until I disposed of that awful thing and jumped on back with her. You have a very special little girl."

"Yes I do," Shane agreed as he rested his head against the back of the couch. "You're pretty special too. Not many women could have done what you did out there. We both know you could have been killed. There was no guarantee your boots would save you and you knew it. But you still risked your own life to save my child, Kristy's child," he paused and sobered. "I was wrong. I never should have kept you from her. I thought I was protecting her, but instead I just hurt her more. She thought you were avoiding her because you didn't like her. That blasted woman filled her mind with nonsense. I never know when something I do is going to validate Kristy's spiteful ramblings."

"Megan told me her mom said she was unlikeable. She believed her and thought her mom was right when I kept avoiding her. I didn't know, or I would have been more careful. How could her own mother say such hurtful things to her child?" Melissa was getting angry again. "I hate that woman. Shane, I never believed I could have so much anger and hatred inside me, but I absolutely hate her. And I don't think I'll ever find it in myself to forgive her for what she's done. Not to me, not to you and certainly not to that innocent child."

Shane smiled. "Join the club," he said ruefully. "But enough about Kristy. She's out of our lives for good. My point is that Megan needs you. I was wrong. My forcing you to stay away from her has only hurt her more. If you won't stay for me, please stay for her. I think you could really help her, if you're willing that is."

"How?" Melissa asked hesitantly. She knew it wouldn't take much for Shane to convince her to stay, even though she truly believed she should go.

"Well, Megan likes you. She respects you, especially now that you demonstrated how fearless you are," he grinned.

"Whatever," she punched his arm playfully.

"You are. I am proud of Megan, she listened to me and did exactly what I told her to do if she ever encountered a snake. But I'm also proud of you. I will never be able to repay you for what you did today. Megan couldn't have lasted much longer. Standing there like that was getting harder and harder for her. She never would have lasted until I got back and Cora wouldn't have made it to the lake. Maybe this will convince her she needs to have that surgery. She's afraid of it, but she knows she needs it. Anyway, I'm proud of you too. I know you Melissa and I know how hard that was for you. Which is why you need to stay. I'd like to give my daughter a chance to get to know you. I'd like her to have one good example in her life. You are the best mother I know. I want Megan to know there are good mothers out there. I also think you can help her understand what her mother told her was nonsense. I didn't know how mean and vengeful Kristy was. If I had, I would have made her go away long before I did. I can't undo that now, but if you're willing to help me out I think you might be the one person that can give Megan back a little self-confidence."

"Shane, that's a lot of responsibility. What if I hurt her instead of help her?" Melissa asked, truly worried.

"You won't," Shane said confidently. "I know you. You don't have it in you to hurt a child."

"You're wrong. I already hurt Megan once." Melissa was still ashamed of herself for that one. "And while we're on the subject I want to apologize to you for everything I said. I was so wrong and I didn't even believe those things. I don't know what got into me. And I don't blame you for hating me for it. Especially now that I've met your mother."

"I've already forgiven you for that," Shane lied. The things she said still hurt, but he knew he'd forgive her in time.

"Liar," she accused. "You don't forgive and forget that easily. But I really am sorry."

"Then you can make it up to me by staying a little longer," Shane pressed. He couldn't explain why, not even to himself, but he knew he had to get Melissa to stay. He felt like his entire future depended on it.

Melissa took a deep breath and let it out slowly. "Okay, I'll stay a little longer. But I won't make any promises about how long. When I feel it's time to go, you have to let me go."

"I'm not making any promises either," Shane said, grinning. "Will you try to stick around long enough for me to smooth things over with Jeremy?"

"I told you, he's mad but he'll get passed it. He never stays angry for long," Melissa said confidently.

"I'm not so sure. He called me a bully," Shane said, clearly hurt by the accusation. "And he said his father told him he never had to be nice to bullies."

Melissa was surprised by that. Maybe Jeremy was more upset than she originally believed. "I'll talk to him tomorrow. Most of it has to do with me. He's so protective of me. You made me cry, so

Jeremy is lashing out. You're not a bully Shane I know that and I'll make sure Jeremy does too. Trust me, things will be back to normal soon. It might take a couple days, but like I said, Jeremy doesn't hold a grudge and he forgives pretty quickly," she smiled. "He gets that from me, not you."

"Point taken," Shane admitted. He didn't forgive easily and he knew it. That wasn't always a bad thing, but sometimes maybe it was. He stood. "I'll get out of your hair. You have a lot of work ahead of you. It looks like you need to unpack."

"Funny," Melissa said, laughing as Shane walked out the door.

Chapter Nine

Melissa sipped her coffee and tried not to be obvious about her ogling. Shane was standing next to the corral in those hunky jeans she loved so much. He was wearing his work boots this morning and a tight blue t-shirt that hugged his muscles and showed off his wide shoulders. She loved the way that man looked in anything really, but especially dressed like he was today. It had been over a month since she'd rescued Megan at the lake. Things were definitely better. Most nights she and Jeremy ate dinner at the big house with Shane and Megan. Shane encouraged Megan to spend time with Melissa whenever Melissa would allow it. From the outside looking it, they almost looked like a happy little family. But Melissa wasn't happy. She wanted more. She wanted Shane. He was friendly and thoughtful, but distant with her. She hated it.

She'd talked to Pete the day before about the plumbing project at her home. He'd told her it would be at least another month. Something about parts that were on back order and at least three weeks out. She couldn't believe the project was taking so long. On one hand, she was grateful for the delay. She kept telling herself if she had enough time she could make Shane love her again. On the other hand, being so close and knowing he was just out of reach was driving her insane. She glanced back at Shane when she heard his husky voice. She was too far away to understand what he was saying, but she could tell it was some kind of warning. He was guiding a teenage neighbor while he tried to train his horse. Shane was good at this. She knew he could be trusted. Somehow Shane always knew when a horse had reached its limit.

Just as she had that thought, Shane vaulted over the railing and approached the duo in the round corral. Melissa watched in horror as Shane ordered the kid off the horse. The boy had just touched the ground when the horse reared up on its hind legs and snorted in anger. Shane was right there, holding the lead rope and trying to calm the large animal. Melissa ran for the pen. Just as she reached the wooden fence, the horse rushed forward. His front leg collided with Shane's shoulder. Melissa let out a gasp. The horse was so big, it could kill Shane if it tried. She was about to call out to him when Matt placed a hand on her arm. She shot him a quick glance then returned her attention to Shane.

"I know it looks bad, but Shane has it under control. Whatever you do, don't cause a distraction. That could be more harmful than anything that horse does in there." Matt lifted a leg and casually placed it on the bottom rung of the corral.

"But..." she started then stopped when she saw the look on Matt's face. She wanted to scream at him, demand he get in the corral with Shane and help him. But she knew Matt was right, any loud noise, any panicked statement from her, could distract Shane. That would give the horse a chance to win this battle. And it was a battle. Both man and beast were jockeying for control. Melissa was confident Shane would win. He wouldn't give up until he did. She also knew his shoulder could be broken in several places. She turned toward the sound of a car and saw Cora slowly make her way toward the corral. Then she saw Hank move from the shadows of the barn and follow Cora.

Cora didn't say a word. She just stood there, face tight, hands clenched, worry written all over her face. At least Melissa wasn't the only one sensible enough to worry about the stubborn man. Just as she was about to look away and concentrate on Shane again, she saw Hank move in next to Cora and take her hand. The reaction was instant. Cora visibly relaxed. The only indication she was still feeling some tension was the tight grip she had on Hank's hand. They both stood there, silent and stoic as they watched Shane try to regain control.

The teenager climbed out of the pen and moved in beside Matt. "I don't know what I did wrong. Everything seemed fine then all of a sudden Shane jumped the fence and told me to get off the horse, gentle and slow. I had no idea Thunder was even upset."

"Don't sweat it kid," Matt said, placing a hand on the boy's shoulder. "Shane could see it in his eyes. You were on his back. There's no way you could have known and you didn't do anything wrong. Thunder's still learning. This happened a lot when we first started, remember?"

"But I thought we were passed all this," the boy countered.

"Not yet. Thunder is testing the waters. He knows what he's supposed to do, he's just rebelling a little. Shane will show him, don't you worry. Shane won't leave that pen until Thunder learns his boundaries," Matt assured the student.

Melissa continued to watch as Thunder jerked at the lead, stomped his front hoofs and snorted. He reared up one more time, then the change began. Slowly, the horse stopped bucking. Then, a ripple ran over the horses back and his nostrils were no longer flaring. Shane walked the horse twice around the pen then, in one fluid motion slid his foot into the stirrup and swung onto the horses back. The reaction was instant. Thunder reared up, then just as quickly stomped his feet to the ground causing dust to swirl around him. Shane winced at the impact, but held on. Thunder tried the move one more time. When that didn't work he began frantically bucking around the pen. He was leaping into the air and arching his back in an attempt to knock Shane out of the saddle. Shane held on. Melissa was now gripping the fence so hard her knuckles were white. She was sure Shane was going to get hurt again, or worse killed.

Her fear turned to annoyance when she looked into Shane's eyes and realized he was laughing. The moron was having fun. He was sitting on close to a 1000 pound monster that was doing its best to kill him and the idiot was laughing. Shane's face sobered when the horse pivoted around and slammed into the side of the pen. Shane's thigh collided with the top rung. He was able to hold on, but just barely. Shane jerked on the reins and forced the horse back into the middle of the pen. A few moments later Melissa watched as the horse begin to calm again. He gradually stopped bucking then he raised his head and shook it back and forth a couple times. When Shane retained his firm grip on the reins, the horse slowed and began to walk calmly around the pen. Shane circled half a dozen times then directed the horse to the middle of the pen and slid to the ground.

He calmly walked to Matt and handed him the reins. "Do me a favor and take him to the barn. He's had enough for one day." Then Shane turned to the teenager, "Good job, Mike. When we started I told you it was important that you follow my direction at all times, no questions, no arguing. Today you saw why I was so adamant on that point."

Mike nodded. "I still don't understand what I did wrong," he was looking at the ground.

"Hey," Shane said and waited for Mike to look up. "You didn't do anything wrong. Thunder's a strong, stubborn horse. We've come a long way with him, but we're not finished here. That's why I haven't let you take him home yet. I won't until I'm sure he won't do that while you're on a pleasant afternoon ride. In return I need a promise from you. I don't want you riding him unless I'm here with you. That's vital. Do you understand?"

"I promise," Mike said sincerely. "After today, there's no way I'd take that kind of risk. I was taken completely by surprise."

"Good," Shane said patting Mike on the back. "Now, head to the barn and help Matt cool down that beauty in there. He's a magnificent horse. When we're done here, you're going to be the envy of all your friends. Part of that is taking care of him first. Always brush him down after every ride no matter what. No rushing off to a ballgame and neglecting him for the guys. Owning a horse means being responsible."

"Yes sir," Mike promised just before he ran for the barn.

Shane turned and spotted Melissa. She was clearly annoyed. He hadn't realized she'd been watching him out there, but there was nothing he could do about it now. He knew he should say something to her, give her some kind of assurance that he was never in any real danger when Cora spoke.

"Get inside so I can care for that leg," then she stomped ahead, clearly expecting Shane to follow.

Hidden Lakes

Shane stepped into the mud room and moved behind a bench. He knew there was a pair of sweats he'd cut off for shorts in here somewhere. He was still searching when Melissa stepped into the house. The daggers she shot him surprised him. She was truly pissed. He wasn't sure what had gotten into her, but he didn't have time to ask. She walked passed him and stomped through the kitchen. Seconds later he heard a chair slide across the tile. She must be waiting at the table. He shot another frantic glance around the room and spotted his shorts. Once he carefully removed his boots, he slid off his Levi's and pulled on the shorts. Then he casually strolled through the kitchen and sat down next to Melissa. His thigh was already bruised. It looked bad now, but Shane knew by the time he shut down for the night it would be hideous. Good thing the women were seeing it now. He never wore shorts, so once Cora satisfied herself that nothing was broken he'd be in the clear.

Cora poked and prodded but eventually declared him free of any breaks. She straightened and went to the freezer to pull out an ice pack. "I know you have things to do but humor me," she said sternly as she handed him the large pack.

Shane placed it on his leg and winced at the cold. He knew it would help keep down the swelling, but he really didn't have time for this.

When Cora moved to the sink and methodically began scrubbing dishes Melissa spoke up. "What about his shoulder?"

Cora whipped around and scowled at Shane. "What about your shoulder?"

Shane gave a shrug with his uninjured shoulder, but didn't say a word.

"Take off the shirt," Cora demanded.

"Cora," Shane protested.

"Don't Cora me," she barked. "A grown man ought to know better," she mumbled as she stared Shane down.

"Fine," he said, glaring at Melissa. The woman needed to learn to keep her big trap shut. He stood, peeled off his shirt and plopped back onto the chair.

Cora moved in and once again performed her poking and prodding ritual. She frowned and pressed backwards. Shane winced. "I think you have at least one cracked bone in there, maybe more. We need to put that thing in a sling."

"No way," Shane said, standing in protest. "You know I can't work in one of those and I'll just take it off the second I get out of your sight. Just slap some of that hot cream stuff you have on it and let me get back to work."

"Stubborn, bull headed, recalcitrant, obstinate fool," Cora said turning back towards the sink.

"Cora honey," Shane said sweetly. "You sound like you're helping Megan with her vocabulary words. I don't need a thesaurus, I need a cook. Any chance I could get some breakfast before noon?"

"Look," she spun and faced Shane with a glare. "Just because you're a headstrong, stubborn fool doesn't mean I'm going to tolerate your sass. Get out of my kitchen. Go fix something. I'll call you when the food is ready. Until then, I don't want to see hide nor hair of you. I need some space before I throttle you."

Shane laughed then moved in close and gave Cora a loving kiss on her forehead. "I love you too Cora and always will," then he grabbed his jeans and headed for his room.

Cora turned to Melissa. "That boy is going to be the death of me yet. When I shewed him off my roof I thought I'd seen the worst of it. Now I know it was child's play compared to the things he tries as a man." She shook her head and began to crack eggs.

Melissa smiled and stood. "I'll see you in a few hours."

"Aren't you going to have breakfast?" Cora frowned.

"Can't," Melissa called over her shoulder as she walked toward the door. "I've got to get to town. I want to catch Pete this morning before he gets involved in something and doesn't have time for my questions."

"Tell him hello," Cora called out then watched as Melissa walked to the cabin and disappeared inside.

It was seven o'clock before Shane got back to the house that night. He was tired and sore and all he wanted to do was suffer through a shower then climb into bed and sleep for days. He wouldn't of course. The ranch wouldn't run itself, but the thought sounded good. He stepped inside and cringed when he saw three pairs of eyes watching him. Melissa was standing by the sink and the two kids were patiently sitting at the table, waiting for him no doubt. He was starving, maybe he could get through a meal without anyone seeing just how much pain he was really in.

"Dad, are you okay?" Megan asked. She'd seen her dad hurt before, but it wasn't usually this bad. "Matt told me and Jeremy how you got kicked by the horse, but you walk like old man Morris," she was frowning now.

"Thanks Meg," Shane winked as he sank into a chair. "I appreciate the vote of confidence. Old man Morris is ninety two." Shane glanced at Jeremy and saw the concerned look on his son's face. "I'm fine, just a little sore. Just a little too much riding after a minor injury, that's all. My muscles have tightened up. I'll be much better in the morning. After dinner I think I'll take a quick shower then drop into bed. I promise, I'm fine."

Melissa set a metal pan on the table and removed the cover. "Cora made finger food," she set the steaming lid on the counter and took her place at the table. "Chicken fingers with that amazing honey mustard she makes, potato wedges with cheese and corn bread. Go ahead and dig in. We're being casual tonight."

The instant Jeremy finished eating he bolted out of his chair and headed for the sink, plate in hand. Shane had noticed this right away. Jeremy was no slob. He assumed Melissa had taught him to clean up after himself. He was probably twenty before he learned that lesson. Megan was pretty good about clearing the table, but since Jeremy had entered their lives she'd been spot on. Shane knew there was still a little competition brewing there, but he figured they'd work it out among themselves eventually.

"After you rinse your plate, I want you to go up and get ready for bed. It's late and you have school tomorrow," Melissa said absently.

Jeremy stopped mid stride. He turned back and looked at his mother. "Am I staying at the big house tonight?"

"What?" Melissa asked. "Oh, yes. I thought we would all stay up here tonight. Shane's having trouble getting around. I think it would be a good idea for me to stay close just in case he needs anything later."

"Okay," Jeremy said as he ran from the room and up the stairs. Megan was close on his heels.

Shane was watching Melissa. This was news to him. He wondered what she had in mind. He was sure Cora had left some of her liniment somewhere. That was really all he needed.

Melissa noticed Shane watching her and smiled. "I assume that is okay with you, isn't it?"

"Sure," Shane agreed, using all his effort to push himself from the chair. "I'm heading to bed myself. I guess I'll see you in the morning." He was as upright as he was going to get so he slowly made his way to the stairs. He had ascended half of them before he realized Melissa was behind him. He would have made a wisecrack, but if he stopped concentrating on walking, he might take a tumble. The very last thing he needed right now was to take a rolling trip down the stairs. Once they were in his room, Shane lowered himself onto the bed. Melissa instantly went into the bathroom and turned on the faucet. She came out mixing something in a bowl. Shane assumed it must be Cora's secret liniment.

"Shane, I needed to talk to you about something if that's okay." She glanced up, but returned her attention to swirling the stuff in the bowl. "I know you're tired but it won't take long."

"Sure," he said wondering how he was going to get his cowboy boots off. Normally it wasn't a problem but he couldn't lean over right now.

"I went into town today," Melissa began. "While I was there, I stopped by and talked to Pete."

"Oh?" Shane asked, looking up to see her face. "How's the house coming?"

"Slow," Melissa said with a sigh. "Pete had to order more parts. He said they are on backorder and the soonest they'll be here is three weeks. Can you believe that? They're guaranteed by six, but I don't think we'll have to wait that long." She glanced up at him and her frown deepened. "You're still dressed."

The corner of Shane's mouth quirked. "So are you."

"Funny," Melissa said, unamused. She walked to the bed and dropped down in front of Shane then immediately went to work pulling off his boots. "Anyway, that's not the problem. Pete had to get into one of the walls. I'm assuming my parents had a mouse problem because the old wiring is covered in that fabric type material and this particular section is a hazard. The mice chewed away a huge area, exposing the wires. Pete thinks it's a fire hazard. He threatened to call the Fire Marshall if I didn't agree to have it fixed on my own. I can't count the number of times Mitch responded to a fire that was caused by electrical sparks from old wiring." She dropped the boots to the floor and stood. Without the slightest warning she began to pull his arms from the sleeves of his shirt. "My point is that I'm going to have to fix the wiring before Jeremy and I can move back in."

Shane was amused and touched at the same time. He couldn't remember a time when anyone had been there for him like this. He took care of his people, not the other way around. He wondered what Melissa was going to do when they got to his pants.

"So, I know it's a lot to ask, but I was wondering if you'd let Jeremy and I stay at the cabin awhile longer." She pulled the shirt over Shane's head then glanced at his pants.

Before she could go to work on them, Shane took her hand. "Melissa, I told you to stay as long as you need to. If I had my way, you'd live there permanently. I mean it. I like having you close by like this. If the parts take six weeks to come in, they take six weeks. I really don't care. In fact, I hope they do."

Melissa took a deep breath then slowly let it out. "Thank you," she finally said sitting on the bed next to him. "I'm not sure what to do about the wiring. Pete thinks that now is a good time to do a complete electrical overhaul too. He might be right. I mean Pete's crew already took out several sections of one wall. If I hire an electrician to come in now, I won't have to repair the drywall twice."

Shane reached out and took her hand. "What has you worried? Is it staying at the cabin or finances? You know I'd help if you need it."

"No," Melissa said adamantly. "I mean I know you would, but I won't let you do that. You're already doing way too much. I'd try to insist you take rent for my extended stay, but I already know you won't do that. I'll pay for the electrician. I just feel like I'm taking advantage of your hospitality. I've already been out here so long."

"Technically, I'm not really doing anything. From the moment you moved here you refused to accept any child support payments. I'd say it all equals out, in fact I feel like I still owe you. How about we agree that you can stay as long as needed. What I mean is if the electrician gets in there and finds a major problem that is going to take months, I don't want you to think you have to come

210

to me and ask permission to stay. The cabin has been vacant for years. I don't have anyone knocking down my door to spend the night there any time soon. It's yours until your house is livable again. In return, I won't pressure you about the support payments. Agreed?"

Melissa considered. She wanted to jump for joy. She wanted to stay in Shane's cabin, on Shane's ranch, for the rest of her life. But she wasn't willing to accept that offer. On one hand, this was what she was hoping for. On the other, it was going to make leaving so much harder. "Agreed," she finally told him. Jeremy was happy here. Even if she hadn't wanted to stay so badly, she would have done it for Jeremy. "Now, are you going to get out of those jeans or do I need to help you with that, too?" Melissa casually glanced around for the bowl she'd been mixing. She couldn't look at Shane, if she did, he'd know exactly what she was thinking and what she wanted. This chemistry between them was going to be the death of her, she just knew it.

Shane stood and unfastened his jeans then he slowly lowered them from his hips. It wasn't too difficult, once the tension was loosened, they fell to the floor. All he had to do was sit on the bed and kick them off his feet. He pushed his way back and rested against the headboard.

Melissa turned around and gasped. "Shane!" She rushed back to the bed and ran a finger over the huge bruise across his upper body. It was at least the size of a basketball. "I knew you should have gone to the doctor. This is horrible."

Shane took Melissa's hand and brought her fingers to his lips. "I'm fine. Just rub some of that gunk on me and I'll be good as new in the morning."

"Not likely," she said placing the bowl on the night stand. She studied him for a long moment before she spoke again. "Are you walking hunched over like that because you hurt your back? I mean I saw how forceful that horse was when it pounded its front legs into the ground. That had to jar your back out of alignment."

"It's nothing," Shane said out of habit.

"Turn over onto your stomach," Melissa ordered.

Shane smiled. "You gonna ride me this time? Because as fun as that sounds sweetheart, I have to tell you I don't think I'm up for it tonight," he grinned. "No pun intended."

"Of course there was. Just turn over. I'm going to fix your back." Melissa gave his side a little shove.

"No offense, but last time I checked you ain't no doctor," Shane didn't move.

"But you are a cowboy. Even your speech is digressing. Shane, just shut up and let me take care of you for a change. You're so good at taking care of everyone else. Tonight, I'm going to take care of you. Now turn," Melissa ordered.

Shane felt another tug at his heart. Melissa just voiced the very thoughts he'd had only moments ago. He slowly pushed himself away from the headboard and lowered his body to the bed.

Melissa immediately straddled Shane. A strange sensation emulated throughout her body. She tried to ignore it. This was medicinal, not intimate. But oh how she wanted intimate with this man. She shook her head to clear the stray thoughts and focused on his back. Then she gently ran her fingers up his spine. "This might hurt a little," she told him before she popped his back into alignment.

Shane was enjoying the feel of Melissa straddling his thighs, he liked the feel of her hands running up and down his back even more. He didn't like the pain that surged through his body at the same time he heard a loud popping sound. "Ouch!" he yelled. "Dammit woman, are you trying to kill me?"

Melissa laughed. "You big baby," she joked. "It feels better now, doesn't it?"

Shane was about to tell her hell no, it didn't feel better when he realized it did. Okay, so she knew what she was doing. That didn't mean he had to compliment her on her bedside manner. "Thanks," he finally said grudgingly.

Melissa was still laughing as she climbed from the bed and went to the bathroom. She returned with a bottle of hot oil and proceeded to give him a thorough massage. Little by little she felt him relax. His muscles were so tight, but not for long she was sure of it.

Shane was skeptical at first, but the longer Melissa rubbed at his back, the more relaxed he got. He was so relaxed he was having a hard time keeping his eyes open. He was pretty sure he had drifted off and wondered how long he'd been out when he heard her soft voice next to his ear. That sexy little breath she let out tickled the sensitive nerve endings and made him want her even more. He may have been tempted to flip her around and have his way with her, but he knew his body wasn't in any condition for that kind of exertion.

"Roll over sleepy head," Melissa whispered. "I still need to rub the liniment into the bruises then you can crash. I need your help for just another minute," then she pressed lightly on his arm and tried to help him roll. It took some effort, but once Shane was on his back, she scooped out some of the goo and immediately applied it to his thigh. She was able to smear it pretty consistently with the small stir stick she was using, but she thought it would be better if she rubbed it in a little. Once his thigh was done, she went to work on his shoulder. They were both bad, but the shoulder looked worse than the leg. She was pretty sure Cora had been right, Shane had at least a cracked bone in there maybe two. The man was impossible. He needed a doctor, but his ego wouldn't let him admit it. Well, she had a solution for that. She happened to know a doctor that made house calls. Well he did for close friends anyway. And she figured he was about due for a social call. She'd have him here tomorrow night for dinner. Shane was at least going to have medication if he wouldn't accept proper care.

Shane moaned and shifted, then fell back into a deep, steady sleep. Melissa wasn't sure what to do now. She'd been on autopilot all night. She cared for Shane the same way she had a million times for Jeremy. It was second nature but now that he was out, she was torn. Should she go down and sleep on the couch? Should she try to stay up all night and watch over him? What? She decided staying up was out of the question. She was too tired and would never make it. Going downstairs was also out. She'd never hear Shane if he needed something. She glanced at the bed and made her decision. It was a king sized bed, there was plenty of room. She'd just sleep with him, fully clothed of course. Her will power was only so strong. She walked around the bottom of the bed, pulled down the blanket and climbed inside.

Shane woke at dawn, the way he always did but froze when he felt a warm body snuggled against him. He couldn't remember the last time he'd awoken with a woman in his bed. Well, actually he could. It had been over eight years ago and it had been Melissa. He glanced over his shoulder and smiled. Memories of the night before flooded his mind. She took all this caretaker junk seriously. The woman was beautiful, especially while she slept. She looked so peaceful and innocent. His hand itched to reach out and brush those silky strands from her face, but he couldn't. If he did, he wasn't sure the touch would end there and he had work to do. He'd been almost useless yesterday. Things that should have taken twenty minutes took half the damn day. He sat up, expecting his back to give him fits, but it didn't. In fact, his back felt fine. Oh, it was a little sore. His muscles were tight and he'd have to be careful but Melissa was a miracle worker. He tested his shoulder and winced. That was going to take longer. He was pretty sure he'd fractured a bone, maybe two or three but they'd heal in time. He ran a finger over the large bruise on his thigh. That one was sore, but luckily nothing had been broken. It felt a hundred times better this morning, but by the time he stumbled in for dinner it might be back to the way it was last night. He shrugged, oh well. He figured this was the price he had to pay for being a rancher. Life could be much worse.

The phone rang and Shane snatched it up before the noise woke up the kids. "What?" he grumbled into the line.

"Good morning to you too," Sheriff Swenson grumbled back.

"Hey Joe," Shane said a little more politely. "Why are you calling my house this early on a weekday?"

"I tried to get a hold of Melissa, but she's not answering. I need her to alter her schedule a little. Do you know where I can find her?" he asked hopefully.

"Just a minute. I'll get her," Shane paused, that sounded like they had something going. "Uh, I had a little mishap with a horse. Melissa and Jeremy stayed at the house to keep an eye on me. You know women, I think she was convinced I'd fall into a coma and never wake up. Anyway, I think she's still asleep. Let me go wake her and I'll have her call you back. You at the office or on the cell?"

"Cell," Joe said casually. "I'm actually at home, but I don't want the ringing to wake the wife. A happy home and all that, anyway have Mel give me a call right away."

"Will do," Shane said, amused. He returned the receiver to the base and glanced over to discover Melissa staring at him in confusion.

"Was that for me?" she asked sitting up.

"Yeah," Shane turned to her, before he realized what he was doing he'd reached out and tucked a strand of hair behind her ear. "You need to call Sheriff Swenson. He said something about a schedule change."

"Well I was right here, why didn't you just give me the phone?" she scowled at him.

"I didn't think you'd want him to know you spent the night in my bed," Shane smiled. "It's a small town. People tend to talk."

"Oh! Right," Melissa said, sitting up. She glanced down at her wrinkled shirt and jeans. One leg was twisted and riding up to her knee. Her t-shirt was also twisted and pulled up just below her bra line. She quickly jerked it down and narrowed her eyes at Shane when she saw he was laughing at her. "Give me the phone."

"Call his cell. He doesn't want the little lady disturbed by a ringing phone," Shane handed her the receiver and left the room.

Melissa wanted to call out to him, tell him to come back. She was curious about his bruises and wanted to check them before he left for the day, but she was too late. Joe's voice in her ear startled her and made her jump. "Oh, hello Joe. Shane said you called about a schedule change?"

Melissa was disappointed when she hung up the phone. She felt bad for Tina's mother. Susan had fallen again and was back at the hospital. Tina was with her and would need more time off work. Melissa had sympathy for them both, but she really didn't want to work another afternoon shift. The last time she'd covered had been almost unbearable. By the time she got home at night, Jeremy was already in bed. She had a little free time every morning, but Jeremy was at school during the day. When she worked for Tina, she always felt like she was neglecting her son. Oh well, there was nothing she could do about it now. She'd agreed to come in late and work the night shift again tonight. At least it wasn't for a full two weeks like last time. Just tonight and maybe another night in a few days when Tina's mother was transferred back to rehab. She could handle that. It would be selfish to complain.

Melissa climbed out of bed and wondered what she was going to do all day. First she was going to call Doc Jones. Hopefully he'd still come over and check on Shane. She wouldn't be here, but he knew Cora. If he knew how important it was, he'd stop by. She was sure of it. That would take all of about five minutes. How was she going to pass the time for several more hours until she went into the office? It was a hot day, maybe she'd go to the lake. She wondered if Shane had a horse she could borrow. She slid out of bed and headed downstairs. Cora hadn't arrived yet but she hadn't expected her. The sun was barely up. Melissa moved to the large windows and sighed. It would be so wonderful to wake up here, in this house, next to Shane, every morning. She had always loved the ranch, but now that she was older she appreciated the beauty and serenity even more. She stepped into the kitchen prepared to make coffee and realized Shane had already taken care of that. She poured herself a cup, dumped in sugar and cream and headed for the porch. The temperature was just right this time of day.

Melissa sank into the comfortable swing and enjoyed the morning. There was a slight breeze in the air. As she looked out over the alfalfa field, she realized it was nearly ready to harvest. The stems were close to three feet tall and the small purple buds were just beginning to form. She thought the purple hue flowing in the wind made the entire field look like it was floating just above ground. The only sounds she could hear were chirping birds and the river flowing softly in the background. Life just couldn't get better than this. She heard a sound behind her and realized the kids were up. Well, so much for a relaxing morning. The next thirty minutes would be hectic chaos. Then, once the bus pulled away the heat would set in and she'd have to find an escape. Today her escape was going to be the lake.

Melissa stood at the end of the drive and watched the school bus clatter down the road. The district really should invest in a new one. They were transporting kids for heaven's sake. Maybe she'd mention it to Shane. He had pull in this town. If anyone could get a new bus for the kids it was him. Knowing him, he'd just buy the darn thing himself. Maybe she'd need to rethink that strategy. She ran a hand through her tangled hair and headed for the cabin. She wanted to change into her suit, pack a few needed supplies then she was heading for the lake. With every passing minute, she seemed to get more and more excited about her plans. She'd take a book and a soft blanket and plenty of snacks and liquid. She had a few hours to kill before she'd need to shower and head for town. Just enough time so she wouldn't be rushed, but not so much she'd get burned and worn out. The only way today could be any better is if Shane was going to join her. Or Jeremy and Megan. But she couldn't justify keeping them home. They only had two days left, then Cora was going to be in for the surprise of her life. Melissa knew firsthand what a handful Jeremy was during summer break.

Maybe spending his time on the ranch would help. And if he behaved himself, Shane might take the kids out occasionally to help with the chores. "One can always hope," Melissa said quietly to herself. She continued up the drive and was surprised to see Cora's car. How had she snuck in without Melissa seeing her? Maybe she entered from the back way and stopped by the barn before heading for the house. Melissa picked up her pace and was just pulling open the screen door when she heard voices. No, not voices, laughter and whispering. Intimate laughter. She looked up just in time to see Hank push Cora against the counter and slide his hands around her waist. His mouth was on its way down to connect with Cora's lips when Melissa bolted. She was so shocked she almost dropped the screen and let it slam shut, but she caught it just in time. She gently closed the door and ran for the cabin. By the time she opened her door and slipped inside she was laughing. Cora and Hank had finally made the move. Well, good for them. According to Shane, Hank had wanted Cora since the moment he laid eyes on her. Cora had been a single mother with responsibilities at the time. Shane assumed she didn't want to expose her kids to a new man in the house, so she rebuffed anyone that asked.

But Cora's kids were all grown now and she was free to consort with anyone she chose. Melissa was glad she chose Hank. You couldn't help but love the man. He was your typical rugged cowboy. All bark and no bite, but man could the man bark. All the men respected him, including Shane. And he was so good with the kids. Megan obviously adored him, but over the past couple weeks she'd noticed that Jeremy was warming up to him as well.

After changing into her favorite bikini, Melissa rushed through the house, packing up the things she was sure she would need. Then she made a second sweep and added things she probably didn't. She glanced at the clock, but realized she hadn't paid attention to the time when she arrived so there was no way to know if Hank would be gone. Maybe she'd just swing by the barn and as nonchalant as can be, do a little inquiring. The moment she stepped out the door, she decided today was her lucky day. She spotted Hank as he turned the corner and entered the barn. The man was whistling and he had a definite bounce to his step. Apparently the kiss had gone well. Now the coast was clear and she could check on Cora, stuff her bag with goodies and head out for a day of fun, fun, fun.

Cora looked up at the sound of the door. She'd expected Shane and was grateful it was Melissa. "Good morning," she called, trying not to sound too cheerful. She didn't want the entire world to know she'd just been thoroughly kissed by the best looking man on the ranch. She grinned. Shane might argue with that and he might be right, but Hank was definitely a close second. "Did you get coffee?"

"Had some earlier," Melissa called from the pantry. "Do you have any cookies in here?"

Cora moved to the walk in pantry and gently pushed Melissa aside. "They're right here. The same place they've been for over thirty years. What's wrong with you today?"

"Nothing," Melissa said, forcing herself not to smile. "And you haven't lived here for thirty years, Cora. Shane's only thirty five. I might be dense about some things, but I do know Shane didn't buy the ranch when he was five."

"What are you doing, anyway?" Cora asked impatiently.

"Now Cora," Melissa turned to face her friend. She feigned surprise at the whisker burns on Cora's cheek. "What's that?" she pointed at the red mark.

"What?" Cora asked as her hand flew to her face. A face that was growing redder and redder by the second.

"Cora, are you blushing?" Melissa asked mischievously.

"No," Cora said as she abruptly turned and moved in front of the stove. "It's just the heat, that's all."

"Really?" Melissa moved in behind her. "That's funny, it doesn't look like the stoves been on yet today. My, my Cora. I have to wonder, why are you blushing? Is there something you'd like to confess?"

"Oh, very well," Cora said in defeat. "I have nothing to hide. Those are whisker burns."

Melissa widened her eyes in pretend shock. "You mean a man? You Cora? You've finally figured out that there are men out there? Real men with whiskers and everything? Men who enjoy a little hanky-panky every once in a while. You did engage in hanky-panky didn't you? I mean what good is a man if you don't at least get a quickie in the kitchen every once in a while."

Cora scowled. "Hanky-panky," she grumbled. "If you ask me, a lady ought not be talking about hanky-panky in the kitchen in mixed company."

Shane grinned. "What kind of hanky-panky? I've obviously missed something good."

"Nothing," Melissa said, opening the fridge to pull out a couple bottles of water. Then she reached around Shane and grabbed an apple.

"Where's the fire?" he asked, amused. Melissa was rushing around, clearly excited about something.

"No fire," Melissa said, turning to face Cora. "I think it's wonderful. That thing we were talking about. I think it's wonderful even if I shouldn't talk about it in mixed company. By the way, don't expect me for lunch or dinner today. I have to work late. So I'll just grab a bite on my break."

For the first time since entering the kitchen Shane noticed Melissa's attire. She was wearing jeans and boots, but she had on some skimpy bikini top and a thin white button down shirt that wasn't buttoned, it was tied across her ribs. She looked hot. And it was all he could do to take a step back rather than forward. Talk about hanky-panky in the kitchen. If Cora hadn't been there, he might just grab that slender waist of hers and teach her all about hanky-panky in the kitchen. He groaned and turned, hoping nobody heard him. "Are you going swimming?" he asked, trying to sound casual.

"Uh-huh," Melissa affirmed. "I was wondering if you had a spare horse I could borrow. I wanted to spend a couple hours at the lake before I have to head to work. By the way, that schedule change was for today. I have to cover for Tina again so I don't plan to be back until around eleven thirty or so. I was hoping Jer could stay up here with you again."

"Sure," Shane said, frowning. "But I don't like you driving home after dark like that. What if you broke down? You'd be a sitting duck once you got half a mile out of town. Maybe I should..."

"Maybe you should nothing," Melissa cut him off. "I'm a grown woman and I'm not stupid. I'm careful and I have a cell phone if I run into trouble. I promise I'll call you if the car breaks down. The chance of that is about a million to one though since the warranty is still good. Cars don't break down until after the warranty has expired. It's an auto industry conspiracy," she turned to Cora. "I stole the leftover chicken, hope that's okay. It travels well." Then she turned back to Shane, "Horse?"

"Uh…yeah," he said, dizzy after that conversation. "Maybe you shouldn't have any more coffee. I think your caffeine meter tapped out a mile ago."

Melissa ignored him. "I'll meet you in the barn," then she bounced out of the kitchen.

"Who was that and what did she do with Melissa?" Shane asked, reaching out to swipe a piece of toast.

"That was Melissa," Cora smiled. "I remember that girl. It's just been a really long time since she's peeked her head out and come alive. I like her that way. I think the last few years have been hard on that girl. It's good for her to get out and have a little fun."

Shane took the egg and cheese burrito Cora had slid onto a plate and considered. Melissa's life over the past few years hadn't been happy. "That reminds me, I dropped off some pictures over with Scott Johnson. I'm expecting him to call any day to tell me their ready. It's kind of a surprise for Melissa, will you make sure you don't tell her or accidentally send her over to pick them up for you? They're important and I want to give them to her at the right time."

"What are they?" Cora asked.

"Her wedding album and some other pictures that got damaged in the flood. She set them out to dry and then dropped the damaged ones into a box, I assume she planned on dealing with them later. I swiped the box and dropped them off with Scott. He was pretty confident he could either repair the damage or scan and reproduce most if not all of the pictures." Shane glanced out the window, he hated to think of Melissa's life with Mitch. "I could tell they were important to her. She was really sad when they got damaged. I wanted to do something nice for her and I think she'll really appreciate having them back."

Cora studied Shane. "Shane, I know how you feel about that girl."

Shane shook his head.

"I know, whether you want to admit it or not. Whether you want to act on those feelings or not is up to you. But I know how you feel," she said sternly. "If you are feeling threatened by a dead man, you're barking up the wrong tree there. Melissa did love that husband of hers. But she also loved you. No matter how good things were with her and Mitch, nobody will ever convince me they were better than those good times, those strong happy days, the two of you had together. It's just not possible. There's no reason to try to compete with a ghost. He's gone and you're here. Don't you ever forget that. And don't miss out on something that could be wonderful because of stupid pride or fear."

Shane forced a smile and turned to head for the door. "I gotta go make up for yesterday. Thanks for the burrito. Next time add a little sausage though."

Cora huffed. "You sound like Hank."

A thought struck Shane as he walked out the door. Was Melissa referring to Hank when she mentioned Hanky-Panky in the kitchen? Then he grinned. Knowing Melissa, she had. Something had happened in the kitchen and Melissa was playing on words. He wondered if Cora had caught on yet. Then he wondered how embarrassed she was going to be when she did.

Chapter Ten

Shane crested the hill and pulled Nico to a stop. Now that his back was in alignment again, he felt almost normal. He'd been able to accomplish a lot this morning. But ever since he'd seen Mel in that sexy bikini his mind had been on the lake. More to the point, on Mel and visions of her lounging by the lake in nothing but that damn suit. Now, here he was and he felt like a voyeur. She was so beautiful. He'd always loved her body and he still did. But even from here he could see she needed to put on a little weight. He'd noticed that the moment he'd seen her standing on her parents front porch. She was the same, but different. Losing her husband had clearly been hard on her.

Now, as he looked down at her, he assessed her again. He'd always loved those long legs and that round little butt. Her other assets weren't bad either but he didn't like seeing her ribs poke out like that. She needed some meat on her bones. He had hoped bringing her to the ranch would help, but maybe their tentative situation was making things worse. Nico shook his head, impatient.

Hidden Lakes

He wanted to run, or at the very least trot. But Shane had other ideas. He slid from Nico's back and dropped the reins. Shane knew the horse wouldn't leave without him. He'd wander a little, and get his fill of grass, maybe move down to the fresh stream near the base of the hill, but he wouldn't leave. Shane took a step forward, intending to walk down and join Melissa on that big soft blanket when he heard the thud of a horse running toward him. He strained to see the rider and recognized Matt.

"Hey boss," Matt called as he pushed his horse even harder.

Melissa heard the horse before she saw it, then she saw Matt rushing toward the top of the hill. As she shifted her attention, she saw Shane. How long had he been there, she wondered. She didn't really care. Shane could watch her all he wanted. That made her smile. Had Shane been watching her? If so, she was definitely making progress. She considered the past few days. There was no doubt things were improving between them. It was slow going, but progress none the less. But would it be enough? Would Shane's attraction to her, the chemistry they had always had for each other, be enough to get passed the hurt and betrayal both of them had felt? She honestly believed she was passed it already. Eight years and Cora's detailed description of long ago events had helped her put all the heartache and pain behind her and look towards her future. It was Shane that rarely forgave and never forgot. Knowing that made her wonder if they could ever have a real chance. But she wasn't giving up yet. Her eyes locked with Shane's, several seconds passed, then he turned and disappeared. Melissa thought about going after him for about half a second. Then she changed her mind. Matt had been pretty serious about something. Shane would be long gone by now and she needed to head back to the house. She was due at work in less than an hour. She hastily gathered her things and climbed on Molly's back. The horse was ancient. She had no spunk whatsoever and Melissa worried the old broad was going to have a heart attack and croak before she could reach the barn. She wished she had her own horse, but under the circumstances that would be a waste. Melissa had no idea how long she'd be staying here.

Just a few days ago, Shane confided in her about Jeremy's birthday gift. Shane had bought him a horse. He was expecting it to arrive any day now. At first Melissa was worried, but she'd warmed to the idea. Maybe she could take Jeremy's horse out next time she needed a ride. Her son would share with her, she knew he would. That would just have to be enough. She reached the barn, climbed off Molly, then she removed her gear and hung it in the tack room. She checked Molly's hoofs, pulled out a rock and spent a few minutes brushing her down. Once that was complete she led her to a stall, doubled checked to make sure there was plenty of water and hay, then headed for the cabin. She only had time for a ten minute shower. She pulled her hair into a pony tail, pulled on some jeans and a polo shirt and rushed out the door. She might be a couple minutes late, but with any luck she'd make that up on the drive.

* * * *

Melissa stepped outside and paused to take in the cool air. It was only nine thirty, barely dusk. She loved this time of night especially in rural Colorado. In Denver, dusk was still busy and noisy. Here in Hidden Lakes, things were so peaceful it was impossible not to be taken in by the sunset and the beauty all around. She headed for her car and tried not to feel guilty about leaving early. Joe was great to work for and she loved her job but the man was bossy. He had called her five minutes ago and told her she'd be fired if she wasn't out the door by nine-thirty. She'd rushed to finish up the letter she was working on and barely made it in time. She was sure the Sheriff would check the log first thing in the morning and she'd have some explaining to do if she disobeyed him. She smiled as she reached her car, then sighed. She hated the ritual she'd been forced to adopt as a matter of routine when leaving the station.

Melissa reached in her purse, pulled out her keys, then proceeded to inspect her car. It had been over a week since the last episode. Maybe the vandal was getting bored with her and had moved on. Not likely, she said to herself as she rounded the car and headed for the driver's door. She was just reaching for the handle when she heard a noise. Melissa pivoted at the popping sound, then her hand flew to her face as pain radiated across her right cheek bone. She felt something wet and realized she was bleeding. Melissa reached out and pulled her door as wide as it would go. As she started to duck inside, another pop sounded and she felt a stinging sensation on her left arm. She glanced down and realized she'd been shot again. She ducked inside and cringed when another pellet struck her window. At least the large pane didn't crack. The impact was more like a rock chip but she had to get out of here.

Melissa pulled her door shut, shoved the key into the ignition and started the engine. Once again she was thankful that she'd been able to keep the Escape when she'd had to sell off everything else. Having an unreliable vehicle in this situation would have been disastrous. She glanced around as she left the area, hoping to catch a glimpse of her attacker, but she couldn't see anyone. The streets were empty. She was sure it was Gloria. It had to be. Shane's mother was the only real enemy she had. Melissa knew the woman blamed her for Shane's hostility, but this was too much. The vandalism had been irritating and Melissa had considered a confrontation with the hag more than once, but shooting at her? Sure, it was only a pellet gun, but fixing the window was going to cost money and what if Melissa hadn't turned her head, that pellet could have struck her in the eye. She could have been permanently wounded.

Melissa fumed all the way home. She had planned to head straight to the cabin, but after the events of the night, she needed to see her son. Jeremy would be asleep already, but she could slip in and peek in the door. Seeing Jeremy sleeping peacefully would calm her nerves just a little, Melissa was sure of it. She pulled up to the front of Shane's large house and shut off the engine. After a quick glance in the mirror she rummaged around in her purse until she found a tissue. There was still blood on her face and she knew chances were good she'd encounter Shane once she stepped inside the house. Melissa was still dabbing at her wound when her door swung open. She screamed.

"Why so jumpy?" Shane asked, amused. His smile faded when Melissa turned to face him and he saw how pale she was. Then he noticed the wound on her face. "What happened?" he asked as he gently pulled her from the car.

"It's nothing," Melissa said, hoping she sounded casual. She was feeling anything but.

"Tell me," he insisted.

Melissa hesitated. How would Shane react if she told him she'd been shot at and she believed his mother was responsible?

Shane took her hand and led her into the kitchen. "Talk to me Mel," he pressured as he pushed her into a chair. He silently moved to the sink where he wet down a small towel and returned to kneel in front of her. He pressed the cloth gently to skin as he wiped the blood from her face.

Well, so much for cleaning up the evidence. "Someone shot me with a pellet gun after I left work," she said softly. "But it's nothing. Really, I'm not hurt that bad."

"Did they only shoot once?" Shane said, forcing himself to remain calm. Who would do something like that to a helpless woman as she left a police station of all places? It couldn't be random, could it?

"No," Melissa confessed as she pulled her shirt sleeve up and revealed the second wound. "I was only hit twice. There was a third pellet, but it hit the windshield. I'm going to have to get the chip repaired before it cracks, but I'm fine. No real damage done."

"No real damage?" Shane exploded. "Someone shot at you three times, Melissa? Did you report this to the police? How do you even know it was a pellet gun?"

"Of course I didn't report it," Melissa said instantly. "It's no big deal. I admit things are escalating, but really I'm not hurt that bad. It's nothing, really. I just wanted to peek in on Jeremy before I went to bed. I shouldn't have come here. Now you're upset. I really didn't mean to worry you. Let's just forget I was ever here."

"What do you mean escalating?" Shane demanded. "What else has happened? Have there been other attacks that you've hidden in the past?"

"Not attacks," Melissa said, cringing. How had she let that slip out? Of course Shane would jump on it.

"Then what?" he demanded.

"A few pranks on my car, that's all. Really, I'm tired and I'd like to head over to the cabin and fall into bed. It's been a long day," she tried to stand.

"Not on your life," Shane said, pushing her back into the chair. He stomped to the phone and punched in several numbers.

"Who are you calling?" she asked, worried.

"Joe," Shane barked. "Hey Joe, I have a situation. Any chance you can head out to my place?"

"That's really not necessary," Melissa argued. "It's late. Joe doesn't need to drive all the way..."

"Yeah, it's Mel. She needs to make a report," Shane paused. "Someone shot at her as she left the station, we believe it was a pellet gun. Uh-huh. We'll be in the kitchen," then Shane hung up.

"I have to warn you, Joe's a little pissed. He wants to know why you didn't call him right away. He says the crime scene has probably been contaminated by now but he's sending one of the guys over to take a look. With any luck they'll be able to retrieve the pellets." Shane narrowed his eyes at her. "I'll wait until Joe gets here before I make you tell me about the pranks. That way you only have to explain it once. But really Mel, this is serious. Why didn't you tell me you were being harassed? We both know Gloria is the most likely suspect."

"That's why I didn't tell you," Melissa admitted. "You are already so angry with her. This just makes the whole situation a hundred times worse. What will you do if she is responsible?"

"Joe will arrest her," Shane said without emotion. "I know it's hard for you to understand. I mean, you have such loving parents you want to believe everyone had a happy childhood. That's just

231

not the case. I don't love my mother, I tolerate her. I barely do that anymore. She doesn't love me either and she never has. She's a good actress when she wants something and now that I have money, she always wants something. But she doesn't care about me, she doesn't care about Megan, she never has. If it wasn't for Cora stepping in when I was a kid, I probably wouldn't have survived."

"It was really that bad?" Melissa asked, horrified for the kid Shane had been.

"It was," he said soberly. "I didn't tell you before because I never wanted you to feel sorry for me. When we were together years ago, all I wanted was your love. I had to know you loved me for me, not because you felt sorry for the poor kid whose mother hated him."

"I did love you for you. But I have to admit I never truly understood back then. You told me a little about Gloria, but I always thought you were blowing things out of proportion, that you exaggerated how bad it was to justify your feelings for her. Since I met her, I know you down played everything. Even if you had been honest back then I'm not sure I would have believed it, not really. I had to grow up and see firsthand the world wasn't what I always thought it was. Working as a dispatcher in Denver was a real eye opener. It taught me to see people for who they really are. I'm fairly certain Gloria is behind the attack. Will it seriously be okay with you if she spends time in jail over this? I need the truth because I won't cooperate with Joe if that is going to upset you."

"It's going to upset me if you aren't completely honest with Joe. If Gloria did this to you, I want her in jail." Shane moved closer and brushed the hair from Melissa's face. They both stood there, frozen wondering if they were going to take that step. Shane's eyes drifted down and focused on Melissa's lips. He was drawn to her and couldn't stop himself. He lowered his head then jerked back when he heard the knock on the door.

Joe knocked a second time, then opened the door himself and stepped into the room. He spotted the two and wondered if more was going on between them than tenant and landlord. But that wasn't his business. What was his business was the wound on Melissa's face. Her cheek was slightly swollen and it looked like a bruise was beginning to form. There was a nasty scrape that started at the side of her nose and ran at least an inch across her cheek bone. "You didn't tell me she was shot in the face," Joe grumbled as he moved to stand in front of his newest employee. He glared at her, growing more annoyed by the second.

"Hey Joe," Melissa said apologetically. "Sorry you had to drive all the way out here so late."

"I'm not," he said, taking her chin in his big hand and jerking her head to the side so he could get a better look. "It's consistent with a pellet," he finally said sinking into the chair to Melissa's left. "So, tell me exactly what happened and then you can explain what you were thinking leaving the scene and driving all the way home before you notified anyone of the incident."

"Actually, I don't think she planned to notify anyone at all. I took her by surprise," Shane began. "I just got back to the house when Mel drove in. It's been a long day. One of the Heifers got caught in a mud hole this afternoon. It took hours to pull her out, the stress sent her into premature labor. She almost lost the calf. We got lucky, saved both mom and baby for now. Although it's touch and go on the little tyke. We won't be sure he'll make it for at least twenty four hours," Shane paused. "Anyway, I was just headed to the house when Mel pulled up. I took her by surprise. Otherwise, I have a feeling she would have snuck in and out then gone home and kept all this to herself." He glared at Melissa clearly not happy about the revelation.

Joe wasn't happy either. "Is that true? Did you plan to report this or not?"

Melissa straightened. "No Joe, I didn't plan on making a report. I still think you're making too much of this. I'm not hurt," she cleared her throat and continued when Joe just stared at her wounded face. "It's minor. You can't honestly tell me if you'd gotten this," she pointed at her face. "That you would have called one of the guys off the road to take a report."

"Actually yes," Joe countered. "I would have. Not because the injury is serious, but because the crime is. Someone shot at you Melissa. I won't have people going around shooting guns in my town. Now, walk me through what happened and don't leave anything out."

"Okay," she took a deep breath then paused when Cora stepped into the room. Of course, Shane said he'd been working all night. Cora would have stayed to care for the children. "Before I start, do you need dinner Shane? You said you'd been working all day. I assume that's why Matt came after you this afternoon. You have to be starving."

"It can wait," Shane said, smiling at Cora. "Cora, come on over here and join us. I want you to know what's going on so you can watch for anything unusual around the ranch."

Cora slid into a chair and nodded at Melissa, a clear sign she should continue.

"Well, I left the office by nine thirty just like you ordered me to," Melissa said glancing at Joe. "It was such a nice night, I paused to enjoy the cool breeze and take in the country sounds, I guess. Sorry, I know that sounds silly. But my shift changed with every bid when I worked in Denver. Regardless of the time, leaving work was never quiet, it was chaotic. Stepping out into the night here at Hidden Lakes is so different from the city, I just had to take a minute to enjoy it, you know?"

"It's not silly," Shane said, taking one of her hands in his. "It's nice. I do it all the time myself and it's been a long time since I lived in the big city. Feeling the breeze, hearing the crickets, listening to the sound of the river never get old, not for me anyway," he paused to give Melissa a reassuring smile. "So, you stepped outside and paused. Then what?"

"Then I headed for the car. I was feeling guilty about leaving early," she hurried on when she saw Joe was about to argue. "I know you ordered me to, but I just felt a little guilty. Anyway, I reached the car and started my ritual. The one I've been going through since this all started. I had just reached the back of the car and started towards my door when..."

"Wait," Joe interrupted. "What do you mean when all this started?"

Melissa glanced at Shane, then looked back at Joe. "A few weeks ago, someone started vandalizing my car while I was at work."

Joe was visibly annoyed by this. "Any reason you kept this from me? I mean hell, being the Sheriff and all, why would I need to know that a vehicle was being vandalized in my own lot? While my employee was inside my station, working for me."

"Joe," Melissa tried to sooth. "It's not that big a deal. Just pranks. Nothing serious."

"Yeah, like the shooting tonight wasn't serious," Joe growled. "Melissa when are you going to let us in? When are you going to stop believing you have to handle everything on your own? You're not alone. This is your town as much as it is mine. You are one of us and always have been. When will you accept that? I'm sure you wouldn't even be staying out here with Shane if it wasn't for that boy of yours. Put aside all that stubborn pride and independence and let us in. We care about you."

A tear rolled down Melissa's cheek and she brushed it away. She felt Shane squeeze her hand in support and she realized they were right. She was trying to do everything alone. But it was habit, one she'd gotten into when she left here eight years ago. One she'd fallen back into when Mitch was killed. She would talk to her parents, but she wouldn't let them help her with her burdens. She didn't even tell them about them most of the time. She'd let Shane help her, only if she could convince herself it was for Jeremy's sake, not hers. She really did keep everyone at arm's length. That's why she didn't have any real friends to confide in. Well maybe Shane, but she didn't even trust him anymore, not really. She trusted Sarah, but she didn't want to burden her with any more problems. Raising three kids was tough enough. "I'm trusting you now, Joe. I'm going to tell you everything, I promise. I know it wasn't my idea," she glanced at Shane. "But now that you're here, I'm going to trust you. I'm going to ask for your help. Because even I realize this has gotten out of control."

"Good," Joe said, patting her knee in a fatherly way. "So, go back to the beginning. When was the first prank?" He used her word, although he didn't think what was happening here was just a silly prank. And he had a pretty good idea who was behind it all.

"It started five, no I think six weeks ago," Melissa began. "I left work to find 'go back where you came from' written on my driver's side window in lipstick. When I walked around the car to see if there was any other writing I saw 'whore' written in big, bold block letters on the passenger window." Melissa paused and reached for her purse. "I actually took a picture of it. The first person that came to mind was Gloria and I wanted to confront her with it and see if she'd admit to doing it."

"Why Gloria?" Joe asked.

"She was pretty angry with me the night my house flooded. I kind of let her believe Shane's daughters name was Marnie and her plan to manipulate Shane fell apart from there. She blamed me. It was obvious that night, but then she commented on it a couple days later just outside the hardware store. She started across the parking lot, but I didn't wait to hear what she had to say. She yelled at me as I rushed to my car. Calling me names and telling me I had crossed the wrong woman. I was on guard after that and expected something. Not this, but a confrontation or a public scene. When I saw the petty lipstick message, I immediately thought of her. I guess I just thought it fit, you know?"

"I agree," Shane nodded. "That sounds like classic Gloria behavior."

"Okay, then what?" Joe asked.

"There was nothing for about two weeks," Melissa said, thinking back. "I assumed it was over. That Gloria had sent her message and moved on. Then, I left the office one day to find whipped cream smeared all over my windshield. Again, nothing serious. Just a minor inconvenience. I wiped enough off to drive around back to the hose and sprayed down the car, then went home."

"But it didn't stop there?" Joe asked.

"No," Melissa admitted. "The next week I found motor oil smeared all over my door handle. I wiped the goo off my hand and decided to do a quick check of the rest of my vehicle. I found a rag shoved into the tail pipe."

"Yet, you still didn't report any of this?" Joe said, annoyed but thinking. He was in cop mode now.

"It still wasn't harmful, just annoying. At this point I planned to confront Gloria and if I got a sense she was responsible I was going to threaten to make a report. But things got busy and I haven't had a chance to track her down. In the meantime, I've started doing a quick walk around the car. You know, checking for problems. Anyway, last Wednesday I left the office and did my routine check. I found about a dozen nails scattered strategically around and under my car. They were placed so that if I didn't find them no matter how I left, I would run over at least a few of them. I took a picture of that too," she handed Joe her phone. "Then the shooting tonight," she finished softly.

"Okay, walk me through tonight. I want you to go step by step. Tell me exactly what happened," Joe said as he scrolled through the photos. "And I want you to email me these pictures. I'm adding them to the file."

Melissa walked them through the events of the evening. "I was a little panicked when I left. I mean, the pellet hit the windshield and didn't do much damage, but I thought it might shatter one of the side windows so I got out of there pretty quick."

Joe studied her face, then her arm. "I need pictures of these and the windshield. I have a camera in the car. Don't move. I'll be right back."

Once Joe left the room, Cora spoke for the first time. "You should have told one of us what was going on, Melissa. I understand you keeping this from Shane. As annoyed as that makes you," she said to Shane. "I understand. I'm not sure I would have reported it to you immediately either. I know better than anyone how you get when your mother is involved. It's personal and you know it. But why didn't you at least tell me?"

"I don't know," Melissa considered. "At first, it was just annoying. I didn't like what was happening, but I wasn't really worried about it. Then, last week I considered telling you. Both of you," she said, looking at Shane. "But then I decided not to. I didn't want to make you angry. I guess I also wondered if you would be angry with me. I mean she's your mother. What if you took her side? What if you blamed me or said I was being unfair blaming her without proof. I've been so unfair to you and your daughter, I just couldn't take the risk. And telling you Cora, would be the same as telling Shane. You would never keep something like that from him. I just thought it would be better to deal with it myself."

Melissa watched Shane. He hadn't said a word. He wasn't reacting at all. He was just sitting there, so still. She could tell he was deep in thought and she wanted to know more than anything what he was thinking about. But she didn't dare ask. Then Joe returned and she was busy moving this way and that, so he could get a clear picture of her injuries.

"I'll call Jason when I leave and see if he found anything at the scene. With any luck, maybe we'll pick up one of the pellets," Joe said in that cop tone he had.

"You called Jason on this?" Melissa grumbled. "Now I have to call Sarah. She'll be just as mad as you are if I don't fill her in immediately. I'll never hear the end of it if she hears it all from Jason."

"I know," Joe said unsympathetically. "It's a real hassle having people around that care. I guess you'll just have to learn to deal with it," then he walked to the door. "I expect to hear immediately if you have any more problems," then he was gone.

"That man loves to give orders," Melissa said lightly.

Cora was watching Shane. He wasn't himself tonight and she was worried about that. She knew he still loved Melissa and having his mother go after her had really thrown him. She stood. "I left your dinner in the oven. It's on low so it should still be warm. I'm sure there's enough for two. Feed that girl, she's skin and bones. Don't let her out of here until she eats something," she kissed Shane's forehead and headed for the door. "I'll check on the kids before I turn in for the night. You take as long as you need. By the way Doc Jones came by. You were busy in the field so he just left some pain meds but he wants you to call him. He was pretty adamant that you need a full checkup and x-rays on the shoulder," then she too was gone.

Melissa watched Cora go then turned to face Shane. She knew he wasn't happy with her and she was worried about that. Things had been going so well between them. Would this be another setback?

Shane stood and walked to Melissa. He studied her for a minute then pulled her into his arms. "I hate that you felt like you couldn't come to me with this," he whispered. "Whatever else is or isn't between us, I thought we were friends. I thought you knew I would always be there for you." He rested his head on top of hers. "I'm sorry you couldn't trust in that."

Melissa took a step back. Being in Shane's arms felt too good. She couldn't think straight if she didn't put a little space between them. "That's not what this was about, Shane." She took a deep breath. "It was about not forcing you to choose sides. I didn't want you to have to pick. You shouldn't have to choose between me and your mother."

"I don't have to choose sides," Shane said soberly. "I'm here for you, Mel. It would always be you." He let that hang there for several seconds before he walked to the stove and pulled out his dinner. "Now, I'm starved. Do you mind grabbing a couple plates?"

Melissa hesitated. She wasn't hungry. She was rarely hungry these days and hadn't been for over a year. At first, it was the grief over losing Mitch. Then the stress over how the loss of Mitch was impacting Jeremy and their dwindling finances. Since she'd gotten back to Hidden Lakes, it was the stress over Shane. Would the men in her life always impact her appetite? She knew she'd lost too much weight. None of her clothes fit right anymore and some days she fell into bed so tired and lethargic. Lack of nutrition was starting to have a bigger impact on her than she liked. So, she sat down and forced herself to eat. Not only for herself, but because she could see Shane needed her to. He needed to feel like he was caring for her, protecting her. She understood that and wanted to give him what he needed.

They had finished eating. Sitting there in silence had been torture. Melissa stood and began clearing the table. She'd just placed the plates in the sink and stepped into the large pantry when she felt Shane's arms encircle her waist. Melissa turned and found herself pressed against Shane's hard body. His mouth lowered to hers. At first the kiss was gentle, so soft and loving. Shane was still trying to sooth her. Melissa wasn't going to settle for soothing. She wanted passion. She pressed her body against Shane and deepened the kiss.

Shane was breathless. Kissing Melissa was like coming home. She was so soft but wild at the same time. He'd always loved that about her. He'd always loved her. He wanted her more than he'd ever wanted anything in his life. But he couldn't have her. He knew that. His body was begging him to lift her into his arms and run up the stairs to his bed, but he couldn't. In his mind he knew he couldn't have her. He knew he would never survive the pain if he allowed himself to give in to the needs of his body. And still, he couldn't make his body stop. Just a little more, he just needed a few more seconds like this. He found himself pulling at her shirt, then his hands were underneath, touching bare skin. He ran them up and down her back as they continued to kiss with so much passion Shane thought he'd explode. This was insane. He had to stop before he completely lost control. He steadied himself and took a step backwards. Then he took another one. The two of them stood just inside the pantry, inhaling sharply trying to catch their breath.

"I've missed that," Melissa finally said. "I've missed you, Shane," she admitted. She was unsure how to explain. How could she make Shane understand that even though she loved Mitch, she had never stopped loving him?

Shane trailed his finger over her face, softly not wanting to hurt her. "I'm sorry about this," he said, his voice still husky. He pulled her close again then kissed her forehead. "I'm really sorry about everything."

"Shane?" Melissa said, looking up at him. She wasn't sure what he was thinking, but she knew she didn't like it. He was taking a step back from her. She'd had such high hopes after that kiss, but Shane was clearly taking a giant step backwards. So, he still wasn't ready to trust her. She guessed she couldn't blame him, but it still hurt. What did she have to do? How could she prove to him that she loved him and always had? For about the millionth time Melissa wondered if Shane would ever forgive her for the mistakes she'd made. Or maybe it was loving someone else that he couldn't forgive. Melissa considered that. If the tables were turned, if Shane had really loved Kristy, if they had gotten married and something had happened to Kristy, would she be willing to forgive him? That was certainly something to consider. "Well, I guess I better get going," she finally said. "You have an early morning and I can see you still have that limp. How's the shoulder tonight?"

"Good," Shane lied. His shoulder was killing him. He had tweaked it earlier dealing with the cow and then again during that kiss. His leg was starting to bother him, too. He needed to get to bed. The pain was severe enough he was actually considering trying the pain meds Doc Jones had left. "Mel?" he asked hesitantly.

"Yeah," she said, studying him closely.

"I have something for you," Shane began. After the night she'd had maybe the photo albums he'd gotten back from Brad would cheer her up.

Melissa paused, confused. "What do you mean?" she asked as she watched Shane open a cabinet and pull out two beautiful photo albums.

Shane set the albums on the table. The old ones were damaged beyond repair so Shane had purchased two new ones from Brad. He hadn't spared any expense. Melissa had been so upset when she thought she'd lost all those pictures. He still hated knowing those books contained memories of another man, but if it made Melissa happy it was worth the heartache it caused him. "I could see these meant a lot to you so I called in a favor," he knew if he told her he had paid for the repairs she would insist on covering the cost. "Bradley Sinclair is a genius when it comes to photo repair and recovery." He gave one of the albums a gentle push hoping she would open it and take a look.

Melissa was floored. Shane had secretly had all the damaged photos of her wedding repaired? She felt him watching her and knew she had to act happy even if she was confused. Was this an act of love, or another message? Was Shane telling her they would never be together because she'd married another man so she should cherish what she had? She slowly opened the first album wondering what she would find. A smile spread across her face when she saw the beautiful blue eyes of her one year old son staring back at her. Shane had done it. He had repaired the reminders of those precious memories. "Thank you," she said, emotion making it hard to speak. She had been so afraid the first seven years of her child's life had been lost forever. Tears formed in her eyes and she began to blink rapidly. How was she ever going to repay Shane for this? She looked up at him and smiled. "Thank you, Shane. You have no idea how much this means to me."

"You're welcome," Shane said with mixed emotions. He knew having the pictures back was important to her. It made her happy and that had been the point, right? He just couldn't get passed the fact that she was happy because she had just been given back tangible reminders of another man. A man he could never compete with. A man she had loved, married and planned to spend a long happy life with.

Melissa watched Shane. She wished she knew what he was thinking, but at this moment she had no idea. All she knew was she needed to get out of here. The albums confused her. She wanted to smile and cry at the same time. It had been a long day for both of them. It was time to head back to the cabin and spend some time alone. She stood, gathering the books under her arm. "Thank you again for these. It was thoughtful of you," she turned, headed back toward the door.

"You okay?" he paused. "I mean....well, you know. Are we okay?"

"Sure," Melissa said, forcing a smile. "If I don't see you in the morning, I'll be over for dinner. Tina's working her regular shift so things should be back to normal."

"Good," Shane said, wanting to move closer. Wanting to pick up where they left off in the pantry, but knowing he couldn't. His heart couldn't survive another blow from Melissa. He'd barely survived the first one. Getting involved with her again was a monumentally bad idea no matter how much he wanted to.

"Okay then," Melissa said, taking another step toward the back door. "I guess I'll see you tomorrow." She pushed open the screen then stopped. "Oh, do me a favor and don't mention what happened to Jeremy. I don't want him to worry."

Shane frowned. "What are you going to tell him?" There was no way he would lie to his son.

"I don't know yet," Melissa paused. "Well, that's not true. I'm going to tell him a version of the truth, but I need to down play it. Jeremy thinks it's his job to protect me. I can't have him driving himself crazy thinking I'm going to get shot, not after what happened to Mitch. He was worried about you by the way. He asked me if you could die. He wanted to know if being kicked by a horse that way could kill you."

Shane frowned. "I'll talk to him about that tomorrow. He doesn't need to worry about me. But I can see where you're coming from. He's a kid, he shouldn't be worried about either one of us dying."

"Exactly," Melissa said, relieved. "I'll let you know what I tell him just in case he corners you about it," then she turned and strolled out the door.

* * * *

Shane dropped his pen and sighed. He leaned back in his chair, rubbing his temple. He was worried about Mel. She'd had to work late again, something about Tina transferring her mother to rehab. He didn't like her being out after dark like this. His mother was cunning and malicious. He'd learned that at a very young age. It had only been two days since the pellet gun incident. He'd like to think it was too soon for another episode, but Joe had paid Gloria a visit. He didn't have enough to arrest her yet, but he'd put her on notice. That in itself could escalate her efforts. Gloria hated dealing with the police. He checked the clock again, ten minutes to midnight. Joe never made her work this late. If she didn't get back in the next ten minutes, he'd drive to the station himself.

Shane jumped at the sound of his cell phone. He grabbed it before the second ring. "Mel?"

"Hey Shane," Melissa said trying to keep the stress from her voice and failing. "I have a problem."

"Are you hurt?" Shane asked concerned.

"No," she said quickly. "I'm fine, but my car isn't." Her voice hitched and she hated herself for the weakness.

"What did she do now?" Shane asked, hearing the stress in Melissa's voice. "Whatever it is, we'll fix it," he added hoping to reassure her.

"My car is a mess and it's not drivable," she admitted. "All four tires are slashed and she hit the windshield with something. It's completely shattered, right above the steering wheel. Shane I hate talking about this as if we know Gloria did it, but..."

"But we do know she did it," Shane interrupted. "Go back inside. I don't want you out in the open. You're too vulnerable like that. Go inside and I'll be there as soon as I can. Did you call Joe?"

"Well...that's the other thing," Melissa hesitated. "I know he said he wanted to know immediately if anything else happened but I just can't call him tonight. He left early. He had this big evening planned for Molly. It's their thirty fifth wedding anniversary. Shane don't ruin tonight for him. Let him and Molly have their special evening together."

"I'll stop and pick up Jason on my way," Shane decided. "Are you back inside?"

"Yes," Melissa said relieved he agreed with her. "I locked the door so you're going to have to call me when you get here. Oh, and try not to wake up all the kids. Sarah doesn't need to be up all night, either."

"Give me a little credit, Mel. I do have kids of my own," Shane wanted to be annoyed at her for the insult, but he was just too worried and angry. "Stay inside no matter what. I'll call your cell when we get there."

"I'm not going anywhere. See you in a few," Melissa hung up and studied her desk. She could pass the time by doing work, but she knew she'd be too distracted. She thought about her car and those horrible words written all over it. The Escape would never be the same again. She hated Gloria for that. The one thing she had left of her life with Mitch was now ruined all because Gloria wanted a free ride and she believed Melissa was standing in her way. Well, if she'd had any doubts before about pressing charges, that had all changed. She stood and began to pace.

Melissa was still pacing when her phone rang twenty minutes later. "Hello," she said after the first ring.

"Come outside," Shane said angrily.

Melissa hung up and rushed to the parking lot. She paused when she saw the furious look on Shane's face.

"You didn't tell me about the spray paint," he barely glanced at her before returning his angry stare to the car. "That woman is going to pay for this," he ran his fingers through his hair in irritation. "She is going to pay dearly, I promise you that," he turned to face Melissa.

She was still standing a few feet away from him. She'd never seen him like this before. He was even angrier than he'd been that night at her house when he believed she was running again. "Shane," she began. Then he was there, wrapping his strong arms around her and pulling her tightly against him.

"Mel," he said closing his eyes and letting the feel of her calm him. He had been so worried about her, then the instant he saw the car he'd been furious. There was a little guilt in there somewhere, too. His mother was terrorizing Melissa. His mother had completely lost her mind. His rejection had nothing to do with Mel, but Gloria was taking it out on her anyway. "I'm so sorry," he finally told her. "I'm so sorry for everything. That is all so ugly. The things she wrote for the world to see. Mel I am so sorry."

"Shane it's okay," Melissa said furrowing her brows. "I don't care about that. But I am furious that my car is ruined. I loved that car. It's all I have. My house is a mess, I'm completely broke and the only thing I had worth anything is that car. Look at it. I have to buy all new tires, replace the windshield and having it repainted is going to cost a fortune. I can't afford that, not after all the trouble at the house. My job pays well, but not that well." The longer she talked the more furious she got. "On top of that, I had to pull you away from home, away from your kids, my kid, at midnight. Jason had to leave his family, Sarah had to get up in the middle of the night and she doesn't get enough sleep as it is. All because your mother wants a free ride and you won't give her one. I've had it Shane. This has to stop."

Shane was smiling now. Melissa had seemed fragile and vulnerable just minutes before. Now she was spitting mad. He liked her better mad. And he was sure she'd regret telling him how broke she was. Well, she wasn't paying for this mess, he was. Gloria was his mother and this had Gloria written all over it. She'd screwed up this time. Shane happened to know this wasn't the first time Gloria had written smut all over someone's car. Really, the woman had no imagination. She'd used the same vulgar sayings on Meredith Carter's car when Shane was six. He'd watched her do it. He was too young to know what most of the words meant, but not all of them. And, he'd had Cora. Before Gloria had finished, Shane had run to Cora and brought her back to see what his mother was doing.

Hidden Lakes

Cora had taken pictures, of the car and Gloria putting on her finishing touches. Shane still had those photos. He figured it might be circumstantial evidence, but it was still evidence against Gloria. No way was she going to get away with it this time.

Meredith hadn't pressed charges. She didn't care about the damage to her car. It was a beater anyway and she'd just landed the hottest, richest man in the county. Corey Martindale took one look at Meredith's car and called the junk yard. Within an hour the thing was crushed into a pancake and Meredith was driving a brand new red convertible mustang. Six months later the two of them were married. Last Shane heard they were still together with grown kids and a couple grand kids to boot. He'd always loved knowing his mother had lost out on that one. Corey was a good man. Which is why Shane had kept those photos all these years. It was a reminder that women like Gloria didn't always win. Plus, they had pushed him to succeed, to be a better man. Now, they were going to help him get justice for Melissa.

"What are you thinking about?" Melissa asked. "You have the strangest look on your face."

"I'm enjoying the knowledge that Gloria just made her first mistake. And it's a doozy," Shane grinned. Then he proceeded to tell Melissa and Jason about Meredith and Corey and the Junker.

"Any chance I can get those pictures?" Jason asked. "I promise, once she's convicted I'll return them." He glanced at Melissa's car and grimaced. "In fact, if you want I'll get you a set of these to go with them. ID's on the way. Why don't you guys head home? Once we've processed the vehicle for evidence I'm going to move it into the lot. I'll do another more thorough search

Melanie P. Smith

in the morning. It's easier to spot hair and other fibers in the day time."

"Jason that's going to take hours," Melissa argued. "I'm sorry about all this."

"Not your fault," Jason shrugged. "And don't worry, Sarah's used to it by now. I'm off tomorrow but I'll come in for a couple hours anyway. I want to process the car as soon as possible. And wipe that frown from your face. This case just gave me an excuse to schedule adjust a few hours on Saturday. Now I get to watch my son's baseball game. We all win, now go home and get some sleep."

Melissa walked over to Jason and gave him a long hug. "Thank you," she said again. "And I'll make sure Joe doesn't give you any hassle about the time on Saturday. I owe you one. Tell Sarah sorry for me."

"Good night," he called, then turned and walked toward the approaching vehicle. Forensics had arrived.

Shane walked Melissa to his truck in silence. "I want you to drive my truck until we can figure out what to do about your car."

"Shane, that's not necessary. I have insurance. It will pay for a rental," she climbed into the passenger seat and watched as Shane closed the door and walked quickly to the other side.

Once Shane climbed in, he turned to face Melissa. "I know that car has sentimental value to you. It probably reminds you of your late husband. I'm sorry for that, too. I'm sorry my mother tainted those memories for you. But I want to make this right. I'll buy you another car just like it if you want. Or if you'd rather, I can pay to fix that one back up just the way it was. I know you want to argue with me, but please let me do this for you. My mother is harassing you. My mother destroyed something important to you.

251

I need to be the one to make this right. The only reason she's doing it is because I won't give her any more money."

Melissa turned to argue with Shane, but when she saw the hurt and pleading look in his eyes, she couldn't. He would need to make this right. Not because it was his fault, even though he wouldn't see it that way, but because it was his mother. "We'll talk about it tomorrow," she agreed. "I really do have good insurance. Let's see what they say then we'll go from there."

"We'll talk about it," he agreed. "But I don't want your premiums going up over this. Insurance companies always raise rates when you file a claim. It would be stupid to involve them when I can so easily take care of it myself."

Melissa smiled. "We'll talk about it."

"And in the meantime, you will drive my truck," he pressed.

"Do you ever stop?" she asked, only half joking. "I already made one concession. If I make one more can that be enough for tonight?"

"Sure," Shane said innocently.

"Then I'll drive your truck."

Shane grinned.

"For now," she added. "But the thing's as big as a tank. The sooner I get back into a car the better."

"I could buy you one," Shane offered.

"Funny," Melissa said, not in the least bit amused. "Don't even think about visiting a car lot without my being there. If I decide to replace the car it's not going to be on your dime, not completely. But I'm sure we can compromise somehow. Can we just leave it at that for tonight?"

"Okay," Shane agreed. That would have to be good enough for now.

Chapter Eleven

Melissa pulled Shane's big truck to a stop in front of the house. It had been over a week since her car had been destroyed. She still didn't know what to do about a replacement. She'd thought a lot about the situation. Shane was still insisting he pay for the damage or replace the car. Especially now that Jason had evidence proving Gloria's guilt. She had left finger prints, but even more damning was the bubble gum she'd chewed then plastered under the door handle. Had the woman never heard of DNA? Now they just needed to find her. Gloria had gone missing. Judge Stone hadn't hesitated to issue a warrant for her arrest and a DNA order once they had her in custody. Gloria was in big trouble. The kind she couldn't get out of by batting her eyes and acting innocent.

Melissa had called her insurance company and reported the incident but hadn't filed a claim. She told her agent that she was waiting to see if the one responsible was going to pay restitution. If that happened, she wouldn't need to involve the insurance company. Her agent had insisted on getting a case number and Melissa was sure he had requested a copy of the police report. For now, that would have to do. If she ended up filing a claim later on, she didn't think she'd have any trouble with the repairs. Shane was still fighting her on that.

His words kept coming back to her. She'd thought about them every night and sometimes during the day. He thought the car was important to her because it was something tangible she had left of her time with Mitch. Sure, she had bought the car while they were married, but they hadn't even picked it out together. Her old car had been falling apart so Mitch had insisted on getting a new one. He'd gone to the dealership while he was working and found the Escape for her. The salesman had agreed to hold it for twenty four hours to give Melissa a chance to test drive it. She'd loved it the instant she'd sat behind the wheel, but Mitch had known she would. Even so, she'd told the salesman they wouldn't be buying it. Mitch had argued with her for two days before she'd finally given in. She didn't think they could afford that kind of car payment. There were some months they could barely pay the mortgage.

Mitch disagreed and insisted he was up for promotion any day now. He wanted her to have a reliable car. He worried about her when he was working and wanted to know her and Jeremy wouldn't break down on the side of the road somewhere. That had convinced her. The thought of being stranded in the big city with Jeremy while Mitch was off fighting a fire for hours was too much to bear, especially if they broke down at night. The instant she gave in, Mitch had driven her to the dealership and less than an hour later, drove home with a slightly used Ford Escape. As much as they'd struggled at times to make ends meet, she'd never regretted buying that car.

Hidden Lakes

She thought about Shane again. Was that the reason he was holding back? Because he thought she still had too strong an attachment to Mitch? Sure, she still loved him and he would always have a special place in her heart. But she loved Shane now. Didn't he know he held a special place in her heart, and always would? Melissa thought about her time back in Hidden Lakes. Maybe Shane didn't know. They had never talked about it and Shane had seen her fretting over memorabilia of Mitch after the flood. He'd even gotten those pictures repaired to make sure she didn't lose them. Shane would never try to compete with a ghost. He'd hold back, like he was. Was Mitch the obstacle she had to overcome to be with Shane? She considered the situation and decided there was a way to take a step toward fixing that misconception. She would get a new car rather than fix the old one. Now she just needed to decide how much of a role she was willing to let Shane play in the new purchase.

It would be difficult to afford a car payment, especially with the charges she'd put on her credit card for the electrical work. Then again, she'd feel guilty if Shane just out and out bought her a new car. How was that any better than what his mother was trying to do? In fact, one of her primary goals had been for Shane to get her a fancy new vehicle. Melissa wasn't sure she could live with herself if she allowed that. She stepped from the car, still unsure how to proceed.

Cora saw Melissa pull in and tried not to let the kids see her relief. Shane should have been back hours ago. Matt and Hank weren't due back until morning. There was a problem with delivery of the new horses and Hank had to drive to Idaho to pick them up himself. Matt had gone with to make the run easier. The rest of the men had already gone home. Once the thunderstorm rolled in, they'd called it a day. Cora didn't have numbers for any of them.

She'd never needed anyone but Shane, Hank or Matt. The past hour had been terrible. Twice she'd almost called Melissa home from work early. But she had stopped herself, Shane would be angry if she called Mel away from work for nothing. She wasn't going to go through this again. As much as she hated it, as much as she feared it, she was going to have to have that surgery after all. She just couldn't take feeling this helpless all the time. If she'd been able to ride a horse, she'd have gone after Shane herself.

Melissa stepped into the kitchen and pulled off her boots. "It's really coming down out there, Cora. Please tell me you have coffee," she stepped into the kitchen and stopped. "Cora, what's wrong?"

Cora glanced at the kids then back to Melissa. "Oh nothing," she tried to sound casual. "I do have coffee, but I was wondering if you could take it to go."

"To go?" Melissa asked, confused. "Where am I going? It's raining buckets out there if you haven't noticed."

Cora turned to the two kids. "You two go wash up. Supper is going to be ready in a few minutes."

Melissa turned to Jeremy in greeting and frowned. He hadn't moved and he was clearly worried about something. "What's going on?" she asked, watching Jeremy closely.

"Dad didn't come back," Jeremy said running to Melissa and wrapping his arms around her waist. "He went out alone to work in the north field and didn't come back like the rest of the guys when the lightening started."

Melissa glanced at Cora, who nodded. Cora wasn't saying anything but Melissa could see she was wound tight and ready to lose it any minute. Lightening lit up the small room then thunder immediately filled the silence, echoing throughout the large house. "I need to change. Cora, put a pack together. I need medical supplies in case he's injured. His shoulder is still bothering him. If he's fallen from his horse...well, you know what I'll need. I also need food and water," she turned to Megan and Jeremy. "You two help Cora. Find your dad's favorite snacks. Fill a bag with some of those chocolate chip cookies you made this morning. Jer, get the small thermos and fill it with milk. I also need the large one. If he's out in the cold he'll need coffee to warm him up." Nobody moved. "Come on, all of you get a move on. I'm going to change but it won't take long. I want to head out as soon as I get back."

With that, the three of them scattered. Melissa darted up the stairs. Her heart was racing, Shane had to be okay. But she knew something was wrong. There was no way he would stay on the hill in this weather. She threw off her clothes and grabbed her thermal underwear. Normally she only wore those in the winter, but she was going to get drenched in this down pour. The additional layer might help with the cold once she was soaked. She pulled on a pair of jeans, grateful for the first time she'd lost weight. They were loose enough to wear over the added layer. Then she pulled on a t-shirt and added her large hoodie. She pulled on two pairs of socks and stood in front of the closet wondering what boots to wear. She didn't have any that wouldn't get soaked in about two seconds.

Cora stepped into the door and held out a pair of rubber boots. "I know they are impossible to walk in, but they might keep your feet dry. I also grabbed Shane's old rain coat. It's going to swamp you, but it might keep you relatively dry. I'm sorry, but I don't have any rain pants. I'm afraid you're going to have to use the coat to keep as dry as you can."

"Perfect," Melissa said, pulling Cora in for a hug. "Don't worry. I need you to be strong for the kids. Especially Jeremy. He's worried about Shane, and now I'm heading into danger after him. He tries to act strong, but he's so vulnerable. Keep them busy and I'll get back as soon as I can."

"There's a small cabin in the woods just beyond the north field. If Shane didn't think he'd make it back, he'd try to go there," Cora explained.

"Do you think he might be safe in the cabin?" Melissa asked hopefully.

"No," Cora shook her head. "There's a radio. If Shane made it, he would have called to let me know. But I think he may have been headed there. If you don't see him along the trail, head for the cabin. You can't miss it. Just head through the woods there's a small dirt path that takes off at an angle, you'll run right in to it."

"Thanks," Melissa said, giving Cora a hug. "Take care of the kids. Shane's going to need to know they're okay."

"Be careful," Cora hugged her back. "And don't worry about those two. I'll keep them busy preparing for your return. If they feel like they're contributing it will help pass the time."

"Oh," Melissa said as a thought struck her. "Have you checked in at home? Are your kids okay?"

"Yes," Cora assured her. "Corrine and Tawny are back at college. They decided to take summer school this year. They figured if they were both there, they could get through it and graduate early. My youngest, Amy is on vacation with a friend. None of them are even in the state right now. My only worry is Shane," she blinked back tears. "Something is wrong. I can feel it in my bones. He wouldn't stay out there in this weather. He knows how much I worry and he wouldn't do that to me or the kids," Cora insisted.

"Cora, Shane is going to be okay." Melissa hoped she was right. "I'll find him. I promise. I won't come back until I do," she smiled. "Maybe you could make us a fresh pot of chicken soup. We're going to be mighty cold when we get back. I know you said you already made dinner but the soup will keep you busy and we can always freeze it for later if we don't end up eating it."

"I'll make the soup, but if you get up there and Shane is hurt, take him to the cabin. Unless it's life threatening, take him to the cabin and wait it out. I can handle the kids until morning. Just let me know you're okay," Cora instructed.

"I promise," Melissa said, then she took the boots and sat down on the edge of the bed to pull the things on. It was difficult to walk in them, Cora's feet were slightly larger than Melissa's. She'd added a third pair of socks to compensate. It helped a little, but she wouldn't be doing much traveling by foot. As she stepped into the kitchen she smiled. "Impressive," she said with a low whistle. "You guys work fast."

"I think we got everything mom," Jeremy said as he set the large thermos into the saddle bag. Then he rushed over and wrapped his little body around hers. "Will you be careful?" he asked, trying to be brave.

Melissa sank to her knees and pulled Jeremy in for a hug. "I'm going to be fine honey," she pressed a kiss to his forehead. "But I need you to do me a favor."

"What?" Jeremy asked, pulling back to look at his mom.

"Megan looks a little scared and Cora's worried because Shane and I will be wet and cold when we get back. I need you to be brave," Melissa whispered. She hated to do it, but she was going to use Mitch's request and hope it gave Jeremy the strength he needed to get through this. "Remember what Mitch told you about being the man of the house?"

Jeremy nodded.

"Well, I need you to be the man of the house while I'm gone," she requested. "Just until me and your dad get back though. Once Shane's home, he'll be the man of the house again. Do you understand?"

"Yes," Jeremy said, forcing himself to stand up straight.

"Okay good," Melissa said, reassured by Jeremy's new posture. "So, get Megan to help you. I need the two of you to get prepared. It's raining pretty hard. The power might go out. You and Meg make sure there's enough firewood inside to last all night. As hard as it's raining, the wood is going to get soaked in no time. Bring it inside or it won't burn."

"Okay," Jeremy agreed, taking a mental note. "We also need flashlights. Cora can help me with that."

"And blankets," Melissa added. "While you have light, set up some beds in the family room. You can push the couch and chairs aside to make room. If the power goes out, everyone should sleep in front of the fire."

"Okay," Jeremy agreed. "Don't worry mom, I'll take care of things here. Go find dad."

Melissa gave her son one last kiss then she stood and moved to Megan. "Hey sweetheart, you doing okay?"

Hidden Lakes

Megan brushed a tear from her face. "Is my daddy going to be okay?" she sobbed.

"I'll find him," Melissa promised. "Cora's going to fix soup for Shane, do you think you can help her? Jeremy also needs your help. He's making beds in the family room in case the power goes out. You stay here and make sure everything is taken care of and I'll find your daddy, okay?"

Megan noticed Melissa hadn't pretended like her dad was okay. She was glad Melissa hadn't lied. Nobody knew if her dad was hurt or not, but Melissa would find him. The same way she'd found Megan when she was at the lake with the snake. She wrapped her arms around Melissa in a big hug. "You be careful too. Jeremy would be really sad if you got hurt," she paused. "So would me and Cora."

"I'll be careful," Melissa told her. "Do you think Hank would mind if I borrowed his horse? I think he's stronger than Trigger. He can handle going out in the rain, the weight of me and all this stuff." She pointed to the two saddle bags stuffed with medical supplies and food.

"Hank won't care," Megan said confidently. "I think he'd like it if you used Bandit to find dad."

"I think so too," Melissa agreed. She moved to Cora and let her slide Shane's old rain coat onto her shoulders. It was huge, but Melissa thought that might help once she climbed onto Bandit. She grabbed the saddle bags and headed for the door. "Be good!" she called over her shoulder. Then added, "I love you," as she disappeared into the rain.

* * * *

Shane opened his eyes and tried to orient himself. He noticed immediately it was raining, hard. He tried to remember where he was. In the north field? Yes, in the north field. Once the lightening started he knew Nico would never make it back to the house. That horse had always been spooked by thunder. He was also a little concerned about the lightening. So why was he lying flat on his back and where was Nico now? He tried to stand and fell back, pain shooting through his entire body. His leg was stuck between a rock and what? A wall of dirt? Well, that meant he wasn't in the field. He moved his head from side to side and realized he was perched on a small ledge overlooking the lake. He didn't remember how he'd gotten here. And he had no idea how to get back to high ground and find Nico before the temperamental fool got himself hurt.

Shane took a deep breath and tried once again to force himself into a sitting position. His shoulder was killing him. He just hoped he hadn't broken the damn thing again. He was finally able to function without pain killers. He gritted his teeth and forced his body to move. Once he was upright, he was exhausted. His head was pounding and he realized he'd hit his head and blacked out. How long had he been unconscious? He closed his eyes and fought off the dizziness. That wasn't working, so he laid his head against the muddy wall of the embankment and tried to think. How was he going to get out of here? With this kind of torrential storm, the ledge could give way any minute. And he didn't even want to think about where Nico had gone. That horse could be anywhere if the thunder spooked him bad enough.

Hidden Lakes

* * * *

Melissa pulled on Bandit's reins and listened. There it was again. She couldn't see very far in front of her, the wind was blowing so hard, the rain whipped at her face and stung her eyes. She decided to get off Bandit and walk. Maybe then she could figure out what kept making that noise. She had finally reached the north field and there was no sign of Shane anywhere. She slid out of the saddle, grateful for Cora's rubber boots and Shane's old rain coat. Her pants were soaked but her feet were dry. Her hoodie was slightly wet, but the raincoat had done its job pretty well all things considered. Bandit snorted and a horse whinnied just a short distance away. Nico? Had she finally found Shane? "Lead me to Nico, Bandit." She gave the horse a little head and let him lead her.

It was slow going because she couldn't walk very fast in those boots, but she finally reached the edge of the field and spotted Nico. Panic struck her instantly when she realized Shane wasn't with his horse. Where could he be? Shane would never leave Nico alone in a thunderstorm. As she approached, Nico reared up and snorted at the air. "It's okay boy," Melissa soothed. "It's alright." The instant Nico's feet hit the ground, Melissa moved forward. She reached out her hand so Nico could smell her, hoping he would recognize her scent. It worked. Nico nodded his head, bumping Melissa's shoulder in greeting. "Good boy," she crooned. "That's a very good boy." She slowly reached out and secured his reins. One down, she thought, one to go. "I don't suppose there's much chance you can lead me to Shane can you?" Melissa asked, not at all hopeful.

At the sound of Shane's name, Nico whinnied again. "Yes, Shane. Can you lead me to Shane?" Melissa knew the horse didn't understand, but he might understand Shane's name. And Nico was one hundred percent Shane's horse. If she gave him his head, he just might lead her to where he thought Shane might be.

Okay, this was not working, Melissa admitted. Nico was just wandering in circles around the north field. She was cold and wet and tired, but she knew Shane could be in worse shape than she was. They had to find him, but how? So far, Nico wasn't much help. She thought about what Cora had told her. Shane would have headed for the cabin at the far end of the north field. So, she'd head back to the road and follow it across the field, looking for Shane. Why did Shane have to own so much land anyway? This place was huge, there was no way she could search it by herself and the storm was getting worse, not better. This was no typical summer thunderstorm. She glanced at the clouds. It could go on for hours and now it was completely dark. Cora was going to be frantic. She just hoped the power was still on. Otherwise Cora would have a hard time keeping the kids busy.

As she reached the roadway another idea struck her. Shane may have been headed for the cabin, but the fastest way wouldn't be all the way to the edge of the field and then a straight line. It would be to cut across from the other side. She turned Bandit around and headed that way. She had just reached the edge of the field when she heard a noise. She stopped and listened again. Nothing. Could that have been Shane? But he wouldn't have gone in that direction. That went to the overhang. There was no way down to the house from there. She shifted Bandit to head in the opposite direction when Nico broke loose and ran toward the ledge.

Melissa ran after him. Would the horse be smart enough to stop when he reached the ledge? How would she ever face Shane if she let his favorite horse fall to its death in a violent thunderstorm? She'd recognized how skittish Nico was every time there was thunder. Somehow he must have thrown Shane, or ran off and left

Shane stranded somewhere. But that didn't account for his whereabouts. If Nico had simply run off, Shane would have either walked to the cabin or started walking down the road toward the house. She pulled Bandit to an abrupt stop when she heard Shane's voice.

"Hey buddy," he said, soothing his horse. "I'm glad to see you."

Shane paused and Melissa thought she heard a moan. She jumped from Bandit's back and ran with him to the edge of the cliff. "Shane!" she yelled when she saw the bloody mess that was Shane's body. "Shane! How bad are you hurt?" she dropped Bandit's reins and fell to the ground. "There's so much blood. I have to get you out of there," she was starting to panic.

"Mel," Shane said, taking charge. He'd never get out of here if she hyperventilated and passed out. "Take a breath."

"What?" she said, shaking herself. "Oh, I'm fine. Shane, how in the world did you get...never mind. I have to get you out of there. That ledge doesn't look all that stable."

"Sounds like a plan," he agreed. "But there's a problem."

"What?" she asked as she dug in the saddle bag for the rope she'd added from the barn. She realized thunder might spook Nico again and without a rider she wasn't sure what Bandit would do. She glanced around until she found a tree large enough to tie the horses securely. Then she returned and peered over the ledge. "I'm going to throw down this rope. Tie it around your waist. If I can't pull you up, I'll use one of the horses to slowly pull you back off that ledge."

"Melissa," Shane said then let out a loud whoosh of breath and another moan. "That's not going to work."

"Why not?" she asked, trying to take in the situation. Then she spotted the problem. "Oh!" she gasped. "Do you think it's broken?"

"I think that's a guarantee," he closed his eyes against the dizziness he was feeling again. "But more importantly, you can't pull me out until I get that leg unstuck from the rock."

Melissa hesitated. If she fell, Shane was out of luck and she'd be dead. The drop was at least two hundred feet down. Thank goodness that ledge was there and Shane had only fallen about twenty feet. She tried not to think about what could have happened if Shane hadn't landed on that outcropping. She considered the dilemma, there was no other option. She had to descend the cliff and try to pry Shane's leg from the rock. "Which horse is more steady?" she called down. "Considering the conditions, which horse is going to be better? Nico or Bandit?"

"Bandit," Shane said without hesitation. "Nico is too spooked around thunder."

"Okay, just hold on for another minute. I'll be right there," she disappeared.

She'll be right there, what did that mean? What in the world was Melissa planning? She wouldn't try to...apparently she would, Shane thought as he watched Melissa lower herself over the cliff. "Are you nuts?" he hissed.

"Maybe," she called back. She couldn't look down or she'd lose it for sure. "That's a good boy Bandit," she called as she gave the rope another slight tug. Bandit took another step forward and Melissa's body lowered several more feet.

Hidden Lakes

Shane watched in horror as Melissa tugged and lowered, then tugged and lowered. Finally, she was inches above him. He reached out and grabbed her foot so she would know she'd reached her destination. Her boot slipped off in his hand. Shane held on, surprised but amused.

"Hey!" she called. "Give that back," she lowered herself down behind Shane and stood on one foot. "You really are not helping," she told him, annoyed.

Shane reached over and slipped the boot back on her foot. The instant he finished, pain shot through his shoulder and he sank against the dirt wall again. He was gritting his teeth, trying to force the blackness away. He lost the battle.

Melissa nearly panicked. Shane was unconscious. It only took her a couple seconds to realize that might be a good thing. She could step over and get his foot loose while he was out. Then she'd wrap the end of the rope around his waist and get Bandit to pull her back up. Once on top, she could back Bandit up until Shane was safely on high ground. She moved slowly, not wanting to disturb the balance too much. With both their weight on this ledge, it could collapse at any minute. She crouched down and studied his leg, then the rock. She could push the large boulder over the edge, but what if the dirt went tumbling with it. She'd better secure Shane before she tried anything. She turned around and went to work. She just hoped she remembered what Mitch had taught her. If she did this right, Shane would be as safe as he could be. Once she'd tied the last knot she moved back to look at her work. It looked pretty good. For a rope harness, it wasn't half bad. She moved back to his feet and pushed at the rock. Nothing. It barely budged. Maybe she could wedge her way between the cliff wall and Shane and push it over the edge with her feet.

By the time she was done, Melissa was a muddy mess, but the rock had come loose. One last push and it would go over the edge. She held her breath, closed her eyes and pushed. The sound was deafening as the boulder struck the side of the mountain, then bounced, then struck and bounced again. Finally, it hit bottom with a loud thud. Melissa opened her eyes and looked around. Well, they weren't hanging from thin air, so that was a plus. She glanced at Shane and saw him watching her. She forced a weak smile. "Now comes the hard part."

Shane looked at the rope and considered. "What did you have planned?"

"I'm going to guide Bandit backwards. He'll pull me up the side first, then I'll be able to control him as we pull you up," she frowned. "I'm afraid I'm going to hurt you. I wish you'd stayed unconscious a little longer."

"Thanks a lot," Shane moaned. "I like it this way better thank you anyway." He considered her plan. "I'm not going to be much help, but I'll do what I can. How are you going to get Bandit to walk backwards? He doesn't know that command."

Melissa smiled. "I'm going to pull the rope."

"That's how you got him to go forward," he shook his head. "I'm not following you."

"That's because you hit your head," she crouched down and pressed her fingers to the base of his skull. "You have a gash on the back of your head and a huge lump. Are you sure you're okay?"

Shane reached up and took her hand. It came away bloody. "I'm going to be fine," he assured her. "Now that you're here. I'm going to be just fine. Show me how you plan to get that stubborn horse of Hank's to walk backwards," he forced a smile. "I'm not ungrateful, but this mud is getting a little cold."

"Oh right," Melissa said, standing. She grabbed a second rope and gave a pull. Bandit took a few steps back and Melissa's feet left the ground. She pressed them against the wall and winced as a large glob of mud fell onto Shane's chest.

"Don't worry about it. Just get to the top," he called.

Melissa gave another tug and once again she was pulled further up the hill. She continued until she was finally able to swing her leg over the side and pull herself to safety. "Okay," she said as she peered over the side. "You ready? It's not a smooth ride, so it's going to be painful. I'm sorry, I can't do anything about that."

"I'm ready," Shane said, wrapping his bad arm around the rope and then grabbing above it with his good hand. He grimaced as the rope pulled and his shoulder struck the side of the cliff. He realized he didn't need to hold onto the rope. The harness Melissa had tied would secure him. He used his good hand to swing his body around so he could see the side of the hill. From there he was able to guide himself up with his good leg and his hand.

Melissa used Bandit to pull Shane up the hill as fast as she dared. She hadn't heard any swearing so either he was doing okay, or he passed out again. She just needed to get him to the top, then they could decide how to get him onto Nico's back. That was going to be even more challenging. She took another step back and saw the top of Shane's head. So, he wasn't unconscious. Just a few more steps and he would be safe. She forced herself to go slow until Shane's butt hit the edge of the cliff, a portion of the ground sloughed off and for a minute she thought Shane was going to go with it. She gasped and took several steps backwards with Bandit.

Finally, Shane lowered his back to the ground and closed his eyes. He was out of danger. Melissa noticed he was breathing hard and she started to worry all over again.

She tied Bandit to a tree then ran to Shane and began to frantically untie the harness. "Shane," she sobbed. "Did I hurt you?"

Shane reached up and tried to take Melissa's hand in his, but he was too weak. He stopped trying and his arm fell back to the ground. "I'm okay," he finally croaked.

Melissa finished undoing the make shift harness and grabbed Shane's hand. She was leaning over him now, tears streaming down her face. She didn't notice, they were mingling with the heavy rain. Her hair was soaked. The hood from the rain coat had fallen off sometime during her assent up the hill. "Shane, I'm so sorry. Shane? Please don't pass out again. I need your help. We have to get you onto Nico. I have to find that cabin and get you out of those wet clothes."

Shane took a deep breath then reached up and brushed a wet strand of hair away from Melissa's face. "You're so beautiful," he whispered as his hand fell back to his chest.

"Now I know you're delusional," she stood, looking around for something to help her lift Shane onto the horses back. "You're in such bad shape, Shane. Do you think you could handle the ride back to the house? I think we should get you to the hospital. You've lost a lot of blood in addition to that head wound."

"Mel," Shane said wearily. He'd waited so long to tell her how he felt she thought he was delusional. Well, he'd rectify that soon enough. "I'm okay. Give me just a minute and I'll be able to lift myself onto Nico."

Melissa shook her head. "No way. It's not possible. Shane, your leg is broken. You can't put any weight on it. And your shoulder is bothering you again. How exactly are you going to climb up onto that high rise of a horse's back?"

"High rise of a horse?" Shane laughed. "I'm not sure how to take that," he paused. "Do me a favor and bring Nico over here."

Melissa studied Shane, then turned and headed for Nico. He was more than happy to return to his owner. Shane tried to stand, but he lost his balance and would have toppled back to the ground if Melissa hadn't been there to grab him. "Okay smart guy, care to share your plan?"

"I don't really have one," Shane admitted. "Nico won't move, so I just need to use my good arm to pull myself up then somehow swing my bad leg over his back."

"Yeah?" she said skeptically. "How exactly are you going to jump ten feet into the air before you swing that bad leg on over?"

"You're not helping," Shane scowled. He grabbed onto the horn of his saddle and tried to pull himself onto Nico, but he couldn't do it one handed and his arm was no use. He didn't have any strength because of his bad shoulder. He tried to grab onto the other side of the saddle for support, but using that arm even slightly had instant pain shooting through his torso. Shane swore and leaned against Nico's side. He was trying to come up with another plan when Nico lowered himself to the ground.

Melissa gave Shane a surprised look. "Did you teach him that?" she asked impressed.

"No," he said as he swung his bad leg over the horse and settled into the saddle. Nico immediately stood, then he looked at Melissa as if to say, "Problem solved, let's go."

Melissa ran over to Bandit and climbed on. "I assume you can find the cabin from here?" She was watching Shane for any sign of distress. "I mean, can you stay conscious enough to find the cabin from here?" she called.

"I told you I'm fine," he rolled his eyes and held Nico's reins as they walked across the large field.

Melissa followed close behind. She wanted to be nearby just in case Shane passed out and started to fall. She wasn't sure what she could do about that, but she wanted to be close. She was so cold and tired. Being wet wouldn't be so bad if it wasn't for the wind and the pain of the rain drops striking her in the face. Other than that, things were good. They finally reached the edge of the field and Shane continued on into the thick woods. Melissa wasn't sure she would have found the barely marked trail without Shane. He had never brought her here, not even before. They had spent all their time at the lake or at Shane's small mobile home. The one he'd brought in years ago for shelter while he got his ranch up and going and built his real house.

They continued along a narrow path that ran diagonally just as Cora had explained. Melissa was beginning to think it was further away than Cora had believed when the trees opened up and she spotted the small cabin. Relief ran through her. Shane was still in bad shape, but now she could at least get him out of those wet, muddy clothes and bandage his wounds. Plus, she was thankful for the radio. She could call Cora and get an update on the kids. Things were finally looking up.

Hidden Lakes

Shane brought Nico to a stop and wondered how he was going to get off the horse. With Melissa's help, he could probably slide down and support his weight on one foot. From there it was going to be a challenge to hop up the stairs and into the small building. Nico seemed to be watching as Melissa climbed from Bandit's back and slowly removed two large saddle bags. She walked to the porch and deposited them next to the door. Then she returned to Bandit and pulled off his saddle and blanket. She left the halter but removed the reins. Then she slipped the rope through the hoop and secured it to the top rail of the hitching post built in front of the cabin. Once she was finished she gathered up his tack and moved it to the front porch out of the rain.

"That's going to have to do for tonight. You ready to give this a try?" she asked, moving to stand next to Nico.

"I'm going to leave my good foot in the stirrup and swing my other leg around. I might need you to steady me if I swing too hard. When I have my leg in position, I think I can just lean over Nico and lower myself down. Once I hit the ground, I'm going to need to lean on you for balance. Then, I think I can hop over to the cabin and we're home free," he smiled reassuringly.

Melissa wasn't buying it. "It's not going to be that easy, but let's give it a try." She placed a hand on Shane's good leg and waited while he tried to swing his other leg around.

It took time, but Shane finally managed to get into position. Then he supported his weight on his stomach, holding onto the saddle horn with his good hand as he slowly pulled his leg from the stirrup. He got stuck, but Melissa was there to help. She pressed her shoulder against his butt as he lowered his body to the ground. Once his foot hit dirt, he gave a sigh of relief. Melissa was there to steady him as he gave Nico a pat. The horse had remained perfectly still throughout the entire ordeal.

The two of them slowly made their way to the front porch. Shane was grateful there were only two stairs and a short distance to the door. Melissa tried the handle then swung the door open. "You don't lock it?" she asked in surprise.

"Why would I?" he said through gritted teeth. "It would defeat the purpose."

"I guess," Melissa said as she helped to lower him onto the couch. "I'm going to take care of Nico then I'll be back. Don't try to move. I won't be long."

Melissa stepped back into the cabin and silently studied Shane. He had his head resting against the back of the couch and his eyes were closed. Once again she wondered if he was conscious. She silently closed the door and moved to his side. He immediately opened his eyes. "Ready to get out of those wet clothes?" she asked.

"You're soaked, too. Get out of that coat and then call Cora. She's going to be worried and I want her to know we're alright," Shane pointed to the corner. "The radio's over there. I'm sure she's waiting by the one in the house, so it shouldn't take long to reach her."

Melissa hesitated, but not for long. She wanted to ease Cora's worry and she needed to know the kids were okay. She picked up the hand piece and pressed the button. "Cora?" she called. "Cora, its Melissa are you there?"

"Melissa?" Cora's voice crackled over the speaker. "Did you find Shane? Is he okay?"

"I found him," Melissa assured her. "He's injured, but he's going to be okay. We're both okay. How are the kids?"

"We're fine," Jeremy and Megan called through the speaker. "Tell dad we love him," Megan added.

Melissa turned to see Shane smile at that. "Tell her I love them too," he said softly. "And thank Cora for me. She's been putting in a lot of overtime. I promise I'll make it up to her soon."

"Shane says he loves you, too. And Cora, he promises you'll get an all-expense paid vacation when he gets back," Melissa grinned at him.

Shane laughed. "That's not exactly what I said, but it works."

"Is the power still on up there?" Melissa asked.

"It's been going off and on for the past hour," Cora said. "But the kids are fine and now that we know you're safe we're going to try to settle down. As long as the power holds I promised the kids a movie. Don't worry about us. We're as happy as clams up here."

Melissa was relieved. "Okay. Goodnight then. I love you all," she paused. "Uh, Cora?"

"Yeah?" Cora asked happily.

"When Matt and Hank get back in the morning will you send them up here in the truck? We're fine, but I'm a mess and Shane's leg is injured. I think it might be broken. I don't want to try to transport him back down on the horses if we don't have to." Melissa hoped she sounded unconcerned.

"I already thought of that," Cora told her. "Hank heard about the storm and called to check on things. I told him Shane was missing, so he said he and Matt would head out early. I'm going to text him and let him know you found Shane and the two of you are staying at the cabin. Don't worry about a thing. The boys will be there to help you get Shane back home."

"Thanks Cora," Melissa said, relieved. "See you in the morning."

"Goodnight mom," Jeremy's voice blared through the speaker. "Goodnight dad," both Jeremy and Megan said in unison.

"Goodnight kids," Melissa answered. "We love you," then the room went quiet. Melissa pulled off the rain coat and hung it next to the door. Next she removed the boots and the first two layers of socks. She only hesitated a minute before pulling off her jeans, then the thermal undies. Finally, she slipped off the hoodie. She was completely undressed, standing there in her t-shirt and underwear, before she thought of the fire. She ran her hand through her hair as she glanced around the room looking for firewood. Then her eyes rested on Shane and she realized he'd been watching her. Her cheeks turned red and she tried to breathe. For some reason the very act had become difficult.

"Come here," he said, holding out his hand.

Melissa moved to the couch and sat down next to Shane. "I need to get you out of these," she pointed to Shane's jeans. They were not only wet, but caked with mud.

Shane smiled. "I used to love to hear you say that."

"Funny," Melissa said, reaching for the buttons. She paused and looked at his shirt. "I think we should get this off first." She moved her fingers to the small buttons on his western style shirt and

277

began to slowly undo them one by one. "How come you wore this today?" she asked, trying to sound casual. She felt anything but. It had been a long time since she'd undressed a man. And even longer since that man had been Shane. "Lately you've been wearing t-shirts. I assumed that was your summer attire."

Shane covered Melissa's hand with his. "You're shaking," he whispered. "Are you cold? I can build us a fire."

Melissa laughed. "You can't even get off this couch without help." Her eyes locked with his and she stopped breathing. She knew that look, Shane wanted her. "I'll do it later," she swallowed hard. "I mean, I'll build a fire after I get you out of these wet clothes. You'll have to tell me where the wood is, but I want to take care of you for a change. Will you let me do that, Shane?" she waited. "Let me take care of you," she whispered.

Shane couldn't speak. He loved this woman more than anything. He had to tell her. To hell with protecting himself. He wanted her to know he'd never stopped loving her. He'd never gotten over her leaving that way. He wanted her to know how much he needed her. He gave her a quick nod then continued to watch as she finished unbuttoning his shirt. Then she knelt on the couch and gently pushed the fabric off one shoulder then the other. The instant she saw his wounded shoulder she inhaled sharply.

"It looks worse than it is," he assured her, not even glancing at the bruises.

"I don't think so," she said, moving her gaze from his shoulder back to his face. "Shane, you're a mess."

Shane smiled. "I know," and he did. He was a mess, in more ways than one. But he'd been that way for years.

Melissa's hand moved to his head. "I didn't see this one before," she gently ran her fingers through his hair, then ran one finger over the large cut on the side of his head. "Did this happen in the fall, too?"

"No," Shane admitted. "That one is responsible for the mess on the ledge."

Melissa furrowed her brows. "What do you mean?"

"Nico is afraid of thunder. Lightning struck the field and then thunder boomed right afterwards. I was paying more attention to the lightning strike than to Nico, worried we were going to get struck with the next one. Before I knew what was happening Nico darted into the trees. My head struck a large limb and I think it knocked me out. The next thing I knew I was waking up, on my back on that ledge. I'm not really sure how I got there. I'm just grateful I wasn't thrown a few feet in either direction. We both know how disastrous that would have been."

Melissa looked at him with wide eyed horror. "I can't think about that," she said, tears streaming down her face again. "Oh, Shane. You could have died."

"But I didn't," he said, pulling her against his chest. She felt good there. He gently ran his hand over her head then down her back. Melissa had been through a lot tonight. He was amazed she'd found him in that downpour. They sat there like that for several minutes, Melissa crying and Shane doing his best to silently sooth her.

Finally Melissa pulled back and wiped her face. "Sorry about that. I didn't mean to have a break down. I think I'm finished now."

Shane ran a finger across her cheek. "It's almost healed," he finally said, still angry at his mother. Joe hadn't found Gloria yet but the entire force was looking. At first they thought she had left town, but William was positive he'd seen her two days ago. She was leaving the grocery store from the back alley. He called to her, but she disappeared before he could catch up. Shane was confident Joe and the boys would find her though. They were determined. Melissa had become one of theirs. And everyone knew you didn't mess with a cop's family. Mel was now family.

"It's fine," she said uncomfortable. She knew Shane was still angry. She was still angry, but it was in the past. Gloria would eventually be caught and punished for her actions. Right now, she needed to focus on Shane. "Let's get you out of those wet pants," she climbed off the couch and crouched on the floor. "First the boots. This might hurt, but I think we should take your boot off. I know with the swelling you're not going to get it back on any time soon, but I want to see how bad the break is."

"I agree, just give it a quick pull. I'll be fine," Shane assured her.

Melissa pulled as quickly, but as gently as she could. She gave Shane an apologetic look when he swore and closed his eyes in pain. "Sorry," she said and meant it. "Let me get the other one off then I'll take a look." She quickly removed Shane's other boot then gently removed his socks. Shane's ankle was black and blue and was already starting to swell. "We don't have any ice," she said, moving to sit next to him. "I think we should get you into bed, then I'll do my best to elevate it. I'm afraid there's not much more I can do for the ankle. I do have some pain killers though."

"I love you," Shane said softly.

"What?" Melissa asked, eyes wide in disbelief. "Maybe I should take another look at that head wound."

"I mean it," Shane said taking her hand. "I've always loved you. I think I fell in love with you the first time I saw you," he paused, trying to gather his thoughts. "I know I messed up. I was so afraid back then. I had so many plans for us. So many grand ideas, but I always knew there was a chance I might fail. Every time I thought about you living in that run down mobile home, working long hours so we didn't lose the ranch I panicked."

"I know," Melissa said, moving in to cuddle with Shane. "I was scared, too. But for other reasons. I never thought I was good enough for you. I was just a small town girl, and you were larger than life. I was afraid you'd get bored. That the chemistry we had would wear off and you'd be stuck with a nobody."

Shane frowned. "I never knew you felt that way. Why didn't you tell me?"

"I guess for the same reason you didn't tell me your fears," Melissa surmised. "I was so in love with you, I was insecure and I was young, I couldn't tell you. What if you agreed? What if you realized I was right and you left me? I couldn't take the chance. I just kept on loving you and hoping that somehow everything would work out. Somehow I would be enough."

Shane kissed the top of her head. "You were more than enough," he pulled her closer. "I never stopped loving you. Even when I found out you married someone else. I thought that was going to kill me. It was hard enough when you left me, but knowing you loved someone else, knowing someone else was loving you, was the hardest thing I've ever had to live through." He was still amazed her marriage had made it into the gossip mill, but Jeremy hadn't.

"Shane," Melissa sat up. "I'm sorry," and she was. Not for marrying Mitch, but for the pain she had caused Shane by doing it.

Hidden Lakes

"I understand," Shane said, pulling her back to his chest. "From what you and Jeremy have told me about Mitch, he must have been a wonderful man. He sounds like everything I wasn't. You don't have to apologize for loving someone else. I deserved that. I betrayed your trust. I hurt you. I certainly don't have a right to complain."

"Shane," Melissa paused. She wasn't sure what to say. He had been victimized but he still believed he had betrayed her. She couldn't argue with him because she wasn't supposed to know anything about it. "Will you tell me about Kristy?" She knew the story, Cora had told her. But she needed to hear it from Shane.

"That's in the past," he said shaking his head. "It doesn't matter now."

"But I think it does," Melissa argued. "I won't apologize for marrying Mitch and I'll explain that to you in a minute, but I need to hear the truth from you." She sat up so she could look him in the eye. "I was too upset and too immature to listen back then. I refused to hear what you wanted to tell me. Please, tell me now."

Shane studied Melissa for a long time then he began to speak. "Like I said, I was terrified of disappointing you. I never knew how you felt, that you were scared too. All I saw was this wonderful, innocent woman. A woman I loved more than I ever imagined possible. You were depending on me. I saw how your parents were with you. I knew you were inexperienced and naive. I loved that about you, but I felt even more pressure because of it. I had become responsible for not only my life, but yours as well. I knew what I wanted, but I wasn't sure I could get it. I wanted you, of course, but I wanted so much more for you than what I had. I wanted to love you, to marry you, to pamper and take care of you. I wanted you to have security and all the things you'd ever wanted or dreamed of."

"I didn't need all those things, all I needed was you," she whispered.

"I think I know that now. Because I know that's all I needed. If I had you, I could get through anything," Shane paused. "But I was scared. I had driven to Bramble and bought you a ring. It wasn't much, but at the time it was all I could afford. When I got home that night we argued. You were upset because I didn't take you with me. I didn't want to propose that way. I couldn't use the ring to smooth out our fight. So I took it back home with me. The next day you were still angry, so I waited. Then, the next day I had that trouble with the building permit. I decided to wait. I couldn't ask you to marry me until I knew I could give you a home. That took weeks. All the while I fretted. Was I doing the right thing? Did you deserve someone better? The questions and worries kept piling up."

"Shane, I wish you had talked to me," Melissa was trying to remember those days. "I know I was naive, but I could have helped."

"I know. I was stupid," Shane agreed. "Then Brad called. I knew you had plans with Sarah that night. Scotty was only a few months old and she didn't get many nights free. The two of you were so excited to finally have some time to spend together. So, I went to the party. I was afraid it might be the last time I saw Trent. He was leaving for Iraq in a few days and so many soldiers had died over there. I didn't want to go party, but I also knew I'd never forgive myself if I didn't. Once I got there, I realized it was just us guys. Brad and Trent of course, but there were a few other guys that I'd met casually around town. That helped me relax. Things had been piling up for so long, I got drunk. I didn't plan it, but that first

283

beer had tasted so good I had another. Then Brad started passing out shots. Before I knew what I was doing, the three of us were having a contest to see who could drink the most tequila. It was a bad idea. You know I've never been a drinker, but I won. Brad and Trent stopped the game, they dropped out. I think they realized something was wrong and they quit prematurely. I had one more shot to prove I won, then I practically passed out on the couch.

I don't remember a lot after that. I remember, vaguely, the two of them helping me up the stairs. Then I remember taking off my clothes and climbing into Brad's bed in just my underwear. I only remember that because at the time I thought I was going to puke and I was grateful I wouldn't get it on my pants. Once my head hit his pillow I was out again. That's it. The next thing I remember is waking up the next morning naked, next to Kristy." He paused to look at Melissa. He hated admitting this to her. He hated what he'd done.

"I jumped out of bed, got dressed and drove home," Shane sighed. "Another mistake. I'm sure I was still half drunk and never should have been driving a car, but I was so horrified by what I'd done I had to escape. I couldn't face you for three days after that party." He closed his eyes, still feeling the pain and disgust with himself almost as intensely as he had back then. "It would have been longer, but you showed up at my door demanding an explanation. I should have confessed then, but I couldn't. I just knew the instant I told you I'd been with another woman you'd leave me. I didn't know how, but I was determined to fix things. So, I kept it a secret and agonized over it every minute of every day. The longer I waited, the harder it was. After a few months I realized it would be worse. You'd never believe it was an accident. You'd never trust me again and I knew I deserved that. So I didn't tell you.

I kept telling myself I would. Somehow I would tell you. But I couldn't ask you to marry me until I came clean."

"Then Kristy showed up and announced she was six months pregnant," Melissa added.

"And I had to tell you," Shane nodded. "I never blamed you for hating me. I knew I deserved that. I only wish you hadn't run off. I'm not sure it would have mattered. I didn't deserve you after that party, but I didn't know how to live without you."

"Shane," Melissa was serious now. "You didn't betray me. Kristy basically raped you while you were unconscious. That's not a betrayal. I wasn't mature enough to hear it back then but I am now," she paused. "Is everything you told me the truth? The absolute, honest truth?"

"Yes, but I am responsible. I got drunk. I let myself get out of control. I was probably three when I promised myself I would never allow myself to drink like that. Mom had dated too many drunks. I knew at an early age it was something I wanted to avoid, but I did it anyway. I let myself down and I let you down. That one mistake ruined my life. I want to say I regret it, but a part of me can't because I got Megan out of that night. But I do regret hurting you. I regret the pain I caused you because I was selfish and afraid."

"And I regret the pain I caused you because I was selfish and afraid," Melissa told him. "I ran away. How juvenile is that? I knew I was pregnant with your child but instead of staying and fighting for the man I loved, I ran. We both made mistakes. I've forgiven you; do you think you could ever forgive me?"

"I already have," Shane admitted. "As much as I wanted to hold a grudge, I forgave you a long time ago," he considered. "I know I haven't shown it, but I love you Mel. I love you with all my heart, I'm pretty sure I always will."

Hidden Lakes

"Then why have you stayed so distant?" she asked. "Why have you only let me in a little? After the thing with Megan, you've been my friend, but nothing else. Why have you held back like that?"

"I guess I didn't completely learn my lesson all those years ago." He gave her an apologetic smile. "You scare me Melissa. You are the only person alive that can destroy me. If it wasn't for Megan, I'm not sure I would have survived losing you back then. But I had to go on for my daughter. I had to get up every day and work the ranch, she was depending on me. I know I failed you but I couldn't let myself fail my baby too. Having you back here has been both heaven and hell. I've wanted you so bad it hurts, but I'm not sure I could survive losing you again. I thought if I held back, it would be easier when you left me. I was afraid I couldn't survive if I gave in to the love and you still left or you simply didn't want me anymore."

"So why did you tell me now?" And why did the moron think she would leave? Because she hadn't done enough to show him how she felt? Because he thought she was still in love with Mitch?

"I thought I was going to die out there tonight," he said soberly. "I was lying on that tiny ledge, stuck in the rain. My foot was securely wedged between that heavy rock and the side of the hill and I just knew I was going to die. I knew Megan would be okay. I was sure you, Hank and Cora would be there for her. I knew Jeremy had you so he'd be alright. Then I realized I was going to die and you would never know how much I loved you. You would never know I hadn't stopped loving you," Shane paused. "I realized that avoiding you, that holding back my feelings from you, was stupid. If I only had one more day with you, at least I had a day. If you left me after a month, at least I had a month. I've been depriving myself of happiness, however temporary, because of fear. And I promised myself if I got out of that mess somehow you were going to know how I felt. I know it doesn't change anything. I know you are still in love with Mitch and I don't expect anything. I just needed you to know, that's all."

Melissa leaned in and kissed him. Not some friendly, chaste kiss either. She gave him a full out, mind blowing kiss that she hoped he would never forget. Then she straightened and studied him. "Does that feel like I'm still in love with Mitch you moron?"

Shane blinked. "Well, no. Actually it didn't," he waited. When Melissa didn't speak, he did. "What exactly are you trying to tell me here?"

"That I'm madly in love with you, idiot." She rolled her eyes and took a deep breath. "Shane, I'm not going to tell you I didn't love Mitch. I did. But I want to try to explain things to you. I'm not sure that's possible but I'm going to try. You said you never stopped loving me. Well, a part of me never stopped loving you."

"I don't believe that," Shane interrupted. "I know you. You would never have married Mitch if you were in love with another man. You loved him."

"I did," Melissa continued. "Now, let me get through this without another interruption and I will do my best to explain. Okay?"

"Okay," Shane agreed.

"When I left here, I was devastated. I knew, without a doubt I would never love anyone the way I loved you. And I was right. No, don't. You agreed to let me talk." She narrowed her eyes when she saw Shane was about to say something anyway. "I was depressed and lonely and terrified. I actually slept in my car that first week. I had a little money, but I was on my own for the first time in my life. I was afraid to use what little I had on rent. Eventually I got a room at a shelter. I only qualified because I was pregnant but it was a nice place. Don't feel bad or guilty, it really was nice and the lady that ran the place was great.

She was a mom herself and she took very good care of me. She also helped me get a job. I was a waitress at this little café in downtown Denver. Before long, I had enough money to get into an apartment. That's where I met Mitch. Of course, he did all the work. I never wanted to speak to a man again. But Mitch lived next door and he was a fireman. He looked out for me. As I grew bigger and bigger, he figured out my story. Well, the basics anyway. He knew there was a guy and I had a broken heart. So he waited. He never pushed me. He was just there. Do you get what I mean?"

"Yeah I get it," Shane grumbled. A million things were running through his head. Melissa lived in her car, then a homeless shelter all because of him. The guilt was increasing by the minute. "Before you go on, I do have one question. How did I get you pregnant? I mean we were always careful. I know we had that one mishap where the condom broke but you were on the pill."

"But I'd had that bad cold, remember?" Melissa asked. "Mom took me to the doctor and he put me on antibiotics. I didn't know that rendered the pill ineffective. We had sex, the condom broke and even though I took the pill religiously, it didn't matter, nine months later Jeremy was born."

"I hadn't thought of that. I mean at the time I didn't know that either. Then when you showed up with my kid, I never put the two together," Shane considered. "I'd say I'm sorry, but I can't regret Jeremy either. So many other things yes, but not Jeremy."

"Stop regretting and just listen," Melissa scolded. "I got used to having Mitch around. He was nice and sincere. I slowly began to trust him. Then one day, when I was six and a half months pregnant, I started to have pains. I was at work, but my boss realized something was wrong and sent me home. I was climbing the stairs, I lived on the second floor, and I had a pain so severe that I collapsed. I was huddled right there in the middle of the stairway when Mitch found me. He picked me up and rushed me to the hospital. I was okay and so was Jeremy of course, you know that now, but I was so terrified that something was wrong. My doctor put me on bed rest. She was concerned enough that my arguments didn't matter. I didn't realize Mitch was still in the room until later.

After the doctor left, Mitch proposed a plan. He insisted on taking care of me. I admit I lost it a little. I had a job but no benefits. I was frantic about the hospital bills and didn't know how I was going to pay the rent. Mitch knew I wouldn't let him help, so he quietly took care of everything. Mitch tried, without success, to get me to move in with him. He wanted to be there to take care of me. I refused, but he didn't give up. Every day after work he came by. He brought me food and silently went through my mail. I was such a mess it took me several weeks before I realized I never got any bills. Needless to say, I was furious with him. I insisted on paying him back. He agreed, but told me he wouldn't accept any money until after the baby was born. I argued, but he wouldn't budge.

Like I said, Mitch was a fireman and he had a lot of friends. In Denver, like a lot of places, he worked a twenty four hour shift then had forty eight hours off then worked twenty four again. On the days he worked, he always sent a fellow fireman over to bring me dinner and make sure I was okay. Once Jeremy was born, Mitch continued to be there for me. He showed up one night when Jeremy was fussy at three in the morning. Mitch found a twenty four hour pharmacy and bought some of that numbing stuff for kids. Jeremy was teething and the stuff did wonders. We were both able to get to

289

sleep within thirty minutes. He was always thoughtful that way," Melissa paused. She wanted Shane to understand, but she didn't want to hurt him more than she already had. "Eventually I came to rely on him."

"Mel, it's okay. I understand, he was a great guy and you fell for him. I don't need all the details." He didn't want the details. It killed him to know she was all alone, that she needed someone and he wasn't there for her.

"That's not my point, Shane." She shook her head. "I know I'm hurting you. I'm sorry, but I don't think I can explain this without giving you the details," she paused. "By this time I had quit my job at the café. It just wasn't possible to work with Jeremy. Mitch got me a job in dispatch. I could usually work out my shifts so I was off on the days Mitch worked. I was grateful but by this time I felt so indebted to him I was a little annoyed. Everyone assumed Mitch and I were together, as a couple. To everyone on the outside I guess it looked that way, but to me he had become my best friend. I was finally able to talk to him about you, about Kristy and about what happened. He was understanding, but didn't agree with my decision to keep Jeremy a secret. Before that time, he assumed you knew and just didn't want any part of our lives. Mitch was very family oriented. He didn't like being a part of what I was doing to you. In fact, he was so angry with me, he stayed away for over a week. I thought I lost him forever. I was the one that went to him. I had come to rely on him and it was during his absence that I realized I had come to love him.

The love we shared was so different than what you and I had, it was hard to recognize at first. By this time Jeremy was a year old. Mitch agreed, reluctantly, to come to Jer's birthday party. It was after that party that Mitch and I started dating. Six months later we got married. But I never really got over you completely. Mitch understood that. We talked about it actually. He explained something that I never understood before. He told me about a girl he dated just out of high school. They went to college together. Mitch was madly in love with her. He believed they would spend the rest of their lives together. But one night, Stacy was walking home from a chem lab, she was attacked and murdered. Mitch still loved her. He told me a part of him always would. They were soul mates, just like you and me. They had chemistry and passion like he had never felt before or after, not even with me. Our love was different. It was soothing not combustible. It was calming and sweet, it's hard to explain. But Mitch understood that you would always have a special place in my heart, the same as Stacy would always have one in his heart. We accepted that about each other.

That didn't mean I couldn't love Mitch or that he couldn't love me. It just meant we were lucky enough to find two special people in our lifetime. It made sense and I stopped feeling guilty about loving you. Does that make sense?" She was worried she wasn't explaining things very well.

"I suppose," Shane wasn't sure how he felt about what she was telling him. Was it possible that Melissa still loved him? And how did Mitch factor into their future?

"I know I'm not explaining things very well. But I want you to know that Mitch never stopped arguing in your favor. He wanted me to come home. He wanted to meet you. He wanted Jeremy to meet you. I couldn't do it. I was afraid I'd have to share Jeremy with Kristy and that about killed me, but I was also afraid of my feelings for you. I loved Mitch. Even if I'd come home and realized I was still madly in love with you, I don't think I ever could have left him. He didn't deserve that. And deep down, I don't think I wanted to know. I didn't want to live with that kind of knowledge. I have to believe things worked out the way they were supposed to.

Hidden Lakes

I had a few wonderful years with Mitch and he was happy when he died. I'm grateful for that, but it doesn't mean my love for you has lessened. In fact, I'm in a much better place now. I'm older and more mature. I think I can handle the explosive, all consuming force that is Shane Chandler a little better now. If you'll have me that is. I think our love can be even stronger and more solid now than it ever was back then."

Shane was studying Melissa. Was it possible she wanted what he wanted? He wanted marriage. He always had. "Does that mean what I hope it means?"

Melissa smiled. "I don't know. What are you hoping? For the record, I won't settle for anything less than forever."

Shane pulled Melissa close. "Are you sure? I can be patient. As long as I know you're going to be here, I can wait," he watched as she nodded.

"I'm sure," Melissa smiled.

"I love you Melissa Peters Carpenter. We are going to have to do something about that name," he smiled. "How do you feel about Chandler?"

"I've always loved it," she grinned.

"Will you marry me, Mel? Will you be my wife? Will you move into my house and let us be a family? I have to remind you that Megan is part of the deal. She adores you. I can't think of a better mother for my little girl."

Melissa was crying now. "Yes, Shane Chandler, I will marry you." She flung her arms around him and realized he still had his wet pants on. "Oh," she sat up. "I forgot. Let's get you out of those."

Shane smiled. "With pleasure," he had that wicked glint in his eye.

"Not tonight stud," Melissa shook her head. "I need to bandage your head then you need rest. I won't make things worse. You're a mess, mister." She reached down and unbuttoned his jeans. "Lift," she said. Once he pushed his hips up, she slid down his jeans. The instant they were off, she frowned. "I brought clean clothes, but you're going to need them in the morning. Let's get you to the bedroom first, then you can change into clean underwear."

"I might need help," Shane laughed when Melissa glared at him in warning.

"I'll help you alright, funny man." She grabbed a bag then moved back to the couch and held out her hand.

Shane took it and realized he wasn't up for the kind of night he'd been hoping for. By the time Melissa got him to the bedroom his head was pounding and he was freezing. He fell onto the bed and wasn't sure he could move another inch.

"If it's not warm enough with those blankets I'll go back out and build a fire," Melissa told him. She studied him for a minute then rushed out the door. By the time she'd gotten back, he'd pulled off his wet shorts and replaced them with dry ones. She walked to the side of the bed and held out two pills. "Take these," she ordered. "I got them out of your medicine cabinet. I also noticed you haven't been taking them as prescribed."

"I didn't need them," but he did now. His leg was killing him, his shoulder hurt and his head was pounding. "Sorry, honey. I think

I'm down for the count. Once those pills kick in, I'm going to be comatose."

"Good," Melissa said, climbing under the covers. "I'm going to take care of you for a change." She pressed her lips to his. "I love you, Shane Chandler. Don't think you can change your mind for one minute. This time, I'm never going to let you go."

"I'm going to hold you to that Melissa Carpenter, soon to be Chandler." He mumbled just before he sank into a deep dreamless sleep.

Melissa watched Shane sleep. She wanted to believe him. She wanted to hope that this time they would really be married. That she was really going to get her happily ever after for good this time. Shane didn't fight fires. His work was a little dangerous, but maybe this time she could grow old with the man she loved. It was worth hoping. She would always love Shane and she had even grown to love Megan. Funny, she never thought of her as Kristy's daughter anymore. Just Shane's daughter and her son's sister. They were going to be a real family. She wondered what she would do with her parent's house now. Obviously the four of them were going to live on the ranch. Melissa wouldn't have it any other way.

Shane woke and felt a warm body pressed against his. It had been a long time since he'd felt this woman snuggled against him. He tightened his grip and enjoyed the moment. They'd wasted so much time. Not only the eight years she'd been gone, but all that time since she'd moved back. He wasn't going to lose another moment. He watched out the window as the sun came up, then he watched as Melissa slowly came to life. She had never been a morning person but that was okay. She didn't need to rise with the sun to be his rancher wife. He would take care of all the morning chores. And if he was lucky, she'd awaken each morning just in time for his break. He smiled down at her as she slowly ran her fingers through her hair.

"I'm a mess," she said sitting up. "My hair was soaked when I fell asleep. I can only imagine the knots."

Shane pulled her close and kissed her. "You're beautiful. You haven't changed your mind have you? Before you answer, remember I'm not letting you get away again. Melissa, are you really going to marry me?"

Melissa smiled. "Absolutely. Well, if we can get back to civilization that is. When do you think Hank and Matt will be here?"

"Probably in an hour or so," he tried to stand.

"Where are you going?" Melissa frowned.

"Bathroom," Shane told her. "I think there's still toothpaste in there."

"Oh no you don't," Melissa jumped up. "I'll bring it to you."

"What about the toilet? You going to bring that to me, too?" Shane joked.

"Well, sure. Okay, I mean you're a guy. You can go in anything, right. I think I saw a mason jar out here. You'll just have to use that. I'm not risking your health again. I wasn't sure we were going to make it to the bed last night." She was out the door before he could argue. Once she handed him the jar, she ran to the bathroom. "Women first. Feel free to go while I go." She closed the door, grinning.

Shane hesitated, then took care of business and placed the jar under the bed. He was just pushing himself into a sitting position when Melissa returned with a toothbrush and a bottle of water. "Get started, I'll grab that old coffee can I saw on the shelf. You can spit in that."

"I'm not sure I like this," Shane said taking the toothbrush. "What if I do something that makes you change your mind," he looked at her seriously. "I just got you back, I don't want to lose you already. Being an invalid is embarrassing."

Melissa rolled her eyes and left the room. Within seconds she was back with the coffee can. "I love you silly, seeing you this way isn't going to change that. In fact, I like taking care of you. It makes me feel needed."

Shane rinsed his mouth then pulled Melissa back onto the bed. "You have no idea how much I need you, baby," he whispered just before he kissed her. When he was finished he was sure she had a better understanding of his needs. "I wanted to ask you about something," he said, watching her closely.

"What?" she asked snuggling in closer.

"I was thinking about your house," he began. "You know, what you could do with that now that you'll be moving in with me. I'd offer to move to town with you, but I can't do that and run the ranch. I hope I'm not being presumptuous or pushy. Before you always loved the ranch as much as me, which leaves an empty house in the middle of town."

"I do love the ranch and I want to make our home there. But, I was wondering about my house too," she admitted. "I'm not sure I can sell it. I mean I have so many memories there. It will always feel like home and what if I hate what the new owners do to it?"

"I agree," Shane said. "I remember years ago when we were together. Mostly we talked about my dreams, but there was that one time at the lake that I got you to share your dreams with me. Do you remember? You told me you would love to open up a bed and breakfast. You thought it would be perfect because you loved people and you loved to bake. You described the place in so much detail I still remember it to this day. I thought maybe we could do that with your parents' house. Turn it into a bed and breakfast. You could bake muffins and Danish for breakfast and we could hire someone to come in and manage the place. Clyde's is the only motel for miles and it's pretty run down these days. Hidden Lakes needs something with more class. I was thinking your house would be perfect and since you are already doing repairs it would be a good time to make any necessary alterations."

Melissa considered it. She actually liked that idea. "I think we might be able to do that. I'd have to quit the Sheriff's Office, do you think Joe will be mad?"

"No," Shane told her. "In fact, I have a pretty good idea for a replacement."

"Oh?" she asked frowning. "Who?"

"Have you met Kathy Thomas?" he asked. "She's the single mother that lives about halfway between the ranch and town. She just moved in a month ago. She's been looking for work closer to home. Right now, she gets her two kids off to school then drives to Henley. I only know because I gave the kids a ride home one day. Kathy got stuck at work and was late picking them up. She was a basket case by the time I caught up with her. Anyway, she used to live in Idaho and was a dispatcher. She told me her husband was a cop. He was killed in the line and she moved out here. She'd be perfect for the job."

Hidden Lakes

"I agree," Melissa snuggled closer. "And I'd like to meet her. Losing your husband is hard. I might be able to help, you know with emotional support." She glanced up, hoping the mention of Mitch hadn't ruined the mood.

"Don't look at me like that," he kissed the top of her head. "I understand things better now. And I admit it was hard to listen to you talk about Mitch last night, but now that I slept on it, I get his point. It is possible to love more than one person. I won't get upset because you loved Mitch. I just choose to believe you love me more."

Melissa laughed. She didn't know about more, but different anyway. Shane could believe anything he wanted to about that. She was just happy they finally had each other.

Chapter Twelve

Shane stepped into the kitchen and wrapped his arms around Melissa's waist. She was still skin and bones, but he was working on that. He dipped his finger in the bowl of icing and licked it clean then reached out for seconds.

Melissa slapped his hand. "No double dipping," she turned to glare at him. "The guests don't want to share your germs."

"Okay," he grinned, turning her around the rest of the way and trapping her between his body and the counter. "I'll just share them with you," then he lowered his mouth to hers and proceeded to indulge himself. "Umm," he moaned. "Better than cake."

"Let go of me," she tried to protest but it came out weak and she knew it. "I have to finish that cake before my parents get back with the kids. The guest will be arriving any minute," she glanced out the door, expecting the neighbors to be standing there watching.

When she turned back to face Shane, he pressed his lips to hers again.

"We still have an hour before Jeremy's party. The guests won't come this early. It's rude," then he kissed her again. This time, he slid his hands under her shirt and caressed her back. As his hands shifted to move to her stomach he felt her ribs and frowned.

Melissa sensed Shane's mood change and wondered what had caused it. "What?" she asked, pulling back.

Shane ran his thumbs over her rib cage. "This," he told her. "Your ribs poke out. You need more meat on your bones." He reached behind her and dipped his finger in the frosting again. Then he pressed it to her lips. "But I think I know a way to get started on a much healthier you."

Melissa licked off the frosting. She ran her tongue over his finger slowly and deliberately. Two could play this game. "How's that?" she whispered, then pulled his entire finger into her mouth and sucked.

Shane's body erupted with desire. He lifted her off the ground and set her onto the counter, then moved to stand between her legs. Her mouth was hot and sweet, his was starving for her taste. He wanted her, now. Right here on the kitchen floor. It was just a good thing his fatherly instinct was so strong. He couldn't risk having the kids walk in on them naked, sliding around in the kitchen. The thought of explaining that one kept things in perspective.

* * * *

Cora moved up the back stairs then paused just before she pulled open the screen door. She'd spotted Shane and Melissa and there was no way she was going to interrupt that passionate moment. She took a step back and turned, only to run into a hard, masculine chest. "Oh," she gasped then covered her mouth.

Hank smiled as he glanced into the kitchen. "I'd say they have it about right," then he pressed his mouth to hers and pushed her up against the wall.

Cora enjoyed the kiss only a moment before she realized where they were. "Hank," she scolded, pushing him away. "We can't."

"Why not?" he was scowling now, too. "I'm tired of keeping our relationship a secret, like we're doing something wrong. This isn't wrong, Cora. I love you. Are you ashamed to be seen with me? Because that's the only reason I can come up with for sneaking around. I know I'm just a ranch hand, but I've got enough money saved, I can provide for you, for us."

"I'm not ashamed of you. I love you too," Cora admitted. She smiled a little at the shocked look on Hank's face. No, she hadn't told him that before. Not out loud anyway, but she thought he should know it by now. They'd been sneaking around for months. "I'm just not sure what Shane is going to think. I don't want him to be upset."

"Shane ain't gonna care, woman." He scowled deeper. "What about the girls? When do you plan to tell the girls we're an item? I told you before, I want to marry you. I want a life with you. At some point, the girls are gonna figure it out."

"I already told them," Cora said softly.

"You did? When?" Hank asked, surprised by the news.

"Last weekend, when they came home for a visit," she admitted.

"Why didn't you tell me?" Hank didn't like that she'd kept it a secret. Everything had to be a damn secret. "And what did they say? Are they okay with it? With me?"

"They're fine," she said, moving away from the door to sit on the large patio chair. "They said they've known all along. They told me I was a fool not to hook up with you sooner. They wanted to know what took me so long. And they said they're happy for me."

"Really?" Hank said grinning. "Well, they're right on all accounts. You were a fool for rejecting me for so long. But I don't mind as long as you don't reject me again. I want to date you, Cora. Out in the open like other folks do. I want you to be my date for Jeremy's birthday party today. It's time for this town to know you're mine."

Cora considered. It was time they brought this thing out into the open. It was a small town and everyone would know soon enough anyway. It might as well be today. "I'd love to be your date to the party. Now, sit down next to me and kiss me again. I think Shane and Melissa might be awhile yet."

* * * *

Shane pulled away, he was breathing hard and so was Mel. "You have no idea the things I want to do to you right now," he whispered as he pulled at her earlobe with his teeth. Then he ran kisses across her neck and over her jaw until he reached her mouth again.

Melissa's body was like Jell-O. Shane always had that effect on her. Once he got started she couldn't remember where she was or what she was supposed to be doing. It was all she could do to remember her own name. She still couldn't believe they were getting married next week. It hadn't taken much to pull a quick wedding together. Melissa's parents were already here for Jeremy's birthday. Being retired, it was easy for them to extend their vacation another week. The wedding would be held here at the ranch, in front of the rose garden. Melissa couldn't have asked for a more beautiful spot.

"I think I'm losing you," Shane said, straightening. "It's probably for the best. Another second of that and I'd carry you up to my bed and have my way with you."

Melissa glanced at Shane's cast. "You think so?" she asked skeptically. "I think it's all you can do to carry yourself up those stairs. I'd never let you risk my life that way."

"Good point," he grinned. "I guess we'd have to lock the pantry and finish what we started in there." He glanced at the door, considered then discarded the idea. Maybe someday, but not until after the wedding. That was fifth or sixth year of marriage material.

"Not on your life," Melissa said shaking her head. "Cora will be here any minute and so will my parents with the kids." She looked out the window and spotted Hank and Cora on the front porch. "Do you think they saw us?" she was horrified.

"Probably," Shane said, casually. He didn't care if they did. In fact, they better get used to it because he intended to kiss Melissa frequently.

"How can you act so nonchalant about it?" she said, still watching them. Then she raised her eyebrows as Hank pressed his lips to Cora's in a sweet, loving way. It wasn't the hot, animalistic kiss she'd just shared with Shane, but it was nice. "Did you know they were seeing each other?" she asked, glancing over at the man she loved.

"Sure," Shane said, grabbing a cookie from the tray. "But they don't know I know. They think it's a secret," he looked out the window. "I guess they finally decided to come out and announce it to the world, or at least the town. I'd say Jeremy's party is as good a day as any."

"Why didn't you tell me?" Melissa asked, taking two cookies from a container and handing them to Shane so he'd stop removing the ones she'd laid out for the party.

"Nothing to tell," Shane said, moving to wrap his arms around her again. "Hank has loved Cora since the moment they met. I think it was almost that fast for her, too. She just resisted because of the girls. Her husband was trash, a mean drunk and completely worthless. Cora wasn't willing to bring another man into her daughter's lives for anything. Now that they're all grown up and on their own, it only made sense for her to hook up with Hank," he smiled. "If you ask me, there's not a better man alive. They'll be good together."

"I agree," Melissa said wistfully. She hoped Cora would find happiness. She'd been so lonely for so long.

"Now, come out to the barn. There's something I want to show you," Shane said, excited.

"Is it here?" she asked. "Did Hank bring Midnight already?"

"He did," Shane said taking her hand. "Let's go see."

"I still don't understand why you made me wait," she pouted. "It's not my birthday present. Why couldn't I see Jeremy's horse before today?"

"Because I wanted it that way," Shane said with a shrug. "And since it's my present, I get to be the boss for once."

"Well, don't get used to it," she joked. "I think I want to wear the pants in this family."

"The honeymoon is over already and we're not even married. What was I thinking?" Shane laughed when Mel hit him. "Now don't go and knock me off balance. Think how bad you're going to feel if I fall over and bend these crutches. Then you'll have to help me recover and I'm pretty sure you're skinny little butt isn't strong enough to pick me up off the ground."

"I already saved your sorry butt once hot shot. I can do it again," but she placed a protective hand on his shoulder for support. The barn was dimly lit and her eyes took a minute to adjust. Shane left her side and moved toward the closest stall. He grabbed a lead rope off a hook and slowly opened the door. Moments later, he returned with a beautiful buckskin. The horse had a black tail, mane and dark boots that stopped midway up his legs. "Oh, Shane. He's beautiful." She reached out to run a hand over its nose and the horse bobbed its head. "But why did they name him Midnight?"

"Her," Shane corrected. "She's a mare and her name isn't Midnight. This is Zander. Well, it's actually Zanderharrah Von something or other, but she likes Zander or Zandra whichever you prefer," he explained.

Melissa looked at Shane, confused. "I thought you said you bought Jeremy a horse named Midnight."

"I did," Shane said handing the rope to Mel. He turned and approached another stall. "Keep a hold of her. She likes to test the waters. She's a bit of a handful," then he stepped out with a beautiful black stallion.

"You bought Jeremy two horses?" she asked, still not understanding.

"No silly," Shane said, as he tied the stallion to a rail. He took the rope from Melissa and tied the mare next to it. "I bought Midnight for Jeremy. He's a perfect gentleman. A good horse for a kid to learn on. He's patient enough to be safe, but he has enough spirit in him to give a young boy a thrill. Later, when he's more experience that is. Zander is Midnight's half-sister. They have the same father but different mothers. They were born a few months apart."

"You got Zander for Megan?" Melissa replied in understanding. "The horses reminded you of Megan and Jeremy and our situation."

"No," Shane corrected. "I bought Zander for you." He turned to her and smiled. "I remembered how much you used to love to ride. The only extra horse I have is Molly. She's great for someone that's never been on a horse, but not my wild beauty. You needed a horse that was a challenge. You needed Zander. Unlike Midnight, she's not a good horse for a kid. Anyway, Megan has Trigger. She loves that sable gelding and he loves her. They're a good match just like me and Nico. I think Midnight is going to be perfect for Jer and trust me, Zander is perfect for you."

"You bought me a horse?" Melissa asked, surprised. "But that was back...you didn't even like me then."

Shane pulled her into his arms. "I always liked you. I told you I've loved you since the moment I saw you. I just didn't want to like you. But as much as I fought it, I couldn't help wanting to keep you here, with me forever. When I heard their story, how they'd been together almost since birth and I saw Zander's spunk, I just knew I had to buy her for you."

"Thank you," Melissa said, pushing onto her toes to press a kiss on Shane's lips. "You have no idea how much I wanted my own horse. I just couldn't justify it. After riding Molly, I wanted one even more. But I convinced myself a horse for Jeremy was enough. He's a good kid, he'd let his mom ride every once in a while. I just kept telling myself I could be happy with that, it would have to be enough."

"I never want you to settle for enough, honey," Shane said kissing her gently. "I want to give you the world," he paused and looked at the mare then back to Melissa. "So I did good?"

"You did great," Melissa grinned. "Now I just need my own saddle and stirrups. Oh, and I want to buy one of those beautiful Indian blankets. You know the ones? They just came in at the hardware store a few weeks ago. There was one I really loved, but I didn't have a horse to put it on. I hope nobody else bought it." She was rambling and she knew it, but she couldn't help it. It was like her birthday, too.

Shane laughed. "I've created a monster." He shook his head when her face fell. "Of course you can go get one of those blankets. You can go get anything you want. I'm rich, remember? We're rich," he paused. "Uh, I wasn't going to ask yet but maybe now is as good a time as any."

"What?" she was smiling again. She was so happy, she couldn't stop. She was going to get married next week and Shane had bought her a horse. A beautiful, spunky horse just for her.

"Well, you used to help your dad out at the hardware store," he hesitated. "I mean, doing the books and stuff."

"Yes," she said, looking at him seriously. "Are we in trouble, financially I mean?"

Shane laughed. "Not even close," he assured her. "But I hate keeping the books for this place. I've done it, for all these years I've done it because there was never anyone else I trusted to take it over. I trust Hank, but he can barely balance his own checkbook. I'd never let him loose on something as complicated as the ranch. Anyway, I was hoping you would be willing to help me. In fact, if you want, I'll let you take that job over completely."

"You'd let me have control of the money?" she asked, speechless. Shane had a lot of money. And he was willing to trust her with all of it.

"Of course," Shane said, furrowing his brows. "Why wouldn't I?"

"Uh, I don't know. Maybe because you're a gazillionaire. What if I'm marrying you for your money?"

Shane laughed again. "You? Marrying me for my money?" he shook his head. "Such a comedian." He rested his hands on her shoulders. "I trust you with my life, my daughter, my son and my money Melissa Carpenter," he frowned. "Melissa Chandler," he nodded. "Yeah, that's better. I trust you. Now will you do me a favor and rescue me from spreadsheet hell? I'll love you forever if you do."

"You'll love me forever anyway," she smiled, "but yes, I'll handle the books. I actually love doing that sort of thing and since I quit my job I've been wondering what I was going to do with my time until we get the B&B up and going. That will help."

"Oh, don't you worry about getting bored. I have plenty of ideas to keep us busy," Shane kissed her again. "I love you."

"You're just saying that because I'm doing the books," she teased, then took his hand and started for the door. "Are we going to leave the horses out like that?"

"Yeah," Shane said as he let her lead him from the barn. "I want to give Jeremy his present now before everyone starts arriving. I think I heard your parents pull up."

Melissa glanced around and saw her mother's new Audi. "Sure did," she said happily. "Jeremy is going to go crazy over Midnight. He's going to want to ride him now."

"Maybe later," Shane told her. "I'll saddle him up and lead the kids around the corral after we eat. Don't worry, I'm not as big a pushover with him as I am with you."

"Almost," Melissa laughed. They entered the house and found Cora in the kitchen, but there was no sign of the kids or her parents. "Cora, do you know where mom went?"

"They stopped in, then immediately went back outside. You didn't see them when you came in?" Cora asked.

"No," Melissa said, looking toward Shane. "Do you think something's wrong?"

"Let's go look. They can't be far," Shane said, taking her hand and leading her back out the door. The instant they stepped outside they knew there was trouble. Connie Peters was rushing toward them.

"Mom, what's wrong?" Melissa asked.

"Shane! It's your mother," Connie said, trying to sound calm but clearly worried. "The kids took off with Frisco the instant we stopped the car. The dog was anxious to get out of the truck, to run around and do his business," she paused. "Anyway, the kids followed. But when they didn't come right back, Jake decided to go look for them. I waited a short time, then I got worried and followed. Gloria was talking to the kids. Jake was hiding in the shadows listening. He spotted me and motioned for me to go back. Maybe we should call the sheriff."

Shane pulled his cell phone from his pocket and dialed Joe's number. He filled him in and closed the phone. "He's only a few minutes out. He's going to expedite. I need to keep her busy until he gets here," he took Mel's hand. "Come on, let's see what we can do. Connie, Cora's in the kitchen if you want to join her. It's a hot day and you look like you could use a nice tall glass of iced tea."

"I'm not a fading violet Shane Chandler, but I will join Cora. She'll want to know what's going on." With that she turned and headed for the door.

Shane approached the end of the drive with caution. He hated that he was on crutches. If Gloria tried to run again, there was no way he could stop her. And he knew Melissa, the woman would chase after Gloria herself. As he got closer he could hear Jeremy talking.

"You're not a nice person," he said. "You ruined our car."

"Not on purpose," Gloria told him. "And that was your mother's fault. I am a nice person. I just wanted to get to know my grandkids. I want to spend time with you and come to your birthday party. That's not too much to ask is it? To let your grandma come to your party?"

"That depends," Shane grumbled. "What does he have to give you in return?"

"Shane," Gloria said in surprise. She knew she'd have to face him, but she hadn't wanted to do it just yet. The kids weren't cooperating. The stubborn boy was angry with her over his mother. And Megan wasn't helping. "I was just coming up to see you," she saw Melissa and grimaced. Well, what had she expected? If the rumors were true, Melissa would be marrying her son in a matter of days. "Hello, Melissa."

"Gloria," Melissa said, moving in to stand next to Shane. "What are you doing here?"

"You didn't tell me you had a son," Gloria said, not answering. "And that he was also my grandchild," she shook her head. "But I guess I'm not surprised. After all you kept that a secret from Shane for years, didn't you?"

"Mother, why are you here?" Shane asked. "You know Joe's looking for you. You've already done enough damage. What do you want now? Or is it just more of the same? Give me money, buy me a new car, buy me a house."

"I never asked you to buy me a house," Gloria countered. "Why can't you believe I'm only here to make amends? All I want is to attend my grandson's birthday party. Then I'll leave if you want me to. I'll take the memory with me and leave," she sniffed. "I won't like it. I'm getting older. You're all I have. You and those two precious kids. Is it really too much to ask for you to let me get to know them?"

Shane paused. If he didn't know her better, he'd be taken in by her attempt at sincerity. "And then what? You get to know the kids, let them bond with you then what? You threaten something sinister if I don't finance your lifestyle?"

"When did you become such a cynic?" she asked, truly surprised. Shane had always been such a happy kid. "You have so much, why are you so hostile towards me? I'm your mother. I love you. I know I messed up sometimes, but I did my best to take care of you."

"Yeah mother," Shane let out an unamused laugh. "Being used as some random guy's punching bag was an act of love."

"The only man that ever touched you was Danny. And you know I kicked him out once I was sober," Gloria protested. "I even let that no good Kevin what's his name move in because he took such a liking to you."

"Oh yeah," Shane scoffed. "Kevin liked me alright. A little too much. The instant he found out I wasn't some timid kid that would participate in his perverted games he was off like a rocket."

312

"That's not true," Gloria protested. "Kevin never touched you." Had he? The story actually made sense. He was horrible in the sack but he had money. That's what counted. But she would never be able to live with herself if she'd brought a man home that had molested her son. She'd never wanted the kid, but she didn't want him hurt either.

"No Gloria," he assured her. "Kevin never touched me. Not for lack of trying, but I wasn't helpless anymore. And I hadn't been for years. Kevin split because I told him I was going to the police. I'm sure he was wanted, but I was too young at the time to realize it. He split and you brought home Creepy Carl. I guess at least you married that one. Remember mother, you were so in love with Carl that you forgot I even existed, literally. The two of you partied night after night and completely ignored the starving kid in the corner. If it wasn't for Cora, I'm not sure I would have survived that one."

"You make everything sound so ugly Shane," Gloria brushed away a tear. "It wasn't all that bad. I bought you food. I made sure you had clothes to wear to school. And after Carl I wised up. I never married for love again. I did my best to find men that could provide for us. Men with money, men with security."

"But that was never enough, was it Gloria?" Shane continued. "Because you didn't marry for love. Those guys didn't mean a thing to you. Did they? Just a means to an end. You never did say, why did Stanton give you the boot? He was a decent guy. Too decent, apparently. He adored you. What did you do that was so terrible he wanted a divorce? I'm sure it has to do with another man. You never could be faithful for more than five minutes."

Gloria didn't answer; she just glared at her son. Was she as bad as he thought she was? She hadn't loved Stanton, but he had adored her. In the long run that hadn't been enough. She needed excitement. She'd needed the thrill. That's why she'd risked it all for that stupid pool boy.

"I thought so," Shane said as he moved a little closer. He was now securely between his mother and his children. He reached back and gave both of them a little push. They moved back next to Melissa, but didn't leave. "Mel, will you please take the kids to the house? I'd rather they not be subjected to this conversation."

Mel took each of the kids by the arm and turned to leave. That's when she spotted Joe and let out a silent sigh of relief. Gloria would be gone soon. Listening to Shane replay his childhood was horrifying. She couldn't believe Gloria would expose a child to such terrible conditions.

"Shane," Gloria began, then she too noticed the police car. "So that's it," she sobbed. "You're going to have me arrested? Was I really that horrible that you would call the cops and have me arrested just for stopping by to visit?"

"No Gloria," he said coldly. "I'm having you arrested for shooting at Mel."

"I never shot at her!" Gloria shrieked. Okay, so she had vandalized Melissa's car and that might have been wrong. She wasn't going to admit that right now, she wasn't completely stupid. But she had not shot at the woman and she would not take the blame. That was Donald, the idiot. She had no problem giving him up to the police. The man was creepier than Creepy Carl, who hadn't been creepy at all. Oh, maybe he was to a kid. Shane had only been six or seven at the time. But Gloria actually cared for Carl. That's why it had been such a blow when he left. He'd been the second man she'd allowed herself to care about. The second man that had left her. The first one, the only man she'd ever loved, had been Shane's father.

Joe stepped forward, handcuffed Gloria then read her the Miranda warning. "We're going to go back to the station and have us a little chat," he told her. "Sorry about the party, Shane. Tell Jeremy Happy Birthday for me." Then he reached in the window and pulled out a small wrapped package. "It's not much, but I think he'll like it."

"Thanks Joe," Shane said taking the gift. "I'm sure he'll love it, whatever it is. And thanks for this," he pointed to Gloria.

"I'll call you in an hour or so and let you know what I get," then he climbed into the car and pulled back out the drive.

Shane turned and slowly walked toward the house. The guests would be arriving soon. They still needed to give Jeremy the horse. Somehow none of that seemed important anymore. Why did seeing his mother, watching her sob, watching her handcuffed and thrown into the back seat of Joe's car, make him so terribly sad? It was his son's birthday. The first party he'd ever attended. He'd bought him a horse, a damn good horse that Jeremy was going to love. So why did he want to jump in his truck and chase Joe down and drop all the charges?

But he couldn't. She had shot at Mel. He might be able to forgive the vandalism, that was typical Gloria after all. But not shooting at the woman he loved. He pushed his hands through his hair as he lowered himself onto the porch swing. He needed a minute before he went in. Melissa would see right through him and she would drop the charges without a second thought. He knew her well enough to know she wouldn't allow his mother to go to jail if it upset him even a little bit. He glanced up when he heard the screen door creak.

315

"I assume Joe took her away," Melissa said, sitting next to him on the swing.

"Yeah," Shane said, stretching out and resting his head against the wall. "It's over."

"Not necessarily," Melissa said, taking his hand. "I think she really is sorry. Maybe not for what she did to me, but all that other stuff. The men, the neglect, all of it," she glanced at Shane, but he was still just sitting there, legs stretched out, eyes closed. "I felt a little bad for her. She's getting older. Her husband just booted her out of the house, her son hates her. She has two grand kids, but she doesn't know either one of them. Her life is pretty depressing, you have to admit that."

"She created it," Shane said, opening his eyes. "I can admit it, but she has no one to blame but herself. Stanton really was a great guy. I could tell that in less than five minutes. She used him. I have no doubt she broke that man's heart. He would have tolerated almost anything but cheating, unfortunately that's what Gloria does best. She gets bored and she takes on a lover. I'm sure poor Stanton came home early for some reason and caught her with the mailman, the grounds keeper, the pool boy, someone. It's what Gloria does."

"Do you know why?" Melissa asked. "I mean, you said she hasn't loved any of her husbands. Why do you think she's never been in love? Or did she love someone that left her?"

Shane considered that. "The latter I think. When I was little she used to tell me about my father, my real one. When she talked about him, it was different. I think maybe she loved him, but when he found out she was pregnant with me, he left," Shane paused. "Maybe I do owe her something. Maybe it's my fault the only man she ever loved, left."

"That's nonsense," Melissa said immediately. "If he left because he had a kid, that's his fault and he wasn't worth squat."

"Agreed," Shane said, pulling her into his arms. "Why can you always make me feel better? I was sitting here, depressed. Feeling guilty because I just had my own mother arrested and after five minutes with you, the world doesn't seem that bad anymore."

"We don't have to press charges," Melissa said, treading carefully. She knew Shane was going to argue.

"She shot you," he said shaking his head. "As much as I might like to pretend none of this happened, that woman shot you. I can't look the other way. I won't. And what if we did. I can't even imagine what that woman would do next time. No, we have to let this one stick. She created this mess, she's going to have to deal with the consequences."

"Shane," Melissa began. "I know this is difficult. How can I make it easier for you? What if we drop the charges on the car stuff and I agree to enjoy my new Escalade without any strings? I will never complain about you spending a fortune on that extravagant, luxury car again," she paused. "I think she needs to pay for the shooting thing. That was dangerous, but the rest was only stuff. Kind of like that other story. Meredith gets a brand new car and the guy. They lived happily ever after. I can live with that, like Meredith; I got the car and the man. Let's just leave it at that."

"I might consider it," Shane said, thinking. "Let's wait and see what Joe says after he talks to Gloria. Then we'll decide what to do, together."

"Deal," Melissa said, looking up to see two vehicles pull in. "I think the monsters are starting to arrive. Put on your party face and go greet our guests. I'll get the kids."

Hidden Lakes

* * * *

Shane, Melissa, Megan and Jeremy approached the barn. Jeremy felt his parent's excitement and wondered where they were going and why. His friends were starting to arrive and he wanted to be there to show them around. He couldn't wait for them to meet Frisco. He'd never had a dog before so he talked about Frisco all the time. His friends wanted to see for themselves if the German Shepard was as smart and friendly as Jeremy claimed. They had been talking about it for days.

Megan couldn't wait to see Jeremy's face when he found out he was getting his very own horse. She'd been there when Hank and her dad unloaded Midnight this morning and then stayed in the barn alone, petting Midnight and getting to know him. She remembered how excited she'd been when her dad had bought her Trigger. Jeremy was going to be just as happy about Midnight. And maybe soon they could go out riding together. It was okay to ride with her dad or Melissa but they were always busy. If Jeremy had his own horse, he'd get better at riding and dad would have to let them explore.

She skipped ahead and then stopped, waiting for her dad to catch up. It was hard to wait while he hobbled along on his crutches. She still hated to think about the night he got hurt. She was so scared. She didn't know what would happen to her if her dad died like Jeremy's other dad did. She didn't have a mom that would love her, she didn't have anyone. She had told Jeremy how much it scared her but he said she was just being stupid. He thought Melissa would still be her mom, but Megan wasn't so sure. Why would Melissa want to get stuck with another kid, one that wasn't even

318

hers? Megan was sure Melissa wouldn't want her. She'd just have to make sure nothing ever happened to her dad. Then she wouldn't have to be alone.

They finally reached the barn and Shane motioned to Melissa to go ahead. He would stay with the kids while Melissa led Midnight out into the open.

"Why did we stop?" Jeremy asked, confused. His friends were here and he wanted to go play. He didn't understand why his parents would make him walk all the way to the barn with them but then not go inside.

"Your mom's bringing out a surprise," Shane said, wishing he could run and get the beautiful mustang himself.

"How come?" Jeremy asked, glancing back into the darkness. "I mean, why didn't she just bring it up to the house?"

"It's too big," Megan laughed.

Jeremy frowned. "If you already know, it's not a surprise," he grumbled.

"It's a surprise to you," she said with a shrug. "Stop pouting, you're going to love it."

Melissa stepped from the barn, Midnight in tow. The instant the horse was out in the open, Megan clapped her hands and began jumping up and down. She was so excited.

Jeremy looked at Megan, then to his father and finally to his mother. He was confused. His mother began to smile and then his father spoke.

"Happy Birthday son," Shane said, placing a hand on Jeremy's shoulder. "What's wrong, don't you like him?"

Jeremy spun around and stared at his father. Was it really true? Did he really have his own horse? "Really?" he asked quietly. "Is he really all mine?" A huge smile began to spread across his face. He had asked his mom for a new puppy, but this was even better. He didn't really need a puppy, he had Frisco. Frisco was Megan's, but she didn't mind sharing. He couldn't wait to show his friends.

"Really," Shane said giving Jeremy a little push. "Go meet Midnight."

Jeremy ran over to his mom and hugged her. "Thank you, thank you, thank you. It's the best birthday present ever."

"It's not from me," she said winking at Shane. "It was all your dad. I saw Midnight for the first time this morning."

Jeremy ran back over to Shane and wrapped his arms tightly around his waist. "Thank you," he said looking up at his father.

Shane started to lower himself to Jeremy's level then realized he'd never get up. Instead he took Jeremy's hand and slowly led him back to the horse. "What do you say you introduce yourself?" Shane wrapped an arm around Melissa and watched as Jeremy began to run his hand down Midnight's neck. His son was hesitant at first, but in no time he was standing in front of the big mustang talking to him and rubbing his nose.

Melissa handed the lead rope to Shane and disappeared. Moments later she returned with a folding chair. Shane kissed her, grateful she'd thought of it. He was finally getting used to her pampering and he had to admit he liked it. Once he lowered himself onto the chair Jeremy moved to stand beside him. He was still smiling and Shane could see the horse was a hit.

Jeremy was so happy he couldn't stand still. He wanted his dad to know how much he loved his present, but he didn't know how to show him. Finally he reached up and gave his dad a hug. He was surprised when Shane lifted him onto his lap, the way he always did with Megan.

"Now," Shane said knowing he would cherish this moment forever. "Owning a horse is a big responsibility. It's up to you to make sure he's fed every day and that he always has water. If he's good, you need to reward him with a treat like an apple or a carrot. You will need to brush him before and after every ride just like Megan does with Trigger. I know you've been helping Hank with Molly, but Midnight is yours. That means no more helping. Hank, your mom or I will help you if you need us to, but you have to take care of Midnight. Do you understand?"

Jeremy couldn't help himself, he leaned in and gave his dad another big hug. "Midnight is the best present in the whole world," he smiled. "I love you dad," then he jumped off Shane's lap and ran to his mom.

"He's mine mom," he said walking around his new pet, pausing here and there to run a gentle hand over Midnight's dark coat. "All mine," he turned to Megan and grabbed her hand. "Let's go get Ted and Bobby. They have to see my birthday present," then the two kids ran off talking excitedly and practically flying they were so happy.

Melissa tied Midnight to a post then returned to Shane. He brushed a hand over his eyes as she approached. Melissa smiled. Jeremy had no idea how much his words had meant to his father, but she did. She slowly lowered herself onto Shane's lap and pressed her palms to his cheeks. Then she pulled him in close and hugged him tight. "I love you too big man," she whispered. "It's a good day."

Shane smiled. He could always count on Melissa to understand him. "It is," he finally said. "It really is."

"Jeremy is going to remember this day for the rest of his life. You do know you're going to have to saddle up that beauty and spend hours giving rides," she glanced down at his leg. "Or maybe I will. You're still an invalid."

Shane shifted Melissa in his lap, pulling her closer. "Not where it counts," he whispered before he kissed her thoroughly.

Melissa smiled at Shane, a little breathless from the kiss. Then she gently rested her head on Shane's shoulder. "Was that the first time he told you he loves you?" she asked knowing it had to be or Shane wouldn't have had such a potent reaction.

"Yeah," he said taking a deep breath as he watched his son and daughter return with three young boys. "I wondered…" he stopped, still choked up.

"You wondered when he would accept you, totally and completely as his father and openly give you affection?" she finished for him.

"Okay yes," he admitted.

"He's loved you for a long time," she said pressing a soft kiss to Shane's lips. "I think he's just struggling with how to show it. I mean, he wants to be macho and tough like his dad, but he also sees how you dote on Megan. She's a very expressive kid. Jeremy is still trying to find his way," she smiled. "It's a good day," she said again. Then she stood and walked back to the horse, worried he might get spooked by so many rowdy kids.

Jeremy approached his dad. He was still self-conscious about how he'd reacted. He'd never told Shane he loved him before even though he had for a long time now. When his dad pulled him onto his lap, he'd just felt loved and wanted his dad to know he loved him too. But his friends were here now, so things were a little awkward.

Shane stood and moved over to his son. He paused then reached down and lifted Jeremy onto his shoulders. "You better hold on Birthday Boy," he said, laughing. "It might get a little rough up there when I start to walk."

Jeremy laughed. His friends gathered around his dad, begging for rides.

Shane moved in next to Midnight and then placed Jeremy on the horses back. "Midnight belongs to Jeremy," Shane said as he turned back to the other kids. "You're going to have to ask him if it's okay."

Jeremy leaned down and gave his horse a big hug. He loved him already. He was so excited he could hardly sit still. He smiled at his friends, of course he'd let them have a ride. He could share Midnight today, he'd have his horse all to himself forever. "They can have a ride," he told his dad. He glanced around, wondering how he was going to get off.

"Did you hear that?" Shane asked. "Jeremy said he's willing to give you a chance to ride Midnight."

Two of the boys raised their hands in the air and gave each other a celebratory slap. "Yes!" Shane heard them say as they all began to talk at once. He took advantage of the moment and reached up, lifting Jeremy off the back of the horse. He held him in his arms for the slightest moment then he leaned in and whispered, "I love you too, son."

Jeremy didn't have a chance to react before Shane set him back onto the ground. The kids had been right. Jeremy did have the coolest dad in the world. "Who should I let ride Midnight first?" he asked, not wanting to cause a fight.

"Why don't we figure that out later?" he said, placing a hand on Jeremy's shoulder. "You have more guests to greet and we need to have dinner first."

"We're not going to ride him now?" Jeremy asked, disappointed.

"We'll do that later," Melissa said moving in beside the two. "Grandma and Grandpa need you guys to go help them bring out the food."

"But mom," Jeremy started to protest. "I want to ride Midnight now. And all my friends want that too. If we wait, it will get too late and then they'll have to go home. Why can't we just do it now?"

"I promise," Shane said, stepping in to avoid an argument. "I'll give all of your friends a ride on Midnight later. Right now your mom's right. We need to get the food out here before the masses start to riot."

"I don't know what that means," Jeremy said soberly. "But you really promise. You won't let their parents take them home without riding Midnight?"

Shane nodded. "I promise."

Jeremy hesitated, wondering if he could really trust his dad. "Okay," he finally said and turned to call to his friends. "Come on guys, we need to help with the food." Within seconds they were gone, racing each other across the large yard, headed for the house. Two of the boys shoved each other playfully. Both fell to the ground. Megan leapt over them, laughing. She fit right in with Jeremy's friends.

"I hope they settle down before they reach the house or Cora is going to tan their hides." He smiled and pulled Melissa close. "Am I in trouble?"

"Nope," she said, wrapping an arm around his waist as they too headed toward the house. "It's nice having backup. He can't be an angel all the time and it is his birthday. I was tempted to give in."

Shane laughed. "Then it's a good thing I was here. He needed to wait, the timing is better after we eat."

"I agree," she said once again marveling at how easy it had been to fall into a family rhythm with Shane.

* * * *

Just over an hour later, Joe showed up. Melissa spotted him first. She headed his way when Shane hobbled over.

"Can we go inside?" Joe asked, soberly.

"Sure," Shane said, turning. "Let's head for the Study." Once the three of them were inside, Shane shut the door firmly behind them. He paused, then reached back and locked it. Joe looked serious and he didn't want any interruptions. "Is Gloria still in jail?" he finally asked.

"She is," Joe nodded. "But we have to talk. I've charged her with vandalism for your car Melissa as well as harassment. I'd charge her with stupidity if there was a code for that," he stopped.

"What about the shooting? Did you charge her with aggravated assault, shooting in the city limits? What?" Shane asked.

"No," Joe said, glancing at Melissa then turning his attention to Shane. "She wasn't the one that shot at Melissa."

"Well of course she would say that," Shane began. "She can be very convincing."

"I'm aware of her history," Joe said soberly. "But it wasn't her. Jason arrested a guy by the name of Donald Singleton. Have you ever heard of him?" He was asking Shane, not Melissa.

"Singleton?" Shane considered. "Might ring a bell. Who is he?"

"Some guy that lives on the outskirts of town," Joe said. "He's on the Henley side, so he's out of my jurisdiction. I've never met him before, but he seems to know you. He was rambling on about some livestock. For some reason he seems to believe you cheated him."

Shane's head popped up. "I remember but that was several years ago," he was trying to recall the details. "Hank and I were at the auction checking out a prize heard when this guy slammed into Hank. We both turned to see him knocking around some woman. She wasn't the picture of innocence or anything but a man shouldn't hit a woman no matter what. Hank and I got involved. We told the guy if he hit the girl again, he'd have to deal with us. The guy wasn't happy, but he moved on. Then once the auction began he started a bidding war with me for one of those prized bulls. I wanted that bull, so I paid top dollar for him. This Donald guy hid behind the barn and ambushed me. Sucker punched me right in the side of the head. Might have done more if Hank hadn't shown up. Why would he shoot at Mel?"

"Apparently Gloria hooked up with him," Joe began. "She was just using him for a place to stay, but after that last attempt to get you to soften up failed she was in a ripe mood. She says she went back to the house and was venting, you know going on about how Melissa was ruining her life and how if it wasn't for her, things would be different. That's when she let it slip that you were her son and that you refused to help her out, with money and a car. Gloria didn't notice Donald's reaction, not then. But that's when he started to scheme. The night he shot at Mel, he was planning to kidnap her. He thought you'd give plenty to get your woman back. He's confessed to everything. We're not charging Gloria in the shooting. She's the one that stopped Donald from grabbing you. By that time she'd become suspicious. Donald was constantly asking her details about your schedule and Shane's. She got there just after he fired the third shot and she went off on him. Basically, she attacked him. Broke his nose. Donald was pissed and gave Gloria the boot. He told her never to set foot on his property again or he'd shoot her with a real gun. She believed him.

She claims that's why she destroyed your car. She was desperate. She couldn't get Shane to help her. She was out of money and attacking Donald to help you, made everything worse. She was forced to spend the night in her run down car and there you were living on the ranch, driving that fancy car. She claims she just lost it. I'm not sure I believe that. I think there was plenty of intent, but I do believe she was feeling desperate. So, Donald is in jail for the shooting. Gloria will do some time for the property damage, but not much. And the two of you have to figure out what to do when

327

she gets out. She says she's going to stick around. Only time will tell, but right now, she's going on about her grandchildren. She told me she's going to take Melissa's advice, get a job, an apartment and hang around here until you forgive her. I hate to break it to you Shane, but we might be seeing a lot more of Gloria Chandler, or Matthews or whatever she's going by these days. I can't keep up."

The group sat in silence for several minutes. Shane and Melissa were taking in the situation, considering their options. Joe finally stood. "Well, I'm gonna head out. Molly's waiting for me. Be sure and tell Jeremy I'm sorry for missing his big day."

Melissa stood to walk him out. When they reached the door she paused. "Thanks Joe," she smiled. "Why don't you stop in the kitchen on the way out? Cora will package up some of her delicious cake for you and Molly."

"I'll do that," Joe grinned. "Cora's cake is the best in four counties. You don't think I'd pass it up now do you?"

"You'd be foolish if you did," Melissa crooned.

"I'll find my way back," Joe said softly. "I think that man in there needs you right about now."

"I agree," Melissa whispered. "Now go on, don't keep Molly waiting."

* * * *

Melissa stood in the doorway watching Shane. He was so stressed, she wasn't sure she knew what to do to help him. A noise caught her attention and she turned. Her mother had just stepped into the hallway. Melissa silently moved from the study and pulled her mother into the kitchen. "I need a favor," she began, hating what she was going to ask. "Can you keep the kids busy for a while? Maybe start a game or something? Most of them are finished eating and they are expecting their horse ride. I really need a few minutes alone with Shane."

Connie Peters studied her daughter. There must be a new development in the arrest. "Of course," she finally said. "Don't you worry about a thing. Your father and I will handle this. It's not as if this is our first birthday party. We've dealt with enough hyped up kids to know how to handle them. I know a couple games that will keep them occupied for a while. You go on and do what you need to do."

"Thanks mom," Melissa said, relieved. Her mother was right. They had thrown huge birthday parties for Melissa every year of her life. Until she got too old to hang out with her parents anyway. She loved her parents and owed them so much. They had been so good to her, better than she deserved sometimes. She just hoped she could be as good a parent to Jeremy and Megan as her parents had been for her. "I'll hurry."

The instant Melissa returned to the study she slid the door silently closed and locked it behind her. Shane looked up when Melissa reached the couch and sank down next to him. She smiled when he reached out and took her hand in his.

"We better get back out there," he finally said as he started to stand.

Melissa didn't move. She waited, when Shane looked at her in confusion she slowly shook her head. "We need to talk."

"It can wait," Shane said, trying to pull her from the couch again. "We have two dozen kids out there waiting for a horseback ride. I made a promise, I won't disappoint them or Jeremy."

"Mom's playing a game with them," she said giving his hand a tug this time. "We have a little time. Let her have some grandma fun. She lives with a bunch of old geezers now. She and dad need this right now. And so do we," she said softly.

Shane slowly lowered himself back onto the couch, knowing Melissa wanted to talk about his mother. But his feelings were even more complicated than that. Melissa had been shot because of him. It was one thing to know she was in danger because of his crazy mother, but it was entirely different knowing her safety was at risk because of some business deal that had occurred years ago. How many other ways had he put her at risk?

"Tell me which thing concerns you the most," Melissa finally said. "There were several things that Joe told us that we need to talk about, so I need to know which one we should broach first."

Shane didn't answer. He was at a loss. What should he do? He loved Mel too much to have her in constant danger because of him. And what about his kids? Were they in danger over business he had conducted in the past?

"Okay," Melissa said, studying Shane. "Then we'll leave the matter of your mother for last. Let's talk about this Donald character."

"Melissa this is serious," Shane said taking a deep breath.

"I'm aware of that Shane," Melissa said cutting him off. "Before we talk about Donald I think we need to talk about you," she paused. She didn't know the right way to approach this.

"What about me?" Shane asked wearily.

"Well," Melissa began. "We need to talk about the way you take the blame for everything. Don't get me wrong, when it's just you and me and we're arguing over something personal, feel free to take all the blame, all the time. It will make things much easier on me."

Shane didn't smile, but Mel could see he wanted to. The left corner of his mouth was twitching ever so slightly. "But outside our marriage this needs to stop," she said seriously. "Eight years ago Kristy basically raped you. Call it date rape, call it taking advantage, call it whatever you want but she forced you to have sex when you were drunk and passed out. It was morally wrong and it was illegal. Sure, it would have been hard to prove but that doesn't make it any less criminal. And what do you do? You take the blame. You carry the guilt and the shame with you for years. In fact, you are still carrying some of it. Sure we talked about what happened but I don't believe for one minute that you have forgiven yourself for what you perceive as a lapse in judgment. Stop it already," she took a deep breath. She was getting angry. "I love you for your values. I love that when you are in the wrong you will admit it and apologize immediately. You were angrier than I've ever seen you when you thought I callously ignored your wishes and took Megan for a ride. You yelled and blustered but the instant you realized you'd read the situation wrong, you came and apologized.

I wish I had that kind of strength, that kind of character. I yelled at you and Megan but when I realized I was out of line, I stressed over it. I knew I had to apologize when I got the chance, but I didn't take immediate action. I stayed home and wallowed because I was horrified with myself. I didn't get in the car and drive to your house and tell you and Megan I was sorry, that I was wrong and I was sorry. We both know that's what you would have done if the tables were turned that night."

"Melissa, I don't know what you are trying to get at, but we really need to get back out there with the kids," Shane pressed. He didn't want to have this conversation. He didn't want Melissa to absolve him of his past sins.

"The kids are fine," Melissa said, brushing off his concern. "They are on a sugar high, they are playing games with my parents and when we get finished they will have a wonderful horseback ride before we send them on their way. We have plenty of time so stop avoiding." She moved a little closer and took Shane's hand in hers. "Do you think I don't know what you were doing when I walked in? You were sitting here berating yourself because some random dirtbag attacked me to get back at you. That thug is a criminal and an abuser, which means he's most likely a bully. So tell me Shane, what should you have done differently that day? Should you and Hank have kept walking? Should you have pretended like you didn't see the abuse to that woman and avoided a confrontation? Clearly she left him. Did you ever stop to think maybe you and Hank's kindness gave her the strength to do something she already knew she needed to do?"

"If that's true that just means it was more personal than I originally thought," Shane said, considering. "If Donald's girlfriend left him because I interfered it's no wonder he came after you."

"And if you hadn't interfered, what do you think would have happened?" she continued. "If you had just walked by and pretended like you didn't see a man hitting his girlfriend what would Hank have done?"

This time Shane did smile. "He would have helped the woman, then he would have tanned my hide himself."

Melissa smiled, too. That's exactly what Hank would have done. "So if you hadn't gotten involved Hank would have anyway. Then what if this Donald guy realized Hank was in love with Cora? Everyone knows how close you are to Cora. If he had tried to kidnap her instead he would have accomplished the same thing. He would have hurt Hank for interfering and he would have walked away a rich man."

Shane wasn't sure where Melissa was going with this. "If you're asking if I would have paid money for Cora's safe return, you know I would have."

"I'm not asking Shane, I already know you would and so does everyone in town. That's my point. If Cora had been the one Donald kidnapped, would you be blaming Hank right now? Would you be angry with him? Would you be questioning his actions, berating him for being so stupid? If you hadn't been at that auction that day, would Hank have purchased that bull anyway? Even with the bidding war?"

"Yes," Shane admitted.

"So, would you be sitting here going over every business deal, every auction Hank ever attended looking for danger?" she pressed.

"No," Shane admitted. "I wouldn't blame Hank."

"Then why do you blame yourself?" Melissa said softly. "I mean really, what's the alternative? Shut down the ranch? Stop buying cattle? Never help someone in need ever again because their attacker might be deranged? Maybe you should just give all that money you have worked so hard for to charity or something because having money will always make you a target."

Shane ran his hands over his face and took a deep breath. He knew she was right. He couldn't stop doing business just because it might make some guy mad. So how could he continue business and ensure his families safety at the same time?

"Shane," Melissa said as she placed a supportive hand on his thigh. "I know it's hard. Before now, you've been enjoying the fruits of your labor. You had a dream and you made it come true. You probably never thought achieving your goals would bring wacko's out of the woodwork. Don't let one guy's greed, one guy who is lazy and deranged, spoil everything you have worked your whole life to achieve. The guy was mad that you bought the bull he wanted. So what? It was an auction. If Donald wanted a sure thing he should have tried to make the purchase from a private seller. And just because he says that's why he did this, it doesn't mean it is. He needed to come up with an excuse. He wanted to make you look bad, so he claimed you cheated him out of a prized bull. Maybe I cut him off one day when he was driving down the road, would that justify shooting at me?" When Shane didn't answer, Melissa did. "No, Shane it wouldn't. Donald what's his name is lazy and opportunistic. He wasn't kidnapping me to get back at you, he was kidnapping me because he wanted a free ride, just like Gloria does. Keep this in perspective Shane and stop blaming yourself for the lack of character in other people. I won't tolerate it."

Shane pulled Melissa into his arms. He silently held her there while he went over the situation in his mind. After several minutes he kissed the top of her head and let out a huge sigh. "You're right," he finally said. "I wanted this. I worked hard for it. Donald is like my mother and I'm not going to blame myself for his bad behavior."

"And Kristy?" Melissa asked softly. "Are you finally going to put that nonsense away and stop blaming yourself for her actions as well?"

"That one is a little harder," he admitted. "The price I paid for going to that party was far too high."

"True," Melissa agreed. "But like you've told me before, if you hadn't gone you wouldn't have Megan. As I see it, the reward for all the trouble is pretty great, too."

Shane pushed Melissa's shoulder until she sat up. She searched his eyes for a clue. But had no idea what he was thinking.

"Do you really believe that?" he finally asked. "I mean I know my little girl is an amazing reward but do you really believe that Melissa?"

"Yes," Melissa said without hesitation. "I love that kid almost as much as I love my own son. She is an amazing, sweet, lovable girl," Melissa paused. "I know our wedding, me moving in and all that has happened so quickly. We all need time to adjust. But I want you to think about something for me."

"What?" Shane asked, curious now.

"You said Kristy signed away all parental rights to Megan. Well, I was hoping one day you would let me adopt her. I know it might take a while before you trust me with her. I know I have made some terrible mistakes, but one day I would like us to be a family. I want Megan to know she is as much mine as she is yours. I want her to feel like this is her family too. Like I'm her mom too. I don't want that girl to ever feel like an outsider. I think if you will let me adopt her...."

Shane was beaming as he pulled Melissa back into his arms. "You would really do that?" he asked, loving Melissa even more for her offer. "I mean we both know who her biological mother was. You could really get passed that and accept my baby girl as your own?"

Melissa slid back and took Shane's hands in hers. "That first night I had a hard time being around Megan. I kept looking for signs. Looking for a reason not to like her, to somehow blame her for our breakup. I think that's why I misread the situation so poorly when I walked into that room. I saw what I wanted to see, what I expected to see. But Megan is nothing like Kristy. She is sweet and loving and amazing. She takes after her father I guess. When I see Megan, I don't see Kristy's daughter. I see an amazing child that needs to feel loved. I see a little girl who is unsure of herself, who would do anything she could to make her father happy. I see a very special little girl who needs a mother. I'd like to be her mother, Shane. Kristy is awful. She's beyond selfish, she's cruel and malicious. I want to help Megan overcome her doubts and show her what a family is supposed to be. Show her how a mother is supposed to act towards her child. I have a great example and she's outside playing with those children."

"I'll call Steve. He's pretty quick with this kind of thing. We'll file the petition this week," Shane told her as he pressed a gentle kiss to her lips. "I love you." He wanted to say more but he was just so happy he couldn't speak.

"Are you sure?" Melissa asked hesitantly. "I mean I don't want to push you. I want you and Megan to be ready for this step."

"The instant I asked you to marry me, I wanted to ask you to adopt my daughter. I thought it was too soon for you," Shane said as he wrapped his arms around the woman he had always loved. "I have the same concerns as you do. I never want Megan to feel like an outsider. But I didn't feel like I could ask. I mean her mother is the woman that tore us apart. How could I ask you to step in and accept her daughter with open arms? How could I ask that of you? It just seemed like too much."

"It didn't take me very long to realize that Megan has nothing to do with Kristy. I mean I will always hate Kristy with a passion. Knowing how cruel she was to that innocent little girl out there makes me hate her to my very core. I just hope I never see that woman again," Melissa said honestly. "Knowing what I might be capable of when it comes to Kristy scares me to death."

"I know," Shane said in understanding. "I've wanted to strangle her myself more than once."

"So we're clear on the Kristy issue then?" Melissa pushed. "The woman is evil and she seduced you while you were vulnerable. She victimized you Shane. I know that's hard for a macho cowboy to accept, but she did. Just like she victimized me and your daughter and probably Cora at some point. That's what Kristy does. I'd like to put that behind us once and for all."

"I'll try," Shane said, it was the most he could promise at this point.

"Okay," Melissa said, relieved. She felt like they really were making progress. "So we're not giving all our money to charity and no more guilt about the past. That only leaves the issue of Gloria to deal with."

"Maybe we should wait on that. I mean we have taken more than a couple minutes in here already. I don't want to take

337

advantage of your parents. They might truly need help out there," Shane started to stand, but Melissa wouldn't let him.

"Chicken," she said with a smile. "This won't take long. I actually have a suggestion. It's not something you can decide tonight so let me get it out there and then we can go enjoy the rest of our son's birthday."

"What kind of proposal?" Shane asked, skeptically.

"I know you don't want to give your mom free money. And I agree to a point," Melissa began. "I mean I saw what happened when I gave her two hundred bucks, she was back asking for more."

"Exactly," Shane said in agreement. "It's not that I'm opposed to helping her out now and again, it's that the demands would never stop."

"Good," Melissa said, turning to face Shane. "I'm glad to hear that because my plan might look like a handout on the surface but it really isn't."

"I'm listening," Shane said, even more curious now.

"Well, Joe said Gloria is planning on staying in town. She says she wants to get to know her family. I don't personally believe her. I mean people can change, but not overnight. Gloria wants to get to know the kids because she wants leverage. She wants to be able to use that relationship to get money from you. I know I could be wrong, but I don't think so."

"I agree. She's not here because she cares about me and the kids. She's here because she cares about Gloria. That's all she's ever cared about," Shane said, scowling.

Melissa could see that Shane was still hurt by his mother's actions but he didn't let it cloud his judgment. He saw her for what she was. He had a pretty clear picture of Gloria, which is why she was never successful when she tried to manipulate him. "I think so too," Melissa began, "but what if we're wrong? The first thing I want to propose to you is that we allow her to come to our wedding."

"No way," Shane said immediately. "I'm not going to let that woman ruin my wedding day. I've waited too many years for this. I want it to be perfect."

Melissa put on her best pouty face. "Everyone has the crazy relative that makes things interesting. Are you really going to deprive me of bragging rights? I mean really, who has Gloria beat? My mother-in-law is a bigger monster than anyone I know."

"Which is why she is not attending our wedding," Shane said with finality.

"We are just going to have to disagree on this one for now because I need to move on," Melissa took a deep breath. "The second part of my proposal has some unknowns for me. I mean I haven't looked at the books yet, so I have no idea how rich you really are."

Shane smiled. "I don't think we're going to starve any time soon." It was cute how Melissa was so self-conscious about finances.

Melissa ignored him. "The amount would depend on how much you can spare, but I was thinking we could put a large sum of money into a CD or buy some bonds, whichever you want. It would depend how long you want to tie up those funds. Anyway, if we had a good sum of money, we could put the interest into a trust for Gloria."

"Why would I do that?" Shane asked, not following Melissa's logic. "That would just be giving her a free ride. Something I've avoided all these years. Plus once we start giving her money, she's only going to want more."

"Because I think this could resolve the problems you are having. Gloria sees you as rich and you are her son. In her mind that means you owe her. Before you blow up, I don't agree so just simmer down a minute." Melissa's mind was running a mile a minute. It had seemed so logical to her, but now that she was trying to explain it she wasn't so sure. "Can you give me a ballpark figure of how much expendable cash you have? I mean, I know to run a ranch you can't tie up all your funds because if the crops are ruined in a hail storm you might have to spend that cash on hay. I know running a ranch is expensive and a ranch this big requires a lot of expendable cash. I'm just looking for an idea of how much you have to play with. How much…"

"Millions," Shane said casually. "I keep an emergency fund for the things you were just talking about. I rarely use it, but it's there and it's substantial. I told you Melissa, I'm rich." He wasn't bragging, just stating the facts.

"Okay, that makes this even easier," she said wondering how she was going to adjust. She was completely broke. She owned a house that she planned to make into a B&B, a car that Shane had bought her and a huge credit card bill. Shane had millions.

"Breathe Melissa," Shane said, smiling. "Don't get distracted."

"Okay," she said taking two deep breaths. "So if I wanted to take, let's say two million and tie it up for five years in a high interest CD, that wouldn't be a problem?"

"No," Shane assured her.

"What if I wanted to take five million?" she pressed.

"Still not a problem," he said flatly.

"Okay," Melissa said still reeling. She knew Shane had money, she hadn't realized just how rich he actually was. "Then here is my proposal. We take five million and tie it up in CD's. That is going to make you roughly two to three percent a year."

Shane already had money invested in CD's, he knew the return on investment he was going to get but he'd let Melissa continue.

"What if we took a portion of that profit, say four thousand dollars a month and we placed that into a trust."

"Continue," Shane said, trying to see where she was going with this.

"You set up the terms of the trust, but there would have to be very strict parameters. I'm thinking a cap on what Gloria could withdraw each month," Melissa continued. "Three thousand tops. That would give her a comfortable living."

"I'm still not sure why I would want to give her that much money every month," Shane was still against this plan. He truly believed it would only make Gloria come back more frequently wanting more.

"Because that is all she would ever get and you would be very clear on that," Melissa told him. "You said you don't have a problem helping your mother out. This would help her out," Melissa gathered her thoughts. "In talking to you and Cora and even Joe, I've realized that Gloria comes to you only when she is desperate. When she's between husbands."

"True," Shane agreed.

"Well what if she never had to be desperate?" Melissa asked. "If she left the money in the trust until her next divorce, when her next marriage ended, she would know she didn't have to come to you and ask for money. She could just withdraw it out of the trust. It might keep her from showing up to con you and if she felt like you were helping her, it might actually improve your relationship. I'm not saying you will ever have a loving mother/ son bond, I really don't think that's possible. But what if when she did show up, she wasn't asking for money? Maybe she was just passing through and stopped in for dinner with husband number eight? She'd leave the next day and we'd joke about the crazy relatives."

"It sounds nice, but you are forgetting one thing," Shane said, considering Melissa's plan. Parts of it did have merit.

"What?" Melissa asked.

"Once you give to Gloria, she always comes back. And the second time around, she wants more," Shane said coldly.

"But then she loses her safety net," Melissa disagreed. "You would have to make it very clear that this is all she gets. Three thousand a month would pay for rent, a new car payment, gas, insurance and even food. Not an elaborate life but a basic one. It's a good deal. I have no doubt in the beginning she would test the waters, but she's doing that anyway. You're not giving her anything, you are running her out of town, and you have to deal with her shenanigans every few years anyway. Make it clear that this is it. It's the only offer she is going to get and if she messes it up, if she keeps coming back for more, if she harasses or terrorizes anyone in this town, the trust will go away. I don't think she'll risk it. She may or may not stop by on occasion, she may just accept the money and go away, or she may stop by now and again, have a quirky dinner and leave town. I just really think this might change the dynamics of your relationship, for lack of a better word. And it might make things a little easier in the future."

Shane started to shake his head but Melissa stopped him.

"I said don't answer me today," Melissa stood and waited for Shane to join her. "We've been in here long enough and we need to go out and enjoy the rest of our son's birthday party. Just think about it. Like Joe said, Gloria might be in town awhile. We're going to have to figure out a way to deal with that. Throw her a bone and maybe she'll surprise us all."

Shane stood and pulled Melissa into his arms. "I'll think about it," he said as he kissed the top of her head. "Now let's go enjoy our son's birthday party. You're parents are gems but they have to be ready for a break by now."

Melissa smiled. "They are, aren't they? I'm so glad they could make it for both the party and the wedding," she paused. "I'm starting to think I didn't spend nearly enough on those flowers. And since you're loaded, maybe I should have added the shrimp platter to the menu. Oh and…"

Shane cupped his hand over her mouth and groaned. "I've created a monster. Ouch!" he said, shaking out his hand after Melissa bit him. Then he pushed her up against the wall, her hands trapped high above her head as he lowered his face to hers. "You are going to pay for that later." He promised as he pressed his body closer, sliding his leg between her thighs. Then he pressed his lips to hers in a long, languid kiss. Shane released Melissa and moved backwards. He paused to give her a cocky wink before he turned and disappeared out the door.

She might pay for biting him later, but he was definitely going to pay for firing her up and then leaving her wanting.

Epilogue

Melissa stood in the large study turned bride's room staring at her reflection in the mirror. Her first wedding had been small and informal. She and Mitch had decided that's what they wanted at the time. Her parents had been there as well as Mitch's parents, his brother and a few close friends from Denver. That was it. They had a small, intimate ceremony at a little chapel down the street from their apartment and a cozy reception at Mitch's parents place. All the firemen had stopped by at one point or another, a couple neighbors and family. Today was going to be so much different.

Today, Melissa was having the wedding she'd always dreamed of. Sarah was her matron of honor. That was one thing Melissa had always regretted at her first wedding. She and Sarah had spent hours in that old clubhouse making wedding plans. They knew exactly what they wanted down to the last detail. Sarah had made her childhood plans a reality when she married Jason. Sarah's wedding had been a celebration just as she'd always wanted. It was beautiful and glorious and perfect. Melissa had put her dreams on hold due

Hidden Lakes

to circumstance. She couldn't invite anyone from Hidden Lakes, if she did they would find out about Jeremy and then Shane would know. So Melissa had altered her plans and settled for something small and cozy.

This time there was no settling. Shane had insisted on inviting the entire town. Melissa didn't mind. She'd grown up here, she knew almost everyone in Hidden Lakes but more importantly, her parents knew them. Like Sarah, Melissa's wedding was going to be a celebration. Her parents were so happy. Melissa hadn't seen her father laugh so much in years. He looked healthy, too. She just hoped having Megan and Jeremy for three weeks wasn't too much for them. The kids were going to head back to Florida while Melissa and Shane went on their honeymoon. Shane still hadn't told her much about it. He wanted most of it to be a surprise. She knew they would be spending tonight in a fishing cabin somewhere out west. Shane had bought the place a few years back and was excited to show it to her. From his description, she thought it would be wonderful and couldn't wait to take the kids there someday. Apparently the rest was up to Melissa. Shane told her she would have to decide if they spent the entire time at the cabin or if she wanted to go somewhere more exotic. He promised to take her anywhere. She was pretty sure they would just be staying at the cabin. There were a lot of places she'd love to go, but she wanted Megan and Jeremy with them on those trips.

Melissa jumped at the knock on the door. "Come in," she said a little breathless. She'd gotten so caught up in the honeymoon she was going to miss her wedding.

Sarah stepped through the door and whistled softly. "You look amazing," she said rushing to Melissa and pulling her into a tight

346

hug. "Mom's outside, she wanted to know if it was okay if she came in."

"Of course," Melissa said, thrilled. Sarah's mother was like a second mother to Mel. She'd spent as much time at the Miller's home as she had at her own growing up.

Darla Miller entered the room, followed by Connie Peters. Melissa froze, desperately trying to hold back tears. Darla rushed to Mel and pulled her into a long motherly hug. "It doesn't look like you need a mother's touch in here. You seem to have everything handled on your own," Melissa laughed as her own mother held her tight. When Connie stepped back, she brushed aside a single tear and smiled at her daughter. Pride was radiating off her face. Melissa wrapped an arm around each of the women, enjoying their comfort for a long moment. "I do need help with this veil," she finally told them.

Connie reached into her purse and pulled out what looked like a tiara. She moved in front of Melissa and gently slid the ends through her hair. When Melissa turned to look in the mirror she let out a small gasp, it was beautiful and exactly right. "Thank you mom. You always know exactly what I need."

Darla went to work securing the veil to the head piece and within minutes Melissa was ready to walk down the aisle.

Sarah sat back and watched the women fuss over Melissa. She might have been jealous, but they had done the same thing at her wedding. It struck her again today, the same as it had so many years ago, just how lucky she and Melissa were. Both of their parents were wonderful. Melissa and Sarah had grown up having two mothers who loved and adored them. Oh sure, they'd gotten into loads of trouble, especially when they were together and bored. But Connie Peters and Darla Miller were two of the best role models a girl could have. Sarah thought of little Megan and fumed. That girl had been through way more than any child should with Kristy around. Sarah knew that Mel would make up for all the bad times. Megan was Mel's now. They were still waiting for that official piece of paper from the courts, but Melissa Peters, soon to be Chandler, didn't need a piece of paper to claim Megan as her own. She'd done that gradually over the last few weeks. Sarah knew Mel's love would be permanent.

The small group exited the study through the back, leaving the large French doors wide open in their wake. Sarah went first and joined her husband who walked her down the aisle. He paused in front, placing a soft kiss to her lips before he turned and took a seat. Connie Peters was next. Hank paused to seat Melissa's mother before taking his place next to Shane. Hank was serving as Shane's best man. He smiled and gave Cora a quick wink before turning to watch Jake Peters walk his only daughter down the aisle. The room silenced immediately as the organ began to play.

Melissa was floating on cloud nine. Her father was by her side, her son was walking slowly in front of her carrying a small pillow with two wedding bands fastened to the ribbons on top. Megan was walking with Jeremy, one arm looped through his the other hand cautiously tossing flower petals from a basket as they walked. She watched the kids for a minute proud as any mother could be, then she glanced up; searching for her man. The instant her eyes met his, the world stopped. She forgot everything and everyone else around her. Shane was the most handsome man she had ever laid eyes on. She absolutely loved him in his tight jeans and cowboy boots, but standing there in a tux tailor made for him, he took her breath away. The look on his face was one of pure love.

Shane stood at the front of the room, anxiously waiting for his bride to exit the house and get this show started. He smiled, as usual Melissa was calling the shots here. He better get used to it, they both knew she had him wrapped around her little finger and always would. Shane felt her somehow before he saw her. She'd insisted he couldn't see her dress before the big day so he had no idea what to expect. Sarah and Jason started to walk forward, then Hank and Connie. He smiled at the kids. He was so proud of them. Jeremy walked confidently toward the front of the room guiding his sister at every step. Meg was more cautious, she put so much pressure on herself to be perfect. Hopefully in time he and Mel could change that but today his kids made him so proud. The music started and he spotted Jake Peters first, then Melissa came into view and his heart stopped. He was sure of it. Several seconds of nothing, then he forced himself to take a breath. She was the most beautiful woman he had ever seen. Her long gown accentuated all those wonderful curves he loved so much. Her hair was flowing loosely over her shoulders but she'd pulled part of it back to hold the veil. He couldn't wait to get that thing off her face. He knew it was tradition, but he wanted to see her eyes. The second Jake reached them, Shane stepped forward and lifted the thin white cloth away from Mel's face. Their eyes locked and Melissa smiled. That was all it took, Shane pressed his lips to hers and closed his eyes. He grinned when the minister cleared his throat. Shane took Mel's hand and led her forward.

"We're not quite to that point Mr. Chandler," the minister scolded. The crowd laughed, Shane shrugged and Melissa blushed. Jake stepped forward to give his daughter away and the nuptials progressed as usual.

Once the ceremony was over, Melissa turned to smile at the crowd. As her gaze traveled from her parents to Sarah's parents to all her friends at the Sheriff's Office they stopped abruptly in surprise. She immediately looked to Shane in question.

349

"I decided to take your advice," he whispered, knowing what had surprised Melissa.

"Why didn't you tell me?" she scolded.

"Because I made the decision while you were in the study getting dressed. You were very clear on that. I was not to come anywhere near that room for any reason today. I had no idea my wife was that superstitious."

"It's tradition," she corrected. "Now let's go catch your mother before she leaves. I want to make sure she knows to sit with the family at the reception."

"She knows," Shane said taking Melissa's hand. "I already told her," they began down the aisle but didn't get very far. Everyone wanted a moment to congratulate the happy couple.

"We're going to lose her," Melissa said, worried.

"Clearly you do not know my mother," Shane said laughing. "Do you honestly believe that woman would leave this party on her own? It's a chance to spend time in the limelight. Trust me, Gloria is outside making sure she gets her fifteen minutes of fame."

Melissa decided Shane was right. Gloria wasn't going anywhere. She was relieved Shane had decided to invite her. They may not get along, but a mother should be allowed to attend her own son's wedding. Shane still hadn't decided what to do about the money, but Melissa thought he was coming around.

* * * *

"Wake up sleeping beauty," Shane whispered in Melissa's ear.

Melissa moaned, shifted and went right back to sleep. Shane laughed as he reached into the car and unfastened her seatbelt. She definitely had a long, exhausting day.

He was lifting her out of the car when her eyes flew open. She immediately wrapped her arms around Shane's neck and snuggled close to his body. "I hope you were planning to carry me over the threshold."

"It seems you didn't really give me a choice, babe. You were sleeping like the dead, well other than the loud snoring that is." He laughed when she punched his arm, annoyed. He was grateful he'd talked to the doctor into a walking cast. He was determined to carry his new bride and that would have been impossible with crutches.

Shane set Mel down and turned her toward the lake. He moved in behind her and wrapped his arms around her waist. "I wish you could see it better, but the moon shining off the water gives you a rough idea tonight. I think you're going to love it in the morning."

"I love it tonight," she whispered as she leaned back and relaxed against Shane's broad chest. "It's wonderful and so peaceful out here. I can't believe you own the whole thing."

"I don't own the whole lake," he corrected. "Across there, to the left there's another cabin that sits up on the hill. They own a small section over there. But the rest is ours. We own the lake honey, not me."

"I think that's a premarital asset," she said grinning as she turned to wrap her arms around her husband.

"Well since you and I are never getting divorced, premarital assets aren't any different than marital assets. They all belong to you now." He gently lifted her into his arms and started for the door. "And there's one particular asset inside that I want to show you immediately."

Melissa giggled as Shane impatiently kicked the door shut and headed for the bedroom. "Well, I happen to have a couple assets I'd like to show you as well."

"Baby I'm very familiar with your assets but you can show them off any time you like."

THE END